PROMISE KEPT

BOOKS BY K'WAN

PROMISE KEPT

K'WAN

BLACK
STONE
PUBLISHING

Printed in the United States of America

First edition: 2024
ISBN 978-1-7999-6143-7
Fiction / Urban

Version 1

Blackstone Publishing
31 Mistletoe Rd.
Ashland, OR 97520

www.BlackstonePublishing.com

PROLOGUE

Pain . . . Mind-numbing pain that spread from the back of his head and over his face was the only thing that told B-Stone that he was still among the living. He slowly opened one eye and found that he had trouble opening the other. As far as he could tell the eye wasn't swollen or damaged. It was like his brain couldn't communicate with that side of his face to send the proper signals to get his eyelid to function.

Pressing the knuckles of both his massive hands into the carpet, he tried to push himself up. More pain shot through his face as half the carpet fabric seemed to come loose in the act. The blood covering his cheeks had begun to dry and cake into a sticky mess. When he tried to sit up, the world swam, and he plunged back down. He lay there like a cripple, breathing heavily as if he had just run laps. He was in worse shape than he initially thought. A murderous fire burned in his heart as he recounted what had happened to him and who had been responsible. He would bring the full weight of his rank down on the head of the white girl and her little friend for crossing him. They'd tried to take him out—and failed. It was a mistake they wouldn't live long enough to regret.

"Take it easy, blood," B-Stone heard a voice say. "You might have a concussion." B-Stone wanted to turn his head to see who was speaking, but he didn't yet have the strength. When a pair of hands took him under both arms and gently began pulling him from the ground, he didn't resist. B-Stone had made it as far as a kneeling position before he motioned for whoever was helping him to stop. His head was killing him, and he felt like he might throw up if he did too much too soon.

"Fuck," B-Stone huffed, kneeling in the middle of the hotel room, rocking back and forth. After a few ticks, the room stopped spinning, and he was able to turn his head slightly. Standing near him was the face of a kid he had seen around the neighborhood, but he couldn't remember his name. He was from the area, but not a part of the crew. At that moment, it didn't even matter. B-Stone was just thankful for the helping hand.

"Damn, big man. You look like shit on a stick," the kid said, running his finger along the thin gold chain around his neck while he watched B-Stone curiously.

B-Stone caught the insult, and normally he would've thrown the young civilian a good beating for speaking to him in such a way, but right then wasn't the time. Besides, all his fury would be saved for the white girl. "Bitches tried to do me in. I'm gonna kill that white whore when I catch her."

"They're long gone. I saw them book it down the stairs before I came in here to see what became of you." The kid sat on the bed, beside where B-Stone was kneeling. "They looked pretty shaken up, especially Promise."

"Fuck that mutt. She wanna be around waving fresh meat in front of a bunch of wolves all night, and then cry foul when one of us takes a bite. When I catch her, she's gonna take this dick before I end her life. She can run, but there ain't nowhere in the Bricks or the state of New Jersey where I won't be able to touch her. Everybody nigga swinging a red flag gonna be hunting honkie!" B-Stone fumed.

The kid let out a sigh of what sounded like relief, hearing that whatever evil deed B-Stone had intended had failed. "I figured whatever you two came in here to do went to the left when I saw her crying. That's when I knew what I needed to do. I had to make sure that the monster was really dead for her to be free."

"What? The fuck is you mumbling about?" B-Stone asked in an annoyed tone. He had only been half-listening to the rambling young man because he was too busy plotting his revenge against Promise. In response, he felt the kid's arm wrap around his neck in a reverse choke hold and pressure being applied. B-Strone was bigger and stronger than him, but he was at a disadvantage because he was kneeling and badly injured. "You know who the fuck I am?" B-stone asked, his voice strained.

The kid pondered it. "Yes, the monster." He produced a knife from his pocket and ripped it across B-Stone's throat. B-Stone thrashed about, desperately trying to claw at his enemy's face but only managing to tear the collar of his shirt. It was no use. Eventually B-Stone stopped his squirming and went still. The kid continued to hold him for a time, like a parent comforting a child. His eyes stared vacantly at the blood splatter on the bed and wall, as if his brain was trying to pick out a hidden pattern in the spray. He could've gotten lost in the mural of blood, but time wasn't on his side.

He heard a familiar female voice echo down the hallway: "I saw him go in the other room with the white bitch. He's breaking her in for the rest of the crew. You better hurry up and get yours before there ain't nothing left. You know blood greedy as hell."

It was time to go. The killer took one last moment to admire his handiwork while he wiped his knife clean on the hotel bedsheet. B-Stone lay on his stomach, head cocked to one side, and frozen on his face was the terror of knowing that he was breathing his last breaths. His killer had wished it hadn't had to come to this, but the minute he walked into that hotel room and saw that there was still life in the man sprawled on the carpet, he knew what he had to do. It was one life measured against two, so he did what he felt the universe would've wanted and protected what he loved.

B-Stone was a foul dude and deserved what had happened to him that night and then some. He was not a good man, but he was a man to be respected. B-Stone was a decorated general in one of the largest domestic armies within the United States, the Bloods. He may not have had any standing to speak of in any official branch of the military, but in the City of Newark, his rank spoke volumes. B-Stone's was a murder that would not go unnoticed or unpunished. The city would bleed for this.

B-Stone's killer crept to the hotel door, silently opening it and conducting a brief scan of the hallway. He was able to match the voice of the girl he had heard speaking with the young lady in the hallway. She was tall, with chocolate-colored skin and hair dyed crimson red. He knew who she was and what would happen if she spotted him coming out of that room. Thankfully, a distraction presented itself. One of the partygoers from the hotel suite three doors down, where the main party was happening, engaged her in conversation. When her back turned to the scene of the crime, the young killer stole across the hallway and escaped down the stairs into the night.

By the time anyone discovered B-Stone's body, he would be gone without a trace—or so he had thought.

The killing of B-Stone had been committed with the intention of saving the life of an innocent, but in the game they played, there were no innocents. His actions would have unforeseen consequences, and in time, he would discover that the blood he had spilled on the cheap hotel carpet would spread beyond the hotel and wash over the city, threatening to drown everyone connected to the crime, including those he had been trying to protect.

It would be two whole days before the murder at the Robert Treat would make the *Star-Ledger*. The journalist covering it had written a small piece about another young Black man who had added to the city of Newark's ever-rising murder rate. The only real lead the police had to go on was an anonymous witness's account of two women fleeing the scene and a strange chain, decorated with what appeared to be gold teeth, clutched in the hand of the victim.

PART I

SHE WITHOUT SIN

CHAPTER 1

The gentleman's club known as Dirty Wine—which was a play on words—was a bit more chaotic than usual that night. It wasn't really a club, more like a bar with a stage built behind the glass horseshoe counter where the drinks were served. Dirty Wine was an out-of-the-way, hole-in-the-wall spot in the Bronx that wasn't the most well-known on the circuit, but it had its nights. Weekends usually drew a decent enough crowd because the drinks were strong and the door cover charge was only five bucks. But at the time, it was only 8:00 p.m. on a Thursday, and there were already a few dozen people in a space only built to hold about sixty. At that rate, they might have found themselves shut down by the fire department before the *real* entertainment started.

For the last thirty minutes or so, patrons had begun trickling in. Most of them were the after-work regulars, coming to spend portions of their paychecks on lap dances and beers and fantasies manufactured by the girls whispering in their ears before returning to their realities of wives, families, and the bills awaiting them.

Women of all shapes and sizes pranced around the small room wearing little to nothing at all. The city of New York had cracked down on full nudity in strip clubs a few years prior, but some of the girls danced dangerously close to the line. One girl, who went by Lita, wore only three pasties which covered her nipples and the opening of her vagina. Her big ass swung freely as she passed one of the tables, stacked with bottles, drawing the eyes of every man sitting at it. There was blood in the water, and Lita had a nose better than most sharks.

Not everyone who came in were locals. There were a few unfamiliar faces sprinkled in. Some mingled with the girls, trying to negotiate lap dances, among other things. Those who were handling a few dollars paid the extra charge for private tables and bottle service. They weren't the heaviest of hitters in the city, but they were players. You could tell by their jewels and designer labels. They took notice of the girls, but for the most part hadn't come for pussy or lap dances. They were there for the listening party that Dirty Wine had been fortunate enough to be hosting that night.

A local rapper who went by the moniker of Inferno would be the guest of honor. He had made his bones as a battle rapper known for scorching his opponents with his lyrics, which is where the name came from. Over the years he had released a series of well-received mixtapes and YouTube videos, which helped to grow his exposure and put him on the radar, but it was his presence that had record labels salivating over him. Inferno had a personality that could fill a room as soon as he entered it, and his music was something that no one could quite categorize. It was a hybrid of rock music and eighties gangster rap, and he had been known to cause riots when he touched the stage.

Most of the larger clubs would no longer book him for fear of the violence that seemed to follow him, which is why he was forced to host his listening party at Dirty Wine.

"Promise, you gonna stand there daydreaming all day or get these drinks over to table five sometime this century?" A voice snapped Promise out of her daze. It belonged to a tall woman who wore a large beehive-style wig that leaned slightly to one side. This was Big Sally, the bartender. She was thick with large breasts and hands that resembled catcher's mitts. She had knocked out more than a few unruly patrons with those fists, and people who came to Dirty Wine were more cautious of Big Sally than they were of the bouncers. During the late eighties and through the early two thousands, Big Sally had been a legend on the pole, but now that she was creeping on fifty, she spent her nights behind the bar.

"Yes, ma'am," Promise said obediently, picking up the tray of drinks Sally had set on the bar. She had to steady herself before attempting to cross the room. She hadn't quite gotten used to walking in the large platform heels that Larry, the owner of Dirty Wine, insisted all the girls wear. Promise was only a waitress and not a dancer, but it didn't matter to Larry. He made his money promoting sex, not comfort.

Once Promise felt confident enough that she could walk without falling flat on her face, she began her journey. Table five was only on the other side of the small room, but it may as well have been miles away. She had practiced walking in the shoes with her friend Mouse back at the apartment, but walking in heels on carpet was nothing compared to the hardwood floors of the bar. "One foot in front of the other," she muttered to herself as she made timid steps. She was focused on her feet, instead of what was in front of her, and by the time she looked up, it was too late to stop the collision with a man who had been crossing the room. The tray holding the glasses went up, and Promise went down.

"Stupid bitch!" the man she had collided with cursed angrily. He was light-skinned and well-built, with a short afro and thick beard. He continued to hurl curses at her while looking down at his cream-colored jogging suit, which was now soaked with brown liquor.

"I . . . I'm sorry," Promise said nervously. She tried to climb to her feet but slipped in the liquor she had spilled and fell back down.

"Sorry ain't the word. This outfit costs more than you probably make selling pussy in this bitch all week. I should break my foot off in your whore ass!" For a second, it looked like he was about to make good on the threat, but thankfully someone intervened.

"Bone!" someone yelled from behind the man and froze him mid-stomp.

From the deep bass in the voice, Promise expected it to belong to someone larger than her attacker or, at the very least, his equal, but the man who stepped into view was neither. He wasn't short, nor was he tall. She put him somewhere around average height. He was quite handsome, with sunburned skin, thin bowed lips, and dark silky hair that was braided into cornrows that stretched well past his shoulders. Blue jeans sagged slightly off his hips, and a gold chain with the Virgin Mary hanging from the end of it rested against his black T-shirt. When his eyes landed on Promise, she felt her heart skip. At first glance, they looked hazel, then danced to a shade of auburn, and finally settled somewhere in between. Even under the threat of being stomped, she found that she couldn't take her focus off those dreamy eyes. Though Promise had never met the man a day in her life, his eyes told her something that his mouth didn't have to. They told her that she was safe. For as long as she was in his presence, no harm would befall her. At least not from Bone.

"What part of low-key didn't you understand?" the man with dreamy eyes asked Bone. The bass was gone from his voice, but the weight of his words remained.

"Sincere, this broad is out of pocket. This is an eight-hundred-dollar Gucci suit she ruined." Bone pointed at the liquor stains on his outfit. He knew that, once you let Hennessey settle into something light-colored, it was a wrap for the garment.

"An eight-hundred-dollar piece that you copped off Treece the booster for three-fifty." Sincere pulled a bankroll from his pocket and peeled off two hundred dollars, which he shoved into Bone's chest. "Get it cleaned or put another buck-fifty on top of it to cop another one. I don't care either way, but I'm gonna need you to stop making us look like lil niggas with no home training, ya heard?"

"You right." Bone tucked the money in his pocket and stood down. He didn't do so because he was afraid of Sincere, but because he knew his brother was right. Stealth was their bread and butter, and his outburst had put eyes on them.

Once Sincere was sure that Bone was no longer in his feelings, he turned his attention to Promise. She was still sitting on the floor, covered in liquor, looking up at him curiously. "Let me help you." He extended his hand. Promise was hesitant. "Don't worry, shorty. I don't bite. At least not unless I'm invited to."

"Thank you," Promise said, finally accepting the helping hand.

"No thanks needed. And please pardon my little brother Bone. He off his meds today," Sincere half-joked.

"I know his type, so it's all good," said Promise. Mr.

Dreamy-Eyed Sincere had no idea who she was and what she came from. His brother was a choir boy compared to some of the dudes she'd encountered in her neighborhood in Newark.

"What I owe you for the drinks?" Sincere went back to his bankroll.

"It was my fault. I should've been watching where I was going. Don't worry about it." Promise said, trying to sound more confident than she actually was. She knew that cheap-ass Larry was always looking for a reason to dock money from the girls' pay. Those five shots of Hennessey she had dumped would hit her check for at least seventy-five dollars, if not more. When girls spilled drinks, Larry didn't give them house prices, he hit them for what the bar charged.

"You say that now, but you might feel different when that slum-ass nigga who owns this place tries to tax you," Bone said with a chuckle. It was as if he was reading her mind.

Sincere shot his brother a disapproving glance before refocusing on Promise. "Just take it." He forced six crumpled twenties into her hand. "If you don't want to put it on the spilled drinks, add it to your tip money."

"Only bartenders and strippers are supposed to get tipped in here. I can take the money, but just keep it low." Promise told him.

Sincere's thick eyebrows curved in on each other. He gave Promise and her outfit the once over. "Shit, you in a strip club hustling and fosho don't look like no janitor I've ever seen. So, if you ain't a stripper or a bartender, what's yo play?" He tugged at her boy shorts.

It wasn't an aggressive gesture, just one that reminded Promise of what she was wearing and how it must've looked to him. Larry had forced them all to wear the platform heels, but she drew the line when he tried to hand out the decree about bikinis. Promise met him halfway on the dress code, coming to work in boy shorts and a skin-tight tank top. The shorts had ridden up her ass when she fell, now looking like a G-string, and the tank top was wet, exposing her silver-dollar-sized nipples beneath. "I wait tables here. Nothing else." She folded her arms across her breasts, ending the free show.

"Easy, lil mama." Sincere smiled at her embarrassment, revealing that his teeth were just as well put together as the rest of him. "I ain't here to pass no judgment. I'm probably the biggest sinner in this whole joint, so I ain't got no room to talk anyhow. I'm just trying to see where you at with it. That's all."

It felt like Sincere was flirting. She was almost sure he was, but Promise didn't want to jump off the porch until she was certain. She was about to hit him with a slick rebuttal when Larry's hating ass showed up.

"Look out, look out." Larry elbowed his way through the small clusters of dancers and spectators who had gathered to watch the spectacle. His coal-black face was covered in a sheen of sweat, though it wasn't that hot in the room. It seemed like Larry was always sweating. He was an oddly shaped man, with long, thin legs and arms and a beer belly that threatened to split the front of his yellow shirt and hung over the front of his too-tight white jeans. He was somewhere in his midforties, but his balding head made him look older. Larry was a bottom-feeder and a crook in his everyday life, but within the halls of Dirty Wine, he was the king. "Fuck going on around here." His eyes flashed from Promise to Sincere and back.

"Ain't nothing, OG. Just had a little accident. That's all," Sincere told him.

"Goddamn it, Jersey! Why is it that, every time there's a commotion in my spot, your ass is at the center of it?" Larry barked at Promise, ignoring Sincere's explanation.

"It was an accident, Larry," Promise reiterated.

"Damn right it was. Just like it was an accident for me to hire your clumsy ass. You can't dance, you fuck up drink orders, and more liquor ends up on my floors than it does the tables! Only reason I even gave your simple ass a job here is because Keisha and Candice vouched for you and they're two of my best earners." Larry turned to Sincere. "Listen, my apologies for whatever damages she's caused. Let me comp you and your boys a bottle on the house."

"Nah, man. It ain't that serious. We pay like we weigh. We don't do handouts," Sincere said, declining the offer.

"Speak for yourself," said Bone, cutting in. "We'll take a bottle of Henny, but please don't have this broad be the one to bring it to us. I ain't trying to get drenched again."

"Say less. And don't worry, this was her last night working here," Larry assured him.

"C'mon, Larry, don't do me like that. You know I need this job!" Promise pleaded. She hated begging Larry for anything, but at that moment, she found herself desperate. When she and Mouse had moved in with Keisha and Candice, the young women had made it clear that they had to pull their own weight to help with the bills or they would be out on their asses. Waiting tables at Dirty Wine was one of several jobs Promise had tried her hand at since moving across the water. She'd put in applications at a few fast-food restaurants and the local supermarket. She'd even been called in for interviews twice. Promise was willing to put in honest work, but with each employer willing to give her an opportunity, she kept running into the same roadblock: her paperwork. Her driver's license and social security cards were fakes. They were good enough for her to skate through a routine stop or purchase alcohol, but she wasn't sure if they would stand up to a thorough background check. With her current fugitive status up in the air, she was afraid to risk it. The idea of going to prison wasn't something that appealed to her, and the threat of street justice for her alleged crimes appealed to her even less.

When working a legitimate job hadn't worked out, Promise got creative. She did mobile food delivery while hustling weed for Candice's baby daddy Vaughn on the side. The food delivery gig had potential, but because she didn't have a vehicle of her own, the drop-offs took forever, and she couldn't cover enough ground fast enough on foot to make any real money. Vaughn's business was only rocking every other week or so. The boy smoked more than he sold. This is how she found herself letting Keisha pull her into working at Dirty Wine with her and Candice. Promise had been working there for about three months, and every time she punched in for her shift at the small strip club, she was reminded of how far she had fallen. Only six months earlier, her biggest worry was not flubbing the *Most Improved Student* speech she was supposed to give in front of her high school graduating class. Now she worried if she would get back to their shared apartment in time to catch a spot on the couch, or if she'd be sleeping on the floor. This wasn't how her life was supposed to play out.

"Tough shit, baby girl. You're starting to become a liability, and I can't afford that. Clean out your locker and hit the bricks!" Larry thumbed toward the door for emphasis.

Promise wanted to continue pleading her case, but she knew it would be a useless effort, especially in front of an audience. Larry had been looking to get rid of her for a while now. Ever since he cracked on her for some pussy and she had shot him down, Promise had been on his shit list. He had only kept her around for two reasons: having a thick white girl working at his spot was a draw, even if she was only a waitress, and the second reason was that he had held onto hope that she would give in and let him hit it. Most of the new girls played hard to get in the beginning, but that was only until they came to discover the benefits of being in Larry's good graces. He was a prick to work for, but he was also a major trick. He didn't mind spending money if the pussy or the head was official. Promise had yet to break down and give in, so in his mind, she was on the clock, and her time was damn near up. This latest debacle was the excuse he needed to be able to fire her and not have to worry about Keisha beefing about him finally getting rid of her play-cousin. Promise lowered her head and was about to begin her walk of shame back to the dressing room area when Sincere's voice stopped her.

"That's too bad. You know me and my boys had planned to come in here and spend some paper." Sincere flashed his large bankroll for Larry to see. "I was hoping Ms. Jersey could attend to our needs personally. If she's no longer employed here, I guess we're going to have to take our business elsewhere." He stuffed the money back in his pocket. "What you think, Bone?" He spoke over his shoulder to his brother. "That other spot off Jerome should be jumping tonight, right?"

"Should be. It's still early enough for us to get out of here and go find out." Bone picked up on the game his brother was playing.

"Hold on now. I don't see no need for you boys to go somewhere else when we got everything you need right here at Dirty." Larry changed his tune at the threat of money walking out the door. "Odell." He snapped his fingers over his head. "Odell!"

The overhead lights under which they were standing seemed to wink in and out as if due to some type of power surge. But this was no surge . . . it was a man whose frame was large enough to block the light out. Odell was the largest man Promise had ever seen. He had to be at least six foot six and almost as wide.

Rocking a short bowl cut with pale skin and sunken cheeks, Odell bore a striking resemblance to the DC Comics villain Solomon Grundy. A half-dozen bouncers were employed at Dirty Wine, but Odell was the first and last line of defense.

Odell loomed silently, letting his eyes drift over Sincere and every man with him. It was like he was putting together a kill list in his head so that he could decide which order the men would die in. He turned to Larry with a questioning look on his face. All it would've taken was a head nod, and Odell would've snapped both the brothers' necks without thinking twice about it. When Larry set him to a task, it was never personal. Every jaw he broke and every neck he snapped on behalf of Larry just brought Odell one step closer to repaying the debt owed to Larry by Odell's late father. He never cared to work for Larry, and he made this apparent to his boss in the way in which he dispatched those he had been set upon. Odell was thorough in everything he did by nature, but he always went the extra mile when it came to doing things for Larry. This way Larry could see what he was capable of first-hand, which would create a lingering fear in the back of his boss's mind and make Larry think twice about ever playing him unfairly. Odell wasn't the sharpest knife in the drawer, but he was no butter knife either. His hands flexed at his sides while he waited for instructions on what to do next.

"Dell, walk these fine gentlemen to one of our tables and make sure they get a fresh bottle of that Dog," Larry said. By *Dog* he meant Hennessey. "While you're at it, be sure that they've also got some of our finest girls to entertain them."

"You know we ain't got but eight tables in this place and they're all booked for the night. People coming out in droves to see this Inferno nigga," Odell said in the heavy southern drawl he had brought north with him from his native Louisiana.

Larry eased closer to Odell so that his reply would be private. "Seat these boys and we'll work the rest out at a later time." There was fresh cash in the room, and Larry needed to taste every dollar that passed through his spot. "Jersey," he said, turning to Promise, "go get yourself cleaned up so you can come back and tend to your business."

"So, I'm not fired anymore?" Promise asked sarcastically.

"Gal, don't get cute." Larry pulled Promise close so that only she could hear what he was saying. "You dodged the hangman's noose, but this can either be a stay of execution or a full exoneration for your crimes. That'll all depend on how you conduct yourself for the rest of the night. No matter how it shakes out, I still get my taste. Now hurry up and get your ass back here so we can get this money." He slapped her on the ass and gave her a small shove toward the dressing area. He waited until she was gone before turning his attention back to his payday. "Now, about that paper you were wolfing about spending."

CHAPTER 2

Promise left the exchange with mixed feelings. She wasn't quite sure what to make of the confrontation or Sincere. She had never seen him at Dirty Wine before, but he handled himself within its walls as if they were familiar. She also hadn't missed out on how willing Larry was to accommodate Sincere for whatever offenses might've taken place. Larry was a cheap son of a bitch and never offered anything for free but game, and that was only when he was applying it. Larry seemed eager to please Sincere, which said that he knew more about him than he let on. She had no idea who Sincere was, but she was thankful for him. He had saved her job—at least for the moment.

"Fucking jerk," Promise mumbled to herself, thinking about how Larry had belittled her in front of Sincere and his group. Taking shit from Larry was hard enough when she was scheduled to work, but it burned her even more when it was voluntary. That was supposed to be her night off, but Larry had called at the last minute. One of the other waitresses had quit, and he needed someone to cover her shift on account of how crowded it would be in the place because of the rappers who would be in the building. Promise would've much rather just kicked back with Mouse and enjoyed her day off, but she was too broke to turn down the extra money. Rent would be due soon, and Keisha would be on her ass for her share.

Promise only had a few minutes to get herself cleaned up, changed, and back out on the floor to work Sincere's table. If she was late, she doubted Larry would've let it slide, regardless of what Sincere said. She had just crossed the threshold which led to the bathrooms and girls' dressing rooms. A line of girls was making their way out as she was going in. She had to jump out of their way to keep from getting knocked over. The dancers were practically climbing over each other like jackals to beat each other to the floor and get a head start on snagging one of the big spenders everybody had been whispering about. Word had it that Inferno's listening party was going to bring out a couple of the record label executives who had been courting him. If what the other girls were saying was right, then there would be so much money flying around that even a klutz like Promise could find herself tripping over a bag.

After the passing stampede, Promise continued into the space that served as the dressing room for the dancers. It resembled a high school locker room, with three wooden benches between three rows of rusted lockers. There were only about a dozen or so, four per aisle. Four of the six overhead lights were blown, and Larry had yet to get someone to come and replace them. The best lighting in the entire room came from the two vanity tables in the back near the three cracked toilets, which sat behind a thin silk screen and included a single shower stall. Promise never fooled with the vanity tables. Larry had made it clear that such luxuries weren't for the likes of her. They were for the money makers like Lita and a few of the others who brought people into the bar. If somebody like Promise needed to do her makeup or fix her hair, she had to settle for a hand mirror and the flashlight on her cell phone.

Promise made a quick stop at the double sink, where she grabbed a fist full of paper towels and began trying to wash some of the liquor she'd spilled off her skin. She wiped down her arms and legs and blotted her armpits, just in case. A shower would've been nice, but she knew, for a fact, that the stall hadn't been cleaned in the time she had worked at Dirty Wine and could only imagine how long it had gone neglected before then. The *ho bath* was probably a safer option.

The dressing area reeked of funk, stale pussy, and chicken wings, which made for an odor Promise could gladly have done without smelling four nights per week, yet here she was. Her locker was on the last row, farthest from the door but closest to the toilets. They called that section of the dressing room "the Projects." It was where the new, temporary, or ugly girls were banished to. Promise knew that she fit two of the three. Maybe all three depending on who you asked. She had suffered from insecurities since she was a little girl and, even as a young woman, found that they still lingered.

She parked herself on the bench that sat in front of her locker, sighed, and turned her attention to the dented metal door. She palmed the thick Master Lock hanging from the handle. It wasn't a regular lock, but one of those thick, industrial numbers that you might see securing the fence of a junkyard with two mean-ass dogs barking behind it. Keisha and Candice always teased Promise when she put the heavy-duty lock on, but her locker had already been broken into twice since she had been working there. She welcomed the thirsty bitches who had stolen her stuff the last time to try their hands with this lock.

Promise only had a few minutes to get herself cleaned up

and back out on the floor, so she had to move swiftly. Though the locker room was empty, she still gave a cautious look around as if she thought someone might be watching before spinning the dial on the lock back and forth, putting in her combination. There was an audible click before the spinner released the lock bar and Promise was granted access. She began to rummage through her mess of a locker for something dry that she could swap out for the wet clothes she had on. She found sneakers, hoodies, several knives, and a can of mace. None of that screamed sexy, and Larry demanded sexy. Just as she was about to abandon her search, she came across her knock-off Gucci fanny-pack. Inside, wrapped tightly in a plastic supermarket shopping bag, was a one-piece bathing suit.

The suit had been a mercy gift from Mouse's cousin, Candice. One day, not long after Promise and Mouse had arrived in New York, Candice and her sister Keisha had gotten a line on something going down at Orchard Beach. Promise and Mouse were still new to the city and were anxious to get out and see what it had to offer. Promise had never been to Orchard Beach or any beach, for that matter. She was a child of North Jersey. It wasn't that New Jersey didn't have beaches, but most of them were in South Jersey. Kids from the North rarely went South unless it was to visit Atlantic City, and Promise had never been there either. This would be a first.

Because of the circumstances under which Promise and Mouse were forced to relocate to the other side of the Hudson, they hadn't arrived with much more than the clothes on their backs. They were hardly equipped for the beach. Mouse, who was petite, was easy to shop for, and they were able to grab something for her at the local shops in the hood. Promise proved to be a bit of a different case. She had a little too much hips and ass for what was on the racks. Promise was fine with hitting the beach in a pair of cut-off shorts and sneakers, but Candice wouldn't hear it. She couldn't roll with one of them looking like a bum. Candice knew of a boutique in Brooklyn that catered to women who were on the curvier side. It was called Charlotte's Closet. She was in and out in less than ten minutes with a bathing suit that she assured Promise would fit and was tasteful. Promise had wanted to try the suit on, but Keisha kept complaining about it getting late, so they headed to the beach. It wasn't until Promise had changed into the suit in one of the bathrooms that she realized that she and Candice had polar opposite tastes in clothing.

The suit was actually kind of pretty. It was all black with a golden Wonder Woman–inspired stitch across the front that led a trail over the hips and down the strip of fabric that went right down the crack of her ass. If this was Candice's idea of tasteful, then Promise could only imagine what tasteless would've looked like. She had only worn the bathing suit the one time at the beach. She was accosted by so many cat calls and uninvited hands of young men that, when they had come back from the beach, she tossed the suit into the bag and shoved it into the bottom of her knapsack, vowing never to wear it again. Unfortunately, she didn't have a choice that night.

Promise took a minute to freshen her makeup in the dingy, oval-shaped mirror that was bolted to the inside of her locker's door. She had never been big on makeup, but in the line of work that she had fallen into, Promise learned that a little lipstick and some eyeliner could go a long way. Promise was a girl of very fair skin. So fair, in fact, that, in the right light, you could mistake her for white, which wouldn't have been completely inaccurate. She was the byproduct of a Black mother and a white father and had inherited most of her father's features, including his auburn eyes. But her hips and lips had all come from her mom. Her lips were one of her most striking features. They were plump, juicy, and curved into a bow. They were the kind of lips that made you want to suck them. People of non-color paid good money for injections to achieve that look, but Promise's were natural. Her thick, auburn curls had grown back in nicely over the last few months, almost touching her shoulders. Promise could remember a time when her hair hung down her back. That was before her aunt Adelle had made her do the unthinkable. She complained that the upkeep of the hair cost too much and insisted that it be chopped off. Promise cried like a baby that day. Her aunt Dell was a mean bitch, but she had to admit that there were times when she missed her. Adelle had her ways, but she and her daughter Brianna were the only family that Promise had. There had been times when she thought about reaching out, but to do so could potentially open a can of worms that was best left closed. At least for now.

After finishing her makeup, she stood, turning her body this way and that to see how she looked in the bathing suit. Other than the fact that the thong felt like it was cutting into her ass, it wasn't that bad. It made her ass look like an apple, ripe for biting. The best part was that it was a one-piece, so it did a good job of hiding her slightly protruding belly. Promise was a little on the thick side. She wasn't quite fat but had the genetics to be overweight if she wasn't careful. She had always been insecure about her weight which is why she often hid her body under baggy clothes. Guys often complimented her, telling her that she was thick for a white girl. In Promise's mind, she was just fat.

"I see you, fresh fish," a feminine voice said from somewhere in the dressing room. Promise spun. At first, she didn't see her, but then she spotted the swelling ember at the end of a blunt. It seemed to swell every time she took a pull. The flame touched her brown eyes softly, giving them a demonic look.

It was almost as if they were glowing. After a beat, she pulled herself from the dark while blowing twin plumes of smoke from her nostrils, resembling a light-skinned dragon. She licked her painted-red lips while giving Promise a playful smirk.

"Donna, you nearly scared me half to death. What you doing skulking around in the shadows like some damn serial killer?" Promise asked.

"Watching," Donna said before fully stepping out of the shadows. Donna was breathtakingly beautiful. She was tall, with banana yellow skin, and wore a long, jet-black wig that touched the center of her back without extensions. The red catsuit, with the ass cut out, hugged her shapely body. She wore a sheer black wrap that hung off her hips, which did little to hide her ass. Donna's body was sculpted by the most skilled plastic surgeons. It wasn't overly done where her legs didn't match her ass, like some of the other strippers. It was just right. Donna tried to pass her body off as natural, but the girls didn't buy it. It was too perfect to not have been paid for.

"Well, ain't nothing to see here," Promise told her.

"I wouldn't say that." Donna ran one of her red-painted nails over the gold pattern on Promise's swimsuit. Aside from Keisha and Candice, Donna was the only girl who worked at Dirty Wine who spared Promise more than a few words that didn't involve sending her to fill a drink order. She had started working at Dirty Wine not long after Promise but was already becoming a big draw at the spot. Some of the girls felt threatened by Donna, as they should've. She was a bad bitch, and she knew it. Donna extended her blunt to Promise.

"Thanks." Promise accepted the weed. She took two pulls and started coughing. It was potent as hell.

"So," Donna said, snatching her blunt back, "you gonna tell me what you were doing all up in Sin's face?"

"Who?" Promise was confused.

"Sin, the pretty yellow nigga with the long braids." Donna nodded in the direction of the main floor. Through the door, you could see the table where Larry was personally seating Sincere and Bone.

"You mean Sincere?" Promise finally caught on.

"That might be what his mama and granny call him, but the streets know him as Sin," Donna informed her.

"I don't know about all that. I accidentally spilled liquor on his brother, and instead of them tweaking out, Sin got Larry not to fire me and even requested that I work his table tonight," Promise said proudly. "How the hell did you even see me talking to him from back here?"

"I see a lot." Donna hit the weed again. "You sure you ready to swim in the deep end?"

"What's that supposed to mean?" Promise asked defensively. She didn't know the girl to be a hater like the rest of the dancers at Dirty Wine, but she thought she felt a little shade coming from her after Promise had shared her news about Sin requesting her for the night.

"Slow down, Jersey. I know that look and ain't nobody trying to piss on your parade." Donna read Promise's eyes. "I know you're still a little green to all this, so you still don't know how to tell the dolphins from the sharks."

"I'm from Newark. I've dealt with plenty of dudes who are from the streets." Promise had grown up around killers and murderers all her life, so she knew what time it was.

"I'm sure you have, but I can guarantee you that none of them were like Sin and his bunch. Them Brooklyn niggas are cut just a little bit different. I ain't kicking no dirt on Sin's name, but the kinds of games I hear that he likes to play are only entertained by folks who know they ain't long for this world and are totally fine with it. I know you're a tough kid, Jersey, but watch yourself when standing next to those dudes."

"It ain't that serious. They just requested me to be their waitress for the night. I get to keep all the tips to myself, and they look like they're handling!" Promise said. She didn't know why Donna was trying to make it so deep. Promise wasn't like the other girls who were trying to get chosen by the men who came in flashing money.

Donna gave Promise a sly smile. "I see you already nibbled at that carrot hanging from the end of his stick. Just make sure you don't bite down too hard."

"I'll keep that in mind," Promise said in the way of thanks. "Let me get back out there before Larry starts his bullshit." She turned to head back to the floor, but Donna stopped her.

"Here, Jersey." Donna pulled the black wrap from around her waist and handed it to Promise. Promise looked confused, so Donna enlightened her. "Show them the trailer." She gave Promise a firm pat on the ass, making it jiggle slightly, before pulling the wrap over her hips and tying it about her waist. "If they wanna see the whole movie, then they need to pay the price of admission."

Promise smiled up at the taller girl. This was another one of the many jewels Donna had dropped on her in their short time working together. It had been on the strength of Keisha and Candice that Promise had gotten the job at Dirty Wine, but she couldn't have survived it as long as she had without Donna looking out for her. "You got it all figured out, huh?" she questioned, already knowing how Donna would reply.

"Nah, only the important parts." Donna laughed softly and hit the blunt again. "Now get your thick ass out there and get that bag."

CHAPTER 3

"Keep risin' to the top!" Asher sang along with Keni Burke, as the sounds of the old-school classic came through his car speakers. "Risin' to the Top" was a song that Asher knew damn near word for word. It was one of his mother's favorite songs, and she played it a lot. Asher once asked her why she spun the record so much, and she replied, "Because the lyrics remind me of what I need to be out in the world doing, giving it all I got." It wouldn't be until Asher had lived a little more that he would understand what she meant.

He rode slowly up Market Street, moving deeper into the city. He normally wore his dreads braided into two plats, but today he wore them loose, allowing them to spill over his shoulders and flutter in the breeze that came in through the partially cracked car windows. His hair felt liberated to match his mood because that's exactly how Asher was feeling . . . free!

Both sides of the streets were lined with shops and retail chain stores, but at that hour, most of them were already closed or pulling their gates down to close shortly. Sunset always started what Asher referred to as *scary hours*. It was when the working class of his neighborhood would be retiring for the day and turning the reins of the city over to the hustlers and anybody else who earned their living from sundown to sun up. It was a fair exchange and kept interactions between the two classes minimal. For the most part, it worked for all parties involved, especially Asher. It was his crew who held sway at that end of town.

Asher's passing had drawn some stares from the few people who were still milling about the shopping area. He couldn't say that he blamed them. He might've had to do a double take as well if he spotted a handsome young dude, who didn't even look old enough to drink, pushing a cocaine white Mercedes-Benz C-Class with all the trimmings. It was only a 2017, but it was his! Bought and paid for. He knew dudes who had worked all their lives and died never knowing what it was like to own a Mercedes, and here he was at eighteen with his very own. A few months ago, his primary vehicle had been an Accord that his mom had passed down to him after having it for five years herself. It was a testament to how hard work could change the fortune of a man. Hard work, and a bullet in the back of the right person's skull.

Asher had purchased the car two weeks prior. He hadn't wanted or needed the car at the time he dropped on it, but pride had pushed him to the purchase. His best friend Cal had been looking to buy a car because his Cherokee was on its last legs. He hit Asher up and asked him to take him car shopping, which wasn't a problem. Things didn't get awkward until he pulled up at Cal's place and saw that his friend wasn't alone. A chick he had been trying to smash was there with one of her home girls. As a part of his play to get the pussy, he had invited her to accompany him car shopping and just like that, Asher's quick favor for his friend had turned into a double date that ended up taking up his entire day.

One of the spots they hit was a dealership on Route 22, somewhere near Springfield, NJ. Cal slid in and out of various whips, doing his due diligence while the girls trailed him. The broad Cal was courting kept throwing her two cents in while Cal nodded like he was taking her suggestions in. He could've given less than a fuck what she felt or thought, but acting like he did would place him one step closer to the pussy. Asher had left Cal to his devices and busied himself moving back and forth between the lot and the showroom, looking at different cars. Only a few of them really moved him, with the C-Class being one of them. A tall African salesman had attached himself to the group of youngsters, showing them the cars and answering whatever questions they may have had about the automobiles. After about an hour of Cal jumping in and out of cars but giving no real indication that he was going to buy something, the salesman got frustrated, and instead of taking it out on Cal, he turned on Asher. Asher's questions about the C-Class were more out of curiosity than anything else, but the responses he got from the salesman were rude and dismissive. When Asher asked about test-driving the car, the salesman replied, "You boys obviously don't have any money. Why waste both our time?"

The salesman's words burned Asher's ears long after they had left the dealership, with Cal still without a new car. Asher wouldn't have accepted being dismissed by anyone, whether he had money to spend or not, but for it to come from another Black man placed an additional bruise on his already tattered ego. Asher had stayed awake that whole night thinking about how he had been treated. As soon as Asher thought they were open, he jumped in a cab and rode back out to the dealership.

He had two Bravo shopping bags full of bills of different denominations and slammed them on the first table he saw inside the dealership.

"The white C-Class. I'm taking that. Get the tags and shit ready," Asher told the young Black woman who occupied the reception desk. She gave him a confused look.

"Um . . ." she began after a few awkward moments of silence. "I'm just a receptionist. Maybe I can get one of our salesmen to help?" She waved the tall African over. The same one who had been less than warm to Asher the day before. When the African saw that it was Asher, he sucked his teeth.

"You suck them joints on some ho shit again, and I'll make sure that you swallow them," Asher promised. He turned back to the receptionist. "Baby girl, I don't care if you're the receptionist or a janitor, I just need anybody but that nigga to get the commission on this." He stared hatefully at the African, holding the shopping bags full of money.

"Brudda . . ." the African salesman tried to begin his apology after seeing all the cash Asher was holding. By then it was too late.

"Oh, we brothers today? Yesterday you treated me like I was a shit stain on the bottom of your shoe," Asher reminded him. "Nah, nigga. Keep that same energy." He then turned back to the receptionist. "You gonna push this sale through, or do I have to take my money elsewhere?"

The commission from Asher's purchase ended up going to the receptionist. It was the first sale of her career. She also ended up being the first woman he defiled in the backseat when they went out for a test drive. For the first forty-eight hours of owning the car, Asher felt like the man, but then reality set in. He had just blown half his savings on something that he didn't really want or need. He didn't even have anywhere to park it. If the car was left in one of the spaces at the condo he shared with his mom, it would tell everyone who was curious exactly where he laid his head. He ended up having to stash the car in the garage of one of his homies and resumed driving the Accord on the day-to-day. This C-Class was a purchase that he obviously hadn't thought through. Another sign of his immaturity when it came to such things. He was a shot caller in the crew now but still had a lot of lingering soldier tendencies that he had been struggling to break. Engaging in prideful, materialistic bullshit was one of them.

Normally, Asher wouldn't have even bothered with the C-Class, especially in the hood and when there wasn't anything going on. He was in his bag that day though. He woke up that morning and felt like flexing, which was rare for him. He was a low-key kind of dude, but every so often, he found that he had to remind people who he was and how he'd gotten there.

Over the past six months, a lot had changed in the hood. After the unexpected death of their former general B-Stone, things got crazy. Right before his passing, B-Stone had pulled their hood into a war with a rival gang over a personal grudge. There were heavy casualties on both sides, but none heavier than the losses of B-Stone and his second in command, Ab. With no leadership, the hood was thrown into chaos. Asher and his boys found themselves fighting a war on two fronts: the rival gangs and members of their own crew who were seeking to stake a claim to what B-Stone had left behind.

It was a bad time for their neighborhood and looked to get worse unless someone did something to bring an end to it. This is when Asher stepped up. While other members of their set sought to take over through violence, Asher employed subterfuge. While everyone was trying to kill each other, Asher was behind the scenes brokering a deal that would not only stop the killing but change the dynamics of the hood. He brought something to the table that none of the top hitters trying to take B-Stone's spot could . . . a new connect.

No one ever saw Asher's takeover coming. To the power players in the city, Asher had never been considered a threat. To them, he was simply one of B-Stone's young lieutenants who had a reputation as a pussy hound, not a gangster. By the time they realized the error of their ways, Asher had seized control of the neighborhood with barely a shot fired. This isn't to say that his takeover wasn't without its share of bloodshed. There were still those who questioned whether or not Asher was fit to lead. Their questions were answered swiftly and violently. Once the first few bodies dropped, everyone else fell in line. Asher taking over ended up being the best thing that had happened to the hood in a long time. He wasn't a tyrant like B-Stone who had ruled through intimidation and greed. Asher was a businessman who wanted everyone to eat. It didn't matter if you were from his set or not. So long as you weren't an enemy, you could get a seat at the table. Publicly Asher was the man who had taken the throne, but there were unseen forces at work that kept him sitting on it.

"*Incoming call*," the car's Bluetooth announced. Asher looked at the number flashing across the screen on the dashboard. There was no name associated with the number, but it was one Asher was familiar with. His mood darkened because he knew that the person on the other end was likely calling to say something that he didn't want to hear. With that in mind, he rejected the call and kept coasting.

He continued coasting up Market Street and hit a hard right on MLK. This was where the Essex County College campus was located. The school was in the heart of the hood, but only those who lived in the city really understood this. Those who made the commute from other places were oblivious to the dangers lurking only a few blocks away. He pulled the car to a stop near a fire hydrant and put on his hazard lights. He fired up his blunt but made sure to keep checking his mirrors. From the way his head was on swivel, you'd have thought he was on high alert for enemies, which he always was, but in this case, he was looking for traffic cops. They were lousy in that neighborhood and loved to slap tickets on car windshields. Once he'd even gotten a ticket while sitting in the car. Some of them were dicks like that. Hopefully he wouldn't be there long.

As if reading his mind, his man Cal appeared, walking from one of the campus buildings. He had been taking night courses there for the last month or two. There was a knapsack slung over his shoulder and wire-rimmed glasses sitting on the bridge of his nose. On his arm was a pretty Asian girl who was smiling from ear to ear at whatever he was saying. At a glance, you'd have thought that Cal was just another math nerd coming from class, but looks could be deceiving. When he spotted Asher waiting for him, he held up a finger, indicating that he needed a minute while he wrapped up his conversation with the Asian girl. After whispering a few more sweet nothings, he kissed her on the cheek, and they parted ways.

Cal waited until he was in the car with Asher before calling the change. The knapsack was discarded into the back seat with abandon. He slid the glasses off and tossed them into the center console. Gone was the doe-eyed school-kid expression that was plastered over his face; it was replaced by a look so hard it would make a man think twice about testing him. From somewhere behind his ear, he produced a Black & Mild, which he fired up and let the smoke float out of the open window. It was watching Dr. Jekyll turn into Mr. Hyde. This was the Cal Asher knew. The Cal who had stood back-to-back with him in the face of insurmountable odds, and they had still come out on top. He turned to Asher, and the first two words he spoke were, "Sup, nigga?" Asher smiled at the greeting.

Cal, whose real name was Calvin, was Asher's best friend in the world. He'd been given the nickname Calico because he suffered from vitiligo. It was a condition that caused his pigment cells to malfunction and resulted in his skin being splotched with spots that were lighter than the rest of his toffee-colored complexion, causing his skin to resemble the fur of a calico cat. He had been Asher's partner in crime since they were kids, and the men had come to look at each other as brothers. Though they shared no blood between them, they'd shed enough together to make them family. Cal was a full year younger than Asher, but he acted like the older brother of the two. They'd both jumped off the porch and into the streets at early ages, but Cal had been in the streets going full speed ahead since he was a small child. He'd made his first drug transaction at eight, and by the time he was ten, he was already stashing guns for the homies on the block. Cal was a bad seed, but he was as loyal as they came.

"Waiting on your slow ass. What took you so long?" Asher asked.

"What? You ain't got eyes? I'm trying to crack little mama. I ain't never had no Asian pussy. I hear it's the bomb!" Cal said.

"It is. I took down this bad Japanese joint before I flew back yesterday," Asher said with a smile, reminiscing on the episode he'd had with the little freak.

"Sounds like Cali is being good to you. I guess that's why you're always sliding out there," Cal said.

"I can't front, that shit is starting to grow on me. The sunshine, the weed, the money! What's fucking with that? Still, you know my heart is always gonna be in Newark," Asher told him.

"Speak for yourself. I can't wait until my pockets get to where they need to be so I can put this grimy-ass city behind me," Cal said seriously. He had been born and raised in Newark but had always yearned to see the world beyond the Garden State.

"I keep trying to get you to take a trip with me, dawg. I'm getting tapped in with a lot of the movers and shakers out that way. As a matter of fact, this kid I been doing a little something with is supposed to be out here for a day or so, on business. I'd love to put you two next to each other. Dude been around the music business for a while and pulled my coat to a lot of game. He's a street nigga like us, but got this shit figured out on the industry side."

"I'll let you keep playing diplomat. I'm good on making new friends," Cal told him. Every time Asher came back from California, he always chatted Cal up about this person or that he had met in the industry. Asher was built for the Hollywood shit, but it wasn't really Cal's thing. He just wanted to get paid.

Asher shook his head. He loved Cal, but the boy could sometimes be short-sighted when it came to the long game. Cal would never be able to move in the circles Asher had discovered if he didn't shake his street nigga mentality. "I don't know why you fronting on Cali, when you already out here moving on some Denzel shit. I see an Oscar in your future." Asher poked fun at Cal.

"What you mean?" Cal frowned.

"I mean you acting like you actually belong at somebody's university with the rest of them squares," Asher clarified. "I'd definitely nominate you for an Oscar."

"You sound dumb as hell. I got as much to continue my education as any white, Indian, Chinese, or whatever color of the rainbow ass kid on that campus. What, you think playing these corners is the end game in all this? Somebody among us has to be educated enough to show you dumb muthafuckas how to wash all that dirty money," Cal said with an edge of hostility to his tone.

"Damn, I was only fucking with you," Asher said, not understanding why Cal was so offended. The homies always gave Cal grief about him going back to school, including Asher. In the beginning, he thought his friend was only attending to chase the uppity girls who attended, but after Cal had completed the first semester he reasoned that his friend might be serious. Cal had always been a smart dude, smarter than Asher even, but he had given up school long ago to chase paper on the streets. The hood was all he knew and all he wanted to know, but it was obvious that something had changed over the last couple of months. Asher never pressed him about it. He figured his friend would speak of it when he was ready.

"My fault," Cal spoke up after a few beats of awkward silence. "I just got some shit weighing on me."

"That's obvious to a duck. You haven't quite been yourself since we got our promotions. Of all the homies, I thought you'd be the happiest that we finally got some real stripes," Asher said. He and Cal had gone from two corner boys to upper management. When they were kids, that was all they'd ever talked about—getting bumped up beyond the rank of soldier, and their time had finally come. Thanks in part to Cal.

"I was . . . I mean, I am." Cal tripped over his words. "Yo, shit is just different for me now."

"How?" Asher asked. He saw that Cal was hesitant to respond. "Look, if we're going too deep and you don't wanna talk about it, I ain't gonna pry."

"My granny," Cal said. He took a few minutes before continuing. "She ain't been doing too good."

"Word? I'm sorry to hear that," Asher said sincerely. He'd known Cal's grandmother since he was a shorty. He remembered summer days of sitting at her dining room table and eating fried bologna sandwiches. She was a kind yet no-nonsense woman who could either tend to your wounds when you were hurt or slap the taste out of your mouth if you were out of line. Asher hadn't seen her much since he had gotten heavy into the streets, but she had to be getting on in years. "She gonna be okay?" He was hopeful.

"They don't think so . . . not this time." Cal's voice was heavy with sadness. "Granny been fighting the big C for a few years now. For a time, it looked like she had beat it, but then that shit came back with a vengeance. This might be Granny's last ride."

"Bruh, don't even talk like that. I hear stories in the news all the time about people diagnosed with cancer who come back to beat it. We put our money together and get Granny the right care she's still got a shot."

This made Cal laugh. "You sound just like Granny, praying on a miracle. I wish it was so, kid. They gave us a few different options to prolong her life, but Granny ain't trying to go under the knife and after what that chemo did to her the last time . . ." Cal had to pause to compose himself. "Nah, we ain't gonna subject her to that. All we can do at this point is keep her comfortable and happy. That's why I got my ass back in school."

Asher gave him a questioning look.

"Dude, that old lady has been more of a mother to me than my real mother. When my mom was out in the streets getting her swerve on, it was Granny who looked after me and my sisters. Whenever I would get locked up and they needed an adult to come to the precinct, it was always Granny. She loved me more than anyone and all she asked in return was for me to make her proud. And what did I do? I'm out here slanging and banging for all the neighbors to see. I've been a disappointment to that woman for my whole life, and for once, I wanted to do something that she could be proud of."

"So, you jump in school to make Granny think you've finally come in out of the streets," Asher said. Cal's behavior was starting to make sense.

"Pretty much. I mean, Granny ain't no fool. I'm sure she knows that my hands ain't completely clean, but at least this is something she can brag to her friends about. Her grandbaby, the college student. I can't lie. In the beginning, I was only doing this for the sake of Granny, but as I got heavy into this school shit, I ended up liking it. My grades in college are better than they ever were in high school because I'm actually applying myself this time."

"You trying to take this college thing all the way and get out the streets?" Asher wanted to know. Cal had been his right-hand man since day one, and the thought that he might one day lose him didn't sit well.

"Again, there's that short-sided thinking that all you niggas from the block suffer from," Cal joked. "But on some G-shit, being in these classrooms got me looking at the game from angles that I hadn't noticed before. We them niggas in our hood, but who the fuck are we to the rest of the world? I want my name to ring everywhere, not just on West Kinney! I got long-term plans for us, Ash. Bank on that shit."

For the next few blocks, they rode in silence. Whether he knew it or not, Cal had given Asher quite a bit to think about. Up to that point, Asher hadn't put too much serious thought into his future. He lived his life according to the Jay-Z line: *"Fuck tomorrow . . . as long as the night before was sweet."* At only eighteen years old, Asher was handling a bag, pushing a clean whip, and could fuck any chick he wanted to. For him, he had already surpassed his wildest expectations of where he saw himself at that age once he realized he'd never go to the NBA. After speaking with Cal, he began to wonder: Was there more to the world than money and pussy?

CHAPTER 4

"Damn, nigga. Watch that shit!" Sin barked at his little brother. Bone had just sprayed the whole table with the champagne he had spit out.

"My bad, bro, but this shit tastes like cold piss." Bone eyed the bottle of André Brut Larry had one of the girls bring to the table with the Hennessey. "I should've known, once that fuck nigga offered us a free bottle, that it would've been some foo' shit. He must think it's still the nineties, keeping this dump stocked with this."

"Last I checked, we didn't come here for the free alcohol." This was Unique. He was the third member of their party. He was leaning with his elbows on the table and his fingers steepled in front of him, watching the crowd through dark hooded eyes. Every time he shifted, the heavy gold medallion hanging from his neck scraped the table. Unique was a tall, lanky kid who wore his hair in a dark, wavy Caesar with a half-moon part cut into it at the hairline. His sense of style, coupled with his mannerisms, draped Unique in an air that made you feel like he had been hustling out of a Brooklyn crack house in the nineties, been dropped into the new millennium, and hadn't missed a beat. He stank of the streets and wore their coat of arms with the pride of a man strutting into church in his Sunday's best suit.

"Stop acting like you don't keep a pint of something tucked at all times." Bone sucked his teeth in annoyance.

"Yeah, I enjoy a taste here and there but not while I'm on the clock," Unique told him, watching a scantily clad woman saunter past their table en route to a group of young men two tables away. They were popping bottles and talking louder than they needed to. That told Unique all he needed to know about them. They weren't used to money, so he deduced they were either scammers or had recently hit a lick and were enjoying the spoils. This made him crack a gold-toothed smile because the group kind of reminded him of when he and his crew were on the come up.

"What you over there grinning about?" Sin asked, noticing the smirk on Unique's lips.

"Took a short walk down memory lane," Unique answered.

"I'm gonna need you to pull yourself out of the past, so we can focus on the present. How reliable is your source?" Sin asked.

Unique weighed the question before answering. "Nobody is foolproof, but so far, I've worked with her twice, and her info was good. This trick nigga she's dealing with has his head so far up her ass that he fancies himself trying to be her boyfriend."

"Can't wife no ho," Bone interrupted.

"Fortunately for us, he didn't get that memo," Unique continued. "Boy's nose is wide open for that young hole. As it turns out, the only thing he loves almost as much as shoving his face in her pussy is pillow talk. The last two licks she put me onto were as a result of him and his big mouth, bragging about the people he knew and places they like to hang out. This here is a little more personal though. Seems he's been feeling slighted by the cat he works for . . . some internal shit going on or whatever. He's in his bag over it and has been venting to ol' girl about it. He let slip that they'd be here for a meeting tonight. She ran their whole itinerary down, too, while I was throwing cock into her scandalous ass a few nights ago."

"Dog-ass nigga." Sin laughed.

"You're one to judge, like I didn't see how you were looking at that square-ass white broad," Unique shot back.

"So, she's cool with just sitting by while we run down on her trick and his people?" Sin asked.

"He won't be in attendance. She's gonna see to that," Unique told him.

"How?" Sin wanted to know.

"I don't know, and truthfully, I don't care. What's up with all the questions all of a sudden? You getting cold feet?"

Sin marinated on Unique's question before answering. "Nah, just thinking how this dude has to be a special kind of stupid if he hasn't already peeped that him and his girl are the only common threads on both those jobs we did. That, or he's low-key in. Either way, after this business tonight is done you should probably fall back off your girl and her tips. We keep pissing in the same patch of dirt, and it's eventually gonna turn into mud."

"Shit, that's probably all they serve in this bum-ass joint, mud pies," Bone said with disdain.

Sin looked at his little brother and shook his head. "You're the only dude that I know who can find a reason to be angry in a room full of pussy." He loved his little brother, but he was the ultimate pessimist. He was always angry or complaining about something, and it worked Sin's nerves.

"Speaking of pussy." Unique nodded at something just behind Sin.

Sin turned to see Promise making her way across the room in the direction of their table. He almost hadn't recognized her now that she had changed out of the boy shorts and tank top and into something way more revealing. Her hips swayed beneath the black, sheer wrap that obscured the flesh from her waist to upper thigh, but he could tell from the front that the back had to be hitting for something too. Ms. Jersey was clearly far more stacked than he'd earlier assumed.

"Damn, that white girl was hiding all that?" Bone gave voice to his brother's thoughts. Earlier he'd wanted to stomp the clumsy waitress out, but now all he could think about was laying her down. "You think she goes the extra mile like the rest of these bitches." He began counting his money openly.

Sin ignored his brother and kept his eyes on Promise. "For a minute, I was starting to think you changed your mind about taking care of me tonight," he said, greeting her once she had arrived at the table.

"Sorry, I had to change my clothes," Promise explained. She tried her best not to squirm too much under his hungry stare. He was looking at her the same way Asher used to before she discovered that he was really a wolf in sheep's clothing. "What can I get for you guys?" she asked, back on topic.

"How about something that don't taste like pee-pee?" Bone raised the bottle of André. For as much as he complained about the horrible taste, that hadn't stopped him from sipping from the bottle.

"You can bring us another bottle of Hennessey and a few waters," Unique answered for them.

"Okay, I'll be right back."

"Don't take too long, Ms. Jersey," Sin said flirtatiously,

watching Promise as she made awkward steps to the bar. It was almost like watching a baby calf trying to walk for the first time.

"What happened to not being drunk on the job?" Bone asked Unique.

"Aesthetics," Unique replied, tossing a few singles at a girl who was trying desperately to get one of the men at the table to make eye contact with her. She wasn't much to look at, a bit on the skinny side with a dry, synthetic wig. But he allowed her to dance in front of him for a bit.

"What?" Bone didn't understand the word.

"Appearances," Unique said, simplifying it for him while stuffing a few singles into the stripper's top. She tried to sit on his lap, but he waved her away. He was short on sympathy, and the few beats he allowed her to linger had served their purpose. "Three dudes at a table with no bottles and no bitches sends up a red flag. Be active, but on point, feel me?"

"That's a strategy I can get with," Bone agreed. He summoned two passing strippers and had them squeeze into the booth on either side of him. He draped one arm around each girl and started talking dirty to them while flicking.

Inviting a bunch of random chicks into their space wasn't exactly what Unique meant, but it would keep Bone occupied and out of trouble, so he let it go.

A few minutes later, Promise came back carrying a tray that held an ice bucket with a bottle of Hennessey in it, several plastic glasses, and a few bottles of water. Taped to the top of the Hennessey bottle were two glow sticks. Promise had wanted to light the sparklers like she'd seen the other girls do when bottle service was requested, but Big Sally wouldn't let her. It would've been just their luck if Promise had fallen again and accidentally burned the joint down.

"Here you go." Promise carefully set the bucket holding the

liquor bottle at the center of the table, and then sat the waters down. She was proud of herself for not spilling anything. "If there's nothing else, I'm gonna make my rounds, and I'll come back and check on you in a few." She made to leave, but Sin stopped her when he gently grabbed her wrist.

"Wait a second. Where you off to?" Sin asked.

"I . . . um . . . I was just gonna go and check on some of my other tables and spin right back," Promise explained. Larry didn't pay them, and she didn't dance, so she had to depend on the tips she made waiting tables to make ends meet.

"I thought we had an agreement, Ms. Jersey? In return for me saving your job, you belong to me tonight," Sin reminded her, running his index finger over the back of her hand. He could feel the girl shudder before snatching her hand away.

"Ain't no nigga got no papers on me," Promise said defensively.

"Watch that N-word, shorty. I ain't comfortable with no clear folks throwing it around, and you shouldn't feel comfortable saying it," Unique warned.

"That girl ain't no cracker. She's just as much of a nigga as you," said one of the girls who had joined their table. It was Lita. Bone had her in such a deep headlock that Promise hadn't noticed her. Promise couldn't stand Lita, and the feeling was mutual. She was one of the last people that she wanted to see at that table.

Sin looked from Lita back to Promise. He'd assumed that she was white. Her skin had a little hue to it. Maybe he would've given her Spanish, if not white, but Black? There was no way. "Bullshit!" he blurted out, not being able to mask his shock.

"Real shit," Promise confirmed. "My dad was white. Not that it's anyone's business." She cut her eyes at Lita.

"Don't be cutting your eyes at me like you're about that life," Lita said threateningly.

"She might not be, but I am." Mouse's cousin Keisha appeared just behind Promise. She was a tall, dark drink of water who stood at about five eight, but the high-heeled thigh-high boots she wore had her flirting with six feet. She was a strikingly beautiful girl with Hershey-colored skin and lips that looked like they were made for sucking dick. "We good over here?" She was speaking to Promise, but her light brown eyes were locked on Lita.

"Yeah, we good," Promise answered.

"We'd be even better if your big, fine ass joined us," Bone shot at Keisha.

Keisha looked over the trio and gave a little chuckle. "Nah, I got somewhere to be, but thanks for the offer. Let me holla at you for a minute." She took Promise by the arm and led her away from the table before she could protest. "What did I tell you about letting these hos in here walk over you?"

"Lita wasn't walking over anybody. She was just talking shit," Promise said.

"That's how it always starts. A dirty look here and there, talking slick out their mouths. You let shit like that slide, and the next thing you know, they'll be trying to press you for your tips or force you into some dyke shit." Keisha recalled some of her early experiences when she first started dancing. "When these bitches get out of pocket, you got to bank their asses off the rip. This will send a message to the rest of the girls that you ain't having it. Tighten up, white girl. And what is your ass even doing here? You weren't scheduled to work tonight."

"Larry called me and asked if I'd cover Gene's shift," Promise said. A look flashed across Keisha's face. It was brief, but Promise caught it. "Something wrong?"

"What's wrong is, you over there playing in the mud with that bunch." Keisha nodded toward the table where Sin was trying to pretend not to be watching them. "You know you ain't built to be tied up with no *real* gangsters."

"And how would you know what I'm built for?" Promise asked defensively, folding her arms across her breasts.

"Because I was there when your ass showed up on my doorstep with Mouse, broke, dusty, and scared out of your damn mind when you thought them niggas y'all crossed were after you."

"Well, I ain't that same weak bitch," Promise informed her.

"Yeah, you've grown some stones since you've been here. You're tougher than I used to give you credit for, but that doesn't mean you're ready to run in the fast lane, shorty." Keisha was speaking to Promise like she was a child that she was trying to deter from getting in the streets.

"Whatever." Promise rolled her eyes. She wasn't up for Keisha's shit.

"Promise, don't think because you've put in on a few off-brand bitches that you'd stand a chance against this grand champion, so watch that slick shit. I ain't for it. Save that for hos like Lita, who you keep letting punk you. Don't try it with me," Keisha warned. Promise may not have been a fighter, but she had shown that she was willing to get busy. Keisha had seen her whip a few girls out, and it had earned her a bit of respect from the veteran street runner, but not enough to where she would allow Promise to start thinking they were in the same weight class.

Promise glared at Keisha, but her gaze softened. She knew that Keisha was right. She had been out of pocket for popping fly when she had just pulled her out of the fire with Lita. She was wrong and big enough to admit it. "My fault."

"Ain't it though," Keisha replied. "Promise, you've only been in New York for a year, and I know you think you've got this city figured out, but I guarantee you don't." Her eyes drifted back to the table again. "Keep your head down, get your money, and keep it pushing. Serve the drinks, but don't get caught standing too close to Sin."

"What is it with everybody warning me to stay away from Sin? Y'all act like y'all don't want me to get no money," Promise accused. Sin was tipping bigger than anybody she had ever serviced at Dirty Wine, and it seemed like everyone was hating on her.

"Naive lil bitch, you'll find yourself getting more than money fucking with Sin, and I don't mean that in a good way. Keep your distance," Keisha said seriously.

"I got you, Keisha," Promise said, but she had no intentions of letting Keisha or anyone else block her bag. The fact that Keisha was even bothering to try and look out for her came as a surprise. When they were in the apartment, it felt like Keisha was always on her back about one thing or another. Promise went out of her way to try and please the twin, but it seemed like she could never do anything right. Her change in attitude made Promise just a little suspicious. "Oh, and thank you for what you did back there with Lita."

Keisha let out a chuckle. "Don't flatter yourself. That had more to do with me than it did you. You're working here on the strength of me, which means you're riding my G-card. I can't have these whores thinking that I rock with weak bitches. Besides, if I let something happen to you on my watch, I'd probably have to fuck Mouse's little ass up. You know she thinks she's your guard dog."

"Keisha . . . I ain't paying you to stand around and talk shit. Let's get this money!" Larry shouted from across the room.

"Hold your damn horses! I'm coming!" Keisha yelled back. "Remember what I told you, Promise. Focus on your money and steer clear of everything else, especially Sin."

* * *

Keisha's words buzzed in Promise's head even after she had gone. This was the second time that night that she had received a warning about Sin. If the girls had meant to scare her off, the effect was the opposite, and she only became more intrigued by him. Not that she wouldn't heed the warnings and proceed with caution, but she was curious as to what there was to Sin that made even girls as seasoned as Donna and Keisha leery of him.

When she returned to the table, she found Sincere waiting for her. He had an apologetic look on his face. "Listen, Jersey. I didn't mean no offense. I was just a little thrown off because I assumed that you were white from the jump," Sin explained.

"People assume a lot of shit, but that don't make it so," Promise said flatly.

"This one has got a slick mouth!" Bone laughed heartily, slapping his hand on the table, causing Lita's cup of vodka to spill. "My bad, baby. Let me pour you another one." He reached for the bottle, but Lita stopped him.

"Nah, let the bottle girl take care of it." Lita glared at Promise. She was still upset that Keisha had checked her in front of the customers, but she was too cowardly to direct her anger in the proper direction. So she turned it on who she assumed was the weakest link.

Promise matched her stare. "I don't work for you."

"Nope, but you're a bottle girl assigned to this table. And I'm a guest of this table. So, why don't you get to pouring. My throat is dry," Lita said mockingly and slid the cup across the table.

Lita was always fucking with Promise by doing or saying something out of pocket. They had been at odds for the last few months or so. The crazy part about it was that their beef really didn't have anything to do with Promise. This was about Mouse. Not long after the two Newark girls had started working at Dirty Wine, Lita and Mouse had gotten into it. Promise couldn't even remember what the argument was about, but it had turned physical. Lita assumed that, because Mouse was so small, it would be an easy victory, but she was wrong. Mouse had been raised in the trenches, and her combat skills said as much. She whipped Lita's ass on a crowded Saturday night at Dirty Wine, and everybody saw it. This was part of the reason Larry had fired Mouse. Lita had been the one who started it, but she brought in more money than Mouse, so Mouse was the odd girl out. Lita had never really gotten over that beatdown and was always looking for someone to take her aggression out on because of it. She didn't want any smoke with Keisha or Candice, so she chose to give Promise a hard time whenever she felt like it.

There was a heavy silence as tensions settled over the table. Everyone looked at Promise to see how she would respond. You could tell by the burning in her eyes that she was hot. Lita was always picking at Promise, and for the most part, Promise always let it go. Lita had seniority and was one of Larry's *special* girls, so Promise often turned the other cheek to avoid a confrontation that could lead to her getting fired. That night was different though. It was one thing for Lita to talk down to her in front of the other girls, but now she was trying to show off for Sin and his crew.

As if on cue, the DJ spun Crime Mob's "Knuck If You Buck," and set the tone. The two girls eyeballed each other from across the table, Promise looking uncertain. Lita smirked when she saw doubt cross the girl's face, figuring that she had snatched her heart. She intended to make Promise her bitch for all the disrespect she had been made to suffer by Keisha and Mouse's little dusty ass. "Well?" she pressed.

"You got it," Promise said in a voice that said she conceded. She took the bottle of vodka in one hand and Lita's glass in the other. Instead of filling the glass, Promise hawk-spat into it and slid the soiled glass across the table back to Lita. "Sip that, messy ho!"

Lita was momentarily struck by the move. The girls who danced at Dirty Wine had been bullying Promise for so long without any real backlash that none of them had ever stopped to consider what they'd do if she ever grew a spine and decided to stand up for herself. The rabbit now had the gun, and all eyes were on Lita. With little more than her ego dictating her next move, she got up and took an aggressive step toward Promise, but her feet stuttered when Promise's hand snaked around the neck of the Hennessey bottle on the table. It wasn't a threatening gesture, but one that told Lita how far Promise was willing to go over this. Whatever point Lita was trying to make, she would have to bleed to get it across.

"Fuck is this?" Odell appeared. He glowered at everyone at the table, eyes lingering on Promise longer than anyone else. She was still clutching the bottle by the neck, nostrils flaring and eyes burning into Lita as she sat back down.

"Oh, I was just about to freshen the drinks for these gentlemen and skanks . . . I mean ladies." Promise batted her eyes, while cracking the seal on the Hennessy bottle to fill Sin and his boys' glasses.

"Yeah, Odell. It's hard to find good help, but Promise always makes sure she goes the extra mile," Lita said through gritted teeth.

Odell knew bullshit when he smelled it, but he didn't feel like dealing with a catfight at the movement. "Lita, raise up from this table and hit the floor. Some important folks rolling up and through here, and Larry wants you to entertain them personally."

"I'll be along as soon as I finish my drink," Lita told him, plucking a fresh glass and holding it out for Promise to fill.

"Your drunk ass will be along now!" Odell jabbed his index finger into the table for emphasis and almost flipped it and the bottles over.

"I'm coming." Lita rolled her eyes and slid out from under Bone. Her friend continued to linger. "What are you doing?" she asked the girl.

"Larry requested *you*, not *me*." The girl smacked her lips. With Lita gone, she would now be the center of attention at the table.

"Consider us a package deal. Now come the fuck on!" Lita commanded. Reluctantly, the other stripper slid out from under Bone, too. "I'm gonna see your pale ass again soon," she whispered to Promise as she passed her.

"Don't wait on it, ho!" Promise challenged her. Jack had slain the giant, and she now saw Lita for what she really was, and that was a coward and a bully.

Lita and her flunky had gone, but Odell remained. He wasn't saying anything, just standing there, looking over Sin and his crew with those creepy dead eyes. It was a very awkward moment, which would only become even more awkward once Bone opened his mouth.

"Something you need? You done already chased our bitches off. You plan on taking their places?" Bone asked in a challenging tone. Sin's baby brother was a live wire and obviously not very smart if he was taunting a man like Odell.

Promise's heart leaped in her chest as she saw Odell's jaw

clench. His eyes burned a hole in Bone, who defiantly returned his stare. She knew this was the calm before the storm. She wasn't sure if Bone or any of his people had been skilled enough to sneak any weapons into Dirty Wine, but even if they had, she doubted they'd do much good. She had seen Odell disarm, and break, men armed with everything from pistols to machetes. He was the embodiment of *"No weapon formed against me shall prosper."* Just when Promise was about ready to take cover, the most unusual thing happened. Odell smiled. At least, she assumed it was a smile. His lips turned up at the corners, and there was the briefest flash of yellowing, crooked teeth buried in gums of a sickly purple.

"This is my second time having to see about you boys. Third time will be the charm." Odell turned and lumbered across the room.

"Damn, Jersey. Ain't never a dull moment with you, huh?" Sin asked once Odell had gone and some of the tension had fled the table.

"You don't know the half," Promise said with a sigh. Without even thinking about what she was doing, she grabbed a plastic cup and helped herself to a shot from the bottle of Hennessey on the table.

"Feel free to pour up," Unique said in half-jest.

"I'm sorry." Promise covered her mouth in embarrassment. That was so out of character for her. It seemed like the longer she was in New York living with Mouse's cousins, the more their brash ways were rubbing off on her. They were a pack of wild ghetto broads who never needed an invitation to help themselves to whatever they wanted.

"Nah, you good, Jersey," Sin assured her while pouring her another shot and then one for himself. He hoisted his cup, suggesting that they toast.

Promise didn't want to, but she did. The second shot didn't burn as much as the first one. She normally didn't drink while she was on the clock, and especially not Hennessey. The last time she had gone out and gotten drunk, a man had ended up dead and her life upended.

"You better slow down on that yak, Jersey," Bone said, pulling the bottle back before Sin could pour her another one. One thing he hated was a thirsty bitch, and the pale-skinned girl seemed to be just that.

"I'm good," Promise said, feeling sweat beads pop on her forehead. "And would y'all please stop calling me that? I hate that shit."

"That ain't your name?" Sin asked curiously. He had heard Larry refer to her by that name and had been addressing her as such all night.

"No, my name is . . ." she paused. She thought about giving him some lame stage name like the other girls did but decided to just be straight up. "Promise . . . My name is Promise."

"I guess that's a better stripper name than Jersey." Unique shrugged.

"I told you I don't strip. That's the name my mother gave me," Promise told him.

"Why would she name you something like that?" Sin was curious.

Promise shrugged. "Probably because she was psychic and knew that life would play the same dirty tricks on both of us. Ain't neither of us ever met a man who made a promise that he was willing to keep."

CHAPTER 5

Servicing Sin and his bunch hadn't turned out anything like Promise had assumed it would. In the beginning she had been intimidated, especially considering their rocky start. Her introduction had been nearly getting stomped and fired, but her luck had since turned around. The guys didn't keep her too busy. She fetched them refills when they needed them, made sure that the table had enough water, and that their ice was cold. Every time Promise would have to get something for them, Sin made sure she got a tip, much to the ire of his baby brother who seemed to have something to say every time Sin handed her money. Bone hadn't kicked her like he had threatened, but he made it no secret that he didn't care for the clumsy waitress.

With Bone being the exception, everyone else at Sin's table was pretty cool. Sin, forever the charmer, continued to try and flirt with Promise, and she pretended not to notice. It wasn't that she wasn't into him, but playing with a cat like Sin was like trying to handle a tiger. They were cute enough but could still maul you without meaning to. Admittedly, he had game, but so did she. He just didn't know it yet. Promise was able to see all of them clearly for what they were, except Unique. He didn't talk much. He kept his responses to one or two words, and anything that required more than a whole sentence was whispered into Sin's ear. He'd hardly even said anything to the girls, and it wasn't for their lack of trying. The dancers popped it, shook it, dropped and busted it wide open for him but never got more than a few dollars thrown at them or the occasional slap on the ass, and even that felt like just an effort to be polite. Promise heard one of the girls whisper to another, asking if Unique was gay. The question made Promise laugh. There wasn't anything gay about Unique. He had the look of a man with deep focus. She couldn't be sure what that focus was on, but she guessed it wasn't pussy.

Bone, on the other hand, was all in. He helped himself to girls, liquor, and weed in abundance. Throughout the night, he never had anything less than two girls on his wide lap. He was showering them with singles, but Promise peeped that, for every one he threw, he stole two, which he would recycle. He was a straight grease ball. From the way random girls kept making their way over to the table, word had obviously gotten out that there were tricks in the building. Sincere didn't seem to care for all the attention his brother was drawing, and this was obvious by the looks he kept cutting at him. Bone either didn't notice or didn't care because he kept the party going. There was something brewing between them, and Promise made a note to keep an eye on the situation. One thing that she had learned since working the New York underground was the value of information, and plenty of it passed through Dirty Wine on a regular basis. Promise had seen girls come up off overhearing the right conversations, so she made it her business to keep her eyes and ears open, but her mouth shut.

Sin was different from the rest of his team. Not that he wasn't a street cat, because his whole swag reeked of somebody's projects or avenue. He carried the taint, the same as the rest of them, but in a different way. Whereas his brother Bone was boisterous, wanting to be seen, and his friend Unique was low-key, almost invisible, Sin fell somewhere in the middle. He smiled a lot and was a generous tipper. He even threw money at the girls he didn't touch, just to keep his brother entertained. This is the part that irritated Promise a bit. In her mind, she felt like Sin's section was her lick, and she wasn't keen on the idea of splitting money with random strippers that could've gone into her pocket. It was a hard pill that Promise would have to swallow. For as long as she stood on her principle of only serving drinks, and the other girls were willing to cross lines that she wouldn't, Promise would always have to split the baby with thirsty hos.

Sin proved to be a perfect gentleman. In fact, he never so much as tried to touch Promise inappropriately, though she was sure he wanted to. Still, Promise wouldn't allow herself to get so roped into what he appeared to be that she lost sight of what he was. She felt herself slip a few times. Mostly when she looked into those dreamy eyes of his. My God, she could get lost in them. Behind those orbs Promise saw such passion, but she also saw something else. Something sinister. Despite Sin's good looks, slick mouth, and charms that he wielded like a wizard casting a powerful spell, Promise knew that he was a man capable of evil. Sincere was a hot boy, and Promise was a young girl who loved to play with fire. Her experiences, as a result of pursuing Asher, had proved as much. It was easy to get lost in those eyes, but much harder to find her way out. Knowing this and remembering Donna's early warning was what kept her from falling down the rabbit hole that Sin was surely trying to bait her into.

While Promise was watching Sin, he was making observations of his own. When he'd first made the play to save Promise's job, it had been because he felt sorry for her, but as he got to know her, something had changed. He could tell she was obviously a fish out of water and had no business in a place like Dirty Wine, so the fact that she was working there spoke to her desperation. He reasoned that she was probably pressed for cash. He knew the signs because he had been there more than a few times himself, doing something that he hated to keep from going hungry. His original plan had been to trick off a few dollars and call his good deed done for the night, but as he watched her, an idea began to form in his head. Promise was not a favorite among the other girls working in the club. Some of them just seemed to downright dislike her for whatever reason, but the same couldn't be said for the men. Promise had been receiving quite a bit of acknowledgment from some of the regulars. She'd been greeted by at least a half-dozen men that Sin had counted since she had been at their table. The greetings didn't feel sexual, but he doubted they were completely innocent either. Promise was stacked but didn't have a lot of sex appeal. She gave off a good girl vibe with a sultry edge. It was like your play-sister from the neighborhood. You always felt like you needed to look out for her, but the dirty parts of your mind were somewhere else. Promise was like forbidden fruit in a room full of apples, and totally oblivious to how tempting she was. Sin started to see some *promise* in Promise, and his wheels were already spinning about how best to cut into her.

* * *

"Damn, am I that boring?" Sin finally broke the lingering silence between them. Promise was leaning against the table, lost in a daydream.

"Huh?" she answered, confused.

"You just been sitting there looking off into space the last few minutes," Sin explained.

"Sorry." She blushed, realizing how dumb she must've looked. "I've got a lot on my mind."

"I imagine it must be hard carrying all that around?" Sin's eyes drifted to her ass. She bashfully adjusted her position so that her back was to the edge of the booth. "I meant your thoughts. I imagine they're pretty heavy?"

"You have no idea." Promise let out a breath.

"You'd be surprised. I know a little bit about feeling like the weight of the world is on your shoulders," Sin said honestly.

"And what makes you think my shit is that deep?" she questioned.

"Your eyes. They look so . . . sad." Sin reached up to touch her face, and she recoiled as if he had moved to strike her. "Take it easy, baby." He plucked a loose piece of glitter from her cheek and held it up on his finger for her to see. It must've come off one of the girl's costumes. "Why are you so jumpy?"

"I'm not jumpy, just cautious of strangers," Promise told him.

"Well, we've been shooting the shit for almost two hours. I'd think that you'd be able to tell by now that I'm harmless." Sin smiled and exposed the palms of his hands in a submissive gesture. Promise wasn't moved. "Damn, you're a tough nut to crack, huh?"

"Uncrackable." She rolled her eyes.

"I haven't met a safe I couldn't crack or a lock I couldn't pick," Sin capped.

"That's probably because they were poorly built," Promise

countered. "Listen, Sin, you've been straight up with me all night, so I'm gonna return the favor. I ain't off that. So, if that's the reason you're throwing big tips and talking all nice, we can save you some money and me some grief by killing it right here." The way she came at him was cold but necessary. She had seen this movie before, and she knew better than to stay until the credits rolled.

"No disrespect, but you're giving yourself a little too much credit. You're cute and all, but what makes you think you're my type?" Sin asked. He continued before she could respond. "You fine as hell and got cake for days, but contrary to popular belief, it takes more than some light skin and good hair to move me to action. I need a little more to get in that particular bag, and I ain't sure you check all the boxes."

"Oh, so because I ain't trying to fuck-for-a-buck, I'm ugly now?" Promise asked harshly. It was all she could do to hide the hurt in her voice. Rejection was something she could smell from a mile away. She was used to being too fat, too pale, or just plain uninteresting enough to be a boy's first choice. She was used to it by then, but that still didn't stop it from stinging. Every last rejection always felt like the first one, but the ones that packed more punch than the others were the rejections that came when she had convinced herself that she had even a puncher's chance at getting something she wanted. It had been that way with Asher, and now with Sin. Promise was over this shit. "I ain't for this shit," she said before turning and storming off, leaving Sin sitting there flustered.

"Good riddance. The bitch talks too much," Bone said, glad to finally be rid of the chatty waitress. Outside of the fact that she had ruined his sweat suit, Promise represented a distraction. Sin hadn't done much but stare at her for half the night.

"Shut up, Bone!" Sin snapped at his little brother before rising from the table and starting in after her.

"Sin, where the fuck you going? Leave that bitch! It's a thousand other hos in here! You hear me? Sin!" Bone called after his brother, but he was gone.

CHAPTER 6

"Incoming call ... incoming call ..." Asher's Bluetooth announced. Once again, he rejected the call.

"That's the second time since I've been in the car that I've seen you dub that 862 number. Who that? One of your bitches?" Cal asked.

"Something like that," Asher said, but offered nothing else.

He navigated the Benz through the run-down blocks they had to pass on the way to the weed spot. They had decided to make a stop before. They could've gotten the weed in their hood, but all the young dudes had out their way was Sour, Gorilla Glue, and a few Indica strands. Asher was cool with those, but Cal had a taste for something different. Cal was in the mood for some Haze. Normally, they would've driven across the George Washington into Washington Heights, as they seemed to be some of the last few players in the game who still had good Haze. However, there had recently been some chatter about these Spanish kids in Newark that had it now too. They pumped it out of a grocery store off Grove Street, so this was where they headed.

Asher pulled into an empty spot four car spaces from the front of the store. He never parked in front of drug spots, even when he wasn't driving his Benz. This even went for his own drug blocks. It was a lesson he had learned when a buddy of his got photographed some place that he shouldn't have been. The cops managed to tie him into an investigation they had going trying to bust some coke dealers. Asher's buddy was only buying a few grams at a time from them for personal use, but the police had photographed his car at the spot enough times to twist him up into a conspiracy charge. He was eventually able to beat it, but it cost him time and money.

The bodega sat on the corner of the block, right at the intersection. On the outside, it didn't appear to be much different than any of the other four stores it shared space with in a two-block radius, with their tattered awnings and plexiglass windows painted with advertisements of sandwiches and cold beer. One could've easily driven past the spot and not given it a second look, had it not been for the flow. The door of the small grocery store flapped open and closed with the frequency of a project pigeon trying to evade an alley cat who had gotten the drop on him. The fact that hardly anybody was coming out of the store with shopping bags sent a clear message that this was not your average bodega to everyone, including the police. The best part was that they couldn't do too much about it. More accurately? They chose to look the other way. When Murphy legalized weed, it changed the playing field of cities throughout the Garden State. It still wasn't cool to sell it over the counter of your establishment unless you were licensed, but sometimes the low man got a play too. Newark PD had their hands full enough with the bodies dropping around the city due to the influx of gang activity, so sometimes you'd get lucky, and cops in certain districts would figure that turning the occasional blind eye to the unlicensed pounds being moved through spots like the bodega was less hassle than doing the paperwork. So long as you kept things orderly, you could get money. But the minute you jumped out of pocket, Essex County would sic its most hostile peacekeepers on you. From the outset, the Spanish cats who owned the bodega knew this already.

Cal got out and went into the bodega to get the weed, while Asher stayed with the car. He didn't like to go into weed spots. This probably would seem odd to most, considering the fact that he spent most of his days going in and out of trap houses. His phobia stemmed from an incident where he'd almost gotten picked up as a part of a raid several years prior. The only thing that had stopped him from being booked was the fact that the police van was built to sit twelve and he was number thirteen in the sweep. Thirteen, by the way, was also his lucky number and the number he wore on all his jerseys during his days of playing ball. What also helped was that nobody answered the door when he went inside the spot, so when the police picked him up coming out, he didn't have any weed on him. Since then, Asher never went into weed spots if he could avoid it. He either got it brought to him or sent someone else.

While Cal was inside buying the weed, Asher was leaning against his car busying himself with his phone. He had a missed call and a few text messages from his new plug suggesting that he get back with him. Asher had an idea of what he wanted, but he just didn't have the energy right then and there. Dealing with his eccentric drug connect could be taxing, and Asher just didn't feel like dealing at the moment. His connect had the misconception that, because he had played such a major role in taking over, it meant Asher would jump every time he called, but Asher had other ideas. It's not that he wasn't grateful for the opportunity, but Asher was his own man. He kept the peace for the sake of being able to flood his hood with good drugs, but if things continued the way they had, he might have to find himself a new plug. It wasn't something that he was looking forward to having to do, but it was something he might need to prepare for.

Asher was just about to respond to the text and set up a meet time with his connect for the following day, when he felt the hairs on the back of his neck stand. A feeling came over him. It was the same feeling one would have right before something bad went down. He turned in time to see a red Honda pull to a stop and double park next to his car, boxing him in. "Enemies!" the word exploded in Asher's head. He snatched his gun from the hidden compartment and was about to get it shaking when the passenger window of the Honda rolled down. The face he saw inside the car wasn't that of an enemy, but one that left an equally bitter taste in his mouth.

"Sup wit it, blood?" Starla's thug ass greeted him from the open window. She was wearing a baggy black sweatshirt, and she had a bandana tied around her head.

"Big Star, what's shaking?" Asher replied. Starla was a home girl from the set. She was probably one of the hardest broads that Asher had ever met in his life. He remembered one time when a girl Starla was beefing with tried to hit her with a car. Starla rode the hood of the car for over a block, trying to stab through the girl's windshield with a kitchen knife, before finally falling off into the street. Starla was a straight-up gangster and someone you didn't want to fuck with.

"I can't call it." Starla got out of the car. "Sliding through to get some bud."

"Oh, you don't shop with my people no more?" Asher teased her.

"I could ask you the same. I'm sure you ain't all the way over on this side of town to take in the scenery." She gestured to the dilapidated neighborhood. "What's going on other than that though? We don't see you on the block too much since you took B-Stone's position."

"Inherited," Asher corrected her.

"Right, inherited." Starla gave him a knowing wink.

There had been rumors circulating in certain circles about the mysterious circumstances surrounding B-Stone's murder and the timing of Asher securing a new plug, who just happened to be affiliated with one of B-Stone's rivals. Couple that with Ab, a man who didn't do drugs, overdosing and clearing the way, and the whole situation just felt wrong. There was indeed some buzz about Asher possibly having a hand in the turn of events, but two things made the streets hesitant to turn on him. The first being that he had increased the organization's profits by nearly two hundred percent since taking over. B-Stone got more people killed than he made rich during his personal war. The second thing was that the one remaining person who could've possibly exposed Asher for what he truly was had gone missing. If Asher had it his way, he would remain missing. Though it hadn't been Asher's hands that took B-Stone's life, there was still blood on them, and he planned to keep this fact a secret for as long as he could.

"Well, it was good seeing you, Starla, but I gotta dip." Asher began to walk around to the driver's side of his car. He still had to wait for Cal to come out of the spot before he could push off, but he was looking for an excuse to get rid of Starla.

"I hear you big time. You got an operation to run and all that. But before you dip off, I got a little gift for you," Starla said slyly.

"What could you possibly have for me, Starla?" There was

something about the way she said it that made him uneasy, so he popped the door of his car in case he had to get to his gun in a hurry.

"A blast from the past." Starla knocked on the window of the Honda.

A second woman slid from the driver's side of the car and came to stand in front of Asher. It was a simple motion, but one executed with the grace of a banded sea krait slithering toward its next meal. You knew it was dangerous, but it was so damn beautiful you couldn't help but want to get a closer look, even at the risk of being bitten. Asher had always been turned on by the way she moved. He would sometimes just sit and watch her carrying out the simplest tasks. She looked especially good that day. Better than he'd remembered seeing her look in a while. A crimson red sew-in hung in loose curls down her back and stopped just above her plump ass. Long, toned legs that had moved across trap houses and runways alike extended from the tight shorts she was wearing. The raven-skinned beauty looked more like an exotic model than what Asher knew her to be, and that was a gangsta and former holder of his heart.

Ruby was Asher's ex. They were childhood sweethearts and had dated on and off since middle school. Back then Asher had only dabbled in the streets, as his focus was still on being an athlete, and Ruby was still in her good girl phase. She was a military brat, having moved around quite a bit before settling in Newark. Her mom had started creeping with one of her dad's brothers, and when her dad found out, he snapped. He sprayed his brother's car up while him and his wife were in it. Thankfully, Ruby's mother had lived, but her uncle hadn't been so lucky. For his crime, Ruby's dad had been dishonorably discharged from the military and thrown in prison. Ruby and her mother ended up staying with relatives in Newark until they were able to get their own place.

After what had happened with her ex-husband, Ruby's mom managed to get her shit together and build some type of life for her and her daughter. She secured a two-bedroom apartment in a multiple-family home in the South Ward of Newark that she and Ruby would call home for the next few years. It wasn't the greatest neighborhood, but it was quiet enough and cheap enough to where someone who didn't know the area could be sold on it. Ruby's mom was from Newark, so she knew what the city had to offer and tried to keep her daughter on a short leash so that she wouldn't get caught up in it. But the call of the streets would prove to be too powerful for her little girl. Back then Ruby and Asher had to steal time to be together outside of school, but they had made it work. This was around when Ruby's mom had gotten her into modeling. With her flawless dark skin, fiery eyes, and long limbs, she had a unique look, and the camera loved it. Early in her career, she mostly got booked for small print jobs and was hired as an extra for a few projects. It was a decent start, but Ruby's heart was never as in it as much as her mother's was. She was trying to live her wasted youth through her daughter, so she sometimes pushed harder than she needed to, which only made Ruby more resentful. The more time she spent in front of the camera meant less time she got to spend on the block, chasing the young street punk who had her nose wide open at the time.

When Asher jumped off the porch and got involved in the streets, Ruby followed him. It was the same with gang life. A lot of Ruby's friends who had gotten put on the set did so by sleeping with some of the high-ranking members, but Ruby chose combat as her method of initiation. For as pretty as she was, Ruby was a dual threat. She had hands and could whip most girls, and a few guys. In addition to that, her dad had made sure she was adept with firearms. The skills were his parting gift to his baby girl before the government buried him in a hole, never to be heard from again. Asher filled the void left in Ruby by her father, and the two became the Bonnie and Clyde of the hood. You couldn't tell them that they weren't destined to become ghetto stars, but like Nas said: *"Love changes . . . a thug changes . . . and best friends become strangers."*

A silence hung between them, eyes locked like they were having a staring contest. Ruby took a step toward him, more from reflex than anything, but she caught herself and held her position. His response was to shove his hands into his pockets awkwardly.

"Sup?" Asher finally broke the silence. His tone was dry and somewhat harsh. He hadn't meant to come across that way, but he couldn't help but to wear his feelings on his sleeve when it came to Ruby.

"Damn, it's like that?" Ruby asked.

Asher shrugged.

The dismissive motion cut Ruby deeper than anything that could've come out of his mouth. It made her feel basic. Like she was just another one of countless notches on his belt. Ruby was well aware of the fact that they weren't currently on the best of terms, but had it gotten that bad between them? She expected more . . . no, she deserved more, especially considering their history and the bitch he let derail their future.

Asher loved Ruby, in his own way, but he had never been totally faithful to her during their relationship. He fucked other girls. Some she knew about and others she didn't. In the beginning, when Ruby would hear rumors about Asher being intimate with other women, she would stalk them down and rain hell on them. As time progressed and she got older, she learned to stress herself out less over it. She hated the fact that Asher couldn't control his wandering dick but knew that he would always find his way back to her once he got bored with whoring. She could turn a blind eye to him giving his body away, so long as he kept his heart with her. Physical attachments she could stomach, but emotional ones were a deal breaker. It was an unspoken pact between them. A pact that Asher had honored until he met a girl that moved him in ways that Ruby couldn't. That was the one infidelity, of many, that Ruby couldn't overlook. The slight that her pride wouldn't allow her to forgive. In return, she punished him in a way that neither of them was sure he would ever be able to forgive her for. It had been a while since Asher had seen Ruby. Word around town was that she had got back into modeling and wasn't spending as much time in the hood as she had when she and Asher were still a couple. That was a good thing because seeing her regularly would've made it hard for Asher to honor his promise not to fuck with her like that anymore.

"How you been, Ru?" Asher followed in a kinder tone when he realized he'd hurt her. It hadn't been his intent, but there was an awkwardness between him and Ruby now. During the time when they had split, Ruby had shown Asher a side of her that he never knew lived there. She almost felt like a stranger to him.

She picked up on the fact that his tone had gone from cold to room temperature. "I'm okay. Some days are better than others, but I'm living my life. I'm in a good space these days."

"I can tell." Asher studied her face. "You got a little glow going on or whatever."

"That's because I cut a lot of stress and bullshit out of my life," Ruby said.

"Except Star," Asher joked.

"Fuck you!" Starla had heard the slight.

"You know that my bitch is forever going to be by my side," Ruby said confidently. She and Starla had been best friends since they were kids.

"Star is as loyal as they come," Asher said genuinely.

"I'm thankful for my girl. Very rarely do you find someone who comes into your life and loves you exactly how they said they would." Ruby spoke into his eyes when she said this. She didn't mean anything by it, but from the frown that crossed Asher's face, it must've translated wrong. "I didn't mean it like it sounded."

Asher shrugged. "You don't owe me no explanations. I granted you your freedom a long time ago, remember?"

"How could I forget when I still wear the scars on my heart?"

"A person who shoots themselves can't be a victim," Asher said slickly.

"Really, Ash? What was I supposed to do? Sit back and play dumb while you embarrassed me with yet another side bitch? A busted white ho at that?" Ruby snapped.

"I told you that I never slept with Promise."

"I find that hard to believe. You fucked that bitch, and you would've kept fucking her had she not got run out of the hood," Ruby accused. "She just better hope that the police catch her before I do because it's still on sight!"

"Ruby, it's been a year, and you're still carrying that grudge? Let it go!"

"How the fuck can I when she blew up my life?"

"And you tried to blow hers up. Call it even and leave that shit alone," Asher said with a sigh of annoyance.

"Look, even now you're still defending a bitch you claimed not to have slept with. I don't know how you can go so hard over that bum-ass chick, especially after what she did to the big homie."

"Tread lightly, Ruby," Asher warned.

"What? I'm not saying anything that everybody else in the hood doesn't already know. That white girl was the last one in the room with B-Stone before they found his body. That girl killed the homie."

"Promise ain't no killer," Asher said definitively. "Even if she was, ain't no way she'd have been able to take B-Stone down. Don't act like we don't all know what kind of animal he was. The man had his throat slit and his skull caved in. That's the work of a monster, and I just don't see that in her."

"Maybe she had help?" Ruby suggested, giving Asher a look.

"Fuck you trying to say?" Asher asked defensively.

Ruby knew how far she could push Asher and pulled back just when she had taken him to the edge. "Look, even the police said there was an eyewitness who saw two people running from that room, one of them being that white girl."

"Right." Asher tapped his chin as if he was deep in thought. "You know, I always wondered where the police would get somebody to stand on that story? Everybody there that night was *gang*." He flashed his set. "All of us are solid. As a matter of fact, if I recall correctly, Ab kept steering the homies out of the hall and into the suite because he didn't want hotel management complaining. B-Stone was killed not long after I left, and there's only one person who I can remember that was lingering in the hall about then."

"Fuck you, Asher!" Ruby said angrily. She hadn't expected him to call her on her bullshit. Asher had always been sharper than people gave him credit for.

"Nah, fuck you and all the bullshit and lies that you bring

to the table. You wanna know the real reason why I cut you loose?" Asher asked. He didn't wait for her to answer. "It was never because I wanted to fuck other bitches or because you didn't make me happy. The reason I walked away from our relationship is because I realized, for the first time, just how dangerous a broad like you is. You lied and tried to get an innocent woman killed. For what? Over your ego? Some dick? Fuck her. Did you ever stop to think that what you did could've kicked off a gang war that would've probably gotten half the hood killed or locked up, including me? I could never spend the rest of my life with a woman who has that kind of treachery in her heart."

His words hit Ruby like a closed fist. For a good while, she didn't speak. Not because she didn't want to, but because she could find no words to counter the damage he'd just done to her. Ruby had always held onto the hope that, one day, she and Asher would get back together. She was getting her life together and becoming more than just a hood rat, like Asher had always wanted her to be. A queen to his king. Once he saw the new and improved Ruby, he would realize that they belonged together. What he had just said to her shattered any hope of that. It was at that moment that something in Ruby clicked.

"Yeah, I might've played a part in lining her up, but not for no murder." Her voice had taken on a dangerous edge. "It killed me to watch you chase that bitch around like a love-sick puppy, so I wanted to show you that she ain't no different than the rest. So, I put her in a position to show her true colors. It didn't have the results I had intended, but . . ." She shrugged her shoulders. "I wonder if you would've still praised her as your White Goddess once the homies got done running through her?"

"You are one twisted bitch." Asher shook his head in disgust. He had never known the circumstances under which Promise left or the details about that night, but hearing Ruby break it down made him feel nauseous. He couldn't believe that he had ever allowed himself to love someone so foul.

"Twisted enough to put your pretty ass in the big chair," Ruby shot back.

"Fuck does that mean?" Asher didn't like where she was going with this.

"Asher, we've been together since we were kids. I know you better than anybody including your mother. You think I didn't peep the way you started looking at B-Stone when you thought nobody was watching?"

"Don't go there, Ruby. You know I had love for Stone," Asher insisted.

"I don't know if I'd call it love. You respected B-Stone, but you hated what he was doing to the set . . . all the drama with his personal war . . . the killing. Violence ain't your thing. You just wanted to get money. I know your heart."

"You don't know me as well as you think you do," Asher told her.

"So you've shown me over the last few months. It was a hell of a coincidence how Ab managed to party himself to death before B-Stone's body was even cold, and you ended up being the one to save the organization from crumbling. These dumb niggas are running around with you on their shoulders like some conquering hero, when, in reality, you're just a damn good chess player. I told you I know you better than your mama!" She cackled madly. Ruby could tell by the look on his face that she had struck close to home. For the first time in she didn't know how many years, she had been able to put a kink in his armor. He was on the ropes, so she figured she might as well finish him. It was only fair that she broke him the way he had broken her. She opened her mouth to continue her verbal assault, but Asher's hand closing around her throat killed the words before she could speak them.

"Little bitch," he hissed, "whatever you think you know, you better unthink it! B-Stone was a casualty of a fucking war that he started, and Ab didn't know his limits. Both deaths were tragic, but that's what it is. Leave it alone before you and your far-fetched conspiracy theories get both of us killed."

"Asher, baby, I was just talking because I'm angry! You know I've always kept your secrets and would never betray you!" Ruby had started crying, both out of fear and the fact that she knew she had gone too far and pushed him further away.

"Ain't no secrets to keep! And you betrayed me the minute you walked into that hotel suite and started all this bullshit. The sooner you get that in your head, the better off the both of us will be." Asher gave her a little shake to drive his point home.

"Ash," he heard Starla's voice behind him. "I love and respect you, but if you don't get your hands off my home girl, you're gonna force me to do something that neither of us will be able to come back from."

Asher looked at Starla from the corner of his eyes. She was standing close, but not too close. Just close enough to where she could get the drop on him if she had to draw her weapon. He turned his focus back to Ruby. Her eyes were wide and fearful. He had gotten his message across, so he released her.

"You good, baby girl?" Starla asked Ruby.

"Yeah," Ruby rubbed her neck. "I just want to go home."

"But the weed—"

"Please. I just want to go home." Ruby dropped her head and got back behind the wheel. Starla didn't follow right away.

"What's good with you?" Starla stepped to Asher.

"Nothing . . . you know how me and Ruby get. We toxic for each other." Asher tried to downplay it.

"That ain't nothing new, but what is new is that shit you just pulled. Asher, I been around you and Ruby for years, and I done seen y'all get into some knock down drag out shit, but never once have you put your hands on her."

"Sometimes you gotta let a muthafucka know where you stand on certain shit." Asher smoothed his clothes over.

"Yeah," Starla let her eyes run over him. "I can see exactly where you stand now. Catch you another time, homie." Starla slid into the car. Before she could even close the door completely, Ruby was pulling off.

Asher watched the car as it sped through a red light and disappeared into traffic. Long after it fled his view, he continued to stand there, stare, and think. Though he had tried hard not to show it, Ruby had rattled him. Was he that transparent? If so, who else had figured out the role he had played in usurping the power structure of his set and drug organization? What concerned him deeper still was Promise.

It was no coincidence that Promise had disappeared immediately after B-Stone's murder. This was even before the rumors started circulating about the white girl seen fleeing the room where B-Stone's body was found. Regardless of how hard he tried to convince himself that Promise had nothing to do with B-Stone's murder, he couldn't argue with the facts. Ruby's little confession had filled in some of the blanks that he hadn't had access to before, and this changed the timeline of events as he'd previously known them, but not the conclusion. Promise had been in that room. In his heart, he didn't think that she had murdered B-Stone, that much of what he'd told Ruby was true, but everything else was still up for question. Was Promise simply a victim of Ruby's bullshit or an accomplice in something more sinister?

There was an unspoken price on Promise's head in the
hood. So, he understood why she had stayed away, but with
this new information, Asher could've cleared her, or so he
hoped. There was still the chance that the homies would be
more concerned with their pound of flesh than the facts. Asher
was running the show, but B-Stone had been a national trea-
sure. Somebody would have to answer for that death. What
complicated things further was the fact that, if Asher presented
what he knew to save Promise, it might put the target on Ruby's
back. Or worse, his! The last thing he needed was somebody
picking at the loose string that could unravel the whole ball of
yarn. Ruby had taken a heaping shit in his lap, and now he was
charged with the task of cleaning it up.

It was crazy how, even after all this time being apart, Ruby
was still able to play on Asher's insecurities to the point where
they started fucking with his head. The truth of the matter
was, Ruby had struck a nerve when she threw his affection for
Promise in his face. He'd never courted a girl for the pussy,
including Ruby. You were either fucking or you weren't. Yet,
he found himself locked in an unfamiliar dance while trying to
get into Promise's pants. He was weak for her, and Ruby saw it.
That's what she was really mad about, that he was willing to go
to such lengths for a woman he had just met when she was the
one who had been there since the beginning. That weakness
could've gotten all three of them killed had it played out differently. What Ruby's anger-fueled revelation had shown was
that, for as tight as Asher's plan had been, there were still some
loose ends that would need to be tied up. A man in Asher's
position couldn't afford to have weaknesses of any kind. He
was the alpha of a pack of wolves, but the fates of B-Stone and
Ab showed him how easily those same wolves could turn on
you. No, he would not be the third name added to a mural

erected in the hood to honor their fallen soldiers. Asher had swum through a river of blood to get to where he was and would be damned if he let a broad pull him under to drown. Before he allowed that to happen, he'd cut the dead weight and let them drown in his place. With that in mind, he had a decision to make . . . swim or drown?

CHAPTER 7

Promise had finally managed to navigate the floor in the heels without killing herself or dousing anyone else with liquor. It was crowded by then, so she had to pick her way through a gauntlet of drunks and strippers prowling for a dollar or two. Her eyes stung from hurt and embarrassment, but she wouldn't allow the tears to fall. Not there. Not in front of the people who had marked her as weak anyway. She wouldn't give them the satisfaction of proving them right. Her thoughts and emotions were all over the place, and anger scratched at her heart. She was so deep in her feelings that, when she passed Larry and he tried to question her as to where she was going, she completely ignored him. She would likely get an ear full over the slight later on, but at that moment, she didn't care. She just needed to get somewhere quiet and collect herself.

In a rare act of kindness, fate had smiled down on Promise and spared her the embarrassment of the first tear falling until she was safely in the privacy of the bathroom. Thankfully, there was no one in there at the time. She paced back and forth, twirling the ends of her hair around her fingers so tightly that she could've pulled it from her scalp with a bit more force. She needed to get herself together.

Promise paused her pacing long enough to stand in front of the mirror over the sink. Her face was beet red, and tears danced in her eyes. She was on the verge of a breakdown, but the worst part was that she couldn't even say why. She didn't know Sin from a can of paint, so whatever he said or felt about her shouldn't have mattered, but for some reason, his words had managed to wound her. It was at that moment that she realized that her current emotional state had more to do with being rejected by yet another man than it had to do with Sin. "Look at you crying over some dick you ain't even tasted. Did you risk everything to come to a new city and still be the same weak bitch?" Promise chastised herself. It was her voice speaking, but in her ears, she heard her aunt Dell's words. Adelle, or Aunt Dell as she called her, was one of the few people who could reduce her to such a state. Six months later and with a river separating them, her mother's sister was still living rent-free in Promise's head.

It had been close to four years since Promise's mother, Fatima, had been killed, but Promise could still remember it vividly because she had been there. It happened on a Sunday. She was certain of this because Sundays were the designated day of the week when she and her mother would set everything else in their lives aside and do something together. More often than not it included watching a movie, be it on the big screen or small one. Normally when they went to the movies, it was in Newark at the Cineplex on Springfield Avenue, but that day they had rode out to the theater in Mountainside. It was one of the select theaters that would be showing some movie that Promise's mother wanted to see. It was called *Broken*.

Promise was tight because normally she got to pick the movie, but for some reason, Fatima had been adamant about seeing that particular film. *Broken* was an indie love story set in some fictional city and told the tale of a Black girl from the wrong side of the tracks who had fallen in love with a white musician from a prestigious family. No one wanted them together, but their love wouldn't be denied. In the end, they borrowed a page from *Romeo and Juliet* and made a suicide pact, but at the moment of truth, it was the girl who alone kept her promise. The movie closed with the musician cradling the dead girl in his arms, weeping over what could've been had he not been so weak.

Promise hadn't been impressed by the film, but it did something to her mother. She knew this because she could remember hearing her sobbing in the darkened theater as the closing credits rolled. It wouldn't be until later that Promise would come to find out why the movie had cut so deeply into Fatima. She explained to Promise how *Broken* had been written and directed by Promise's father and depicted the story of their short-lived love affair, minus Fatima killing herself. Her death in real life had been an emotional one. It had been the film for which Promise's father would build his résumé and go on to find great success in the industry. It was the first time Promise could ever remember Fatima speaking more than a few words here and there about her father, other than to answer the occasional question or tell Promise how well her father was doing in his career out west.

"One day, he's gonna send for us," Fatima would tell everyone. It was the only lie Promise could say she ever heard her mother tell.

After the movie, Promise and her mother had been heading home on 78-W. A pickup truck traveling at a high speed moved to merge onto the highway near the Maplewood ramp and blew through the yield sign. The driver never even bothered to look over his shoulder to check the flow of traffic. If he had, he might've seen the Town & Country minivan that was cruising in the slow lane. One minute Promise had been messing with the radio, trying to turn it from the R&B station to rap, and the next her head was bouncing off the passenger's side door as the car flipped six times before coming to rest on two of the three remaining wheels, only in the oncoming traffic lane. Everything after that came in pieces because Promise was in and out of consciousness, but the one thing she could remember was the vacant look in her mother's eyes. She lay with half her body jammed between the steering wheel and dash, while the other half was through the broken windshield. When the police report came back it would document how the pickup truck had been going almost 80 mph when it tried to merge. The driver had been drunk, and Fatima and her daughter had been at the wrong place at the wrong time. Promise's luck held up better than Fatima's because she managed to escape with only a broken arm, but her mother . . . she wished that she could've said that Fatima died instantly from the impact, but she didn't. She slowly bled out while they waited for the ambulance to arrive. Just like that, the only person in the world who truly loved Promise was gone.

With her mother dead, and her father having never publicly acknowledged her, Promise found herself a ward of the state . . . at least, for a time. There was an uncomfortable stretch where Promise was left floating through the system while the issue of who would look after her was sorted out. This is when Adelle stepped up, and things started sliding downhill. For all Adelle's bullshit, she did pull Promise out of the system. Mainly because of the pact she had made with her late sister,

Fatima. They'd promised each other that, in the event something happened to either of them, the surviving sister would
take care of the kid the other left behind. So, when her time
came, Adelle did so, but grudgingly.

In the beginning, Adelle was the picture of the grieving
sister who only wanted the best for her orphaned niece. Whenever she sat with a social worker, or if she had an appointment
at the Public Assistance office, she kept a poker face that J.
Edgar Hoover couldn't even have cracked. Once the state
approved the checks, and the food stamps started hitting that
card, it became a different ball game. Adelle never made it a
secret that she allowed Promise under her roof more out of
obligation than love.

Adelle and her daughter Brianna had been exceptionally
cruel to Promise. She was treated like an indentured servant,
having to basically slave for Adelle and her brat for her room
and board. There were three rooms in the place, but Promise
was still made to sleep in what was essentially a storage closet
that hadn't been insulated. She burned in the summers and
froze in the winters. Her auntie and cousin treated Promise
like a dog, verbally and physically. Their biggest kicks came
from attacking her physical appearance. Promise was a bit
on the chubby side, and they reminded her of this by calling
her Ms. Piggy or Fat Bitch. Her weight was a regular topic of
conversation, and it shredded her self-esteem. At one point, it
had gotten so bad that Promise had considered taking her life
to be free of the constant abuse. It had been a year since Adelle
had kicked her out into the streets. Sometimes it felt like a lifetime ago, and others it felt like the events had just taken place
yesterday. Promise didn't miss Adelle or her bitch of a cousin,
but she'd have been lying if she said they didn't cross her mind
from time to time.

She braced her hands on the sink and let out a deep sigh. That was a different time, and she was a different person now. "You are strong," she said confidently to her reflection. Behind her the bathroom door opened. She quickly wiped her eyes and tried to clean herself up, not wanting any of the girls to see her vulnerable. That was the last thing she needed. To her surprise, it wasn't one of the other strippers who came into the bathroom, but Sin. "What are you doing in here?" She didn't turn to face him but spoke to his reflection.

"I came to check on you," Sin told her.

"I'm good. And in case you hadn't noticed, this is the ladies' room," Promise pointed out.

Sin shrugged. "They ain't got nothing I've never seen before." It was then he noticed that her face and eyes were red. She had been crying. "You sure you're okay?"

"Thanks, but I don't need your pity twice in one night," Promise said sharply.

"Check this fly shit out. Whoever that nigga was that broke your heart and is causing you to channel all that anger in my direction, I ain't him!" Sin had finally had enough of Promise and her shitty attitude, and it was time for him to check her.

"You don't know me!" Promise shot back. He had hit a sore spot for her.

"Nah, I don't know you, but I know your type. You're one of those girls that's so used to dudes dogging you out that you don't know how to accept kindness from a man. You're broken, baby girl, and I ain't in the fixing business. When you get yourself together, you can go on and bring me the bill for the night, so we can settle up," Sin turned and started back toward the door. Her next words stopped him.

"I'm sorry," Promise said softly. Sin had been nothing but nice to her the entire night, and she was repaying him by being a bitch. "You're right. I was out of line for coming at you sideways for something that has nothing to do with you. I got some issues I'm still trying to work through."

"Ain't no shame in that. We all got issues. You just can't let whatever is going on with you block them blessings when they come," Sin told her.

"Blessings?" Promise chuckled. "I work in a hole-in-the-wall strip club for tips. I hardly call this a blessing."

"You don't like your life? Change it!" he challenged.

"That's easier said than done. I'm eighteen, with no work history, sleeping on my friend's cousin's couch in a city that's alien to me." Promise hadn't meant to spill all her business like that, but she needed to get it off her chest.

"My dad used to call that *hitting your bottom*," Sin said. "The good thing about hitting your bottom is that there's nowhere to go but up from there."

"I sure hope so," Promise replied.

"Who knows? Maybe one day a handsome young man will walk through those doors and offer you an opportunity that might change your life." Sin spoke like he was prophesizing things to come.

"In this dump? I seriously doubt that. I can't see anybody who's *really* about something, hanging out in here." Promise chuckled. After she said it, she recognized her slight to him. "My bad. I didn't mean . . ."

"No apologies necessary." Sin cut her off. "I guess it's easy to make assumptions about people based on how they're dressed, rather than what they got going on." He eyed the thong bathing suit.

"Touché."

"But seriously, don't let my thug nature fool you. I'm about a dollar, baby. I'm only putting it out there like that because I feel like you ain't quite picking up on my generosities tonight," Sin flexed a bit.

"Yeah, I guess you all are handling or whatever. I wasn't really clocking like that." Promise lied. She'd had Sin pegged within the first hour. He wasn't a trick, but he also wasn't shy about spending if the ends justified the means. This is what he had been fishing at for half the night, and she knew this but let him keep casting his line.

"Of course, you were," he countered. "All that flash and cash will get anybody's attention, which is why I do it when I'm in places like this. It's a vetting process I like to use when I'm thinking about putting money in somebody's pocket. See, most of these other women in here are trying to fuck me or swindle me out of my paper. You were the only one who was willing to work for it. That tells me that you got some principles about you."

"First of all, I told you that I wasn't on no flat-back shit. Second, who said I need you to put anything in my pocket?" Promise snaked her neck, arms folded.

"You did! Or was that somebody else telling me how miserable they were working for tips, and sleeping on somebody else's couch?" Sin replied. He saw in her eyes that the remark stung, so he tried to clean it up. "I'm not judging you, Promise. We all do what we gotta do to eat, but why stay at a place where you hate being?"

"So I guess this is the part when you sell me on the idea of how I can come up if me and you get together?" Promise asked sarcastically.

"Chill, shorty, it ain't even that type of party." Sin laughed. "This ain't about no pussy, this is a potential business arrangement. At least, for now it is." He winked.

"Sin, your ass is crazy. I don't even know what you do. For

all I know, you could be a dope boy, and I'm not with selling no drugs," Promise told him.

"I don't sell dope. And as far as what it is that I do . . ." Sin paused, thinking how he wanted to word it, but doing a poor job. "It's hard to explain. I can show you better than I can tell you."

She thought of Donna's earlier warning when he said that. "I appreciate the offer, Sin, but I think I'm gonna thug it out here for a while longer."

"Well, if you change your mind . . ." Sin pulled out a twenty and scribbled his cell number on the bill. ". . . hit me up."

Promise stared at the bill for a time before accepting it and stuffing it into the Crown Royal bag she used to hold her tips. She had already been to the dressing room once that night to empty the bag of singles into her knapsack, and it was almost full again. Considering the way her night had gone so far, she might have to find something bigger to hold her cash for the night. As she was tightening the string on her bag, the bathroom door swung open, scaring both of them. Big Sally stood in the doorway, looking from Promise to Sin with an expression that said she had just caught them with both their hands in the cookie jar. "Girl, you know how long I been looking for you? I needed you to cover the bar for five minutes while I use the bathroom. I ain't had a pee break since I started my shift!" Sally brushed between them toward the stall. She didn't bother to close the stall door when she flopped her big ass down on the bowl. You could hear a loud stream of piss spraying from her gash into the toilet. She was watching Promise with a sly grin on her face.

"I better get back to my table. Don't let me leave without us exchanging info, Promise," Sin told her and exited the bathroom.

Promise lingered, checking herself in the mirror. She would need to throw some water on her face and reapply the mascara she had cried off before going back out on the floor. As she was doing this, Sally came out of the stall. She stood next to Promise and began fixing her big wig in the mirror. Promise could feel the energy coming off her, like she had something she wanted to say but was working herself up to it. Promise wouldn't have to wait too long to hear what was on the old woman's mind.

"Little Miss Garden State got a little sin in her after all, huh? No pun intended," Sally shot.

"We were just talking. You know I don't get down like that." Promise finished fixing her face and made to leave.

"Neither did I, at one point. You just make sure you remember Big Sally's rule about me getting twenty percent of whatever pussy gets sold at Dirty Wine," Sally said over her shoulder.

Promise was about to respond but decided it would be pointless, so she just left.

CHAPTER 8

When Asher finally arrived in the hood, he found the usual suspects posted up. It was a cluster of young men and women who were either from the neighborhood or employed by Asher. They were in their usual spot, playing the corner in the shadow of the liquor store. Some were hustling, and others were just hanging around, which wasn't unusual. The strip was like ground zero for the neighborhood, and everything that went on in that section of town ran through those few blocks between Lincoln Park and downtown Newark.

It wasn't out of the ordinary for the front of the liquor store to draw a crowd on a good night, but for some reason, it seemed thicker than usual out there. Asher scanned the faces, watching from the Benz as he and Cal rode past. Some of them he knew, but there were quite a few who he had either never seen before or weren't known for hanging out at that end of the block. Something was up.

"Fuck is all these new niggas?" Cal spoke up as if he had been reading Asher's mind.

"We about to find out," Asher assured him. He pushed the car past the liquor store, instead of pulling up right out front like he normally would. He drove an extra block up to Longworth and pulled into a spot at the corner of the block.

Cal was the first one out of the whip. He had helped himself to the spare .22 that he knew Asher kept hidden in the car, as he didn't have his own gun with him. Cal rarely traveled without a pistol, but he'd had class that day, and he never carried on campus. That was asking for a problem.

Asher was close behind him, 9mm tucked in the back of his pants. He'd had the gun for over a month and had never fired it. He only hoped that the streak would continue. One of the dudes in the crowd he had recognized was one of his lieutenants, a kid named Milk, who was supposed to hold the block down when neither he nor Cal were around. From what Asher had just witnessed, he was slipping. Everybody who slung drugs for him knew his rule: no large gatherings. Seeing a bunch of dudes huddled up in a high-traffic area was all the cause police needed to get in their business. Soldiers holding drugs or guns played one corner, and social hangers-on from the hood played the other. It was one of the first laws Asher laid down when he had taken over, and they were in violation.

"Yo, boss man on deck!" Milk announced when he saw Asher approaching. Milk was as black as tar, so how he had gotten the nickname was one of the great mysteries of their hood. He was a boisterous cat who sported a mouth full of permanent gold teeth. At one time, they had been removable caps, but he had to get implants when someone knocked almost all of his teeth out with a pipe. In one hand, he held a red plastic cup and, in the other, a bottle of Hennessey.

"What the fuck is this?" Asher cut to the chase. He was clearly irritated.

"Relax, big dawg. Ain't nothing but a little celebration." Milk hoisted the cup. Asher slapped it out of his hand, splashing Hennessey on both their sneakers.

"Nigga, you ain't getting paid to party when you're on my clock!" Asher fumed.

"Damn, my nigga. Why you wound up so tight? You used to love a good celebration, same as the rest of us. I guess spending all that time with them suit-wearing niggas has dulled your sense of fun." Milk laughed, trying to lighten the mood.

"Who I do business with isn't your business. Keeping the block jumping is," Asher checked him.

"Shit, you don't see that line?" Milk pointed to the fiends who were standing single file while one of the young boys served them. "This shit ain't only jumping, but doing backflips too!"

"Yo, Ash. Chill out, bro. It ain't that serious." A young solider on their payroll who went by the name of Sean tried coaxing him. He was a good dude, and Asher had never had an issue with him, but this wasn't the time for niceties.

"This is above your paygrade, shorty. Stay in your lane," Cal warned him. Sean wisely fell back.

"Milk," Asher picked up, "why do I have to keep telling you about having all these random niggas in the mix when we're out here trying to get a dollar?"

"Asher, I know how you feel about unfamiliar faces, but this ain't that type of party. These is all homies. It ain't like them dudes from up the way were allowed to start coming down this end to hustle," Milk said. Had he not been drinking, he'd have probably kept that remark to himself.

"Oh, you trying to lose your bottom teeth, too, huh?" Asher invaded his space. His nostrils were flared, and his jaw was clenched. He'd never cared much for Milk, and it didn't have anything to do with him slipping on the block. Not long ago, Milk had tried to touch something that Asher had laid claim to, and word got back to Asher. The girl in question hadn't been Asher's girlfriend, but somebody he felt like he had a real connection with. Everybody on the block knew what time it was, but Milk still tried his hand. In Asher's mind, Milk was indirectly telling him that he could help himself to whatever Asher laid claim to. In return, Asher tried to fuck every bitch that he saw that Milk was interested in.

Asher and Cal had a conversation once about why Asher was suddenly so cold on Milk, and when Asher explained his theory about why Milk needed to be humbled, Cal thought that he was bugging. Asher didn't give a shit what Cal thought; Asher knew a flex when he saw one. One thing he had learned from his predecessors was to pay close attention to the habits of the men he fed. When those habits started to change, it was a sign of a potential problem. B-Stone had missed the signs with Asher, and it had cost him his head and his operation. Asher would not repeat his mistakes.

"It was my fault." A deep voice broke the tension. There was a man standing in the doorway of a liquor store, watching the exchange between them. He was wearing gray sweats that looked to be a size too small and a black hoodie. The man's hair was twisted into short dreads that looked like they could stand to be retwisted. His dark chocolate face was handsome enough but bore the scars of whatever life he had been living. The most prominent mark was the small gorilla head tattooed on his cheek, just below his right eye. He paused, waiting to see what Asher's reaction would be to his initial words before continuing. "I'm just a few days back in the world, and the homie was only trying to show me love. We ain't mean no disrespect to whatever you got going on."

"I hear you, my nigga, and though I appreciate the apology, he's supposed to know better," Asher thumbed at Milk. "It's protocols out here that gotta be observed and respected," he told the dark-skinned dude.

"Protocols, huh?" The dark-skinned dude smirked as he mulled the word over.

"Something funny to you?" Cal didn't like the look of him. There was something about the dude that was tugging at his brain, but he couldn't put his finger on it.

"Slow down, Calico. It ain't whatever you think it is. You know, I had heard Asher was out here running the neighborhood now, but I didn't believe it. I don't mean no harm; it's just weird for me to see the dude who had the NBA-ready jump shot running a corner. That's all."

"Homie, I'm running more than just the real estate you standing on. You better ask somebody about me, ma. For real." Asher checked him. "And why you talking like we know each other?" He studied the man's face. Though it was familiar, Asher couldn't place it.

"Atilla?" Cal asked in surprise. That's what it was eating at him about the man. He knew him.

Atilla Jordan, who would later be dubbed *The Hun*, was a blast from Asher's past. He was the only son of a family from West Africa who lived in the same condo complex as Asher and his mom, Society Hill. Back then, Atilla was a quiet kid who rarely came outside and mostly kept his head buried in a book. There were a few times when he would come to the local basketball court and shoot around with Asher and some of the other kids, but mostly he kept to himself. His father was very strict and didn't allow his kids to run the streets like some of the other parents. This changed around the time his father got into some trouble and was deported back to Africa. Atilla's mother had to raise the boy and his sisters on her own, which wasn't an easy task.

With his father no longer around to police his movements, Atilla started hanging out more. Because he was African and spoke with a thick accent back then, Atilla was picked on a lot. He wasn't much of a fighter, but to his credit, he never backed down from a fight. Asher had seen Atilla get his ass kicked and come back for a second helping. They eventually stopped picking on Atilla, and he became one of the gang. But he still hadn't had his introduction to the streets yet. That would happen when he came to the attention of a dude named Ab.

Ab was Asher's OG and B-Stone's second in command. B-Stone had been a certified monster in the streets, but Ab was more of a predator. He was good at playing on people's needs or weaknesses and using them to his advantage. This is how he had recruited most of the soldiers who followed them into their gang. The same had been true for Atilla. He knew the young African's story about his dad being deported and his mother struggling to keep food on the table, and he had used that to pull Atilla in and put him to work on the block. Atilla wasn't a street dude, but he was a dedicated hustler. He was always the first one on the strip, the last one to leave, and his money rarely came up short. Those few times that it did, no matter whose fault it was, he worked the debt off without complaint. He was just happy to be able to help his mother out. Then the other shoe dropped, and Atilla found himself locked up.

Atilla had never been in trouble a day in his life. He had only been working for Ab for a few weeks when he took his fall, so being locked up was alien to him, and he was terrified. Some of the older guys on the block were making bets as to whether the boy would snitch or hold it down. To their surprise, Atilla never once opened his mouth about his affiliation with Ab or anything else about the organization. He took his time like a man.

Most of what people knew about Atilla's time behind the wall was hearsay. It was rumored that he had plugged in with some guys from the neighborhood who had come under the guise of being friends but had ulterior motives. Being naive to prison and how things worked, Atilla happily accepted favors and goods from these guys, never knowing the heavy price he would have to pay for them. The first leg of his bid had been a rough one. When he couldn't pay back the favors, the guys began extorting him by having his mother either send him packages that they would confiscate or put money on their books. The months when she couldn't afford to send him anything, Atilla was beaten. He tried to fight back, but he was alone, and they always came with numbers on their side. Atilla realized that if he had any hopes of surviving the jungle, he would have to adapt to its laws. He began hitting the weights and brushing up on his hand skills, so he could better defend himself against attacks. Atilla would slide even deeper down the rabbit hole when he hooked in with a gang of dudes who hailed from different parts of New York, New Jersey, and Philly. They called themselves the Apes and were among some of the worse that the prison had to offer. By then Atilla was a young bull whose name had begun to ring out throughout the prison. He had knocked a few dudes out on the prison yard, and one story told said that he'd broken the jaw of a CO, which is how he had gotten time added to his sentence. One story told even said that he had killed a few dudes while he was away. Prison had snatched away Atilla's innocence. When Atilla left, he had been a 130-pound doe-eyed kid. He returned to the world four years later as a 220-pound gorilla.

"Damn, blood. I ain't seen you in forever." Asher hugged his old friend.

"One thousand four hundred and eighty-two days," Atilla told him. "Feels like a fucking lifetime though. I hear you're out here doing big things, man."

"I'm getting by," Asher said modestly.

"Shit, looks like you're doing more than getting by," Atilla remarked, watching the steady flow of drug traffic. "I know you're a busy dude and all, but I need to bend your ear about something."

"For you? I always got time. Let's take a quick walk." Asher led Atilla around the corner and away from prying ears. "What's good?"

"Right now? Not too much of anything," Atilla said honestly. "I don't know if you knew it or not, but my mom and one of my sisters went back home while I was away."

"Nah, I didn't know that. I hadn't seen them in a while, but you know your mom always played it close to the crib anyhow. What made them leave?"

"Look around you." Atilla motioned to the neighborhood. There were fiends shambling up and down the street, and kids hanging out smoking weed and drinking. It was live out there. "My mom never knew anything outside of the small city we grew up in until my dad dragged her to America. When he got sent back, and she had to damn near kill herself for fifteen hours a day at shitty jobs and still barely made ends meet . . ." He shook his head sadly. "It was too much for her. Me getting locked up didn't make things any easier. My sister getting pregnant by some knucklehead nigga who dipped off on her before the kid even got here was the last straw. She felt like she had to get out of Newark to save what was left of our family."

"Damn, so they just left you out here for dolo?" Asher asked.

"It wasn't like that. Mom offered me a ticket to come be

with them when I got out, but ain't nothing in Africa for me. I ain't been back, even to visit, since I was a shorty, so I can barely even remember what it was like. Imagine me trying to go out there and start over. I'd be like a fish out of water. Africa will always be in my blood, but Newark is where my heart is."

"I know that's right," Asher agreed. "So, what's your plan now?"

"Feast or famine, and starving ain't an option." Atilla rubbed his hands together. "I was hoping that you could find a spot for me on the team since you're running the show now?"

"Atilla . . ."

"Just hear me out before you answer," Atilla cut him off. "Dawg, you've known me since I was a shorty, and I ain't never ran around with my hand out. I ain't asking you to bless me with nothing. I just want an opportunity to earn. I don't care if I gotta get out here and go hand to hand on the corner."

"Bruh, you know I'd never put you on one of these corners. We got too much history. The thing is, you're fresh home from prison, so you're hotter than a firecracker. You're a smart kid. Why don't you square up and get a job?" Asher suggested. He was quite serious. Atilla had always been smarter than most and a hard worker.

Atilla laughed at the suggestion. "Homie, my days of being a square ended when I got this." He pointed to the gorilla tattoo below his eye. "Now, I know I've been gone for a while and you're naturally suspicious, which you should be. I'm just saying, if you can't find a spot for me, I'm gonna have to get out here on some ape shit and get it how I live. I'm trying to avoid that because, if I do, it ain't gonna be good for nobody."

Asher measured what Atilla had just said. It wasn't a threat, but a statement of fact. He had heard the stories about how Atilla was moving behind the wall, so he understood what he meant by getting on some *ape* shit. It was going to be open season on corner boys and anyone holding a bag. If it came to a point where Atilla started fucking with Asher's money, he would have him gunned down in a heartbeat, friend or not. Still, Asher would rather not go down that road. He truly wanted to help his friend out, but it had been a while since they had been in each other's company, and Asher wasn't sure how much he could trust him just yet. As he thought about it, an idea formed in his head.

"Look, I might have something that I can pull you in on. Not no street shit, but something that's on a different level," Asher told him.

"Bet, run it down!" Atilla said excitedly.

"Not yet. I'm still trying to work the kinks out. Just know that, if I can flesh this out the way that I need to, you might never have to work a corner again a day in your life. In the meantime, I need you to stay out of trouble," Asher said seriously. He pulled his bankroll from his pocket and peeled off a thousand dollars and held it out to Atilla.

"Bruh, I told you I don't do handouts." Atilla refused the money.

"This isn't a handout. Think of it as a retainer for your services. I'm about to dive off into some heavy shit, but the risks will be worth the reward. I'm talking long-term money. I need good, solid niggas around me that I can trust and that don't mind getting their hands dirty," Asher said seriously.

Atilla reluctantly took the money. "Ash, I'd bust a nigga's head for you just on the strength of how far we go back, but for a chance to see the kind of paper you're talking about, I'll paint this whole city with blood."

"I'm going to hold you to that." Asher looked at his watch. "I got some moves to make, but come by my crib tomorrow morning about eleven, and we can chop it up. You remember where I stay, right?"

Atilla laughed. "We've been neighbors since we were short-ies. How can I forget?"

"Bet, so pull up and ring my bell, and we'll discuss this further. You're still in the apartments down the block, right?"

"Nah, moms gave that crib up when she bounced. Since I got no address, I'm paroled to a halfway house in Irvington until I work my living situation out."

"Nah, that ain't gonna do. I'm gonna holla at my home girl who rents out rooms in the city and get you a proper place to lay your head. She can provide you with the paperwork you'll need to convince your PO that you've secured a steady roof over your head. It ain't gonna be the Ritz, but at least, you ain't gonna have to worry about bedbugs or niggas stealing your shit while you're sleeping," Asher half-joked.

"After what I've been made to suffer through over the last few years, a Motel 6 will feel like a penthouse," Atilla said.

"Follow my lead and that penthouse will be a reality sooner than later. On that note, I gotta make a move." Asher gave him dap. He was about to leave, but Atilla stopped him.

"Before you go, I need to ask you something." From Atil-la's tone, he knew that, whatever the question, it was a serious one. "What really went down with Ab?"

Asher wasn't expecting that question, but he should've been. Ab was the one who turned Atilla out to the streets and fed him when he didn't have anything. "Honestly? All I know is what the streets are saying. He was partying with some bitches in AC and overdosed."

"Yeah, I'd heard that too, but it never felt right in my spirit. Ab didn't do drugs. Yeah, he drank and smoked weed, but anything heavier wasn't his thing. That was B-Stone's lane."

"You think it was foul play?" Asher asked, trying to see where Atilla's head was.

Atilla weighed the question before answering. "I dunno. Maybe I'm reading too deep into it, and maybe I'm seeing what nobody else is."

"Yesterday is yesterday. We need to focus on tomorrow." Asher tried to ease his suspicions.

"You right, and I'm definitely trying to focus on getting this paper. Still, there is something about what happened to Ab that won't let me rest. I had a lot of love for that dude. Ab offered me a hand up when nobody else would, same as he did with you. This is why I need to know for sure. If I find out his death didn't play like what's being said, somebody is gonna feel me," Atilla vowed.

"If that's the case, then they ain't just gonna feel *you*; they're gonna feel *us!*" Asher assured Atilla. Though he sounded sincere, in his heart, he knew that it was a promise that he wouldn't be able to keep.

PART II

THE DEVIL YOU KNOW

CHAPTER 9

At about 10:00 p.m., the man of the hour finally showed up at Dirty Wine. He strode in, hair freshly braided in cornrows to the back and a gold chain swinging from his neck. He was an underground rapper who went by the name Inferno. He had a dozen mixtapes under his belt, some of which were hailed as street classics. Inferno was a highly skilled MC and could've probably been a big deal in the mainstream, had he not come with so much baggage. He ran with a rowdy bunch, and they were known for busting up clubs and heads. While a lot of dudes rapped about the life, Inferno was really out there living it.

Promise had never met Inferno in person, but she had seen his videos and experienced how his music could change the mood wherever it was played. Whenever Inferno dropped something new and the DJ spun it at Dirty Wine, Odell found himself working overtime to keep folks from tearing the spot up. People who played his records at their establishments did so at their own peril. Inferno was like the Pied Piper, leading all the children into the center of the town square where they would pummel each other while screaming his lyrics. With all this in her head, Promise expected more when he touched down than what she got.

Instead of the mob he was notorious for running with, there was only one other person with Inferno. He was a high-yellow Puerto Rican cat who wore his hair in a wavy, tapered cut. He had hazy green eyes and pretty pink lips, so it was easy to mistake him for a pretty boy at a glance, but he was from the bottom. He might not have worn it on his sleeve like most of the guys he grew up with, but he carried it in his heart. This was Inferno's best friend and business manager, Finesse.

As soon as the DJ announced him, Inferno found himself flocked by groupies, male and female. He had to stop every few feet to sign autographs or pose for a selfie. Inferno may have not found mainstream success just yet, but in ghettos across America, he was a young legend.

Inferno and Finesse were met by two people who Promise hadn't even seen enter the club. They'd likely slipped in while she was in the bathroom. One was a short man wearing a black T-shirt and a heavy gold chain. Promise felt like she had seen him before but couldn't place him. The other was a woman. Or at least, Promise thought it was a woman. It was hard to tell. She was dressed in baggy jeans, boots, and a loose-fitting sweater with dark glasses covering her eyes. Whoever the duo was, Promise could tell that they were dangerous. It had nothing to do with anything that they had done since she spotted them. In fact, they seemed to be all smiles, but their body language told a different story. Promise had been around enough killers, and it was easy for her to spot one, even from across the room.

Larry greeted the rapper with his lips pulled back into an ass-kissing smile. Inferno nodded in acknowledgment but didn't say much. The Puerto Rican did most of the talking. After the pleasantries, Larry led the rapper and his people to a booth that sat in the shadow of where the DJ was set up. It was the largest booth in the spot and was always reserved for VIPs or big spenders. With a snap of Larry's fingers Odell appeared. He had Lita, Donna, and two other girls who weren't worth mentioning in tow. The girls were a gift for the rapper and his crew. After getting them situated, Larry made hurried steps toward the bar.

"Jersey . . . Jersey, why the hell you just standing around like you ain't got nothing to do?" Larry started right in.

"I'm not standing around, Larry. I'm getting more waters for my table," Promise replied.

"Whatever." Larry waved his hand dismissively. "I need you to do something for me, and I need it done now. Sally!" He slapped his palm on the bar top to get the attention of the older woman who was trying to flirt with a dude who was half her age.

"What, nigga?" Sally spun on him with an attitude. She was the only one in Dirty Wine who didn't take Larry's shit.

"I need four bottles of bubbles! Not that cheap shit we slinging to everybody else. Dip in the stash and pull out the good stuff. Give them to Jersey to take over to Inferno," Larry demanded.

"But I'm working Sin's table exclusively tonight, remember?" Promise reminded him. Working Sin's table had proved to be not only easy but pleasant and profitable. She didn't want to be bothered with the rapper and his crew and put in a situation where she would likely be groped or worse, for just a few funky dollars.

"You wanna be the first bitch to get fired from the same job twice in less than three hours, or you gonna do like I asked you to?" Larry challenged.

"Fine," Promise said in a huff.

"You need to be showing me gratitude, instead of giving me attitude. Them two down south bamas with Inferno gonna take one look at that fine white skin of yours and lose their shit, and their bankrolls! Do you have any idea who that big head lil nigga is?"

"No," Promise said honestly. From his swagger, she reasoned that he was either a rapper as well or a drug dealer.

"Of course, your square ass wouldn't," Larry capped. "All you need to know is that they're notorious for spending big bread when they hit a spot. Not like them fronting-ass niggas you been catering to who trying to stretch their budgets as far as they can, so they can look good. If I check the receipts or ask the few girls they've tipped, I'll bet it won't come up to more than a thousand dollars, including them lil funky bottles they bought for window dressing." Larry had dissected Sin's whole facade. "As a matter of fact, they're starting to smell like trouble. I see them over there watching everybody all sneaky and shit. I know one thing, they try and act up in my spot, and I'll have Odell bounce all three of their asses out on their heads."

"You done?" Promise asked, tiring of Larry's rant. Big Sally had just placed a serving tray on the bar. Atop it sat a bucket of ice with two bottles of Moët & Chandon Nectar shoved inside.

Larry eyeballed her as if he was thinking about going into another rant. "Yeah, I'm done. Carry your ass over there and deliver these bottles. Make sure you put a little jiggle in your wiggle, too. Then you can go back to them larcenous-ass niggas at your table. When you do, be sure to let them shifty niggas know that, if they ain't spending, then they best be preparing to tip on out, so we can free up that booth."

"Sure." Promise turned to collect the tray holding the

buckets and bottles. When she tried to lift it, she realized it was heavier than she had anticipated. "Am I supposed to carry these over there by myself?"

"Jersey, you twice the trouble as any girl in here, so you should be able to handle twice the workload. Work it out or walk out, and I'll get somebody else to do it. The choice is yours," Larry offered.

Promise was ready to go in on Larry and tell him where he could shove his job and those bottles, but she held her tongue. In the last couple of hours, she had made more waiting Sin's table than she normally did in a whole week at Dirty Wine. The night was still young, and she didn't want to rock the boat and mess up her money. She gripped the platter by both ends and tried her best not to drop anything as she crossed the floor with it.

"I swear, sometimes I wonder how I let Keisha talk me into hiring that dizzy-ass girl," Larry vented to himself. As he was watching Promise's pale ass jiggle in the thong while she tried to cross the room, he remembered just why he had hired her.

"Because you wanted to fuck," Big Sally answered as if she could read his mind.

"That girl holds that pussy tighter than a clam that don't wanna be shucked. She ain't giving nothing up." Larry recalled the different occasions when he'd tried to proposition Promise for sex and had always been declined.

"That white hole you lusting after ain't as exclusive as you think." Sally snorted.

"What you talking about? Somebody done busted her out?" Larry asked like a man who had just heard that his wife had been out tipping.

"I caught her and pretty boy with the braids in the bathroom looking real suspect." Big Sally motioned toward Sin.

"He fuck her?" Larry asked, almost uncertain that he really wanted the answer.

Big Sally paused for dramatic effect before speaking again. "Maybe so, maybe not. All I can tell you is that, when I walked in, they were looking real acquainted." Big Sally knew nothing had gone on between Promise and Sin, but it was fun for her to fuck with Larry's head.

"Funky yellow bitch!" Larry cursed. He couldn't believe that, after all he had done for Promise, she had the nerve to play stink finger with the first nigga who came to the club waving a few dollars. His ego was bruised, and the fact that Big Sally knew this made it even worse. "I'm gonna fix her little ass. You watch."

"Whatever business you got with Promise may have to wait. Seems like you might have a bigger problem on your hands at the moment." Big Sally was looking toward the door.

A man had just walked in and caused quite a stir among the girls. At first, Larry thought it might've been another rapper, as a few of them were supposed to be there that night. As he craned his neck to get a better look, he realized that this was no rapper, but a certified problem. "Find Odell and tell him to get his ass to me right away," he told Sally before plotting an intercept course with the newcomer.

CHAPTER 10

Finesse sat at the VIP table Larry had provided them with, burning blunt pinched between his fingers and one arm slung lazily over the back of his chair. Though he looked completely at ease, he was on point. The club security had allowed Finesse to bring his gun inside, but they were still out of bounds. Not in the sense that they had enemies in the spot, at least not that he knew of, but Finesse never allowed himself to be at ease when he was that far from his hood. On his home turf, he knew the shooters, the bullshitters, and the problem starters. That made trouble a little easier to spot, but in a place like Dirty Wine, he'd never see it coming.

Several dancers had been placed on loan to him and his party by the club owner, Larry. While they were pretty enough, only a couple of them really stood out. One was a girl who called herself Lita. She was cozied up to him, whispering some real nasty shit into his ear. Finesse was only half-listening. Any other time he'd have been trying to figure out how best to convince her to let his dick play stick ball with her tonsils, but he was preoccupied at the moment. From under weed-hooded eyes, he was observing the exchange going on a few feet away from him.

Generally, Finesse was the mouthpiece when it came to things involving P.B. Entertainment, but in their present company, he decided to let Inferno take the lead. It wasn't because he didn't have the words. Finesse could talk circles around most executives and even street niggas, making off with a bag before they even knew that they had been fleeced. That was his thing, the reason they had started calling him Finesse. He was a good talker. The reason he played the background during the opening of the conversation was because he feared that anything he said would've betrayed the shock he felt when he realized who Inferno's backup plan had been. Of all the men he could've foreseen himself sitting down to negotiate with, Trap wouldn't have been one of them.

Trap sat perched atop the backrest of one of the padded seats that enclosed the table they were sitting at, looking like a little menacing black gargoyle. His head bobbed to track number four of Inferno's latest project, while a blunt that was three times the size of the one Finesse had been smoking dangled from his lips. Sitting between his legs was Donna. She had staked her claim to him as soon as Larry had dropped them in the section. Trap showered the well-built stripper with dollar bills and ashes.

Forever at his side was his sibling Moochie, nestled deep under Keisha's rear end getting a lap dance. Mouse's cousin had her long legs wrapped around Moochie's waist, grinding on her lap and talking shit into her ear. The way Keisha moved back and forth, had Moochie had a dick, she would've probably cum in her jeans. Keisha was just that good with the way she moved. Moochie was Trap's big sister, but you couldn't tell at a glance. She was a woman that was shaped like a middle linebacker and who hit twice as hard. She normally kept her thick black dreads pulled into a ponytail, but that night she wore them free, letting them spill over her face and shoulders. If you looked at her head-on, behind her sweeping locs were eyes so dark and sinister, you felt like you were looking into two caves that had been carved into the side of a mountain. Her black pools watched any and everybody who came within five feet of Trap. She had been protective of him since they were kids, so when he was on the come up, he figured, why not let her get paid for it? Moochie was Trap's unofficial enforcer and road manager.

Finesse tried not to get annoyed at the nonchalant way Trap had been carrying on. He was acting like he was more interested in the atmosphere than what they had come there for, which was getting to the business. They had been in the private section for nearly half an hour, and in that time, the DJ had spun some of the hottest cuts from Inferno's project, so he knew Trap had had a chance to digest some of the music, at least, in part. But he'd said nothing. Outside of a bit of small talk to break the ice and a bit of catching up, the subject of the album hadn't been broached yet. Trap was playing with them, and Finesse knew it. He wouldn't give him the satisfaction of feeding into the game; unfortunately, Inferno had no such hang-ups.

"So, what you think?" Inferno asked Trap.

Trap stared at him for a beat before responding. "Joint tight," he said in his southern drawl.

"Man, this shit is more than tight. This is gonna be the next big wave. Watch what I tell you," Inferno said confidently. Nobody with eyes or ears could deny the effect the record was having on Dirty Wine. The strippers were on the pole going crazy, while bills flew, and Inferno's lyrics could be heard being repeated throughout the spot.

"I can appreciate your enthusiasm, big man." Trap bumped fists with Inferno, but there was something about it that didn't have the intended effect. It was more like a pat on the head than a compliment.

Inferno fought the urge to challenge the issue further. "Yo, I wanna thank you again for taking the time to slide through and check out my latest project. I know you're a busy dude and all."

Trap smiled, dim club lights kissing off his gold-plated teeth. Along the left side of the top row "305" was etched in diamonds. "Ain't no thang, lil bruh. I had business in the city anyway, so it wasn't taking away from nothing. I gotta admit. I was kinda surprised when you reached out."

"I know you have an ear for music, so I figured maybe your label could appreciate it," Inferno said.

"I've always had a good ear. I had a good ear back when we first sat down and you acted like my plate was too small to eat off. Why the change of heart?" Trap already knew the answer to the question, but he wanted to see how Inferno would answer. That would determine how he would deal with him from then on.

That was the elephant in the room that Finesse had prayed no one noticed when he discovered Trap's was one of the labels Inferno had planned to meet with. He and Inferno had first met Trap nearly two years prior. He had recently moved his operation from his native Miami to Los Angeles. Inferno had been booked to do a show at the House of Blues, and Trap represented one of several labels that had come to check him out. Inferno was in the middle of a cross-country tour, tearing down venues from state to state. That night at the House of

Blues had been no different. They'd only made it through three songs before the police came and shut it down.

Later that night, Trap's people had taken Inferno and his entourage to an after-hours spot for some drinks. This is where Trap made his pitch for Inferno to sign with his label. Trap had a solid game plan, but the money wasn't quite what Inferno had been anticipating. The rapper knew that his stock was up at the time, so, as he should've, he tried to milk the situation. Inferno's plan was to get the labels into a bidding war for his services. It was a sound plan, but what he hadn't anticipated was that being a game that Trap wasn't willing to play. Trap was a man who did the squeezing, not get squeezed, so the deal never got done. When they parted, it was on good terms, or so Inferno foolishly believed, but Finesse knew better. You didn't slight a man like Trap and expect him to forget. This is why Finesse made sure to keep his head on swivel during their dealings with the Florida gangster.

"C'mon, man. You know how that shit go—" Inferno was about to say something that would likely lessen them further in Trap's eyes, but Finesse saved him the embarrassment.

"That was my fault," Finesse threw himself onto the sword. "Your offer was a fair one, all things considered. It's just that, at the time, your label was still really new, and we weren't sure that you would've been able to give the project a big enough push. Wasn't meant as no slight to you, simply a business decision that I made in the best interest of our company."

For a few beats, Trap said nothing. He just stared, as if his brain was trying to decipher the hidden message beneath Finesse's words. "I can respect an honest man. Truth be told, with the trajectory Inferno *was* on, I probably didn't have the necessary resources to give him the push he needed, but it would seem that we now find ourselves in a reversal of fortunes.

Your name has been trending, my friend. Not necessarily in a good way, either."

Inferno made a dismissive gesture. "You know how them blogs be hyping shit when you come from what we come from. I got a reputation, so whatever I do, they're always going to try and paint the worst picture of me."

"I know, probably better than most, what it's like to be constantly haunted by things you've done in the past," Trap said honestly.

Trap was a gangster from down the bottom of the map. He was beloved in his city as a hustler and later as a hometown hero before he got his shine as a rapper. The hood loved Trap, and Trap loved the hood. He wasn't one of those guys who posted turkey giveaways on Instagram for clicks, he was really in the trenches with his people. Back then, Trap hadn't been a rich man, but he never hesitated to break bread with someone in the neighborhood who needed something. He was literally the people's champion.

Around the time that his rap career started gaining traction, a tragedy in his neighborhood truly put his mantle of people's champ to the test. A serial rapist had been preying on women in the area. Over the course of three weeks, he had claimed two victims, and there was a lingering fear that he would claim a third if he wasn't caught. Since Trap's neighborhood was one of the poorest in the county, the police hadn't made catching the rapist a priority. It wasn't until his next victim, a girl of about twelve years old, was found in an alley, sodomized and beaten to within an inch of her life, that the neighborhood had finally decided they'd had enough, and Trap took the law into his own hands.

With the help of his best friend and running partner, a shooter they called Nutty, Trap led a manhunt to find the animal. It hadn't proved to be as hard as he had anticipated, once he put word out that he was offering a reward for the identity and location of the rapist. Trap and Nutty tracked the man to the home that he shared with his mother, which ironically was less than a mile from the street they lived on. They'd assumed that it was someone from outside the neighborhood violating the women, but it had been one of their own the whole time.

Needleless to say, Trap and Nutty *retired* the rapist and allowed the mothers and daughters of their neighborhood at least one decent night's sleep. The rapes disgusted Trap, but what he found almost as disturbing was the number of people who chose to remain silent about what they knew until there was cash involved. Had they only come forward sooner the women could've been spared the indignities forced on them by the rapist. Trap lost just a little more faith in humanity because of that, but it would be the events that followed the execution that would show him just how fucked up the world they lived in was.

The execution of the rapist had made Trap and Nutty somewhat folk heroes around the neighborhood. They already had the respect of the streets because of how they put their thing down in the game, and now that they also had the love of the community, it only made them that much stronger. For as many people there were who loved Trap and Nutty for what they had done for those women and the little girl, there were twice as many who found even more reasons to hate them. Jealousy can sometimes bring the most thorough cats out of character, as was the case when a rival of theirs tried to knock them out of the box by making an anonymous call to the police about the vigilante execution. All it took was the next-door neighbor picking Trap and Nutty out of a mug book to corroborate the tip they'd received, and it was enough to charge both Trap and Nutty with murder.

Even with paid lawyers, the case was looking shaky for them. Under the circumstances, their lawyers were sure that, if they took it to trial, they could find a sympathetic jury. They could argue that, for killing a child rapist, the boys should be given medals, not prison sentences, and there was a slim chance that they could get the case to swing favorably. Still, this was murder, and they were young Black men in the state of Florida. Even if the defense team got the charges knocked down, there was no way they were going to walk without doing some time. It was then that Nutty made the ultimate sacrifice. He agreed to eat the whole murder under the condition that they give Trap a lesser sentence. Nutty was a repeat offender and already had an open case for a shooting in Orlando. He was going to have to lay down, regardless of how it went. The DA didn't scoff at the idea. In his mind, he was getting a two-for-one, a rapist and a killer off the streets in one shot. And so it went. Nutty was given fifteen years, and Trap was spared so that he might continue to build on the dream they had started.

"So," Trap continued, "reputations aside, what were you boys thinking about the direction you wanna go in with this project?"

"To the top of course," Inferno answered.

Trap let out a short chuckle at Inferno's ever-mounting cockiness. "And I believe that this project has the potential to do just that. It just needs a little push and some polish."

"Polish? What you mean? Everybody knows that I'm a top-five MC and the production on this is tight. If you ask me, this is a project that's ready to go," Inferno insisted.

"Which is why I'm not *asking* you. I'm telling you what I know. Hear me out before you jump in your feelings," Trap said in an almost soft tone. He sounded like a parent who was about to try and simplify something for their child. "You got a gift that doesn't come along often. Nobody could ever take that from you but God. Now, for as tight as your lyrics are, your production could use a little work. I'm not saying that your beats are bad, but they aren't clean. I can hear the difference in the level of your vocals on certain songs. It's subtle, but it's there. That's what happens when you try and save a few dollars by hiring a cook to cater your dinner, instead of dropping the extra bread and bringing in a chef."

"Damn, sounds like you're trying to tell us that our project is some no-frills shit," Inferno said defensively. Trap had been dead on with the accusation though. After recording costs and other expenses, they didn't have much left in the budget to bring in one of the high-profile producers they'd worked with in the past or book high-tech studios. This project had been a grassroots one. The fact that Trap knew this meant that he was either paying closer attention than they thought or they were that transparent. From the way the meeting had gone so far, Finesse suspected that it was the latter.

"No disrespect intended," Trap clarified. "I'm just saying that I'm not that far removed from cutting corners to save a buck. We do what we gotta do to get where we gotta go. Now, with a machine behind you, it would alleviate some of those headaches."

"And this is what has brought us to the table tonight." Finesse stepped in. Where Trap was about to go with the conversation was more his lane than Inferno's. This was about to be a battle of wits. "Trap, we've known each other for a little minute now, so we ain't gotta dance around what is and what ain't. Whether it's a little raw or not, the project is still dope. Everybody in this shitty strip club knows it. In a minute, everybody on the streets are going to know it too. My guy reached out to you out of respect to offer you an opportunity to be a part of what's about to happen, but for the sake of transparency, you need to know that yours isn't the only label interested in this project."

"And who says I'm interested?" Trap asked.

"You did, the moment you agreed to take this meeting," Finesse said confidently. "You're a man who can smell an opportunity from a mile away, which is why you didn't tell Inferno to fuck off when he reached out. I haven't insulted your intelligence, so you need to put some respect on mine."

"And you need to take some of that bass out of your voice, before you turn this into something you don't want it to be," Moochie threatened. No one had even noticed that she had removed Keisha from her lap and was glaring at Finesse and Inferno. Moochie had a short fuse, and putting in work was one of her favorite pastimes.

"Take it easy, Moochie. The man is just speaking his mind." Things were starting to get a little choppy, and he knew how Moochie could get. "Let's everybody take a beat and have a drink. Whatever happened to the bottles ol 'boy claimed he was sending over?"

On cue, Promise appeared. Though she had gotten walking in the heels down to a science, doing so while carrying a heavy tray full of bottles proved to be a different kind of struggle. Crossing the room had been like walking the Green Mile. A few times, she felt her ankles trying to give out but held her balance. To get to the private table, she had to cut between the DJ booth and the coat room. It was a straight shot with her only obstacle being the strip of moldy old carpet that had probably been there since Larry took ownership. She cleared one foot with no problem but had to adjust for the weight of the bottle tray when she planted the other, and that's when things went wrong. Her ankle buckled, and she felt the buckets begin to slide to one side of the tray. Instead of trying to save herself from falling, she tried to protect the bottles from breaking, which threw her even further off balance. That split-second decision she'd made to put Larry's bottom line before her own personal safety would cost her. Her eyes snapped shut as she fell, waiting to hear the bottles crash to the ground, which would surely be followed by Larry bouncing her out on her ass. She was prepared for the worst, but not for what would happen next.

CHAPTER 11

There was no embarrassing crash, only a few loose cubes of ice
bouncing from the bucket and landing harmlessly on the floor.
Promise found herself swathed in the shadow of a man she was
sure hadn't been there when she'd started her spill. When she
opened her eyes, she spied five slender fingers balancing the
tray that she had nearly dropped. She followed the trail from
the hand to the wrist and eventually up an arm covered in soft,
black fur. Its counterpart was snaked around her waist, holding her suspended like a ballerina mid-move. She didn't dare
try and turn to see who had saved her from a second embarrassing moment until she was sure that she wouldn't spill onto
the floor. Once the danger of falling had passed, Promise was
gently released to stand on her own. When she turned around to
thank her savior, she found herself staring at a man who looked
like an angel that had lost his footing and fallen from heaven.

Calling him an angel might've been a stretch, but he was
a beautiful man. His skin was of a pecan color, and there was
a cute dimple carved into his right cheek that deepened when

his rosebud lips curved into what may or may not have been a smirk. It wasn't a smile. He showed just enough of his teeth to let her know that he hadn't judged her for her clumsiness. Beneath his fur coat, he wore a baggy, tattered sweater that looked like it had come from the thrift store but was really a $1,200 top. Promise knew this because she and Mouse had seen a fashion designer wearing it on TV, so they googled the piece and couldn't believe how much they were trying to charge for the rags. Atop his head was a rolling mop of rich, black hair that sat high at the top and lightly tapered on the sides. With no facial hair to speak of, he looked like a boy, but the print against his leg through the tight black leather pants said that he was all man. Maybe too much man. Against her better judgment, Promise spared a look into his eyes. That was the cold water splashed on her face that woke her up. On the surface, he was a beautiful man, but his eyes were dark and cruel. It was his eyes which told the story of what he really was, and it was no angel.

"You think you got it from here, lil mama?" the man in the fur coat asked.

"Yeah, tripped over this stupid carpet." Promise jabbed her heel at the moldy hump.

The man in the fur looked down at the dirty carpet they were standing on and twisted his lips slightly. "Yeah, this carpet can be detrimental to your health. So can everything else in this place, if we're being honest about it." He took in the estab-lishment and its dated decor. When he was done with his inspection, his gaze drifted back to Promise. "I don't think I've seen you here before. Has Larry finally decided to step up his quality of life, or you just passing through?"

"I . . . uh . . ." Promise fumbled. "I need to get these bottles to the table." She wasn't sure what else to say. There was something about the way the man in the fur coat was looking at her that made her uneasy.

"It seems we've both got business at this table, but by all means . . . you first," he half-bowed and motioned for Promise to go in ahead of him.

Not really sure what to make of what was going on, Promise entered the private section and began going about her job of getting drinks into everyone's hands. As she was popping the corks on the bottles, she couldn't help but feel the tension in the air. Promise had thought the man with the fur coat was a member of Inferno's party, but it became obvious that he wasn't from the confused looks everyone was sending his way. The man with the fur didn't speak. He just stood, letting his eyes silently assess all parties gathered. Promise wasn't sure what was lingering between the groups, but she knew she wanted no part of whatever was about to transpire. She did her best to get the bottles opened and the glasses filled, so she could get out of that nest of vipers before they started biting each other.

"Bro, you lost or something? This is a private party," Moochie spoke up, breaking the uncomfortable silence. She hadn't left her seat but slid forward to better position herself if she had to spring into action.

"No, love. I'm just a shepherd looking for one of my flock that has gone astray," the man in the fur coat said. He looked to Donna, who was trying her best not to make eye contact with him.

This time, Moochie did stand, and when she did, her full height was a few hairs taller than the man in the fur coat. When she spoke, her tone left no room for misinterpretation as to what she meant. "I don't know about no sheep. You won't find nothing but wolves over here."

The man in the fur looked at Moochie, cocking his head

to one side, then the other, while he stared at her as if she was an alien and he was trying to guess what planet she was from. After a time, he smiled, hands clasped in front of him at his waist and taking a confident stance. "Let me guess? You're the problem of the group, huh? They let you jump off the boat to see how deep the water is? I can respect a stand-up bitch." He gave a mock salute. "Honestly, big bones, I ain't got the time or brain cells to entertain you. I'll take what's mine and be out of your way so you all can get back to your night." He looked to Donna, who was nestled deeper between Trap's legs. "Baby, you really gonna make me say it?"

"Christian, please don't start." Donna put a name to the face.

"Donna, you ain't in no position to make demands or requests. That pretty face of yours still being intact after you call yourself putting shit in my game is the one and only blessing you'll get tonight." Christian was to remain a gentleman about it, but Donna was testing his patience. "Now you sitting up in here like Queen Shit and trying to pull me out of my character, but we both know I'm too playa for that. However, before I let you piss on my head and try to convince me that it's raining, I'll knock you off that throne I put you on. Let's go." He reached for her, but Trap deflected his hand.

"You need to chill, homie. Whatever you're tripping on ain't that serious," Trap said. It wasn't that deep for him. Dude could've done whatever he needed to with the girl, but he had to do it away from Trap. Donna wasn't his girl, but she was in his company. To allow her to be touched would be a slight to him. At least, in his mind. So, against his better judgment, Trap stuck his nose somewhere it didn't belong.

Christian looked at Trap with deadly intent in his eyes. "Friend, we don't know each other, so I'm not gonna take you touching me personally. I see your angle. This bitch is entertaining you. Got you all turned on with the notion of getting between them legs and seeing what that pussy do. Naturally, there's some part of you that feels the urge to protect her. At least, until you get to the pussy." He went on as if he was a profiler, breaking Trap down. "I get it because I'd probably feel the same if the shoe was on the other foot. Only problem with that is, you got no clue what my gripe or my right to this whore is. From one gangster to another, please stay out of this."

"Gangster?" Moochie gave Christian a comical look. "I probably got a bigger dick than you do." She grabbed her crotch. Her eyes rolled over Christian, the beautiful head of hair, the tight pants. If she didn't know any better, she could've sworn that he was wearing makeup. He was no threat. At least that's what she had assumed. The fact that all the strippers in their section had moved themselves out of harm's way should've told her differently.

Christian matched her stare. "Then how about we both pull out our cocks and compare notes? Your dick might be bigger, but mine is going to make for a much more exciting ride." He undid the zipper of his pants. As he was doing so, his sweater rode up exposing the pearl-handled pistol he had concealed.

Moochie smirked at her underestimation of the seemingly soft man. Maybe he was more than just a pretty face after all. "That's a bet I might be willing to take." She lifted her sweater to show her gun. This was Moochie's type of party.

The tension in the air had gotten so thick that Promise felt like she was suffocating. The big girl with the dreads looked like she didn't play any games, but the man called Christian didn't seem phased. It reminded Promise of an old western she had watched with her aunt Adelle where the villains would have the hero outnumbered and outgunned, but somehow the hero would win the day. She wasn't sure who was the hero or the villain in this standoff, but if she had to bet, she'd put her money on Christian.

"Okay, break this shit up." Larry appeared. Odell followed closely behind him with one of the other bouncers. "What's going on?" He looked back and forth between Christian and Moochie.

"Nothing much, Larry. I've just come to reclaim my property," Christian told him.

"I don't belong to you, Christian. I'm my own woman," Donna said indignantly.

"*Own woman*? Bitch, I built you!" Christian chuckled. "When you came to me, you were a scrawny flat-backer turning tricks on Backpage for a hundred dollars per lay. I turned you into a star. You don't wanna leave with me? No problem. Give back those tits I paid for, that ass I flew you out to the DR to have worked on, and that new nose that you call yourself trying to look down on me with. I'm also gonna need back the bread I spent to get your junkie of a mama into that rehab facility up in Westchester. If you can do all that, then consider our business concluded. If not, get the fuck up and let's go!"

Donna looked to Larry with pleading eyes. He knew that trying to snatch one of Christian's girls would be a problem when he hired her, but when he looked at Donna, all he saw were dollar signs. "Christian, I can't have you in here strong-arming my girls. How about you come back tomorrow and we can sit down and work things out like gentlemen?"

Christian snorted. "Nigga, you ain't no gentleman. You're a chili pimp and a fucking thief. It still amazes me that you can find bitches desperate or dumb enough to come work for you."

"Fuck all this chatter. How we gonna carry this, Larry?" Odell asked in a menacing tone.

Christian looked up at Odell studying him. "I had heard stories about the brute Larry had on retainer. I have to admit, Larry, he is a truly fascinating specimen. I imagine this one can do some real damage with those brawny hands of his. Unfortunately, my monster is bigger than yours."

A shadow appeared over Larry and Odell. When Larry turned his eyes went wide. Up until then, Odell had been one of the largest men he had ever seen, but the owner of the shadow dwarfed him. He was six eight with wide shoulders and a head that was deformedly large. Zig-zagging down his forehead was a scar that resembled a lightning bolt. He bore a striking resemblance to Mary Shelley's fictional monster, which is how he had gotten his nickname, Frankenstein. Larry had heard tales about Christian's enforcer and had always dismissed them as far-fetched. Seeing Frankenstein in person, Larry realized that none of the stories had done him justice. He was a truly terrifying sight to behold.

Frankenstein didn't say a word. He just stood there, glaring at Larry and Odell with dead eyes. He turned his attention to Christian, awaiting the kill order.

Larry was literally caught between a rock and a rock. Odell was a gladiator. He had proven it time and again, but Frankenstein was ripped straight from the pages of a horror novel. It was possible that Odell would be able to take him, but at what cost? Odell was too valuable to Larry to have him sidelined. In the end, the kind of problems Christian was capable of creating weren't worth it. Not over a girl that he should've known better than to deal with in the first place. "Donna, get your things. You're done here."

"What?" Donna's eyes got wide. She was just as surprised as the other girls who had gathered to watch the spectacle. They all knew that she had been Larry's favorite, so it was a shock that he would cast her aside so easily. A few snickers came from some of the girls, happy to see that the self-proclaimed queen of Dirty Wine had been knocked off her throne. "Fuck you, Larry." She sprang to her feet. It was all she could do to fight back the tears of embarrassment. She made to storm past Christian, so she could go to the dressing room to collect her things, but he grabbed her arm.

"And where are you going?" Christian asked.

"I'm going to get my shit from my locker," Donna told him.

"No, ain't nothing that carries the taint of this dump getting in my ride. You're fine just like you are," Christian told her.

"But I'm half-naked and it's freezing outside!" Donna pointed out.

"Call it penitence for your betrayal," Christian told her. "Frank, walk this lame bitch out. I'll be along in a second."

Frank hesitated, not sure he wanted to leave Christian alone, but he reasoned that his boss had it under control. "C'mon, Ms. Donna," he said in a voice so gravely that you almost had to strain to make out what he was saying. He reached for the girl's hand, but she jerked away.

"I can walk on my fucking own!" Donna snapped at Frank. She wasn't mad at the big man. He had never been anything but kind to her. Her anger was directed toward Christian, but to address him further might've led to her having to spend a night or two in his playpen. She would've rather taken an ass whipping than that. With her head held high, Donna strutted from Dirty Wine, ignoring the mocking laughter from the other strippers that followed her.

Christian waited until Donna and Frank had gone before addressing Larry. "I'm only going to say this to you once: steal from me again and you die. Won't be no drawn-out speeches or back-and-forth conversation between us. You'll just quietly leave this world."

"Is that a threat?" Larry questioned.

"Fuck you think?" Christian popped the collar of his fur and gave Larry his back. "My apologies for disrupting your night," he addressed the rappers. "If you ever find yourself in my neck of the woods, pop into my spot and allow me to make it up to you." He handed them several black business cards with the word *Hades* etched across the front in gold letters. "That goes for you too, beautiful," he told Promise. "Me, you, and that alabaster skin can make a lot of money. If you ever get tired of working for a nigga who can't teach you shit outside of how to suck dick and try and steal crumbs from another man's table, come see about me. My name is Christian, and I make stars out of meteors. Ask around about me." He winked and was gone.

CHAPTER 12

"Look at them. They're like fat little pigs, begging for us to run spits through their asses and twist them over an open fire. You boys up for some barbecue?" Bone asked, half-joking. The crowd had begun to thicken by then, and there were some players in attendance rocking nice jewelry. He was paying particular attention to Inferno's group. Among them was a short dude rocking a bald fade. Around his neck was a thick gold chain and on his wrist was the bracelet to match.

"Mind that your eyes don't get bigger than your belly, Bone," Unique cautioned. He looked to Sin, who was inconspicuously watching the group over the rim of his glass. Unique could see the wheels in his head turning, making the necessary adjustments. "What you thinking?"

"That I'm starting to question the validity of your source," Sin replied.

"Nigga, you know my sources are always on point. These extra jokers showing up with Inferno are unexpected twists. That's all," Unique said.

"Man, I don't give a shit how many of them there are. I say we bank all them niggas," Bone said.

"That ain't what we were hired to do," Sin reminded him.

"I forgot, we gotta play it straight because of this mysterious client of yours that got us out here on a witch hunt. You still ain't said much about who dropped the bag. You fill us in from top to bottom on every other job, so why you playing this one so close, Sin?" Bone wanted to know. He had been curious about it since Sincere had brought the job to the table. Somebody wanted a nigga done filthy, which wasn't out of the ordinary. That's what the crew did—take shit that didn't belong to them and put the hurt on people. This situation was different though. It felt more personal than about the money, and the fact that Sin was being so secretive only made Bone more curious.

"All you need to be concerned about is getting cashed out when the job is done. Anything else, leave to me," Sin told him.

"Big bro, you on some bullshit. Them niggas is over there looking like free money right now. From the way they just let that faggot play them out of pocket, we can probably book 'em all with little to no hassle," Bone spat.

"*El príncipe de la noche,*" Unique said.

"Say what?" Bone didn't understand.

"The prince of the night," Unique translated. He'd heard stories about the dark prince of the underworld, but this was his first time seeing him in person. "That's what they call Christian. He might be a lot of things, but somebody we wanna tangle with ain't one of them. That pretty muthafucka is as cold as they come. One story I heard was about these Eastern European cats who tried to muscle him on a deal. Ol' Christian laid them boys low with nothing but an umbrella at his disposal."

"Bullshit. I can't see that candy-ass laying nothing down,"

Bone said disbelievingly. There was no way Unique was going to convince him that a cat who dressed like Prince was a murderer.

"That's his gift—deception. Dudes like him you never see coming until it's too late," Unique warned.

"Good thing we spotted him first then, huh?" Sin asked. To him, Christian was yet another obstacle that he might have to overcome to reach his goal. And despite his laidback demeanor, Sin would cut through Christian and ten more muthafuckas who looked like him if they got in the way of his target.

"Does seeing your little bitch over there giving them niggas the attention you thought was all yours got you in your feelings?" Bone noticed his brother glaring at Christian as he invaded Promise's space. The girl didn't seem to mind either. "What? You too good for sloppy seconds now?" he laughed. It was meant as a joke, but the look Sin shot him was a serious one.

"Don't ever disrespect my character. How about you keep your mind on this business and off my dick?" he said sharper than he had meant to.

"Calm down, Sin. Baby bro is only fucking with you," Unique said, defusing the situation. "I don't think it's a secret to anybody at this table that you seem a little bit invested in this broad." It wasn't an accusation, just an observation.

"You know there's always a method to my madness. For all you know, I might be the one who put her up to cutting into them dudes," Sin said cockily. Truth be told, he really was into Promise, but his interests were twofold.

"I'd say you hit a two-for-one tonight and neglected to tell us," Unique said with a knowing smile. "Knowing you the way I do, it wouldn't surprise me. You keep a trump card up your sleeve, this we all know. Only . . . she seems a little green to me."

"And that's the best part. Niggas are always looking for

greener grass, until they find out there are snakes lurking there too," Sin said.

"So, what's the play?" Bone asked. "We gonna keep sitting here burning money or get some? We been here for hours, and Nique's info ain't proved good yet. That don't mean the night has to be a total waste. I say we strip these rap niggas of their goods and get in the wind. What's good, bruh?"

Sin didn't reply right away. He continued to stare across the room at the rappers, but he could feel the eyes of his brother and best friend on him. When they'd first started running together it was agreed that there would be no singular leader of their crew. Every man would have a part to play. Sin was their strategist, the one whose job it was to explore every possible outcome of a caper and factor in the probability of them pulling it off successfully, before undertaking it. Though he took the lead most of the time, he didn't *officially* wear the title of leader. Still, he was one they all looked to for reassurance that they would make it home to their respective families after a job. He looked at his brother and his best friend and saw an all too familiar look in their eyes. The wolves were hungry and depended on him to make sure that they ate. This was not how Sin planned the night would go, and he hated to go off script, but in this case, he had to put the good of the team ahead of his personal feelings. The client would be disappointed by the turn of events, but Sin didn't have any other choice other than to play the hand he had been dealt. It was either that or leave with his bankroll in the red, and this he couldn't have. "Fuck it," he relented. "Go see if that bitch left our package where she said it would be."

"About fucking time!" Bone said before getting up and heading to the other side of the bar.

"You sure you wanna follow Bone's greedy ass on this play?" Unique asked once the big man had gone.

"Not really, but he's right about us leaving here empty-handed. I'll talk to the client and let them know shit went left," Sin said.

A few minutes later, Bone came back to the table smiling like a kid who just realized he had been left alone in a candy store after closing. He slid awkwardly back into the booth, waving off one of the girls who was trying to get Unique to spend a few dollars with her. Sin could tell from the mirth in his eyes that the package had been there. His insider had done their part, and now it was time for him to do his. He gathered his team around him and began running down the new plan.

"Everybody clear?" Sin asked after having gone over the plan twice.

"Yeah, man. This is gonna be light work," Bone boasted.

"That's just the type of attitude that'll get you killed, baby bro. I ain't gonna be the one to tell Pops that you died on my watch. Don't put that on me. We give each target the same measure of respect, and it puts the odds in our favor to all make it back whole." It was one of the first lessons his father had taught him when he was a kid, right before he started taking him along on robberies. By the time Bone was old enough to get involved in the family business, their dad had gotten himself retired, and Sin was the one feeding the family.

Sincere watched while Bone divided the stash of guns he had retrieved, using the tabletop as cover. They were all small handguns: a .380, a baby 9mm, and a .38. They usually rolled heavier on jobs, but it would've been kind of hard for his insider to stash a machine gun in the paper towel dispenser on the wall. Bone kept the baby 9mm, gave Unique the .380, and slipped the .38 to Sin. He was still in his feelings over his big brother scolding him, and leaving the pop shooter for Sin was proof of that. It didn't matter to Sin because, in his mind, all bullets burned the same when they cut into a man's chest. Still, in light of recent developments, the smaller guns would put them at a disadvantage if they ended up having to bang out. The job they had planned for was supposed to be quiet, a simple snatch and go, but Sin knew in his heart that this new twist wouldn't go down like that. They would have to be fast and coordinated if they hoped to get out alive, let alone pull it off successfully. He knew he could count on Unique to do his part, but he wasn't so sure about his drunk-ass brother. Everything in him screamed to call it off, but they had come too far to turn back.

Just as Sin was about to give the signal for his guys to take up their positions, a commotion broke out near the front door. He watched Larry hot-foot it across the bar in the direction of the entrance where a small crowd had started to gather. Odell was right on his heels. Strippers had abandoned their poles and lap dances, surging in the same direction. From the way they reacted, you'd have thought someone had just tossed a bag of money into the joint. When the crowd finally parted and Sin was able to see who had just come in, he realized that someone had. At least in a sense. He breathed an audible sigh of relief when he realized that he would no longer have to go off script. He looked to Unique, who was smiling at him knowingly.

"You still wanna question my sources?"

"You can gloat on it once we're out of here and in one piece, Nique," Sin replied. This was as close to an apology that Unique would get, and he was fine with that.

"This shit went from a meal to a buffet," Bone pointed out. "We not only got two millionaires in the spot, but if we decided to turn this whole place into meat, they ain't got the muscle or firepower to stop us! We could feast and go to sleep tonight with our bellies overflowing and—"

"Or stick to the script and not let greed trick us into taking unnecessary chances," Sin cut him off. "We plan and execute, not overplay our strokes. That's how we've always won, feel me?"

"Whatever you say, *boss*," Bone grumbled.

Sin was about to check his brother about his attitude when the sound of breaking glass caught his attention, followed by shouts. It was coming from the section where Inferno and his guests were seated. At first, he thought that a fight had broken out, until he spotted Promise at the heart of the disturbance. Her eyes bulged and what little color she had to her skin drained away. Larry was barking something at her, but her eyes were glued to the newcomer. When she finally turned to address Larry, she said something that seemed to shock him. The next thing Sin knew, Promise was galloping on her stilettos toward the dressing room. Sin called after her, but she never broke her stride or spared him a look. It was as if she had the devil on her heels. Sin stood to follow, but Unique stopped him.

"This ain't the time for that, Sin. You gonna chase this bag or that bitch?" Unique questioned.

Reluctantly, Sin returned to his seat. Unique was right. They were at Dirty Wine with a purpose that night. He tried to stay focused on the task at hand, but he couldn't help but wonder what the hell had just gone down with Promise.

CHAPTER 13

Long after Christian had gone, his presence could still be felt throughout the entire club, but especially in Inferno's section. Donna had been replaced by two more strippers, and the drinks continued to flow, but it was obvious that the vibe had changed. There was a nervous energy that hadn't been there previously. Promise could feel it acutely, and she could tell from their body language that the others did too.

Moochie had lost interest in Keisha, settling instead to brood over the bottle of champagne clutched in her large mitt. Trap was a little more at ease. With Donna gone, Keisha was now the object of his affection. He showered her with bills while whispering sweet nothings into her ear. He tried to appear not to have been rattled by the confrontation, but Promise peeped how he kept casting glances over his shoulder anytime someone passed too close to their section. It was like he was expecting Christian to come back to continue their conversation and wanted to see him coming. Promise hadn't been in Christian's presence for more than five or six minutes, but it was enough time for her to agree with the sentiment. He certainly wasn't a man you wanted sneaking up on you.

Inferno seemed the least concerned, which was understandable. Stranger and more intense things happened whenever he showed up somewhere. The fact that this incident hadn't played out in violence was nothing short of a miracle, considering that chaos and, at least, a beatdown always seemed to follow the young rapper anywhere he went. His partner Finesse was a different case. The standoff between Trap and Christian had made him uncomfortable. Promise could tell because of the way he kept glancing at his watch as if he had someplace else that he needed to be. Promise would've been lying if she said that she felt anything close to fear coming from him. It was more like the energy in the room was now off, and he was anxious to get away from it. She couldn't say that she blamed him because she was feeling the same thing. In fact, she decided to take that as her cue to leave and get back to Sin.

"So, listen . . . if you guys are cool for right now, I'm going to clear some of these empties and go check on my other tables," Promise announced. She began gathering empty water bottles and discarded drinking glasses from the table, tossed them into a bin, and tried to make her exit.

"Hold on, baby. Where you rushing off to? Larry said you girls would be with us for the night." Trap blocked her path with his arm. He already had Keisha on lock, but apparently one girl wasn't enough for him.

"I ain't a part of that package," she told him and forcefully moved his arm so she could pass, but he grabbed her by the wrist.

"Don't act like that, lil miss. I ain't hard up for bread. Stop playing with me and put a number on it, so the real games can begin," Trap said suggestively.

"She said she's good. I'm all the woman you'll need for the night, Daddy." Keisha tried to draw Trap's attention from Promise, who was clearly uncomfortable.

"I got deep pockets and a big appetite," Trap told Keisha before turning his attention back to Promise. "C'mon, shorty. Name your price and I got you." He fanned a bunch of bills in front of her.

Promise looked from the bills to Trap's smirking face. "One lesson my mother taught me before she passed was all money ain't good money." She snatched her arm away and spun. It was then that she got into her third accident of the night. "Fuck," she cursed while bending to pick up the empty bottles and glasses that had fallen. Thankfully they were all empty and none of them had broken. As she was cleaning up her mess, she noticed the feet of the man she had bumped. He was wearing a pair of crisp construction Timberlands, untied, laces running free. She wasn't sure why but something about them rang familiar. Her eyes traveled up the black jeans, over the black sweater, and landed on the medallion swinging from his neck. It was a gaudy Rottweiler head covered in black diamonds with two rubies where the eyes should be. Promise felt her mouth go dry and she had to force herself to finish the visual journey that she had started. When she looked into the face of the man she bumped into, she suddenly found that she could no longer breathe.

He was tall. Not as tall as Odell, but well above average height. He had broad shoulders that suggested he worked out or, at least, had at some point in his life. The slight belly peeking through his sweater said that he no longer hit the gym as often as he once had. A well-kept black beard covered most of his face, and his eyes were hidden behind dark sunglasses. Promise didn't have to see the eyes to know that they were boring into her, undressing her.

As he continued to eye-fuck Promise, she could feel the burger that she had eaten earlier shift in her stomach as it threatened to free itself through her mouth. "No," she let out a weak gasp. There were few people who could connect the dots of her old life to her new one, and he was one of them.

"Damn it, girl! Why is it that, every time I turn around, you seem to be on your ass!" Larry barked. Promise didn't know where he had come from, nor did she care. She couldn't pull her eyes away from Don B.

"Take it easy, old-timer. This isn't the first time a bitch has fallen out in my presence, and it won't be the last. The Don can be somewhat overwhelming," Don B. boasted. He extended a hand to Promise in order to help her back to her feet, but she was frozen. All she could do was stare. "What is she? Retarded or something?" he asked Larry.

"Up, gal." Odell took Promise by her arm and pulled her to her feet as if she weighed next to nothing. He could see the embarrassment plastered across her face and wanted to spare her a bit of dignity. "You okay?"

Promise nodded. She didn't trust herself to speak. Her mouth had gone completely dry, and her tongue felt like a sandbag. She dared glance at Don B. and found him staring at her quizzically from behind those sunglasses.

"Damn it, gal. This klutz shit with you is getting old!" Larry barked.

"Larry, I didn't mean to . . . I'm sorry, but—" Promise began, but Larry cut her off.

"You always sorry. Shit, you can't dance for shit, you spill one out of every three drink orders before they get to the tables, and you ain't fucking. You don't belong here!" Larry went in on her. It was obvious that the girl was experiencing some type of episode, but he was too busy trying to show out for the rappers to notice. Even if he had, it was doubtful that Larry would've cared.

Promise was finally able to pull her eyes away from Don B. and turned to Larry. He was still screaming at her as if she was a child, but his voice had faded to white noise. The only thing she heard clearly was his statement about her not belonging there. Once again, she was being rejected by a man she had come to depend on. That was the last straw for her. "You know, what? You're absolutely right, Larry. I don't belong here." She tossed the few empty bottles she had collected back onto the floor. This time, one of them did break, causing Larry to jump back from the spray of glass. "Fuck them bottles, fuck this raggedy-ass club, and mother-fuck you, Larry. I quit!" she announced before storming off.

"You janky bitch! Don't bring your ass back here begging for no job because I ain't got shit for you! You're done here!" Larry called after her. It was more for show than anything else because anyone who had witnessed what just happened knew that Promise's time at Dirty Wine had come to an end. "My apologies, gentlemen. You know how it can be sometimes to break in these new bitches. They all want the money, but ain't got the patience to let me build them into stars."

"No apologies necessary, old head." Don B. was addressing Larry, but looking over the sea of strippers lingering at the fringes of the VIP rope hoping to get chosen. He plucked one from the crowd, gave her the once over, and sent her back. "Something that I learned a while back, stars aren't made,"—he plucked another girl from the crowd, younger and more to his liking—"they're born."

"Fuck was that about? With the bottle girl?" his manager, Tone, asked. He was a brown-skinned man of medium build. He had a preppy look about him, with his pale gray blazer, blue jeans, and white Nike Airs. Tone had been stopped at the front door by a broad he used to fuck while Don B. went ahead, so he only arrived at the table after the incident. All he had to go on was seeing the girl flee and knowing his friend's reputation.

"Fuck if I know," Don B. said honestly. He flipped through his mental Rolodex trying to place her but couldn't right away. "I definitely feel like I've seen shorty before. You don't forget an ass like that, especially on a white girl."

* * *

Promise moved with half the speed and all the grace of a fawn who was just learning to use its legs. It was all she could do to get her feet to cooperate with the rest of her body and keep her balance while she made it to the dressing room. Her ankles were twisting this way and that, threatening to dump her on her face. She cursed herself for not snatching the heels off earlier, but that would've taken time. Time in which Don B. might've had a chance to remember where they'd met before. She needed to put some distance between herself, Dirty Wine, and the demons of her past.

When she passed Sin's table, it was like a blur. She heard him call her name but didn't stop. She couldn't stop. If she had, she would've likely given Sin all that anger she had bottled up for Larry, sprinkled in with her own self-hating shit, and he didn't deserve that. The game they were playing with each other needed to be one of emotional stability. At least, on her part, and she wasn't quite there at the moment. To make matters worse, she knew that she had been doing Bozo shit all night. From the spilled drinks to her daddy issues manifesting themselves in public, no sporting nigga in their right mind would've taken her seriously. And if they did, she would've had to question their judgment because she knew, for a fact, that night she had presented herself as the hot mess that she was.

For once in her life, her luck held, and she had crossed the threshold of the dressing room before she finally lost her balance. Clutching the wall kept her from hitting the ground, but her tender ankles had had enough of the heels. Sitting on one of the benches, she snatched the shoes off and tossed them into the trashcan. Now, free of the cheap plastic, Promise managed to hobble to her locker. It took her two attempts to get the combination right. She snatched the flimsy locker door open, spilling her small makeup bag onto the floor. She ignored the brushes and CVS lipsticks and dug out her cell phone and the sweats she had worn to work that night. She hit the last number she'd called. Actually, it was the only number she'd called, outside of the Chinese restaurant, since she had gotten the phone. It only took two rings before someone picked up on the other end.

"Yo," a low voice came over the phone as Promise was pulling her sweatpants on. In the background, you could hear the "Land O' Lakes" joint by Conway the Machine and Busta Rhymes knocking in the background.

"It's me," Promise said into the phone.

"Like I didn't know that. What's goodie?" the gruff voice questioned from the other end.

Promise slipped into her Air Max and was pulling her sweatshirt over her head when she replied, "I need a solid."

CHAPTER 14

"So, you think homie is solid?" Cal asked once he and Asher were back in the car.

"Atilla?" Asher thought on it before answering. "I haven't seen him in a minute, but you know he's always been crew, even if not officially. We grew up with the dude."

"Yeah, but like you said, you haven't seen him in a while. Time changes a man. Especially prison time," Cal pointed out.

"I don't disagree, which is why I wanna keep him close for a little while. Feel him out, you know?"

"You trying to bring him in?" Cal asked suspiciously. He and Asher had always kept a tight circle, but it got even tighter once Asher was promoted.

"To this?" Asher motioned toward the city. "Nah, these little niggas already on edge with all the new faces hanging around lately and adding one more to the mix probably ain't gonna help to ease the tension. I got something else in mind for homie."

"You better be careful with that one. Handling Atilla is like playing with a loaded gun," Cal warned.

"And that's exactly why I want him close. I got love for him because we got history, but me keeping him on is as good as having my own personal attack dog. He's young, hungry, and fiercely loyal."

"Which is also what makes this such a bad idea. How do you think he'd react if he finds out what you did to Ab?" Cal questioned.

"You mean what *we* did to Ab," Asher corrected him.

The story Asher had given Atilla about Ab having overdosed in Atlantic City was true, but it was also incomplete. After B-Stone was killed, Ab, as his second in command, inherited his position. Ab proved to be a competent enough leader, though a reluctant one. He and B-Stone had been in the streets for years, but while B-Stone embraced the gangster lifestyle, Ab had begun to shy away from it, even prior to B-Stone's death. Ab was more focused on getting his music management company off the ground than building a drug empire. He had been trying for years to get B-Stone to see his vision, but Stone was in too deep, with no interest in getting out. He loved the streets so much that he didn't mind dying in them, and he did. However, Ab had different ideas.

Not long after, Asher found himself playing the position that Ab had only recently vacated, an ambitious young man with his own vision of the future. Ab was the boss, but Asher was the one in the trenches with the soldiers. Between trying to break into the music business and keeping the operation up and running, Ab was a man trying to dance between two worlds, and their business on the street was beginning to suffer because of it.

Asher was the one charged with taking care of the day-to-day operations, from keeping their workers supplied with drugs to settling disputes when they arose. Asher was tapped into the streets in a way that Ab hadn't been in years. This allowed him to see the playing field from a different angle, but so long as his OG kept a leash around the young superstar's neck, he would remain powerless to make the necessary adjustments to ensure that their business didn't get swallowed up by the competition. The only way Asher would ever be able to do what he felt in his heart was best for his gang was to cut the tether. And so, he did.

To Asher's credit, he had tried diplomacy in the beginning. Ab obviously had little to no interest in sitting at the head of a drug gang or the work that would go into making sure that it flourished. Empowering Asher while Ab played in the background but was still the boss in name would've given both what they really wanted. But Ab's ego wouldn't allow it. He was too worried about how it would look to let one of his young boys steer the boat, that it would be seen as a weak move, or him not being able to handle what B-Stone had left behind. He would've rather continued sitting on the throne until it rotted out from under him or was snatched, instead of doing what was right for the gang. This didn't carry a lot of positive favor with the homies who saw what was going on. Ab had broken one of the cardinal rules of gangbanging when he put his self-esteem before the needs of the organization.

The way Asher saw it was that either he or one of the other lieutenants would give Ab what was waiting for him and take over, and Asher wasn't too enthusiastic about serving another general. It was his time, and everyone knew it. It was then that Asher started to plant the seeds of an uprising.

Toppling Ab would require a slightly different set of circumstances than the ones that had taken B-Stone out. Stone was a man with one speed and one intent: conquer as quickly as possible. It was easy to steer a dude like him into some bullshit that he might not survive. There might've been speculation about Asher's involvement with B-Stone's murder. He wanted him dead . . . no, he *needed* him dead for the sake of his own life and that of his mother's. Someone was hanging a cartoon anvil over Asher's head and threatening to cut the rope and Daffy Duck his ass if B-Stone didn't eat dirt first. Thankfully, before Asher could even begin to wrap his mind around the task, someone had beat him to it. The universe had thrown him a lifeline with someone else killing B-Stone before he was forced to, but there would be no such blessings when it came to Ab.

Much like with B-Stone, it had been Ab's one-track mind that opened him up to Asher's treachery. Because Asher was his little homie, Ab would often boast about the things he had going on just to impress him. Little did he know, his one-time protégé used this information to find kinks in his armor. Ab's proudest accomplishment was his management company. He would go on and on about how he had legit shit popping beyond what was going on in the hood. He started thinking that he was Dame Dash and started drilling his ideals into Asher. He challenged him to boss up but denied him the resources he needed to really make a move. Unbeknownst to Ab, his bragging and treating Asher like a lil nigga had the same effect as letting a domesticated pitbull taste blood for the first time. Everything you taught them flew out the window and their base natures took over. They wanted more.

By the time Asher began laying his trap for Ab, he had already started broadening his view beyond Essex County. One thing he learned was that "what one man won't do, another man will." Whereas Ab kept his investments close and only fed Asher enough to keep him alive, his new silent partner opened him up to something different. He introduced Asher to cities like Miami and Los Angeles, where the real action happened. Asher found himself moving in circles of people with real money, and he wanted to be a part of that life. Asher was still the low man on the pole, riding his partner's coattails, but he knew how to work a room. He might not have cut into the larger Hollywood connects, but he managed to establish great relationships with their assistants and entourages. One such relationship had opened the door that Asher would walk Ab through where he would meet his end.

During one of Asher's trips west, he had become friendly with an up-and-coming dude with ties to the music industry. Much like Asher he was from the streets and trying to hustle his way into bigger things. He was doing well for himself, having established a few lucrative businesses and the buzz surrounding his fledgling record label had been steadily growing, but he was still knee-deep in the streets. Also like Asher, he sought to serve two masters and didn't care about them. Their mutual love of the drug game and the glamour that came with being a boss was what had established their bond, but discovering each had an itch that the other could scratch was what proved to be the glue that would bind it.

One night, Asher offhandedly mentioned to Ab how he had met this big-time music guy on one of their trips to Cali and told him about a play they were working on putting together. Asher had already predicted what would happen long before he opened his mouth, and Ab didn't disappoint. He spent the next hour or so picking Asher's brain about his new friend. He presented it under the guise that he was trying to help his protégé plot the best way to cut into his new West Coast connection, but it was really just a ploy for him to poach Asher's opportunity. Being the gracious big homie that Ab was, he offered to front the bill for Asher to fly his people out and would even put them up in a hotel in Atlantic City.

"This will give you some clout in them Cali niggas' eyes," Ab had explained. He was really laying it on thick for this one. Ab was so thirsty to cut Asher's throat that he didn't think twice about it when Asher mysteriously came down with a case of food poisoning on the day they were supposed to drive down to Atlantic City to meet the guys from the label. Ab was all too happy to take the point in the meeting and bring Asher up to speed after. Less than a week after Ab's body was discovered in a hotel room, Asher was the new king of the hood.

"I backed your play," Cal said, recalling the part he had played in the coup, "but it isn't like you were exactly forthcoming with what you intended to do."

"I told you exactly what I planned to do. Remove Ab from power so that the organization could flourish. You agreed that it was the right thing to do," Asher reminded him.

"Right! You said you had plans to *remove* him, not *murder* him," Cal pointed out. Asher had revealed his plan to replace Ab with himself, but he had presented it in a way where Cal believed he was going to coax him into retirement or, at worst, find a new connect to undercut Ab's prices. That had been half-true because, through Asher's new bestie, He had managed to get a better quality of product at a friendlier price. Cal was cool with that, but murder? That was something Cal would've never signed up for had he known that had been his friend's plan. Asher had probably known as much, which is why he kept Cal in the dark about it until it was too late for him to do anything to stop it.

"I ain't did nothing other than what you did, and that's look the other way when it went down," Asher said.

Cal opened his mouth to respond, then clipped whatever he had been planning to say.

"What?"

Cal wasn't going to respond at first, but he couldn't hold what he was feeling. "Bruh, with a dude like B-Stone, I was able to turn a blind eye to him getting clipped and his killers never really being held accountable. Ab, though?" Cal shook his head in disappointment. "His hand didn't call for it. We should've found another way."

"Like what? Sit down, make nice, and try and do the right thing? I tried that approach, and for my trouble, he tried to snake me out of every opportunity I created, including that fake-ass deal I put together in AC!" Asher was getting frustrated. Cal was his right hand and the eyes in the back of his head, so he was the last person Asher felt he should have to keep explaining himself to. "Bro, I'm not sure what's going on with you lately, but we're in the long game now. Me and you." He tapped Cal's chest for emphasis. "If I ain't learned nothing else from those two egomaniacs who came before me, I learned that, if I don't wanna go out like they did, I gotta be willing to do and say some things that ain't gonna gain me many popularity points."

"Being unpopular also played a hand in their downfalls," Cal pointed out. "That's something else I meant to talk to you about. I know you're running around starting new businesses and getting fitted for suits now, but don't take your ear away from the streets."

"Fuck is you talking about? I'm always in the hood," Asher protested.

"Being in the hood and being aware of the politics are two different things. I feel like you might be forgetting that, which is why you keep acting like you see that nigga Milk in your rearview. He been chatting real big lately."

"Fuck Milk," Asher said as a matter of fact. "He just in his feelings because I knocked a bitch off that he was sweet on. Me and him have had a love/hate relationship ever since. Why? He saying some shit that I need to hear?"

"I'm not concerned by what he's saying. It's what he's not saying that's got me looking at him funny," Cal clarified. "We ain't the only niggas in the hood who been moving different since the power has shifted and everybody's gotten promotions. You don't feel it because you're not tapped into the day-to-day antics anymore, and I'm only on deck long enough to make sure all of our spots are running accordingly, then I usually skate. We trust our lieutenants to make sure business is running smoothly, and it's Milk they look to when we're not around. He's the voice most of our soldiers hear every day."

"A monster of my own creation." Asher already saw where Cal was going with this. And he was right. Milk was one of the original knuckleheads who had come under B-Stone and Ab when everybody was getting put on the hood, but he had never been a part of the hierarchy as Asher and Cal had been. He was a dude from the hood but had never put in any work of note. Asher had given him his new position on the strength that Milk was someone familiar. He had been around longer than anyone in their new regime. Milk had taken his new position and started running with it. Asher would be lying if he said that he hadn't noticed the subtle flexes here and there, but he had never given Milk enough credit or respect to deem him a threat. The fact that Cal had mentioned it meant that there was something that, in all his arrogance, Asher had missed. He knew firsthand the fates of men who made those kinds of mistakes. "I'll take care of it," he assured Cal.

"Incoming call . . ."

"Fuck!" Asher cursed and hit the reject button again.

"Damn, shorty must be thirsty as hell for all the times she's called you. Either hit the bitch back or pass her off to your boy," Cal joked.

"Trust me, you don't want no parts of that one," Asher

said honestly. "Speaking of bitches, I got that thing up and running." He changed the subject.

"Say word?" Cal's mood picked up when the topic switched to money.

"Yeah," Asher confirmed. "It's slow motion right now, but I officially hit the go-button on it."

"Damn, kid. I thought we were supposed to christen that mofo together?" Cal was tight that he had missed out.

"We were, and we will. This is what I call a soft launch. I'm just trying to see where we're at with it and what them numbers are going to read like. This is foreign soil we're about to play on, and I wanna know what's what before we plant that flag."

"Smart." Cal nodded, rubbing his chin. "Keep it off the radar so that it doesn't attract the wrong attentions."

"It's gonna come out eventually, so there won't be no avoiding that. Still, I wanna do it on my time, my way. Feel me?"

"Yeah, I feel you, but I can't say that I like it," Cal admitted. "Dark times we're living in where you gotta hide your wins, so people don't take them as a reason to add to your losses."

"Unfortunately, that's the nature of a hater," Asher said.

"So, you trust him?"

"I don't trust nobody," Asher said in a tone that suggested it might've applied to Cal too. "The thing working on my side is that I got him over a barrel because of a bit of advanced planning on my end. Quiet as kept, I put some shit in motion that burned all his bridges so that mine is the only path he has left to walk. I'd be a fool to think that he'll play fair because that ain't in his nature, but he's going to play nice because that's the only way he can stay in the game."

"Cold as ice," Cal remarked.

"Cold above ground is better than cold under it. Even the most skilled snake handlers get bitten. That's a given. The trick is to make sure you have the antidote long before the strike comes. To be honest, this is probably one of the last dudes I'd have placed this much faith in if I didn't have to. The fact that he's been successful at this before and already friendly with the locals makes him a necessary evil."

"I get that, but honestly? I can see him becoming a problem one day. His ego won't allow him to play it any other way," Cal pointed out.

"You know I know. It's like I said; playing fair ain't in his nature, but thankfully it isn't in mine either."

Cal wouldn't say it, but he couldn't have agreed more with Asher's statement. Since seizing the reins of power, Asher had shown him time and again that he was willing to color outside the lines to keep it. This wasn't the same kid he had come up with who had been all about getting money and chasing women. Asher was becoming something else right before Cal's eyes. What exactly he was becoming was still up for question.

Instead of going to Asher's house to smoke like they normally would, Asher suggested they go to Cal's. His mom, Linda, was off from work that night and was probably in the house. It wasn't that Linda minded them smoking in the house. She was a former gangbanger herself and cooler than most moms when it came to their vices, but Asher claimed he didn't feel like her being all in their mix while they were trying to chill. Cal suspected that it was really because Asher wanted to be away from the hood for a time.

A few minutes later, they were pulling up to Cal's place, which was located in North Newark. He had started renting the place when he and Asher had started seeing real money. Unlike his friend, he was smart enough to move his family from the thick of where they did their dirt. He was out of the way, but still close enough to where he could be back in the block within fifteen minutes if he needed to be. It was a two-story rental house with a finished basement that could be accessed through a side door. Cal claimed the basement as his own, so he could come and go as he pleased, and left the women to the upper levels of the house.

"This shit again," Cal said when he noticed shadows moving around on his darkened front porch. They could smell the weed smoke long before they got out of the car. Through the open door, they could hear music, as well as several other voices. Either one of his sisters or his mother must've been entertaining again. They seemed to do that a lot since Cal had been promoted and was able to upgrade their quality of living a bit. They now carried themselves as hood royalty, making sure that all their friends knew about their good fortunes. This irritated Cal to no end because he was so low-key. The whole point of them moving was so that they would be off the radar, but the women in the house insisted on leaving a trail of golden breadcrumbs to their doorstep. Cal had confided in Asher about how he often thought about moving into a place of his own and leaving them to their shenanigans but feared that his mother and sisters would end up pissing the house away and end up piled into his grandmother's apartment on Clinton again. He stayed for the sake of her peace of mind, or so he said. Cal might've popped a lot of shit about his ghetto-ass mother and sisters, but Asher knew how deeply he loved them.

Asher followed Cal through the front gate and up the short driveway. They could make out Cal's oldest sister, Bernadette, one thick ass cheek resting on the rail of the porch. She had on a tight polka dot dress with a high split that showed off way too much of her meaty thighs. She sipped from a plastic cup, talking to someone pressed into the shadows. From the way she was throwing all thirty-two of her teeth, Asher figured she must be talking to one of her old boo-thangs, or a new one. It was hard to keep track of Bernadette's revolving door of men. Whoever she was talking to must've pointed Asher and Cal out in the driveway because she turned, lazy smile on her lips.

"Hey, baby brother," Bernadette greeted him. She moved to greet them, but almost lost her footing when one of her heels hit the chipped concrete steps the wrong way. Thankfully, Cal caught her before she fell.

"What did I tell you about having random niggas over here?" Cal held her by the arm. He was speaking to his sister, but his eyes were locked on whoever she had been speaking to in the shadows. Cal still couldn't make out the face, but he did recognize that there were two of them.

"Random?" a familiar voice called from the darkness. The man Bernadette had been smiling at stepped out into the moonlight, so the two youths could get a look at him. He was tall and handsome, draped in a forest green suit with a white shirt beneath, and the first three buttons undone. His dark eyes took in Cal and landed on Asher, who stood frozen in place. If the devil truly did walk the earth, there was no doubt it was in the skin of this well-dressed man. "And here I thought we were friends."

"What are you doing at my house, Zul? Wait, better question, how did you even know where I lived?" Cal cut his eyes at Asher, who was just standing there, looking dumbfounded.

"Thank your sister. I ran into her earlier. She gets real chatty after a few drinks." Zul gave him a wink. "I had planned to pay a call on your lovely sister eventually, but you can thank your boy Asher for expediting the appearance."

Cal looked to his sister for an explanation, but she appeared too drunk to have noticed the remark. Was Zul taking his sister down?

"Had he answered his phone, I wouldn't have had to pop up unannounced, and we could've avoided this little awkward meeting. You owe me money, Asher? That's the only reason that I can see for you to be ducking my calls."

"Zul, you know I'd never do you like that. What happened was—" Asher began but was cut off.

"If you try and spin me like I'm one of your bitches, me and you are going to have a misunderstanding tonight," Zul warned. As if on cue, his henchman, Snags, came off the porch. He was an older dude with patchy, dark skin and a missing tooth in the front of his mouth. Snags was a headache, and he loved to do Zul's dirt for him.

Asher swallowed his response. He wasn't a sucker, but he was no Zul either. The man could be very temperamental, which was a nice way of saying *psychotic*. He had to be handled with the greatest of care or else you could run the risk of setting him off. Asher had seen what he was capable of when he was like that, and Asher didn't want to risk bringing that down on Cal or his family.

"Smart man," Zul remarked of his silence. "Let's take a ride." He plucked Asher's car keys from his hand and started for the Benz.

"Where we going?" Asher asked with uncertainty in his voice.

"To hell if we don't pray!" Zul called over his shoulder before sliding behind the wheel.

Asher didn't feel good about this, and his face said as much.

"I'm riding too," Cal told Asher. He was still pissed about Asher's antics leading to Zul showing up at his house. That was a man whom you didn't want knowing where those you loved laid their heads. Still, angry or not, Asher was his best friend, and he wouldn't leave him hanging.

"Nah, man. This one is on me." Asher gave him an appreciative smile and was off to whatever fate awaited him.

CHAPTER 15

"I see you haven't lost your touch with the ladies, Don," Trap said with an amused grin.

"And I see you still have a talent for showing up at places uninvited," Don B. shot back.

"Funny, the last time I showed up somewhere uninvited you were singing my praises, or have you forgotten about Miami just that quick?" Trap taunted.

Miami was one of several run-ins that Don B. and Trap had over the years. They were rivals of sorts: two young up-and-comers from the same backgrounds with different levels of success. They were both street cats who had built their respective empires on foundations of blood, but this is where the similarities ended. Don B. managed to crack the Matrix code of the industry and take Big Dawg to a global level, but Trap always played with one foot in and one foot out. He was an underground legend, but Don B. was a superstar. Throughout their careers, their paths had crossed, and there had always been slick, yet respectable, banter trying to outdo each other, but Don B's flex was always bigger. That was until that one night in Miami when the scales were unexpectedly tipped.

Don B. had been a regular in Miami. His roots and his heart would forever be in Harlem, but the Don loved the 305. So much that he even owned a condo in a small suburb a few miles outside of South Beach. He would shoot down there at least twice every month or so. This last run-in between him and Trap had been during a random week when Don B. had come down for a business meeting, but as was his style, it had shifted from business to pleasure. He had spent so much time in Miami that he had started moving with the same ease as he did in Harlem. This is why it had been so easy to catch him slipping. Don B. found himself in a bad way and had it not been for Trap showing up unexpectedly, he'd have suffered a fate which he felt would've been worse than death. Don B. had always known that Trap was holding a marker that would, one day, be called in. It had been the guillotine hanging over his neck since it happened, and he had lived in fear of it one day falling. And now, here was Trap wearing the executioner's mask and holding the rope that would release the blade.

"Sup wit ya peoples looking at me like they're thinking about doing something?" Trap asked playfully. He was peering past Don B. at one of the men in his small entourage. Trap had always known Don B. to roll heavy, especially in New York. That night they were only four deep. Tone he already knew, but the others were unfamiliar. One was a large and menacing-looking, light-skinned cat that looked like he was ready to get it shaking. Trap could see the impression of the bulletproof vest under his shirt, so this told him that the sour-faced man was likely security. "You know? I can't remember the last time I saw anybody except Red Devil watching your back out in public, Don. He ain't with the team no more?"

"Devil has never been a part of the team. He's family," Don informed him. "Sammy is new to the organization, but just as efficient. I'll be sure to tell Devil you asked about him."

"You be sure to do that. Devil is a man I've always respected. With him, you always knew what to expect, but this one . . ." Trap tapped his chin in thought while eyeballing Sammy. "I'm not sure how I feel about how he's looking at me."

"Pay Sammy no mind. He's got a built-in *'fuck nigga'* radar, and you probably just set it off." This comment came from the second unfamiliar man, a thin, short joker with coco skin. His youthful face was marked with tattoos, the most prominent being a black diamond with a Z inside. At a glance, you could've mistaken it for the Superman emblem, but the symbol represented the House of Zod in the Superman comic books. A chain similar to the one Don B. wore hung from his neck, adorned with a Rottweiler head as well, only his hound sported ruby-speckled horns sprouting from its head. His Atlanta Braves fitted was cocked ace-deuce on the side of his head, and there was a thickly rolled joint behind his ear. Like Don B., he too wore sunglasses though it was night, and they were indoors. It was obvious where he got his style and attitude from. Trap had never seen him in any of the Big Dawg circles, but the fact that he even had the balls to address Trap said that he thought he was someone.

Trap pondered how best to respond to the half-ass insult. In the end, he decided that laughing it off was a better solution than slapping the dog-shit out of Don B.'s little friend. "Don, I know you haven't started trolling circuses to plug them holes in your crew?"

"Did this nigga just call me a clown?" the kid in the Braves hat asked no one in particular. It was his delayed reaction to Trap's crack. "Homie, I'll split your wig." He took a step toward Trap, but Don B.'s voice halted him.

"Zod!" Don B. called his name in a stern voice. Zod opened his mouth like he wanted to continue the argument, but a look from Don B. silenced him. "Excuse my nephew, Trap. He's young and a little on the wild side still, but we're working on smoothing out some of those rough edges and teaching him the business."

Zodiah, known as General Zod to his enemies, wasn't actually Don B.'s nephew, but his cousin's youngest son. He was a native New Yorker but had been living with his mother in Atlanta for the last couple of years. Zod had been a wild boy since the day he came into the world, fighting, stealing, and being an overall menace. Zod was a bad seed, but he was a saint compared to his older brother Terror, who was a stone-cold killer. Most people in the neighborhood were scared to death of him, which is why it came as no surprise when he turned up dead one day. They found him in a project stairwell, shot and with his throat cut, and had no real leads as to who had done it. Terror had been Zod's hero, and when he received the news, he went ballistic. Zod was already a loose cannon, but he had gotten ahold of a PCP-laced cigarette, and it turned him into a demon. Since no one knew who for sure in the neighborhood had killed Terror, Zod waged a personal war on the whole block. He had made it rain blood in the hood for a few days, twenty-four hours straight before he was finally brought down by the police, and even then, it took pumping his ass full of bullets to stop him. Zod lived but found himself locked up for his actions. Don B. kicked out the money to hire a team of lawyers to defend his cousin. Because of his age and the fact that he had been high on angel dust at the time, they were able to use an insanity plea, and instead of spending the next twenty years in prison, he rode out four years in a mental institution. No one knew what he had endured in the institution, but it was clear that Zod wasn't the same kid when he came out as when he had gone in. Upon his release, his mom took him to Georgia to try and keep him out of trouble, but it didn't help. If anything, it made him worse. Atlanta had never seen anything quite like young Zod, and it was only a matter of time before he had a price on his head for the things he was pulling down south. Desperate and out of options, she sent him back to New York to stay with Don B.

Don B. started Zod out doing odd jobs and running errands. He mostly shadowed Tone and some of the other executives as they went about the day-to-day business at Big Dawg Entertainment. Young Zod might have been a violent sadist, but he was also incredibly intelligent. He mostly ran errands or spent his day shadowing Tone or one of the other Big Dawg executives while they went about handling the day-to-day operations at the label. Zod was like a sponge and soaked up everything he saw. He hadn't been there for a month before Don B. recognized that his cousin's talents were being wasted on coffee runs and rolling weed. The kid had a great mind for business, so Don B. promoted him to an A&R position and let him work with some of the newer acts. Some of those projects Zod had worked on were the only things keeping Big Dawg afloat. Though Zod would still need a little grooming, when the time came, Don B. planned to use him as the bridge between Big Dawg Entertainment and the new generation of artists that the label had previously struggled to tap into. Zod was in line to be Don B.'s heir apparent, if he didn't let his mouth or his temper get him killed first.

"I can dig it," Trap said after a pause. "I used to have the bad habit of speaking out of turn too until somebody punched me in my shit and knocked a few of my teeth out." Trap hooked his finger under his lip to show off his mouth full of permanent gold teeth. "I can refer him to my dentist because he'll likely need him soon enough at the rate he's going."

"Fuck all the subliminal threats. What you doing in my city, Trap?" Don B. changed the subject. "Better question . . . what the fuck are you doing at my meeting?" he was speaking to Trap but was throwing disapproving looks at Inferno and Finesse.

"I'll take the blame for this." Finesse raised his hand. "I know how busy the two of you gentlemen are based on how long it took us to arrange a sit-down with either one of you. It was just a stroke of luck that you both happened to have holes in your hectic schedules on the same night, so I figured we'd kill two birds with one stone."

"Shorty, I came here out of the kindness of my heart to see if there was any star potential in you, and you repay me by inviting this snake-ass nigga to the table?" Don B. glared at Inferno.

"Watch your mouth, homie," Moochie said, coming to her brother's defense.

"It's cool, Mooch. Ol' boy didn't mean anything by it. This is just a little friendly competition. Ain't that right, Don?" Trap addressed his rival.

"Competition?" Don B. chuckled. "You doing your little thing, Trap, but don't forget who sits at the top of this music food chain."

"Right, the notorious Big Dawg Entertainment, where artists go to get fucked over or murdered under mysterious circumstances. You the only nigga I know outside of Suge Knight who has made more money off artists' posthumous music than the ones who are actually still alive," Trap accused.

Don B. took it and didn't flinch. When he spoke, his tone was icy. Not just cold, but final. "It ain't cool to make light of the dead. You popping fly about situations that are above your pay grade. Now, the fact that we've suffered some tragedies over the years is no secret. Still, for every soldier who has fallen while waving a Big Dawg flag, there is a family who'll be taken care of for the rest of their days on earth. With some of my artists, if they were smart, it'll be at least a generation before any of their loved ones will ever know what it means to work a nine-to-five. So, yes, I've lost some cats that were dear to my heart, but I've also made sure that their legacies live on. At Big Dawg, we leave no man or family behind, but let Nutty tell it. You wouldn't know anything about that."

For the briefest of instances, Trap allowed his mask to slip. It was a rare loss of self-control for a man who lived every moment of his life wearing a poker face, but he was quick to recover. "There was a time when you and I would've had a misunderstanding about that crack. One that might even lead to bloodshed," Trap said in a deadly tone. This caused members of both crews to take up defensive postures around their respective leaders. Trap looked from Moochie to Don B.'s entourage. It was two against four, but favorable odds as far as he was concerned. A part of him wanted to take it there and humble Don B. in his own backyard, but he checked his ego and turned his attention back to the business at hand. "But that was when I was a lil ignorant 'jit, and putting a nigga on his back meant more to me than putting money in my pocket. This is a new day." He made a sweeping gesture with his hands, letting everyone know that all was well. Some of the tensions eased, but both crews remained at the ready in case things changed. "Look, there's too much testosterone in the air right now, and that can lead to poor decisions. Ladies, why don't you entertain the troops while the generals walk and talk? Let's see if we can't come to some type of understanding."

"Fuck that. I ain't letting you out of my sight with King

Creep," Moochie protested. Despite his clownish behavior, she held no illusions as to how dangerous the Don of Harlem was.

"I'm with the dyke on this one, Unc. I ain't cool with you sliding off with this joker," Zod chimed in. Luckily for him, Moochie was so focused on Trap and Don B., she let the slur slide.

"Since when we start doing business in back alleys?" Tone asked suspiciously. Unlike Zod, he wasn't worried about Trap trying Don B., at least not in the tristate. He was more concerned about whatever money might get discussed during that sidebar conversation. As far as Big Dawg was concerned, Don B. was in charge of the flash, and Tone the cash. Not a coin was exchanged unless he checked the date on it first.

"Since the beginning, my nigga. Or y'all been in rooms full of lawyers that you've forgotten how much money has been made over intimate conversations?" Trap jabbed. He picked up on them being suspicious of his motives, so he decided to have a little fun with it.

"We got a private room in the back where you guys can talk," Keisha offered.

"That'll work. If the Don is okay with it?" Trap asked. The opposing group still looked skeptical, so he decided to play on Don B.'s notorious ego. "What y'all worried about? This is Don B.'s backyard, so I'd be a fool to play it foul. I'm the lone frog in a gator pond. But if your Don feels like he needs some muscle around to feel comfortable, by all means, tag along," he offered.

"Even before I was the richest nigga in rap, I was still the don and never needed to move in a group," Don B. proclaimed. "Lead the way, shorty."

CHAPTER 16

The first ten minutes of the ride felt like the longest ten minutes of Asher's young life. Zul was, in general, a chatty muthafucka, but that night, he was unusually quiet. Quiet for Zul wasn't a good sign, because that meant that his brain was working and usually on something sinister. Asher imagined Zul wasn't happy at the fact that he hadn't picked up his calls, but that wouldn't have been the first time Asher had looped him, and certainly not cause for Zul to come all the way to North Newark to track him down. No, he had something else on his mind, and the fact that Asher didn't know what it was made him nervous.

Every so often Asher would let his eyes go to the rearview mirror. He could see Fangs following closely behind them in Zul's truck. For as near as he could tell, Fangs was alone in the truck and not riding with the Lynch Mob. That was the nickname given to the crew of killers that he kept at his disposal. They were a nasty lot who didn't believe in traditional murder. Zul's hitters would often come up with especially cruel ways to dispatch those who had run afoul of Zul. Asher had once been in a car with them when they had run down a kid who had been talking crazy about Zul. The only thing that Zul took more seriously than his money was his name, and to kick dirt on it would guarantee you a first-class trip to the afterlife. Asher knew, from the time they had picked the offender up, that he was as good as dead, but he hadn't been prepared for the method of execution Zul's twisted mind had come up with.

"Since you like to run your mouth, let's see if your legs can keep up," Zul told him before binding the man's wrists and tethering him to the back of his truck.

To the offender's credit, he had the stamina of a high school track star. He managed to keep up with the truck for four blocks and probably could've gone further had he not lost his footing and fell. Zul dragged that boy from Market and William Streets all the way to Lincoln Park before having one of the mob get out and cut him loose. They left him there to die in the middle of the street like roadkill. Miraculously, the offender survived, but lost most of the skin on one side of his body as well as an eye. That was the first time Asher really understood what kind of devil he had made a deal with. The two things that Asher remembered most about that night was the extent of the offender's injuries and how eerily silent Zul had been up until passing the death sentence. It was a silence much like the one that filled Asher's Benz that night.

Zul pushed the Mercedes deeper into the hood. Asher initially thought they were headed for the block, but Zul passed the neighborhood where they got money and rode further still. They were now moving up Frelinghuysen. The two- and three-family houses had started to give way to a more industrial section of Newark. There were garages on one side and the park on the other, but at that hour, all the businesses were closed, and the park was still. Asher knew, from past experience, that this is where they went when they wanted to get rid of something or someone. His eyes drifted to the gun he had stashed between the driver's seat and center console. Zul was focused on the road, so he reasoned he could reach it in time, but even if he did manage to kill Zul and avoid dying shortly after the car crashed, there would still be the issue of having to deal with Fangs. Part of him wished that he had accepted Cal's offer to ride along.

Zul made a movement, which caused Asher to jump nervously. Zul gave him a quizzical look, before grinning sinisterly. "Relax, I was just turning on the radio. Too quiet in here." He hit the button, and Funk Master Flex's voice filled the speakers. He was deep into his Friday night mix. "What's with you, Ash? Why you so jumpy?"

"Ain't nobody jumpy, man. I'm just high," Asher lied.

"Not off anything stronger than weed, I hope?"

"Zul, you know I been stopped fucking with them pills once I started getting real money in the hood. I gotta stay focused," Asher said, which was partially true. He had limited his ecstasy trips to only those occasions when he was trying to break a new bitch in and wanted to show off.

"That's a good thing. Them pills ain't no good. I've had my fair share of fun with them back in my day, but that was before we knew where the shit was coming from and what was in it. They're tainting all this new shit with fentanyl, so there's always a fifty-fifty chance that your next high ends up being your last. Sometimes it hurts to see how far your generation has fallen."

"I never understood why you looked down so hard on pills, but ain't got no problem putting them on the streets," Asher said.

"My moral compass and bottom line are two things that'll never intersect. One of the first things I noticed when I got out of prison and got back in the game was that the landscape was changing. Sure, people still want the brown and the white, but there is also a great demand for opioids. I'd be a fool not to get my slice of that pie. And based on this beautiful machine you're riding around in, I'd say it's safe to say that you agree."

"You know me, man. I'm about a dollar," Asher told him.

"Indeed, my sly young friend. You'd cross your own mama if there was a bag in it for you. That's a quality that makes me both admire and detest you, Asher. If I'd been as ruthless as you are when I was your age, I'd either be way further ahead than I am now or dead. A worthwhile gamble at any rate, which is why I can understand why you sometimes do shit that makes me scratch my head about you."

"Zul, you know I hate it when you talk in riddles. If you've got something you need to say to me, then come out with it. We ain't gotta dance around the issue."

Zul flashed him an amused look. "You've gotten real ballsy since I put that crown on your head. I'll bet it makes you seem like hot shit among the homies, huh? Their beloved prince, feeding the hood again. I wonder if they'd still love you if they knew our twisted history and how you really came to power?"

It was a threat, and Asher knew it. The thing that he feared most about Zul was not his team of shooters, or the fact that he was a bloodthirsty maniac. Every man could bleed, no matter how untouchable he thought he was. B-Stone had been proof of that. No, what Zul had access to could do more damage than any weapon forged against Asher. It was the information he held that could bring Asher's little kingdom crashing down on his head.

Only a few people knew the real connection between Asher and Zul, and most of them were dead. He and Zul's relationship went back to when Zul and B-Stone were still on good terms. Despite the war between them that had rocked the whole city, the two men had been friends at one time. They were from two different gangs, but bonded over sports, with both of them having played football for Central High School. This was back when a kid named LA had been the one supplying the hood. Ironically enough, it had been B-Stone who introduced Zul to LA. Thanks to the introduction by B-Stone, LA had started to sell Zul weight directly, much to the displeasure of B-Stone. Someone who B-Stone had always seen as lower than him on the food chain was now his competition.

The difference between B-Stone and Zul was that, although they were both gangbangers, Zul was a businessman first and foremost. He had a different understanding of the game than B-Stone did and set up his crew to run like a well-oiled machine, instead of a bunch of trigger-happy dope boys. Zul's business began to flourish, and he eventually knocked B-Stone out of the box as LA's best customer. He was moving major weight while still flying under the radar of law enforcement. Zul was bringing in double what B-Stone did, with access to only half the real estate.

What started out as a business relationship between LA and Zul developed into a friendship. LA took a liking to the suave and ambitious young man. He saw that Zul was ready to step out onto the big stage and was about to open things up for him. Unfortunately, before LA could put Zul in position, he was removed from power. When LA went, so did his connect. The next thing you knew, the hood found itself in the middle of a drought. No drugs meant no money, and it created chaos. Nobody knew where their next dollar was coming from, so the homies started getting it how they lived. Violence was now at an all-time high and everybody knew that whoever found the next connect would be the next king of the hill.

Zul was the first one to break luck and find a halfway decent supplier. It wasn't the best work, but he was the only one holding a bag at the time. This meant that anyone who wanted to buy drugs had to get them from Zul's people, including B-Stone's crew. Zul always looked out for B-Stone and never charged him the same thing he charged everybody else, but B-Stone couldn't bring himself to get comfortable eating from Zul's hand. He wouldn't admit it, but he was jealous. The extent of his jealously wouldn't fully show itself until B-Stone managed to secure his own connection. This is when B-Stone would fire the first shot in a war that would last an entire summer.

The battle between the two former friends proved to be one of the nastier ones that Newark had seen in recent years. To those on the outside looking in, the war looked like it would end as lopsided as Custer's last stand. Zul had a handful of loyal men that all got busy, but B-Stone commanded an army of savages that lived to put in work. B-Stone rained some biblical shit on Zul's head, but in the end, the odds tipped in Zul's favor because he understood something that B-Stone thankfully didn't. Wars weren't won by whichever side knocked off the most people, but the side that killed the *right* people. While B-Stone had his boys executing drive-bys, the Lynch Mob was strategically assassinating everyone who had a position in B-Stone's power structure. Even outnumbered, Zul had his childhood friend against the ropes. Out of desperation, B-Stone crossed a line that he couldn't come back from. He broke the rules of engagement and used Asher to do it. It was Asher's act of treachery that had been the nail in the coffin that carried Zul into prison and opened up the lane for B-Stone to become the undisputed boss of their section of the city.

"We still on that? I thought we was good?" Asher reminded Zul.

"In for a penny . . . in for a pound," Zul replied.

"And after what I've already done, my scales ain't balanced yet?" Asher questioned.

Zul laughed. "Young nigga, you a Judas twice over, and I still gave you a play. Name me one hustler on the planet who was double-crossed into prison and, when he gets on his feet, shares his bag with the joker who put him there? Either I'm stupid or I see something in you that makes me keep banging my head against the wall."

And there it was. The thing that Zul had been holding over Asher's head that had gotten him into this whole mess in the first place. The thing that forced Asher to betray his set. During the war, it had been Asher who B-Stone used to get close enough to Zul to plant the gun in the car that he went down for. Asher was a part of B-Stone's crew, but Zul and Asher's mother had come up together, so even while the two sides were fighting, he never viewed Asher as a threat, which had proven to be a mistake. He turned out to be the most dangerous one in the whole lot. Zul didn't figure it out until he was a few months into his prison bid, and when he did, he had several years to plan his get-back. When he was released from prison, the first stop on his revenge tour had been to Asher's mother's house. Asher had almost shit himself on the day he walked in and found Zul in his kitchen making pancakes. It was time to pay the piper. Zul had given Asher two options: make things right by killing B-Stone, or his mother was a dead woman. With little other choice, Asher agreed.

Shortly after Asher made yet a second deal with a devil, B-Stone was found murdered. The thing was, it hadn't been Asher who had killed him. Zul had charged Asher with the task of killing B-Stone. When the time came to make good, Asher found that he hadn't had the stomach. He had known B-Stone forever, and besides that, the man was a stone-cold killer. Still, Asher found that he wasn't up for it, but he would have to if he wanted to keep him and his family safe. By the time Asher had gotten up the nerve to go through with it, he found that someone had beat him to the punch. Zul had just assumed that Asher had been the one to do the deed, and Asher didn't bother correcting him. In truth, to that day, he still had no clue who had murdered B-Stone, so he had ridden the lie straight to the top.

With B-Stone dead, Asher thought that he would finally be free of his debt to the homicidal Crip, but little did he know, the puppet master had only just begun to jerk at his strings. Asher told himself that he wouldn't indulge in any more of Zul's sick games, but this was before Zul made him an offer that would prove too tempting to pass up.

"I let you live, even after what you did, because I saw a lot of me in you," Zul continued. "Yeah, you're a dishonorable little piece of shit, but you're also a charming bastard who knows how to get a dollar. What better shepherd to lead my new little flock than one the sheep already trusted? I made you a hometown hero in the eyes of your set, but you and I both know you ain't shit but a snake."

"Then why keep dealing with me?" Asher asked.

Zul paused before answering. "That's a question I've been asking myself more and more lately."

He steered the Benz toward a scrap yard on a darkened street. It was after hours, and the place was closed, but Asher could still see men milling about. Zul flashed the headlights in a pattern, and a few seconds later, two members of the Lynch Mob appeared and pulled the gates open. Seeing that Zul's head squad was on deck filled Asher with uncertainty. The only thing that he now knew for sure was that Zul tracking him down was way bigger than a few missed phone calls. As the luxury car crossed into the yard, Asher's mind again went back to his hidden gun.

Asher could feel his heart attempting to creep into his throat when Zul pulled to the back of the lot and killed the engine. Fangs parked the truck directly behind the Benz, boxing them in. Asher was trapped. "Zul, what's this about?" he tried to keep his voice even.

"You'll see," Zul told him and got out of the car. As an afterthought, he added, "And leave the gun. You won't need it."

CHAPTER 17

Asher walked silently behind Zul, hands shoved deep into the pockets of his jeans. Standing near a ruined car, holding an assault rifle, was a tall, light-skinned man who wore his hair in a fade with skulls tattooed on both sides of his head. They called him Whisper, and he was one of Zul's top killers and a member of the Lynch Mob. They called him Whisper because he rarely spoke and you never heard him coming before he snuffed your life out. Whisper gave a curt nod, watching the group as they passed. Seeing him there only made Asher more uncomfortable, and he just hoped that, if he was to die that night, it would be at the hands of Whisper. At least then, it would be quick and unexpected.

Fangs trailed a few paces behind him. Every so often, Asher would look over his shoulder and find the man smiling as if he had a secret that he couldn't wait to tell. He had never liked Fangs. No matter how Asher's night played out, he promised himself that, whatever trip he was going on, he would take Fangs with him, if no one else.

"So, other than ducking my phone calls all damn day, what you been up to?" Zul asked as they approached the entrance of one of the storage containers that sat in the yard. It was smaller than a garage, but larger than a garden shed. The structure was just big enough to hide some truly devilish shit inside.

Asher shrugged. "Out here chasing a dollar. Same as always."

"From the looks of things, you out here doing more than chasing dollars. You're catching them!" Zul said good-naturedly. "You out here shining, baby boy . . . jewels dripping, skin looking all good. That California sun must be agreeing with you?"

The remark hit Asher like a playful slap. It was no secret that Zul had turned him onto the scene in California. It was Zul who had introduced him to the players, but it had been Asher's low-key wheeling and dealing that put him in the game. None of the moves he was making conflicted with anything Zul had going on, but Asher hadn't exactly been transparent about his latest venture either. Zul wasn't a man who made random statements, and his bringing Cali up meant that he'd gotten wind of something and was fishing. Whether Asher would make it away with the bait or end up on the hook would depend on his response. "Cali has been good to me, but I got you to thank for that. Before that first trip you took me on, the farthest I had ever traveled outside Jersey was to New York."

"Right, I did pluck you out of the slums and try to show you something different, didn't I? They embraced you like a real ghetto celebrity out west. Laid the world at your feet. I guess that's why you started making trips without me, huh?" It was more of a statement than a question.

Asher had seen this coming, so he didn't try and deny it. "Yeah, I slide out there from time to time when I feel like I need to get away from Newark. Mini-vacations, you know?"

"More than you think," Zul replied. They had stopped just shy of one of the storage containers that sat on the yard. It looked like just the right place where one could partake in some truly dastardly shit, and knowing Zul, that was likely its purpose. He placed one hand on the sliding door handle but paused and turned to face Asher. "You've been a busy boy, Asher. Busy doing everything except the right thing. After all I've done for you, I can't figure for the life of me why you continue to go out of your way to disappoint me. That changes tonight."

Asher didn't have to run around to know that Fangs had moved directly behind him. He could smell his breath from over his shoulder. In Asher's mind, he could see Fangs looming at his back with his pistol drawn, waiting for Zul to give the word. When Asher first opened his mouth to speak, he found his gums dry and his lips sticking against them every time he tried to part them. He swallowed once or twice to try and generate enough saliva in his mouth that would form the words to plead for his life. "Zul—" he began but was abruptly cut off.

"I told you earlier that, if you tried to spin me like one of your broads, we were gonna have a problem, and I meant it. You are a great fucking earner, Asher, but your problem is that you think you're always the smartest nigga in the room. You've gotten so cocky in your new position that you've lost the qualities that put you there in the first place. That ego of yours has made you sloppy, and this is what has brought us to this point."

Asher stood frozen as Zul pulled the doors to the storage container open and exposed what was hidden inside. As Asher had suspected, it was something truly dastardly. Something that only Zul could've devised. There was a treadmill set up in the room, with a man naked and bound to the front of it. His legs pumped at a light jog trying to keep up pace. His back was covered in a film of sweat that ran down his spine and dripped through the crack of his ass onto the treadmill. From how heavily he was breathing, Asher figured he had been at it for a while. He would run until he died of a heart attack, which was a far more merciful death than what waited for him if he stopped. At the back of the treadmill, Zul had set up two power saws that he'd purchased from the Home Depot. Their blades spun menacingly, daring him to stop running. Whenever he seemed to find a rhythm at one pace, the juvenile demon working the control panel of the treadmill would increase the speed a bit.

This was Zul's protégé, Baby Blue. He was from out of Irvington. Asher hadn't spent a lot of time around Baby Blue but had heard his name mentioned enough to know what he was about. At only sixteen, Baby Blue was already a headache, but once Zul had gotten ahold of him and started poisoning his brain with his ideologies, it turned Baby Blue into something that there currently was no classification for. He was just a rotten kid. His own mother didn't want anything to do with him, but Zul embraced him like the bastard spawn of the devil that he was.

Asher was about to ask what kind of twisted shit Zul had invited him to witness, until he caught a glimpse of the jogging man's face and his mouth went dry again. The man's name was Danny. The last time that Asher had seen him had been on Market. Asher had been sitting low in a car while he watched Cal place an envelope full of cash—which Asher had provided—in Danny's hand and tell him to get missing. The fact that Danny was now in the custody of Zul meant that he either hadn't listened or Asher's luck was just that bad.

"Big homie, he been at this shit at least a half-hour. If he wasn't such a fuck nigga, he might've been able to make the Olympics," Baby Blue told Zul with a chuckle.

"You can run from a lot of shit in this world, baby boy, but karma is the one bitch who will always catch up with you, no matter how fast you are," Zul replied.

"Zul . . . please, man. I've told you what I know . . . enough," Danny pleaded. He was breathing so hard that he could barely get the words out.

"I'll be the judge of that," Zul told Danny. He then turned to Asher. "From the expression on your face, I take it that you and this piece of shit are acquainted already?"

Asher had considered lying, but Zul wasn't a man who asked questions that he didn't already know the answers to. "I've seen him around before. Ran with Saud back in the days, didn't he?"

"He about to be running with God," Baby Blue snickered, adjusting the speed on the treadmill. "Let me make him do the hundred-yard dash one time, big bruh."

"Cut it the fuck out, Blue. We on business," Zul scolded him before turning his attention back to Asher. "Fangs ran down on this nigga on the humble. He was in Wiggles tricking off and trying to get a couple of Spanish broads to spend a night or two with him and his over in New York. Couldn't stop talking about all the money they were getting up there in . . ." He couldn't remember the name of the city.

"Mount Vernon, boss," Fangs offered in his best house-nigger cadence.

"Right," Zul snapped his fingers. "So, we all know Danny been a bum-ass flunkie his whole life, and nothing short of God could've changed him dying in that same position. Yet, here's this lifetime yes-man, flashing cash and showing out."

"Zul, what I got to do with some off-brand nigga who stumbled into some good fortune?" Asher asked. He didn't really want an answer, but he needed to say something to buy his brain some time to think up a deflection for whatever Zul was about to say next.

"Glad you asked. After my little conversation with Danny, I discovered that my suspicions about him now being able to wipe his ass without someone telling him where the tissue went were confirmed. This is where you come in. What part of *clean house* didn't you understand when we came to our little arrangement?" Zul asked Asher.

"Fuck you talking about? B-Stone and Ab are gone. I saw to that. There's no one left to challenge your claim to the hood," Asher told him.

"Now, it's *my* claim? Thought we were in this together?" Zul gave Asher a suspicious look. "But that's for another conversation. What I need to know is, if you were instructed to get rid of every member of B-Stone's inner structure, why is that sour old bastard Saud still alive and openly pissing on my name?"

Saud was an old-timer, a holdover from B-Stone's reign. But long before he was B-Stone's consigliere, he had been the king of the neighborhood. Asher had been barely a child old enough to cross the street on his own during Saud's time at the top, but his name rang in the ears of the young and old alike. Saud had been a legend until a prison bid knocked him out of pocket. After doing almost two decades behind the wall, Saud was back on the streets. By then, LA was still top dog, but he was on his way out. Everyone thought it only natural that Saud would seek to reestablish himself as king, but he didn't. Saud no longer had any interest in wearing the crown. Unlike a lot of hustlers who reached his age and were still trying to relive their glory, Saud understood that it was now a young man's game. So, instead of positioning himself to become king, he became a kingmaker. His whispers into the ears of prominent underworld figures had led to more bloodshed than his trigger finger ever did. Saud may have no longer had aspirations of wearing the crown, but he knew he stood to benefit by manipulating whoever would sit on the throne next. This was how B-Stone came to power, and Saud his trusted right hand.

"Zul, B-Stone and Ab are gone, and Saud is an old man scraping the bottom of the barrel, trying to hold onto what little he got left. How much of a threat could he be?"

Zul gave Asher a look. "That was the same thing I said until he put the battery in B-Stone to cross me. It may have been your bullshit that landed me in prison, but it was Saud who set that plan in motion. I know his style, and B-Stone wasn't smart enough to come up with something that creative on his own. I warned you, no loose ends. Saud should be laying in a hole next to B-Stone and Ab right now, but you acted like he went so far underground that you couldn't get a line on him. I've seen you track and clip niggas in different time zones, so you'll have to excuse me if I have a hard time believing that you couldn't find a man living less than an hour away. If that's the case, you're either dumber than I thought or smarter than I've been giving you credit for. Which one is it?"

Asher was too smart to respond. It was a loaded question, and no matter how he answered, it would either call his loyalty or competence into question. He remained silent. What only a few knew was that Asher not only knew where Saud had been laying low, but it had been him who plugged him in with the dudes that he was currently eating with in New York. When Zul first gave the order to have Saud hit, Asher had every intention of carrying it out, but then he got to thinking.

It had been Saud who turned out to be the X factor in the war between B-Stone and Zul. He had been one of the few people able to outwit Zul during their game of strategy. Zul's ego couldn't and wouldn't allow Saud to live and run the risk of him creating another B-Stone, which ironically was the same reason Asher had allowed him to live. He had planned to use Saud as his trump card that would finally get him out from under B-Stone's thumb for good. So, instead of killing Saud, he set him up on a nondescript block in Mount Vernon that he was supplying with drugs behind Zul's back.

* * *

"Sounds like funny business to me, homie," Baby Blue added, playing with the speed on the treadmill again. Danny's legs pumped harder, and his chest heaved. At one point, he stumbled but didn't fall.

"Fuck you," Asher snapped at Baby Blue.

"Fuck yo mama!" the teenager matched his tone. Blue slid from his perch at the controls, as Asher moved toward him. It was only Zul stepping between them that stopped fists from flying.

"Blue, don't let that disrespectful-ass mouth of yours have you waiting outside with the rest of the Mob. You out of line," Zul checked him.

"Zul, you got nothing to worry about. I'll take care of this thing with Saud," Asher assured him.

"So you've been promising, but have yet to deliver. Sadly, it's out of your hands at this point. I'm putting someone more qualified on this shit with Saud. I need Saud dead, but first I need answers, specifically how he not only managed to evade my crowned prince, but how he was able to land so effortlessly on his feet so quickly. His life is now in the hands of the Outlaw."

That was a name that Asher had not expected to hear, and the fact that Zul had hired him spoke to how desperate he was to get rid of Saud. John Outlaw a.k.a Johnny Black, was somewhat of a folk hero to those who knew the name. He was the hood's version of Billy the Kid—young, armed, and reckless. He'd get into it with anybody anywhere. Asher knew that Saud was old school gangster and as tough as they came. He'd done more time in and out of prison than Asher had been on earth, touring through some of the most brutal prisons in the state of New Jersey, and it hadn't been able to break him. But this wasn't the prison system. This was the Outlaw. He had ways of making the most thorough dudes talk when he applied the pressure. Zul having captured Danny was unnerving, but there wasn't too much that Danny could say that would damn Asher. Saud, on the other hand? Asher was fairly certain that, when the Outlaw was done with him, Asher's name would be the last thing that crossed Saud's dying lips. This was a conversation that Asher couldn't allow to happen. He needed to get to Saud first.

"If we're done here, I need to get back to the streets. It's almost time for shift change." Asher turned to leave but found his exit blocked by Fangs. Asher looked to Zul.

"You can't leave just yet. We've still got unsettled business here," Zul told him with a knowing smirk.

"You've said you know where Saud is and already told me that I'm off the job of getting rid of him. I don't see what anything else involving that situation has to do with me at this point," Asher said in as calm a tone as he could muster. He felt like the walls were beginning to close in on him and desperately wanted to get out of there.

"According to what Danny has shared, this has everything to do with you, my man," Zul told him.

Impossible! Asher had never had any direct dealings with Danny, or even Saud, for that matter, after their initial bargain had been struck. There was no way that Danny could connect Asher to any of this unless Saud had told him. Even still, he'd be hard-pressed to prove it. Zul was either lying or reaching. "You're crazy if you believe anything that comes out of this cocksucker's mouth about me. He's lying to save his miserable life."

"How can you be sure if you haven't heard it yet?" Zul raised an eyebrow. "Even before this clown started bumping his gums, I had an idea that this had been an inside job. The only way Saud could've managed to avoid my traps was if he had help from someone who knew where I had laid them. I'm going to ask you a question, and I'd advise you to think on it very carefully before answering. What would you do if you were betrayed by someone you'd come to love?"

All eyes in the room turned to Asher. Fangs still lingered in his blind spot. Baby Blue was glaring at him like he was just waiting on Zul to give the word to end Asher. Then there was Zul. His face was devoid of emotions, but his dark eyes bore into Asher expectantly. Mentally drained and out of lies, Asher went for the truth. "I don't know."

"And that's the saddest part." Zul shook his head in disappointment. "Danny, my young prince says that you're a liar. This is your chance to prove him wrong. Leave this world with some dignity and keep it one hundred for once in your life. Speak the name of the dead man who's been feeding you and that pussy Saud."

Asher tensed, waiting for the coward Danny to pass the death sentence over him. If he was lucky, they would just shoot him and not subject him to the Home Depot blades. Asher was a young, pretty nigga and all the women who came to mourn him deserved the gift of seeing his face one last time. Asher was vain, even on the threshold of his death. The insanity of the thought made him chuckle.

"You think this is a joke? Wait until you hear the punchline," Fangs whispered in his ear.

"On my kids' lives, I told you the truth!" Danny insisted. He was struggling to keep up with the ever-changing speed on the treadmill and having a hard time of it.

"Humor me and repeat," Zul said, eyes on Asher.

"Fuck . . ." Danny huffed. "The money . . . the money Saud has been using to bankroll the New York operation came from . . . fuck!" he screamed before losing his footing.

Danny slid down the treadmill, nails digging into the track, futilely trying to prevent the inevitable. Blood sprayed on everyone in the room, including Baby Blue, who proceeded to retch up whatever he had eaten that day. Even Fangs had to turn away from the sight, but not Asher. Asher *wanted* to turn away from the sight unfolding in front of him but found that he couldn't. He watched in an almost trance-like state as the Home Depot blades ripped Danny to pieces. It happened so fast that Danny barely had a chance to scream. Long after he had passed from this life, the blades kept spinning, cutting his corpse to ribbons. Asher chuckled inwardly, thinking at how the universe had finally decided to look favorably on him by dragging Danny to hell and, with him, whatever secrets he'd been planning on spilling.

"Damn you, Blue! I told you to stop fucking with the machine!" Zul cursed, wiping blood from his face with the silk napkin that had been in the pocket of his suit jacket. "I had my dramatic performance all set up and you ruined it!"

"How the fuck was I supposed to know his ass wouldn't be able to keep up?" Blue asked, between gags.

"Maybe if you hadn't been running him like a fucking nag at the Kentucky Derby, he would've," Fangs offered.

"Idiots . . . I'm surrounded by fucking idiots." Zul shook his head. When he turned to Asher, he found the young man trying to suppress a smile. "I guess you think you've dodged a bullet, huh? Think again. Danny already told me what I needed to know, but I wanted to see your reaction when you heard it for yourself that it was your boy Cal who crossed me by throwing in his lot with Saud."

"What?" Asher was shocked. This was something that he hadn't seen coming.

"Yes, it was your right-hand man who was feeding that snake. You didn't know?" Zul questioned.

"I . . . um . . . no, that's not possible. He had to be lying," Asher insisted.

"I thought so too at first. Ironically enough, Fangs is fucking one of the chicks who works at the sneaker store in Market where Danny claims the last transaction took place. I had her pull the tape and saw Cal meeting Danny with my own eyes. You know what has to happen, don't you?"

Asher was too stunned to speak. This was his bullshit, and in his scheming, he had put his best friend's life in danger. He had fucked up in a major way.

"I knew that patchwork-looking muthafucka had larceny in his heart from the moment I met him. I wanted to have you cut him loose when I handed you the keys to the city, but I figured you'd keep him under control. Apparently, I was wrong."

"Zul, this has got to be a mistake. Let me talk to Cal. I can straighten this out," Asher pleaded.

"The time for talking is done, homie. When I first showed up at Cal's house earlier, it was my intent to murder that back-stabbing fuck and his whole family, but then I had a better idea. This doesn't look good on you, Asher. For as close as you two are, I find it hard to believe that you didn't know what he was doing. If you did, that makes you a traitor as well, and you'll be the next one running laps for Baby Blue. If you didn't, then you're incompetent and unfit to lead anymore. Neither conclusion is a favorable one. At least, not for you, but there's an alternative. You want to prove to me that you're not a complete fuck-up? Make this right. Balance the scales."

"Cal is like my brother," Asher said barely above a whisper.

"Did Cain not slay Abel? Either way this shakes out, those blades are going to have a second helping. Whether it's you or Cal that gets served up is totally up to you," Zul said flatly.

What Zul was asking of him was impossible. He couldn't kill Cal, yet he wasn't quite ready to die either. There had to be a way out of this, he just needed time to come up with a plan. "I'll take care of it."

"Of this, I am sure. Until then, Milk will be running the show," Zul informed him.

"Fuck you mean, Milk? Milk ain't fit to run shit but his mouth. With all due respect, this is my city, Zul. I earned it."

"No, it was handed to you," Zul corrected him with the simplicity of a child who had just mispronounced a word from a book they were reading. "I own Newark, Asher. You're just the landlord. Don't let me have to remind you of that again. You don't like my decision? Do something to change my mind. Until then, get the fuck out of here. I don't wanna see you again unless it's to tell me Cal is dead, or I'm consoling your mama while she's putting flowers on your casket."

Asher opened his mouth to speak but didn't trust what

would come out of his mouth. If Asher had been strapped, he would've put a bullet in Zul right then and there, but he wasn't. He held his anger and made to depart the shed. Zul had some parting words for him though.

"If you try to drag this out like you did the business of getting rid of Saud, I'm going to let Baby Blue put a bullet in your head. Clock is ticking, young prince. You'd better get to it."

Asher didn't respond. He just lowered his head and started for the exit. He could hear Baby Blue behind him snickering. *Laugh now, lil nigga,* Asher thought to himself as he stepped out into the night air. Once again Zul had put him in a trick bag of his own making, and this one wouldn't be so easy to lie and scheme his way out of. Betraying B-Stone and even Ab had been choices that he had been able to live with, but Cal? They had been best friends since they were kids. Besides his mother, Cal was the closest thing he had to family and that lunatic had just ordered Asher to kill him. It was either that or end up suffering the same fate as Danny or worse. Asher loved Cal, but enough to die for him?

CHAPTER 18

"I would've died for him," Trap said once they were out of earshot of their respective entourages. Keisha had led them to a back room where the girls did private dances, among other things. It was small and dimly lit, with the only light coming from the few LEDs that lined the ceiling and the exit sign over a fire door in the back. The air was stale, reeking of smoke and sex, and the floors were sticky. But it allowed the two men privacy.

"What's that now?" Don B. asked, shaking a used condom from the bottom of his boot.

"Nutty, my homie that you threw up in my face a while ago. I would've gladly died for him if I had it to do all over again. I should've seen it coming, and if I had maybe I could've stopped it. It's one of my greatest regrets. You ever do things in your life as a young nigga that you looked back on as an OG and regretted?"

"Can't say that I have. The Don does as he pleases and lets the chips fall wherever," Don B. said with a shrug.

"That's that Harlem shit. Y'all gotta be some of the most

cocky and egotistical muthafuckas that I've ever encountered."
Trap chuckled.

"I make no apologies for my confidence," Don B. said.

"Maybe not now, but in time. In time."

"So, what's up? You said we can come to some kind of
understanding. What you talking?" Don B. wanted to get right
to it. There were a few broads at Dirty Wine that he planned to
put on his late-night dinner menu, so he wanted to conclude
his business, so he could get to the pleasure.

"The rap nigga, Inferno. He's got a real gift, don't you
think?" Trap asked.

"He a'ight." Don B. downplayed it.

"Don't bullshit me, Don. The boy is wild, reckless, and
one bad decision away from either going to prison or getting
himself clipped. He's perfect Big Dawg material."

"Which is why you're trying to poach him from me," Don
B. accused.

"In part, yes. I knew you had your eye on Inferno, so part
of me meeting with him was to get under your skin. That's the
pettiness coming out of me. Old habits and shit. To keep it
one hundred with you, the boy has got some skills, and I could
sure turn a profit from his music, but Inferno doesn't really fit
the mold of where I'm trying to take my company these days."

"Since when did you start shying away from controversy?"
Don B. asked.

"Since the music business started becoming more dangerous than the streets," Trap said honestly. "I've gotten into more
shit since I got into the music business than I ever did in the
streets. Every time you turn around, there's a young nigga
trying to prove he's the hardest muthafucka ever born. I got in
this game to get rich, not dirty. I've cleaned up enough blood
to last me a lifetime. I'm off that gangsta shit and just trying

to get to the bag. This is why I'm going to let you have Inferno and everything that comes with him."

This took Don B. by surprise. For as long as he'd known Trap, the man had been like a pit bull on a bone when he wanted something. Him bowing out gracefully didn't sit right with Don B. "So, you did all this just to let me have him free and clear? I ain't buying this shit, Trap."

"You and I both know that nothing in life comes for free. What I'm suggesting is a trade of sorts. I let you sign Inferno without trying to block the deal, and in exchange, you let me have an artist on the Big Dawg roster," Trap suggested.

"I knew you was on bullshit! No way in the fuck I'm giving you one of the stars I created in exchange for an underground rapper who may or may not move units in the mainstream."

"Don, you and I both know that boy has star potential. Once you sprinkle some of that Big Dawg black magic on him, that boy is going to blow up. And I'm not asking for one of your stars. I knew you'd never go for that. I'm talking about one of your castoffs. Word is that you've got a talented young producer tucked away out on the West Coast. Goes by Locks or some shit."

"You mean Keys?" Don B. asked. Keys was a young guy he had discovered from out of Newark. He had been managed by a dude named Ab that Don B. had done business with. "Yeah, the boy has got an ear for music, but the single he released a few months ago never caught on. Nobody wants to hear that depressing-ass shit he was laying down."

"Then you shouldn't have a problem letting me have him. I'm even willing to buy his contract from you as a sweetener," Trap offered.

Don B. thought on it. When he signed Keys, he had high hopes for the kid, but so far, he had been a disappointment.

He hadn't even earned out his advance, not that he would with the way Don B.'s accountants played with the books. The boy was a decent enough musician, but he sucked as an artist. This raised the question as to why Trap wanted him. He obviously had something up his sleeve. Inferno was just the type of artist that Big Dawg needed to get back on top. Still, something felt fishy about Trap's proposition. "What's stopping me from saying 'fuck you,' keeping Keys, and just outbidding you for Inferno?"

"Two things. The first being you ain't got the kinda cash to outbid me. Everyone knows that Big Dawg ain't moving the type of units it was when you had True and Animal. The second being, if you don't do this deal, your little movie will be on every internet blog by morning. You think your company is struggling now? Big Dawg will become the laughingstock of the whole fucking industry when that tape drops. I know we live in a forward-thinking world, but it wouldn't play over too well with the gangsters to see the notorious Don B. hog-tied with a rubber dick in his ass!"

"You a dirty nigga, Trap!" Don B. hissed.

"And that's your problem, right there. You been hob-knobbing with these crackers so long that you've forgotten that ain't no honor amongst thieves. One way or another, I'm leaving here with an artist. Whether it's Inferno or Keys is up to you."

Don B. could've killed Trap right on the spot. The little fucking troll and the tape in question had been a pain in his ass for years. During a trip down to Florida, Don B. had the misfortune of hooking into a stripper named Reign who worked at a club called Purple City. Reign was one of the finest women he had ever seen, but she was also bat-shit crazy. Don B. had done a lot of foul shit to women over the years, but his only offense against her had been being from New York. It had been a man from New York whom she held responsible for her baby sister's death, so she took revenge on every man that she came across who hailed from the Rotten Apple. Instead of the freak session Don B. had been expecting, Reign kidnapped and tortured him. It had been Trap and Moochie who stumbled upon the scene and rescued Don B., but not before taking the video of him in a compromising position. Reign was long dead by then, so this left only Trap and Moochie with the knowledge of how he had been shamed. Don B. had been plotting on killing Trap and Moochie ever since, but the only reason he hadn't yet was because he had no idea where to find the tape. It was a small Hi8 recorded with an older model camcorder.

"And what happened to you being off that gangsta?" Don B. questioned.

"This ain't gangsta; it's strategic. Now do we have a deal or not?"

"You got it, Trap. I'll let you have Keys, but you gotta hand over that tape first," Don B. insisted.

"C'mon, Don. You know I just been trying to get you uptight. I'd never leak the tape. That would be gangsta." Trap laughed.

"Fuck that. You include the tape in the deal, or I'll take my chances. I might end up getting exposed, but you leak that tape and that umbrella you've been using to stay dry all this time will be gone, and make no mistake, I'll use whatever pull I got left on these streets to make it rain blood on you and everything you love. An all-out war with me and the Dawgz ain't something you want, Trap."

That much was true. A war with Don B. wasn't something he really wanted. Trap was well-respected in the South and building a reputation on the West Coast, but Don B. was a global gangster. His reach went beyond anyone that Trap had access to. At least, at the moment. Between his connections in the music business and the fools who followed him blindly on the streets, Trap knew that, if Don really put his mind to it, he could make shit real uncomfortable for him and his team. "A'ight, done deal. I'll have Moochie take care of it as soon as you sign over Keys's contract." He extended his hand.

Don B. hesitated for a moment before shaking it. When Trap went to pull away, Don B. tightened his grip and pulled him closer. "And if you try and get cute and make copies of it to keep in the stash, I'm gonna have Red Devil pay a visit to that auntie of yours that you've been taking care of in that nursing home down in Tampa."

This took Trap by surprise. Outside of his family and a select few others, no one knew about his auntie. This was further proof of Don B.'s reach. "That's cold," he said in an icy tone.

Don B. smiled. "It's like you said, there's no honor amongst thieves."

CHAPTER 19

Sin moved inconspicuously through the crowd at Dirty Wine. Girls were trying to get his attention, but Sin's focus was on the door Keisha had escorted Don B. and Trap to a few moments prior. He had been hoping to catch Don B. alone at some point, or maybe even in the company of one of his crew, as he had no beef with the other rapper. Don B. was the main course, but Trap would find himself on the menu by default.

A few paces behind Sin was Bone. Where Sin was gracefully moving through the crowd, Bone was damn near shoving people out of his way. Sin blamed that on the fact that he was tipsy, which was the same reason that he was with him, instead of at his original post, which was to be covering their exit. Sin switched things up and had Unique on it. Bone wasn't happy about Sin changing the plan, but Sin wasn't happy about him having so much to drink while they were on a job. Had he not been so preoccupied, he'd have cut Bone's drinking short. His brother wasn't drunk to the point where Sin felt like he couldn't handle himself, but he didn't want to leave something as important as securing their exit to chance.

Sin cast a glance toward the VIP section where Inferno and his guests were sitting. Tone was talking to Inferno and Finesse, and Zod was trying to finger-bang Keisha while stuffing dollars down her G-string. The Big Dawg crew seemed pretty much preoccupied, but Moochie was a different case. She had a girl on her lap and two hands full of ass cheeks, but her attention was more focused on the door her brother had disappeared through than the tits being shoved in her face. She was going to be a problem, and Sin knew it. He looked to Unique, who was perched on a bar stool near the door, pretending to sip whiskey. When Sin made eye contact with him, Unique nodded in Moochie's direction letting Sin know that he was already on point. This was why Sin trusted Unique to cover their backs, instead of Bone.

Sin had almost reached the door when it swung open and the two label CEOs came out. Sin stopped so abruptly that Bone ended up walking into him. His little brother opened his mouth to say something, but Sin raised his hand and silenced him. Don B. wore a look of irritation on his face, while Trap beamed like he had just gotten the best hand job ever. Something had changed in that back room, including Sin's plan. He continued to watch them with the intensity of a leopard hunting two unsuspecting antelopes as they crossed the floor back to their respective crews. Trap said a few words to Finesse, which left Inferno with a bewildered look on his face, before collecting his sister and leaving Dirty Wine. Don B. exchanged a few words with Tone before taking a seat directly across from Inferno and Finesse, crossing his legs confidently and addressing them. Sin was too far away to hear what was being said, but he could tell from the look on Finesse's face that he wasn't feeling it.

"What the fuck is going on?" Bone asked Sin.

"Change of plans," his big brother informed him, continuing his surveillance. He wasn't totally certain what had transpired between Don B. and Trap, but if he had to guess based on the two men's body language, he'd say they had come to an uncomfortable understanding. Their party was officially over. "We're gonna have to take him outside. Go get Unique and y'all two post up across the street. Wait for my signal."

"What signal?" Bone asked, irritated. He was itching to get to the action, and this spy shit his brother was on was blowing his.

"You'll know it when you hear it," Sin told him and moved closer to his mark.

* * *

Tone was the first one to his feet when Don B. and Trap returned. Trap was wearing an easy smile, but Don B. was wearing a look that Tone had become all too familiar with over the years. Whatever had gone on in that back room hadn't landed in Don B.'s favor, which was why Tone didn't want him going off alone with Trap. "Everything cool?" he asked Don B.

"Right as rain," Trap said and gave Don B. a sly smile. Don B. flashed him a murderous look. "No pun intended. Me and Don B. have come to an understanding. That said, our business is concluded and we gone." He motioned for Moochie to get up.

"Wait, you're leaving? I thought we were in the middle of a negotiation?" Finesse asked. He'd prepared a whole speech in his head that he planned to use to put Trap and Don B. in a bidding war over Inferno.

"Unfortunately, our pockets aren't quite as deep as Big Dawg's, so we're going to have to respectfully decline signing your artist. Sorry, kid. And good luck to you, Inferno. I'm sure you'll make a fine addition to the Big Dawg roster." Trap winked. "Don, I'll be on the lookout for your email sooner rather than later."

"I'll have Tone get on it ASAP," Don B. assured him.

"Have me get on what?" Tone was confused.

"Get the lawyer on the line. I've got something that needs to be handled in a timely fashion," Don B. told him.

"But it's after midnight," Tone pointed out.

"For what we pay him, I don't give a fuck what time it is. Wake his ass up and have him start drafting a transference of rights agreement."

"But Don—"

"Tone, stop working your mouth and work that phone," Don B. ordered.

Inferno sat there with a bewildered look on his face, watching the exchange between Don B. and Tone, while Trap waltzed out of Dirty Wine, along with the promise of whatever advance he might've been about to offer. He wasn't sure what the hell had just happened, but Don B. would happily fill him in. The Big Dawg CEO took the seat directly across from him and folded his legs. "What's this?" Inferno asked.

"This, my young friend, is the universe smiling favorably on you," Don B. answered. "You see, for as long as me and Trap have known each other, we've never been able to agree on much, but the conclusion we both came to is that his label can't do for you what Big Dawg can. Trap is good for breaking local artists, but I create global stars, which is what I intend to make you once you sign with me."

"With all due respect, Don B., we haven't exactly come to any type of understanding as to where Inferno will sign," Finesse said.

"The understanding is that, without a label, your boy will

be dead in the water. Word is out, and the thinking around the industry is that Inferno is a liability. The shit you've been stirring up over the last few years has these industry people afraid to touch you. Luckily for you boys, the Don does not do fear," Don B. boasted. "Now, I'll have Tone send you boys over a contract to review. It's pretty simple and standard, so don't go out of your way getting a lawyer to review it."

"We don't sign anything blindly," Finesse told him.

"Of course you don't. Knock yourself out and do whatever you gotta do, but this opportunity won't be on the table forever."

"Okay, send the contract over and we'll follow up in a few days," Finesse told him. He felt like the situation was spinning out of control and he needed to slow things down.

"Twenty-four hours," Don B. announced. "That's how long you have before I rescind what I think you'll find to be the most generous offer you'll get since the only other game in town walked out of here leaving you holding your dick."

"Don B., it'll take at least a week to get the contract reviewed. Twenty-four hours is not a reasonable timeline," Finesse said. Don B. was trying to muscle them, and he didn't like it.

"Maybe not, but it's what you have. Now, you can either sign with Big Dawg and let me show you the world or turn down the deal and spend the rest of your youth doing shows in shitholes like this. On that note, it's time for the Don to take his leave." He stood to leave. Sammy led the way, with Tone behind him, still on the phone. Don B. brought up the rear. He made it a few steps before realizing that Zod wasn't with them. He was still cuddled up with Keisha. "Time to roll, nephew," Don B. called to him.

"Y'all go ahead. I'm trying to see what's good with shorty.

I'll catch an Uber back to the spot," Zod told him, never taking his hands off Keisha's ass.

"A'ight, young thirst trap. See you back at the crib." Don B. laughed before joining his crew.

"Lil boy, I don't think you're ready for what I got between these legs. This pussy is for bosses, and near as I can tell, the head nigga at Big Dawg just walked out the door," Keisha told him.

Keisha's slight wounded Zod, and he wasn't yet skilled enough to mask his emotions. "Fuck you." He pushed her off his lap and onto the floor. "My time is coming, and it'll be sooner than you think. When it does, you'll wish I had let you suck this dick," he declared before storming off.

CHAPTER 20

Asher's brain had switched to autopilot after leaving his meeting with Zul. It was through the grace of God that he had made it out of that shack on his own two feet, instead of having his body being carted out in separate bags, which he was sure they had done to get rid of Danny, if there was even enough left of him to fit into bags. After what he'd seen those buzz saws do to that man's flesh, he figured the mess could've probably been cleaned up with a hose and a mop. Danny had gone out bad, and Asher had no intentions of having his story end even remotely close to how Danny's had.

He had spent his young career in the streets, playing fast, loose, and one step ahead of his undoing. He had come up under conditions just as bad as any man standing to his right or left on any given day, but unlike some of his comrades who gained their notoriety with pistols, Asher had made his bones with his brains. He was no stranger to bloodshed, as he had proven during his ascent to his current position, but that had very little to do with his success. His greatest strength was always being smarter than the most dangerous man in any room he entered. This tactic had served him well up to that point, but Zul was a different animal. For Asher to come out of this with his brains still intact, it would take more than a few well-spun lies. Breaking the rules wouldn't do. This time, he'd have to rewrite them. This is what brought him across the Hudson that night.

With his latest scheme, Asher had made a mess of things. A mess that he would need to clean up with haste. Zul demanded blood for Asher to land back in his good graces, and this was nonnegotiable. Asher had fed more than a few souls of those he had claimed to respect, and in some cases love, to the demon he had foolishly bound himself to. What was one more back to step on in his rise to the top? But this wasn't an expendable piece on the chessboard . . . this was Cal. Asher would meet Zul's asking price of blood, but whose life would settle the debt was still up for question.

His first order of business was to get with Saud. He doubted that word of Danny's untimely demise had reached him yet, but Asher needed to look him in the eyes to be sure. Based on his meeting with the old head, Asher would be able to determine what he would need to do next. He had no love for Saud, but at the moment, he was an important part of Asher's expansion plan. He couldn't risk Saud getting knocked off, at least not before he put a backup plan in place. When that time came, he would be food.

Asher hit Saud before he left Jersey, on his way to New York, to let him know that they needed to talk. Saud agreed without even asking what about, which was the first red flag. Saud was one of the most suspicious dudes he knew, especially when it came to Asher, because he had seen the young man's body of work. Asher tried to call Saud back as he got closer to the city but got no answer. He tried twice more and got the same results. That was red flag number two. Something was definitely up.

Asher's next call was to a chick named Shelly. Saud had been seeing her off and on since he had been tucked away in New York. He had been courting the young girl for some weeks, and he felt like he was making progress. Saud was notorious for running game on chicks that he planned to turn out and thought that he was roping Shelly in. But it was actually the other way around. What he didn't know was that Asher had been the one who put her onto him. Asher knew that he couldn't fully trust Saud, so he wanted to make sure he had eyes on the man even when he wasn't around. It had been Asher who had arranged the *chance* meeting between the two, trusting Saud's thirst and Shelly's body to do the rest. So far it was working just as he had planned.

He learned from Shelly that she and Saud were supposed to hook up that evening, but he had unexpectedly canceled saying that he had something to take care of. When she asked what was more important than spending the night with her, he said, "business," and left it at that. After doing a bit of snooping, she found a flyer in a pair of his pants advertising some sort of music showcase at a hole-in-the-wall strip club. Asher knew the place she named by reputation but had never been there personally and doubted that he would ever have a reason to. The way he'd heard it, the place was a shit hole, but also a prime feeding ground for a predator like Saud. He did most of the recruiting for his side business at off-the-radar clubs like the one Shelly was speaking about. He would scour the clubs for desperate girls that he could put to work in whore houses. He'd had a similar situation going in Newark before Zul had murdered one of his favorite girls and shut the spot down.

Saud prowling for girls wasn't suspicious, but his blowing off the man who had been feeding him these last few months was. Asher's gut told him that something wasn't right. He had already been blindsided once that day and wouldn't set himself up for it to happen a second time. This is why, before he left Jersey for New York, Asher stopped and picked up an insurance policy.

When Asher hit Atilla up and asked him if he wanted to hang out that night, the recently released man reacted like the ugly girl who had been asked to the senior prom by the star quarterback. He was beyond thrilled and smiling from ear to ear when the Benz pulled up in front of the house where he was staying. Asher had made sure to set it out for him, too. There was a fresh bottle of Hennessy in the back seat and several blunts already rolled up. Atilla accepted the offerings without question. The whole ride into the city, Atilla chatted about his life during his time away. He spoke about prison with the fondness of a summer vacation. It was weird to hear a man speak of spending years in prison as if he missed it, but Asher understood. He had met plenty of dudes like Atilla. Men who were average at best on the streets but larger than life behind the walls. These types of dudes were usually ones who went back and forth through the system like a revolving door. Men who felt more comfortable incarcerated than they did free because being free no longer felt normal to them.

"So, how come you didn't invite Cal out with us tonight? That boy has been like your shadow since back in the days, so I'm a little surprised he ain't rolling," Atilla said.

Asher shrugged. "Cal ain't never been big on strip clubs, so I didn't bother to ask him to come along. Besides, this ain't exactly a pleasure trip. There's some business that might need to get handled, and the less people who know, the less likely we are to fuck around and end up in prison if this takes a bad turn."

"You make it sound like a nigga might need to get his brain pushed this evening," Atilla said. Asher didn't respond, but the look on his face made Atilla probe further. "Ash, if you need me to ride, imma ride, but don't come at me in riddles. If it be war, let me prepare properly, so that I can live in infamy or die in glory. This is the law of the Apes."

Asher not only heard but *felt* Atilla's statement. Any reservations he may have previously had about how useful the man could be to him were erased. Atilla was a weapon of mass destruction, of which Asher now had his finger on the button. Asher paused for dramatic effect before speaking. "Before I share this with you, I gotta know you can be cool about it. At this stage of the game, the only way to win is to be able to compartmentalize our personal feelings when it's time to stand on business. Can I trust you to see the bigger picture?"

"Asher, you can't count on me to do nothing but react accordingly to whatever it is you're playing cat and mouse with me over," Atilla said seriously.

Asher could tell, by the way Atilla's brows furrowed, that he was boiling to hear whatever it was that he was about to reveal. Asher wouldn't have had it any other way. Atilla's volatile nature would be the glue that bound him to Asher, which is what he had counted on before inviting him to take the ride. "If we being honest? Us coming over here wasn't really about no bitches, but some bitch-ass niggas. You might've been onto something with that rumor we spoke about. The one where Ab's death was more than a random overdose. I just need to look in this nigga's eyes before I can believe the things I'm hearing."

"A homegrown hit?" Atilla said with disgust. He was already going through his mental Rolodex of men who could've made

Ab comfortable enough to let them rock him to sleep like that. "Since we're being honest and all, let me lay something out for you. I knew from the minute that I asked you about what happened to Ab that you knew more than you let on. I just needed to hear you say it, so I could decide whether to deal with you with an open hand or a closed fist." He held up one of his scarred knuckles for emphasis.

"What? You don't trust me?" Asher asked, half-joking.

"This ain't got nothing to do with me trusting you. This is about me *seeing* you," Atilla said with a wink.

Asher didn't have to read too deep in between the lines to get his meaning. Apparently, Atilla was sharper than Asher had given him credit for. It wasn't a bad thing, but it was unexpected. This revelation definitely gave Asher something to consider when he next moved that piece on the board. There were no more questions for the rest of the ride. Atilla had sent his message, and Asher had received it. Atilla would be a willing companion on his slow walk into hell, so long as he could eat his fill of souls along the way. And Asher planned to shove lives down his throat until he was good and bloated.

The minute Asher pulled up to the small bar Shelly had directed him to, he immediately got a bad feeling. It was getting late, so by then dudes were out front parking lot pimping, trying to catch the stray girls who hadn't made enough money during their shifts to turn down any side offers of pay for play. Asher turned a few heads when he and Atilla slow-coasted by the spot in his pretty Benz with the New Jersey plates. Mostly from dudes trying to figure out if he was a lick or a player. The wolves were circling, but Asher was no sheep.

He parked the car a block and a half from the spot, and he and Atilla walked back. He tried calling Saud again, just to check his temperature, but still no response. He had spotted

Saud's Cutlass parked on a side street, so he was certain that he was there. Everything in Asher's gut told him to turn around and go back to Jersey, but this was a time-sensitive matter. He needed to look into Saud's eyes before deciding whether or not to turn Atilla loose on him.

"I don't like this shit," Atilla said as if he was reading Asher's mind.

"We in and out, bruh," Asher assured him.

"I still think you were tripping about leaving the gun in the car," Atilla said. He didn't like being that far from home unarmed.

Asher didn't respond. He skipped the line and went straight to the door where he whispered something to the doorman before slipping him $200. The doorman let them in with no hassle like they were VIPs. They slipped inside and found themselves a position at the bar, where their backs were protected by the wall and they had a clear view of the entire joint. Asher scanned the crowd but couldn't seem to pick Saud out. He ordered two drinks, a Corona for himself and Henny with ice for Atilla. Atilla threw his glass back as if it were a shot, while Asher sipped his beer and studied the different faces. The bar/strip club was filled to near compacity, which was odd considering Asher wasn't too familiar with the rapper who was advertised on the marquee. He better understood when his eyes drifted to the private booth sitting in the shadow of the DJ. Sitting with the unknown rapper was a man who was almost as infamous as the diamond-flooded Rottweiler chain swinging from his neck.

His first and only time meeting the notorious Don B. had been at the Robert Treat in Newark. This was back when Asher had been Ab's unofficial protégé, shadowing him while he was trying to figure out how to turn drug money into rap money. He had a meeting with Don B. to pitch a potential artist to him, a local kid named Keys. Asher knew from that first and only meeting that he didn't care for the New Yorker. Don B. was brash, arrogant, and disrespectful, but he was also well-connected, which is why Ab was trying so hard to plug in with him. Don B. had peacocked through their city that night like he owned it, and not everyone was happy with it. Some had been so vocal in their displeasure of Don B. being in the hood that, at one point, Asher feared the night would take a turn toward violence. Thanks to Ab, it hadn't.

Ab stepped in and negotiated an uneasy truce between their crew and Don B.'s entourage. That was Ab for you. He could talk the most volatile men off the ledge, and he often had in his years of being B-Stone's second in command. He had always been the more diplomatic one of their crew. That was Ab's thing. He'd rather make a dollar than war. There was no telling who Ab could've gone on to become if given the opportunity to have a longer run in the game. But Asher didn't have time to wait for Ab to recognize his greatness when he was already so familiar with his own.

Asher had continued watching Don B. as he spoke a few last words with some folks in the section, gathered his entourage, and prepared to leave. Asher considered approaching him to try and see if he could pick up where Ab had left off. Technically, Don B. was an enemy of the state, but Asher was about a dollar, not gang politics. In the end, he decided against it. There was no question that, had he been able to cut into Don B., the record executive could've opened doors to Asher that would've taken his new business venture to new heights. But at what cost? From the stories Asher had heard, he was just as likely to catch a bullet standing too close to Don B. as he was a break.

Reluctantly, Asher let that ship sail and turned his attention back to the current order of business, which was Saud. There was still no sign of him, and Asher was beginning to think that Shelly had fed him bad information. She and Asher were cool, but Shelly was more about a dollar than loyalty. It wasn't too far-fetched of an idea that maybe Shelly had woken Saud up to Asher's bullshit and had directed him to the bar as part of a trap. The more Asher thought on it, the less comfortable he felt. He had just opened his mouth to tell Atilla that he was calling the whole thing off and that they were leaving, when he spotted someone crossing the room that derailed his train of thought. The club was dark, and she had grown her hair out and put on some weight, but she had a face that he would never forget. How could he when he dreamed of that face more often than not since the night she had fled from his life?

CHAPTER 21

Promise checked her phone to see how long she had been sitting in the dressing room. It had only been about a half-hour or so, but it felt like far longer than that. She had planned on waiting outside for her ride to show up, but to get there would require her going back out on the floor, and the prospect had given her anxiety. It would mean having to face Larry again, and after the way she had styled on him, there was no doubt in her mind that he would have some choice words for her. She had gone big on Larry, but he deserved it. There was no way she was going to keep allowing him to talk crazy to her like she was one of his whores. For as much as she valued her job at Dirty Wine, she valued her self-respect more. Fuck Larry and his country ass! If she never saw him again, it would be too soon. Larry, she was sure she could deal with, if necessary, but it was the prospect of possibly crossing paths with Don B. again that gave her pause. What if he had recognized her from that night in Newark and decided to play a game of connect the dots? If the wrong people found out that she was now living in New York, it could make an already complicated life downright dangerous.

Several of the girls had just come off the floor and gone into the dressing room. Among them was Lita. She was stuffing singles inside a Crown Royal bag. When she noticed Promise standing there, she flashed her a dirty look and shook her bag. It was stuffed, but it was chump change compared to what Promise had made just off Sincere's group. Promise shook her head and chuckled. It was time for her to get out of there before she did something crazy, yet deserving.

Promise kept her head down when she came out of the dressing room and began making her way across the floor. She spared a glance at the area where the rappers had been sitting and found that the group had thinned out. She didn't see Don B., thankfully. He was either gone or in the back crossing the line with one of the girls. Didn't matter to her, so long as she didn't run into him again. Larry was at the bar, barking instructions at Big Sally. His back was to her, so he didn't notice her, but Odell did. His thick lips pulled back into a grin as if he had a secret that he couldn't wait to tell. Odell had always been nice to her, but his presence still creeped her out, and she was happy that she wouldn't have to see him again.

She moved through the crowd in a blur. Over the loud music, she thought she heard Sin calling her name. Promise didn't bother to look back or stop. She wasn't in the headspace to deal with him right then. She was just focused on getting the hell out of Dirty Wine. Promise breathed a sigh of relief when she pushed through the side door and the cool night wind washed over her face. She couldn't remember a time since she had been living in that cursed city that she had been so happy to smell its stale air. Promise huddled in the shadows, wishing that her ride would hurry up. The last thing she needed was to bump into anyone else she knew. No sooner than she had the thought, she heard something that would shift her night from bad to worse.

* * *

For a long while, Promise just stood there, gawking. A million things to say ran through her mind, but she was too stunned to speak. There was a time when her heart would've been aflutter at the sight of him. She would find herself flushed to the point where she would sometimes get dizzy, but that night, there were no butterflies. Back then she had been a silly girl in love, but what she was feeling at that moment wasn't love. It was fear.

"What's up, Promise? You gonna keep standing there staring at me like I'm Jack the Ripper or show ya boy some love?" Asher moved in for a hug, but Promise backed away. It occurred to him that she was afraid of him. "Damn, it's like that?" His eyes flashed genuine hurt.

"What are you doing here, Asher?" Promised asked in a not-so-friendly tone.

"I was supposed to be meeting someone, but I don't think they're gonna show," Asher told her.

"One of your bitches stood you up?" Promised asked smugly.

"Nah, it wasn't a female I was supposed to meet. I was getting with one of the homies about some bread. That's the only thing that would've brought me to this shit hole," Asher said, and regretted it when he saw the look on Promise's face. "I didn't mean . . . I'm sorry. I didn't know you danced here."

"I don't. I'm a waitress. Well, I was," Promise corrected herself. "I quit tonight."

"Good on your part. A girl like you ain't got no business in a place like this." Asher motioned at the bar. "Shit is a far cry from the dreams you used to tell me about, going to college and all that. What happened?"

"You happened!" Promise said emotionally. "Why are you standing here trying to pretend that my life in New Jersey wasn't burned down and it wasn't your ass who lit the match?"

"Promise, I heard what B-Stone tried to do to you, and I'm sorry it happened. That's on my mother. But I wasn't the one who hurt you. You can't put that on me!" Asher argued.

"Can't I? It was you who brought me to that party! You who strung me along and had me caught up in that twisted-ass love triangle with your crazy girlfriend Ruby, and it was you who looked the other way while your people were trying to have me and Mouse killed for defending ourselves when your boss tried to rape me!" Promise spat. "I have nightmares about it almost every night. Did you know that? I can still smell the stink from him when he had me pinned down and was forcing himself inside me. And where were you while all this was happening?"

Asher didn't respond.

"Oh, let me remind you. While B-Stone was taking something from me that I wanted nothing more than to give you willingly, you were in the next room trying to make sure your other bitch was okay." Reliving the memory of that night caused the tears to flow down Promise's cheeks in rivers.

"I'm so sorry," Asher said sincerely. This was the first time he had ever heard the details of what had gone on that night, and it was tearing him apart inside. He truly did care for Promise, but back then, he had been trying to have his cake and eat it too. His greed had cost not only him, but her as well. "If I had it to do all over again—"

"But you don't," Promise cut him off. "To be honest with you, Asher, I can't even be mad. I brought this on myself. I was a stupid girl in love with a nigga who never saw me as anything but another notch on his belt. Because of me being naive, I was defiled in ways that you can't even imagine. It wasn't only my life that was ruined that night, but Mouse's too. My poor sweet friend who would never hurt a fly now has to live with the fact that she killed a man for the rest of her days. She didn't mean to kill him, this much I'm sure of. I can only imagine what was going through her mind when she came in and found B-Stone on top of me. She just reacted when she hit him with that lamp. She was just trying to protect me."

"Lamp?" Asher asked.

"Yeah, she clocked him over the head to get him off me."

"Promise, B-Stone didn't die from the head injury. Sure, it fucked him up, but according to the police, B-Stone bled out from his throat being slit!" The pieces had now all fallen into place, and Asher had the whole story. His suspicions had been right, and Promise was innocent of the murder.

"What are you saying?" Promise asked, sure she had heard him wrong.

"I'm saying that you can finally stop running."

Promise couldn't believe it. The whole time she and Mouse had been fugitives, they had been under the assumption that the police, as well as the homies, were after them for B-Stone's murder. She couldn't count the number of sleepless nights she and Mouse had spent stressing over what they thought they had done in the hotel room. From what Asher was telling her, that wasn't the case. But if Mouse hadn't killed B-Stone, who had?

"You hear what I said?" Asher snapped her out of her shock. "The police can't put this on you, Promise. You can come home!"

Home . . . the word exploded in Promise's head. She hadn't had a place that she could truly call home since she had been living with her aunt Dell. That said a lot. Going back to Adell's house was out of the question, but she could finally go back to New Jersey and get out of the unfamiliar city. Maybe she could even go back to school and stay in a dorm like a normal teenager, instead of crashing on Keisha's raggedy couch. For a second, she allowed herself to be hopeful, but then reality came crashing back. "I can't go back to Jersey, Asher."

"Why the hell not? I just told you that the police can't pin this on you."

"It's not the police that I'm worried about. Word on the street is that me and Mouse were the last ones seen leaving that room before they found B-Stone's body. They might not be able to prove in a court of law that we killed him, but the courts have no say so in the streets. I doubt that the homies would welcome me and Mouse back with open arms. Ab would have us killed the moment we set foot on that side of the Hudson."

"That's the best part. Ab is gone, and I'm running the neighborhood now. I can make sure you're safe," Asher assured her.

"Like you did at the hotel?" Promise snorted. "Thanks, but no thanks." She tried to walk off, but Asher grabbed her arm. "What are you doing?" She looked at his hand as if it was a snake that had just bitten her.

"Trying to keep from making the same mistake twice," Asher said sincerely. "I don't regret too many things I've done in my life, but letting you slip away when I should've been holding onto you for dear life is something that has haunted me for a very long time. When I should've been there for you, I wasn't and I'm gonna have to live with that. Things are different now. I'm different."

"I've heard all this shit before," Promise said with a roll of her eyes.

"I know, which is why I want you to let me show you, instead of telling you," Asher countered. "The same corners I used to sling work on for Ab and B-Stone now belong to me. I'm finally in a position to where I can set you up with the life that you deserve."

When Promise looked up at Asher, she was surprised to find tears dancing in the corners of her eyes. There were only three things Promise had ever prayed for in life. To have her mother back, to know her father, and for Asher to love her. Since the first time she had laid eyes on Asher, she had never seen any man but him. She so desperately wanted to believe him. There was nothing that would've made her happier than throwing herself into his arms and letting him whisk her away, but that was the old, naive Promise. The girl who had been stupid enough to enter a room full of thirsty gangsters and not pay attention to where she set her drink. That was the Promise that Asher may have remembered, but it was no longer who she was. "I can't trust you not to hurt me again. And this time, I may lose my life instead of my virtue."

"I'm not asking you to give me your trust. Make me earn it. Can I get, at least, that?" Asher asked. Promise opened her mouth to say something when Asher unexpectedly plucked her cell phone from her hand. "Don't answer right now." He waved her silent and tapped away on her screen. "Live with the question for a minute. You got my number now, so hit me when you come to a decision."

"You know I'm probably never going to call you, right?" Promise told him honestly. She had already sampled the fruit of the poison tree once and had found it too bitter for her tastes.

Asher shrugged. "If you do, I'll know that you listened to my heart and not my words. If you don't, I guess we chalk it up to a shared moment in time. Nothing more."

"You and that silver tongue," Promise said, unable to fight the smile that forced itself to her lips. Asher was the fucking devil, and she knew it, but a handsome one. From the way he was shining, his time at the top had surely been kind to him.

"Act like you know, lil mama." Asher poked his tongue out suggestively. The blaring of a car horn broke up their flirting. A gray Honda Civic pulled to the curb just shy of them. The windows were heavily tinted, so Asher couldn't see who was driving, but he could feel eyes on him. "I guess that's your ride?"

"I guess so," Promise replied. She continued to stand there for a beat as if she had more to say, but held it and opted for, "It was good seeing you, Asher."

"It was better seeing you, love," Asher replied coolly. He continued standing there while she walked to her ride. He couldn't help but feel like she had put a little something extra into her strut, because that ass was moving under those leggings. She wanted him to see how much she had grown. Promise had barely closed the passenger's side door before the Civic peeled away from the curb. The driver didn't seem to be in the best of moods and Asher's ego hoped that he had been the one to sour it. He reasoned the driver was whatever lame guy Promise had shackled herself with since her move to New York. It hadn't occurred to him to ask her if she was seeing anyone. In truth, it wouldn't have mattered to him one way or another. Lightning rarely struck twice, and if given a second chance, he wouldn't squander it.

CHAPTER 22

Sammy had gone ahead to get the truck, while Don B. and Tone stood out in front of Dirty Wine. Tone was happy to finally be out of that place. He hated seedy joints like Dirty Wine. They were death traps that allowed people in from all walks of life and didn't have the most reliable security. Don B. was a millionaire who had no business in a bootleg strip club full of gangsters. It was asking for trouble. He'd tried to explain this to Don B., but of course, the Don wouldn't hear it. He insisted on taking the meeting with Trap in the club, instead of having him come to the office like Tone had suggested. Don B. had said it would've been in poor form not to accept the invitation from Inferno, but for as long as he had known Don B., he never cared about offending people, especially an unknown like Inferno. Tone knew this was more about Don B.'s ego than it was him worrying about how Inferno would take the slight. For the last year or two, he had been going out of his way to prove that he was still a gangster, and putting himself, and Tone by extension, in questionable situations. It was like his friend was going through a midlife crisis of sorts.

"You wanna tell me what all that was about back there?" Tone finally asked.

"Us getting what we came for," Don B. replied, without looking up from the blunt he had been trying to unsuccessfully light on the windy corner. "By this time tomorrow, Inferno will be a Dawg."

"But what did it cost us?" Tone questioned.

Don B. finally got his blunt lit and took a deep pull before answering. "With a nigga like that, we don't have to start him out with a big advance. About a hundred thousand and a new car should keep him pacified for now."

"I'm not talking about the advance, and you know it. This ain't our first walk in the park with Trap, and I find it hard to believe that he conceded in letting you have an act he was interested in because he didn't think he could beat us in a bidding war. I've seen our books, and we ain't as liquid as we were five years ago."

"All the more reason we needed to sign Inferno. Streets been starved for that brand of ignorance for a long time, and who better to feed them than Big Dawg?"

"I don't disagree. Inferno is definitely going to give us a push in the right direction, but that same push could've been the nudge to put a smaller label like Trap's over the hump. So, again I have to ask, what did you have to give him in exchange for letting us sign Trap?" Tone pressed.

Don B. exhaled a cloud of smoke, watching Tone from behind his shades. Tone knew him better than most and could see that whatever he had done in that back room was weighing on him. "Keys. We're gonna sign Keys's contract over to Trap in exchange for him not trying to block us getting Inferno."

"Are you fucking high?" Tone asked in disbelief. He knew letting Don B. go in that room by himself with Trap would come back to bite him in the ass, and here he was bleeding.

"Calm the fuck down, man. We got the better in this deal. You know like I know that Keys didn't do shit as an artist," Don B reminded him.

"Yeah, but that was on us. We threw an eighteen-year-old kid with zero knowledge about this business into the deep end of the pool and then were surprised when the lil nigga ended up drowning. This is why we usually have people around to develop these artists before we try putting them out to the mainstream. We cut corners with Keys. The boy is a self-taught musician who also writes some decent songs. Over time we could've shaped him into something special."

"Time is something we ain't got a lot of!" Don B. snapped. "It's like you said, you've seen the books, and we're in desperate need of capital, which is just what I went in there and got us! Ain't nobody got time to develop Keys when Inferno is ready to go right now. What's done is done, Tone. You just make sure Trap gets that paperwork."

Tone knew, at that point, that there was no more arguing about this. Don B. had done something that night that Tone hadn't seen him do since they were in the streets trying to build their dream. He made a business decision out of desperation. It was just further proof of how far down the rungs of the ladder the once mighty Big Dawg had slipped. Tone had been trying to hold the company up as best he could, but his shoulders were getting tired.

"Say, ain't that the bitch from the club?" Don B. got Tone's attention. The clumsy white stripper from back at Dirty Wine was standing in the cut a few feet away from them. She had on a baggy sweatshirt and leggings, but Don B. could still spot that ample ass. She was having a heated discussion with some dude who looked familiar, but Don B. was too focused on Promise to pay him much mind. He couldn't shake the feeling that he had seen her somewhere before. When she shifted and the streetlight fell across her face, Don B. was able to get a good look at her, minus the stripper makeup. That's when it finally hit him where he had seen her before. "That's the bitch from Jersey!"

"What bitch from Jersey?" Tone asked coming to stand next to Don B.

"The white broad who Keys almost got himself murked for that night we went to Newark to hear him play," Don B. reminded him.

Tone squinted. "Nah, that can't be her. That broad is probably halfway across the world. I heard the homies are looking to have a not-so-nice conversation with her over that shit that happened with B-Stone."

Don B. shook his head. "I still can't see it. B-Stone was a real-life goon, so him getting killed by a bitch don't make sense to me. Maybe I should reach out to our friends on the other side of the Hudson and see what it's worth to them to find out where their little snowflake has landed." He rubbed his hands together sinisterly and continued to watch her until a beat-up Civic pulled up to the curb and she disappeared inside, leaving the guy she had been talking to standing there smiling like the cat who swallowed the canary. "Lucky bastard." He chuckled knowing the guy had done what he couldn't and pulled her.

Tone was about to say something to Don B. when a flicker of motion caught his eye. The shadow moved so fast that Tone probably wouldn't have even seen it had he not been looking directly at it. "Don!" he shouted, but he wasn't sure if Don B. had heard him over the boom of the gun.

* * *

Sin moved with the stealth of a jungle cat while he skirted the edges of Dirty Wine. His eyes were locked on Don B., who was just wrapping up his meeting with Inferno. From the look on Finesse's face, their night hadn't gone as expected. Little did they know, Don B.'s wouldn't either. Sin noticed that, when Don B. and the others made to leave, the young dude they'd come in with stayed behind. From the way he was pawing the stripper in his lap, it looked like he had opted to keep the party going, instead of leaving with his crew. It was probably for the best. At least, for him.

He was careful to wait a few seconds after Don B. and his crew had gone before making for the exit. Sin wanted to give them time to make it outside, so he didn't risk bumping into them in the foyer and making this job even more complicated than it was already turning out to be. As he was slipping out the door, he noticed Odell watching him from the other side of the room. He gave Sin a knowing smile, before turning his back. Sin wasn't sure what the gesture meant and didn't have time to dwell on it.

Luck must've been on Sin's side because he found Don B. and Tone absent of their bodyguard. He'd likely gone to fetch the car, and Sin wasn't sure how long that would take, so he had to make his move quickly. He spotted Unique and Bone across the street, right where they were supposed to be. Bone looked anxious. Unique was his ever-even self, but Sin knew, once he gave the signal, that would change, and Unique would be the first to react. Don B. and Tone had their backs to him, so that put the element of surprise on Sin's side. They were preoccupied with something outside his line of vision. He slipped a bandana from his pocket and tied it around his face, before drawing the baby 9mm and easing forward. He kept his body low and his steps quick. He was so close to Don B. that he could spit on him if he wanted to. Sin raised his gun and pulled the trigger.

"Don!"

Hearing his name, Don B. instinctively turned his body. That's when he felt the searing pain across his neck. It was like someone had cut him with a white-hot knife. Don B. had been shot enough times over the years to know a bullet when he felt one.

"Got that ass!" a masked man growled, advancing on Don B. with a small gun.

"Fuck!" Sin cursed when the bullet he had been attempting to put in Don B.'s head grazed his neck. The lucky bastard had turned at just the right moment and fucked up a perfect hit. Didn't matter. Sin was too close to miss a second time. He fired again.

Don B. got low, and the bullet shattered the window of a passing car, causing the driver to swerve and hit a parked car. It was officially lit! Don B. tried to scramble away, but Sin was on his ass. Sin was too close to miss. Don B. called on one of his nine lives, and it manifested in the form of a girl from the club trying to get out of harm's way. Don B. grabbed the unsuspecting girl and placed her between himself and the man who was trying to kill him.

Sin tried to target Don B., but every time he moved, so did his target. He was hunkered down behind the girl. Sin had heard stories of how low down the Don of Harlem could be, but seeing it firsthand with him using the girl as a shield turned his stomach. "You serious right now? And you got the nerve to call yourself a gangsta."

"I call myself a survivor," Don B. snickered, pulling the terrified girl closer to him. He was daring Sin to take the shot.

"Please . . . I got a kid," the girl pleaded.

"Fuck yo seed!" Don B. tightened his grip. He knew he was

foul, but he'd sacrifice the innocent girl and a hundred more like her, if it meant the Don would live to see another day.

Sin was trying to figure out his next move when something slammed into his side with almost enough force to knock the gun from his hand. He found himself struggling with Don B.'s manager. Tone was a scrappy son of a bitch, but no match for the battle-tested Sin. Sin pulled Tone's jacket over his head and whacked him in the back of the head with the gun, sending him into a face plant. Tone was out of the fight, but Sin had a mind to shoot him anyway, just off the strength that he was dumb enough to risk his life over a scumbag like Don B.

The screeching of car tires drew Sin's attention away from Tone. The bodyguard was back, and unlike Don B. and Tone, who had been caught by surprise, he was on point. He threw the car door open and came out blasting an automatic. Had he been a shooter, instead of just another nigga shooting a gun, he would've torn Sin's ass up, but most of Sammy's bullets had been wasted on the club. Sin scrambled behind a car for cover. From his hiding spot, he scanned the area for Don B. The rapper was sprinting down the block, leaving the screaming girl sitting on the curb. Sin couldn't let him get away.

When the shooting finally stopped, Sin spared a careful glance through one of the broken windows of the car he had been sheltering behind. He spotted Sammy, slapping another magazine into his weapon. He knew that he had Sin trapped and wanted to capitalize on this. Sammy had been so focused on the task of killing Sin that he never saw Unique walk up behind him. Sammy's brains jumped from his skull and stretched across the yellow lines in the middle of the street. Sin knew he could count on Unique.

Once freed, Sin took off after Don B. His prey had at least a half-block's head start on him, but Sin's determination added

speed to his legs and began to close the distance. Don B. did a
Three Stooges–like skip when he rounded the corner. He wasn't
moving as fast, a result of all the blunts he smoked catching
up with him. Only a few yards separated them now. Sin could
taste sweet justice on the back of his tongue. He slowed, raising his gun level with the rapper's fleeing body. "It's done." He
wrapped his finger around the trigger. Then something unexpected happened.

Sin was about to knock Don B.'s wig off when someone stepped out of the shadows between two cars just
ahead. He was followed by a second figure coming from
somewhere in the doorway of one of the buildings. They
had Don B. in a sandwich. One of them pulled a gun,
and there was an exchange between him and Don B. The
exchange was a brief one, and based on the end result, not
a friendly one. Sin saw a muzzle flash, followed by two
more. By the time Sin realized that someone had robbed
him of the opportunity to kill Don B., the rapper was
already stretched on the cold concrete. The shooter was
on the move, and his accomplice followed closely behind.
As they crossed under a streetlight, Sin was able to catch a
glimpse of their faces. The shooter was an older guy who
Sin was sure he had never seen before. But the accomplice
he recognized. His face was unremarkable, yet familiar, though with his adrenaline pumping the way that it
was, Sin couldn't focus enough to figure out where he'd
seen him. He waited until the two men had gone before
moving toward Don B.'s prone body, and that's when he
saw the familiar flashes of red and blue lights closing from
the other end of the street. He raised his gun with the
thought: One bullet, that's all it would've taken for him to
say honestly that he had shot Don B. But what points did

he get for shooting a dead man? Sin was too gangsta to live his life with a fraudulent charge on his jacket, so he stayed his trigger finger. It bothered him that he hadn't been the one to end Don B., but the fact that his evil taint had finally been washed from the world was a fair exchange.

CHAPTER 23

"Finally!" Promise said when she was inside the car. "What took your ass so long to get here?"

"I was handling something in Brooklyn when you called," Mouse told her. Mouse was as short as her name suggested, but she had the heart of a lion. She was the one person in the world that Promise knew that she could depend on in any situation, which is why it was Mouse that she called to rescue her from Dirty Wine. "You could try showing a little gratitude," she said, adjusting her rearview mirror. Something was going down in front of Dirty Wine. A few seconds later, they heard the first gunshots. "From the sound of things, I got you out of there right on time."

"Girl, you don't know the half," Promise said with a sigh. "Shit was getting too crazy for me, and I had to cut it short."

"For as heavy as that bag is looking, it had to be serious for you to cut your night short. What you got? A few grand in there?" Mouse asked.

"We can count that shit up once we're back at the crib and away from this place," Promise said.

"And was that who I thought it was?" Mouse asked once they were away from the club. The dude Promise was talking to when she pulled up bore a striking resemblance to Asher, but Mouse refused to believe it was him, because of what it would mean for them if it had been.

"Yeah, that was Asher," Promise confirmed.

"Shit, Promise! How did they manage to track us down? Better question. Why ain't you hog-tied in somebody's car trunk on the way back to Newark for Ab to deal with?" Mouse asked frantically. Seeing Asher standing out there had spooked her because of the period in their lives he represented.

"Ab is gone," Promise began before briefing Mouse on her conversation with Asher and the revelation about B-Stone's true cause of death. By the time she was done, Mouse felt like her head had been screwed on backward.

"All this time I been out here thinking I had a body under my belt, and I ain't did shit but give a nigga a severe concussion." Mouse laughed. She wasn't laughing because she found it funny, but because she found it unbelievable. She had been carrying that weight for so long that, now that it had been lifted, she wasn't sure how to react.

"Asher says that we can come home now if we want," Promise told her.

"And you believed him?"

"Why would he lie?" Promise questioned.

"Because it's Asher! That's what he does," Mouse countered. "Promise, you might've lived in the neighborhood, but I'm *from* the neighborhood. I grew up around those guys my whole life, so I know how they think. B-Stone was like the pope to them. The kind of dirt we got on our names ain't gonna wash off so easily, even if Prince Asher seems to think it will. Fuck Asher and fuck Newark. We did too much to escape for me to willingly stick my ass back in the lion's den. Let the past stay where the fuck it's at and let's focus on our futures."

"Asher wasn't the only blast from the past that popped up today." Promise told Mouse about her encounter with Don B.

"You think he remembered you?" Mouse asked nervously. She knew better than anyone what connecting certain dots could bring down on them.

"I don't think so."

Mouse shook her head. "You bumping into not one, but two demons in the same hell-hole on the same night is a bad sign. I think you need to fall back from Dirty Wine for a minute."

"Two steps ahead of you. I quit tonight," Promise informed her.

"Girl, Keisha and Candice gonna flip when they find out you quit and ain't gonna be able to come up with your part of the rent."

"What I got in that bag should keep them off our backs. At least for a little while. It's really only Candice we have to worry about because Keisha was there when I told Larry to go fuck himself."

"What? My cousin was in that club and they out there shooting! We gotta go back!" Mouse insisted.

"No, we don't. Keisha can take care of herself. The last thing we need is to get caught up in some shit with the police, especially if we're not one hundred percent sure whether we're still hot or not. Keisha was inside, and the shots sounded like they were coming from outside the club. I saw Don B. out there before we left, so nine times out of ten whoever was shooting was popping at him. If we're lucky, they hit him and he's dead."

"When has our luck ever been that good, Promise?" Mouse questioned.

The two girls drove the next few miles in silence. Mouse was focused on the road, and Promise decided to count the money she had made rather than wait. To her surprise the crumpled bills of different denominations added up to just over $1,700. For girls like Lita, Donna, and even Keisha, that was probably light, but for Promise, that was the best night she had ever had at Dirty Wine. Maybe she had been a little hasty in quitting.

"You think we gonna have to run again?" Mouse asked after they had been driving for a while.

Promise thought on the question before answering. "I hope not. New York ain't exactly been kind to us, but at least we've been able to survive. I doubt starting over in a different city will be as easy as it has been here, unless you got some other cousins tucked away that I don't know about?"

Mouse shrugged. "I don't know. I guess, after hearing about you running into Asher, I'm just a little worried about the fallout that might come on the heels of that. He knows where we are now, so what's to stop him from telling the others? Ain't but a bridge and a few tunnels separating us from the people who want us dead. Maybe we ain't ran far enough?"

Mouse had said what Promise had been thinking, but afraid to say. She didn't think Asher would tell anyone that he had found her, but why chance it? Blindly trusting Asher had been what forced them to run in the first place.

"I'd do anything for you, Promise. You know that, right?" Mouse said quite unexpectedly.

"Of course. And I'd do anything for you, too, Mouse," Promise assured her.

"I been knowing. You know you're one of the only people in the world who ever been nice to me. Not even my own mama could stop chasing her fix long enough to pay me a kind word, but you always did. Even though you were dealing with your own shit at home, you always made time for me. I love you for that, more than you probably understand. I like New York, but if we gotta run again, I don't mind it."

"Mouse, we're not gonna have to run. I got us, like always," Promise said. "So, what were you doing way out in Brooklyn, anyhow?" she said, changing the subject.

"Trying to make a dollar," Mouse told her, using a loose McDonald's napkin to wipe the remaining lipstick from her mouth.

Promise had been so focused on getting away from Dirty Wine that she hadn't even realized that Mouse was wearing makeup, which was something she rarely bothered with. When her face was made up was the only time that she didn't have the appearance of a fourteen-year-old child. By the way she said, "Trying to make a dollar," Promise knew that she didn't mean packing groceries. "Mouse, what did I tell you about that shit?"

"Nah, it wasn't like that, Promise. This was one of Candice's people. I didn't have to sleep with him. The old man just wanted the company of a pretty girl for a few hours," Mouse told her.

"Then why the fuck didn't Candice keep him company?"

"You know, she just had a baby and all . . ."

"Girl, that baby is almost three months now. Candice's pussy is back in working order, so she can't keep running that. And I'll bet she made you break her off a piece of what you earned for the plug-in, didn't she?" Promise asked. Mouse's silence gave her the answer. Candice wasn't as mean as Keisha, so that made her a little easier to deal with, but the girl was lazy and sneaky. She was always lining Mouse up to do some dumb shit for her. "I should've known something was up when you pulled up in Vaughn's car without him. Did one of them at least go out with you to watch your back?"

"It's like I told you, P, he was one of Candice's tricks," Mouse repeated.

"Girl, one day, you're gonna have to wake up and stop being so fucking naive!" Promise chastised her, as if that wasn't the pot calling the kettle black. Mouse got quiet and turned her attention back to the road. She didn't have to say it for Promise to know that she had hurt her. For as tough as Mouse was, she was also a very emotional young woman. "Mouse, I ain't trying to come down on you. It's just that . . . I don't want to see anything happen to you."

"You know I know how to move in these streets." Mouse pulled a switchblade from her bra, flipped it open, and closed it expertly before putting it back in its hiding place.

"I don't doubt that, seeing how we grew up in the same fucked-up neighborhood. I just want you to be safe. Can't have you going and getting yourself in a jam before we have a chance to get Junie back."

Mouse's eyes lit up at the mention of her baby sister's name. Besides Promise, Junie was the only other person that Mouse could honestly say that she loved. With Mouse's mother always out chasing drugs, more often than not, it fell to Mouse to look after the little girl. Mouse did as well as could be expected considering she was a teenage girl looking after a child, making sure she was fed and out of harm's way. There were even times when Mouse would go without eating to make sure that Junie didn't go to bed hungry. Things got a little better for the sisters when Mouse started working for Ab, selling drugs. She became the woman of the house, taking care of Junie and their mother alike. Mouse was by no means rich at that point, but under Ab she was bringing in enough money to do a better job of provid-ing for her little sister than their mother ever had. All Mouse ever talked about was how she planned to take Junie and get out of the hood once she turned eighteen, but unfortunately it wasn't to be. Thanks to Promise and the bullshit she had pulled them into with B-Stone, Mouse became a fugitive, and life on the run wasn't one fitting for a girl as young as Junie. With a heavy heart, Mouse left her with some distant relatives they had in South Jersey before they fled to New York. She vowed that one day she would return for her baby sister, and Promise was going to be right by her side to help. It was the least she could do.

"How's she doing?" Promise asked.

Mouse shrugged. "Okay, I guess. At least according to my auntie Bernice. I check in every few weeks with Bernice to see how Junie is doing or to find out if they need anything, but I ain't spoke to Junie since not long after we dipped."

"Why not?" Promise asked.

"Because I know that she's going to have questions that I don't have the answers to yet," Mouse said sadly.

"This life we're living ain't the one meant for us. Trouble don't last forever, Mouse. That's what my mom used to always tell me." Promise tried to pick her spirits up.

"Maybe not, but that muthafucka has sure overstayed his welcome." Mouse mustered a weak smirk. "So, I know you made a few dollars tonight, but how long you figure that's gonna last us? If you can't pull your weight, Keisha and them gonna bounce you out the crib. You got any ideas on what you're gonna do for money when that runs out?"

Among the cash Promise had been counting, she found the twenty-dollar bill that Sincere had written his number down on. "I might."

CHAPTER 24

It was almost 3:00 a.m. when Sin pulled up on his block and parked the car. They'd fled the murder scene at Dirty Wine hours prior, but he wasn't ready to take it down just yet. He needed to clear his head. He dropped Bone off first at his spot in the Bronx before taking Unique to Harlem. His brother wanted to hang out and celebrate a successful hit, but Sin wasn't up for it. The whole ride Bone kept going on about being upset that he wasn't there when Sin murdered the rapper and kept pressing him for the details. Sin modestly declined to talk about it. Unique picked up that something wasn't right with Sin but didn't press him about it. He knew his partner well enough to know when not to pry. It wasn't until after Sin had dropped everyone off and was in the car alone that he was able to really breathe.

Sin spent the next hour or so bending corners. He didn't have a particular destination in mind, he just wanted to keep moving and thinking. He found himself driving down the West Side highway as far as Canal Street and then back up to Harlem, where he kept an apartment. He parked and sat in the car for a few minutes, twisting up a blunt. He fired it up, let the smoke fill his lungs, and held it to the point where he started coughing. The weed calmed him some, but he was still wound up over how things had played out.

For the first time since they had all started pulling jobs together, Sin wasn't completely honest with his crew. Withholding the information about why Don B. had been marked for death was something small that he could live with, and so could they so long as they got paid. Sin's stash was going to be a few grand lighter since the money was coming out of his pocket and not the imaginary client he'd told them about. It was a hit he'd gladly take rather than telling them the truth. They'd both likely have still been all in on it and probably would have done the job for free if he'd been honest with them, especially Bone. A part of him wanted to share his motives, but he decided against it. That was his cross to bear.

What really bothered Sin was him taking credit for a murder that he hadn't committed. Sin hadn't exactly said that he was the one who killed Don B., only that it was done. They'd assumed the rapper had died by his bullet, and he just didn't correct them. Sin wasn't a man who took credit where it wasn't deserved, but how was he supposed to explain to his crew that some random nigga did what he had tasked himself to? He punched the steering wheel in frustration. Don B.'s life was his to take, and he had been robbed of that. His mind played the turn of events over and over, Don B. and the shooter's exchange. Catching a glimpse of the shooter and his accomplice under the streetlight after Don B. had fallen. The accomplice's face continued to nag at him. Where had their paths crossed before? All the facts went into a potluck soup, and Sin was just trying to figure out how the flavors meshed. He was too tired to sort it all out. At least right then.

Sin tossed what was left of the blunt out the window and slid from the car. Ambling toward his building, he spotted a cluster of youths loitering out front. They were locals, and Sin was familiar with each one. The oldest couldn't have been more than sixteen or seventeen. At that hour of the night, they should've had their asses in bed, instead of being in the streets looking for mischief to get into. All their young eyes turned to Sin as he approached, with a few of them straightening their posture and trying to put on mean-mugs. Sin knew that was more for his benefit than anything else. Since the young boys had jumped off the porch, they were always trying to impress Sin in hopes that he would pull them into what he had going on.

"Sup, OG?" one of the youths greeted Sin as he approached the building. He was short and a little on the chubby side. They called him Shake because, when he was little, the older heads used to give him money to watch him do the Harlem Shake. For a chubby kid, he could dance his ass off.

"Ain't shit. About to take it in." Sin gave him dap. "What y'all lil niggas doing out at this hour looking like y'all trying to catch a lick?"

"Trying to catch a lick," another of the youths spoke up. His name was Darryl, and he lived on Sin's floor. Of all the young knuckleheads who took up space in front of Sin's building, Darryl was the one who was most likely to make a mess of his life. He was always into some shit and generally pulled whoever was standing next to him into it as well. Sin wasn't as close to Darryl as he was with some of the other teens who hung in the neighborhood, but he had an amazing relationship with Darryl's mother, Sherita. Pour a few drinks down her throat and she'd show you some shit that made you question everything you thought you knew about oral sex.

"I hear that," Sin said, suppressing the memories of him

nuts deep in Sherita's throat. He wondered if she was still up at that hour.

"Oh, shit! Y'all seen this?" one of the other boys in the group suddenly blurted out. He was looking at something on his phone. The other boys gathered around to take a look. "Niggas tried to air the Don out." He was reading a headline on a gossip blog. In the age of the information highway, news traveled fast.

"I ain't surprised. I heard that's a foul dude," Shake said.

"Shit, if all it takes is to be a little foul and I can live like he does, I'll take that all day. Fuck it," Darryl said.

"Not me, man. My soul ain't for sale," Shake said. "What you think on what happened to dude, Sin?"

Sin shrugged. "I think it's time for me to take it down for the night. Y'all be cool." He headed inside the building. A few seconds later, Shake caught up with him. From the look on his face, Sin knew the boy had something on his mind that he didn't want to discuss in front of his friends. "Sup?"

"You give any thought to what I asked you about?" Shake questioned.

"What's that?" Sin played dumb. He knew what Shake was referring to but didn't have it in him to have that particular conversation after the night he'd had.

"C'mon, Sin. You know I been on you for a min to let me get money with y'all. Why you playing me to the left like I'm some little-ass kid?"

"Because you are," Sin replied. "Shake, you're a good kid, and I like you, but at your age, you should be focused on school and not getting yourself thrown in jail or killed."

"Fuck school. Man, I can't hear them teacher over my stomach growling!" Shake said seriously. "Sin, I ain't never been no begging-ass nigga. Even when we was shorties and everybody would press y'all for dollars, you never saw my hand out. I always wanted to earn that candy money."

This was an old argument, and Sin had been having it with Shake for years, but Shake had doubled his efforts in the last few months since he had turned seventeen. Shake was from the block, but he didn't have the same mentality as the kids he ran with. Unlike his friends, who would all more than likely die on that very same block, Shake had the brains and the drive to be something more than a statistic. This is why Sin could never understand why he was always pressing him to get in the game. "Lil bro, why are you in such a rush to throw your life away?"

"Because I'm too grown to keep having my grandmother try to budget my school clothes into her SSI check," Shake said seriously. "Sin, I get it. Don't nothing good come from that game you out there playing, but it's killing me to sit around and watch my granny keep busting her back and ain't shit I can do to help. If I bring twenty dollars' worth of groceries in the house that woman shows the same amount of appreciation as if I'd just brought her a new car. Granny humble like that, but me? Fuck that! I know she deserves more, and I'm going to give it to her."

"Shake—"

"Before you hit me with the same spin like I'm too young to understand what's out there, let me stop you." Shake cut him off. "Sin, I've been off the porch since I was fourteen. You see me and my little crew, how we out here moving, so you know I'm in the streets. Now, I can keep fucking with niggas like Darryl's crazy ass and hope that I figure this shit out before I catch a case over something stupid, or you can teach me how to fish. Whether you put me on or not, I'm gonna get to it, Sin. I ain't got no other choice at this point."

Sin studied Shake for a time, trying to find the right words to say. He ran through a thousand speeches in his head that he could've fed Shake to try to further deter him from playing a loser's game, but the look in that young man's eyes told Sin that, no matter what was said between them in that lobby, Shake had made his choice. "I'll see if I can find something for you to do."

"Thanks, Sin. All I need is a chance, man. The rest is on me," Shake said gratefully.

"You just be cool until I get back with you. And that means no more funny shit with Darryl. Whatever that nigga has got planned for the night, remove yourself from it," Sin told him.

"I'm cool, man. I'm just gonna hang for a while, finish this blunt and this little bit of drink, then I'm taking it in."

"Do that." Sin gave him dap before heading for the elevator. During the ride to his floor, Shake's words played over in his head. Sin could identify all too well with what he was going through. That feeling of helplessness while watching someone you loved sacrifice so you didn't have to go without. He would help Shake if it was within his power to do so. He was a good kid and didn't deserve whatever fate running with Darryl and his gang held in store for him. Of course, Bone was going to scoff at him bringing in an outsider, but this wasn't something that would be up for debate. Saving one young soul would hardly balance the scales for all the evil Sin had done in his young life, but it was a start.

* * *

When Sin entered his apartment, he found it dark and quiet, as it should've been, considering the hour of the night. Still, sometimes you never know. On any given night, you could find either occupant of the apartment pacing the floor like the ghosts of

Christmas Past. The thing about carrying around demons was, they rarely let you rest. That curse didn't afflict everyone under the roof that night. The soft glow of the living room television illuminated the face of a sleeping figure on the couch. She was a light-skinned girl of about twenty or so if one had to guess. Her thick lips were hung open, and there was a trail of slobber running from her mouth and onto one of the couch's cushions. She was down for the count, but her eyes fluttered behind her lips. Sin watched her for a time, wondering if her sleep was as fitful as his.

"Yo." Sin nudged her with his finger, making sure to keep a safe distance. It was the gentlest of touches, but she was immediately up with her hand sliding under the cushion she'd been slobbering on. "It's Sin, baby girl," he identified himself.

The sleep still hanging heavily on her brain caused her to look at him as if he was lying about his identity. When she was finally awake enough to recognize Sin, she sucked her teeth. "Why you creeping through here like a cat burglar?" She sat up on the couch, rubbing her eyes and stretching.

"I wasn't creeping. Your ass was just slumped, and I see why." Sin's eyes went to the plastic cup on the coffee table. "You know how I feel about you getting sloppy when you're over here, Bubbles."

"Nah, it wasn't even that type of party. I had a half-glass of wine, but after the night I've had, I deserve it," Bubbles told him.

"That bad?" Sin asked.

"Wasn't the worse, but shit getting harder. You got your hands full, big bro," Bubbles said with a shake of her head.

"I know," was Sin's response.

"What time is it?" Bubbles grabbed her phone from the coffee table beside her drink. It was after 3:00 a.m. and she had ten missed calls. "Damn, Sin. I told you I couldn't make this a late night. My baby daddy is with the kids, and I know his ass gonna trip off the time I'm coming in."

"My fault, Bubbles. The night went a little longer than I expected it to. If your dude gives you an issue, I'll talk to him. And I'll throw something extra on top of what I owe you for the night." He pulled some money from his pocket and started counting out bills.

"I'll gladly take the extra, but that nigga ain't my daddy, so you don't owe him no explanation." Bubble snatched what she felt like she was owed for the night. "Just be straight with me." She waved her cash before shoving it into her purse.

"You got that," Sin agreed. He waited for Bubbles to grab her things and walked her to the door. "You need me to call you an Uber?"

"Nah, I'm only going to the next building. I'm already late and in the doghouse, so I may as well make a night of it," Bubbles told him.

"You love walking on the wild side, baby sis." Sin leaned against the doorframe of the apartment while Bubbles stepped into the hall.

"That's the only side I know." Bubbles winked and disappeared into the staircase. Her life moved too fast for her to wait on elevators. She never knew what could be waiting on the other side of that automated door.

Once Bubbles was gone, Sincere secured the apartment. He locked the door, put away the wine glass, and checked the lock on the door again. He made his way down the hall and stopped at the first bedroom. The door wasn't completely closed. From inside he could hear soft snoring. He let himself into the darkened room. On a queen-sized bed a woman slept. She lay at a fitful angle, one leg thrown off the bed and the blanket hooked around the other. He moved softly across the room and perched himself on the edge of the bed. She stirred when he adjusted the blanket to cover her but didn't wake. When she shifted positions, the moonlight coming through the window illuminated her face, soft and still beautiful, even at her age and after what she had been through. The only signs of her suffering were the small scar on her forehead and the dark circles beneath her eyes. She'd carried her burdens and everyone else's for so long that the least Sin could do was shoulder some of that weight.

His eyes fell to the picture on the nightstand. It was of a younger version of the sleeping woman, hair all done up in long black braids. She was standing in front of what used to be a recording studio in downtown Manhattan, hugging a little boy to her chest. He had long hair and the smile of an angel, but something darker lurked in his eyes. The woman in the picture was smiling, but you could see the worry on her face. It was a look that Sin wouldn't learn to recognize until he was older. Had she known that far back the tragic turn that her life would take? Or would the demons who would eventually ride her into her current condition already have taken hold?

"Sincere?" A soft voice tore his eyes from the picture. She was awake now and looking at him quizzically.

"Hey, Lil Lady. How you living?" Sin touched her face gently with the back of his hand. Her given name was Cynthia, but Lil Lady is what everyone called her, including Sin. It was the only moniker that he ever felt comfortable using when it came to her.

"I'm okay. Just having a hard time sleeping. The way your girlfriend snores ain't help either," Cynthia told him.

"You know Bubbles ain't my girlfriend. I keep telling you that," Sin reminded her.

"She's your *something*. Don't no woman look at a man the

way she looks at you if he ain't been inside her," Cynthia said with a sly chuckle.

"Go ahead with that, Lil Lady." Sin nudged her playfully.

"I know that look. It's the same look I used to give your father when I wanted him. That man's love was like a drug, and I was strung out." Cynthia laughed, her mind going to some memory that Sin didn't want to hear about. "Speaking of that snake. He come by here earlier. Said he wanted to drop some money off for you children, but of course, when he left, all I had to show for it was a wet pussy and an empty purse."

"Ma, you and I both know he ain't been nowhere but the prison yard for damn near a decade," Sin corrected her, but she ignored him and kept with the broken memory.

"Boy always came like a thief in the night, and gone just as fast," Cynthia said with a suck of her teeth. "Your daddy got a whole church of kids out here that he poisons as it suits him. But that ain't nothing you don't already know. Your sister, Carol, is the only one still running around with blinders on about him. Where she at? Out there parked in front of the television?"

Sin didn't answer at first because he wasn't sure how to. "Ma, Carol ain't here no more, remember? She been gone a while now."

"Gone where? I just seen her this morning? Fixed her some breakfast before she went to school," Cynthia insisted. "Let me go check her room." She made to get up, but Sin stopped her.

"Ma." His grip on her arm wasn't aggressive, but firm. "Carol died in a car accident thirteen years ago." He hadn't meant for his tone to be so sharp. The doctor had encouraged Sin to be patient with her, but the worse her condition became the harder it was. Cynthia was suffering from dementia, so sometimes she slipped between what was and what is. If she had it in her genes, it's possible that it would've started to show signs as she got older, but to attack her at the young age of forty-two seemed cruel. It showing up so early was attributed to a head injury she had suffered on the night Carol was killed.

Carol was Sin's sister. She was younger than Sin, but older than Bone by a year or so, a product of one of their parents' many break-ups. Every few years, Sin's dad would get his mother pregnant, they would break up, and then he would disappear to live his best life before returning to repeat the process. Carol had been the result of one of those breaks. Sin's father fucked other women. That's just who he was, but he crossed a line he could never really come back from when he fathered a child during one of these brief affairs. For years Cynthia wouldn't so much as utter Carol's name. It was too painful. So, one could imagine Sin's surprise when he discovered that Carol's mother had overdosed, and the toddler would be coming to live with them. The first few months weren't easy, with Carol being a constant reminder to Cynthia that her man had given himself to someone else. Cynthia made it work, and even when Bone came along and there was an extra mouth to feed with a daddy that couldn't sit still long enough to do right, Cynthia still treated Carol as if she had come from her womb.

Sin's words brought back memories that settled on Cynthia's shoulders like bricks. She sagged back on the pillows as if she could no longer support her own weight. "She shouldn't have been there . . . shouldn't have been with me . . ." Cynthia dragged the admission out. "Proper place for her that hour of the night was in the house, but she cried so bad every time I tried to leave. I was only going there and coming right back, so what could it hurt? Then . . ." Her words trailed off as the memories came back. She crumbled in on herself and began crying.

Carol's last night on earth had been spent in the company

of Cynthia. She was having some issues with her boss over her paycheck and had to go to the office and straighten it out. Sin was about nine, and Bone five or six. So this landed Carol in the middle, at seven or so. Cynthia had intended to leave her in the house with just the boys, but the girl wouldn't stop crying for her, so she took her along. They drove to midtown so that Cynthia could hash it out with her boss. It was to be a short trip that would take a tragic turn. Years later Sin began to put the pieces together what happened. To that day, he still didn't have all the details, but just thinking about it made him physically ill. Based on her boss's reputation, which he later discovered through the grapevine, he didn't have to be a genius to figure out what had gone down. There was only one thing his mother's boss could've done that would have put her in such a state. When Cynthia left the office, she was damn near in hysterics. She was in no condition to drive, but that didn't stop her from jumping back behind the wheel. She was so caught in her trauma that she neglected to check for traffic when she gunned the small Ford Hatchback from its parking spot and out into the street. She never even saw the SUV that hit them coming. All Cynthia could remember was waking up with a cracked skull, two paramedics pulling her out of what was left of the car, and Carol nowhere to be found. In her haste, she had forgotten to put the little girl's seatbelt on. Carol went through the windshield and was dead before she hit the pavement. Things changed in their family after Carol was killed. Sin's dad stopped coming around as much, and Sin started hanging in the streets more. Cynthia's guilt pushed her into depression and eventually drugs. Between the head trauma and her getting high, Cynthia's brain had begun to deteriorate at a rapid pace, and before Sin knew it, he had moved from the role of a child to that of a parent. He didn't mind taking care of his mother, but it hurt him to know that there was nothing he could do to stop what was happening to her.

"That was an accident, Ma. That wasn't on you." Sin gathered his mother in his arms and tried to soothe her.

"Might as well have been," Cynthia said sadly, reliving those last few moments before she pulled out into traffic. "I'm gonna have to pay for that one day."

"No, you won't. The sins of this family are mine to carry now, Lil Lady. The scales are balanced, and your soul is clean." Sin tucked Cynthia back under the covers and kissed her on the forehead.

"My sweet Sin." Cynthia smiled up at him. The only time she called him that was when she knew that he had done something she wouldn't approve of but understood why he had done it. She was in her right mind again. At least for the moment.

Sin waited until he had finally coaxed Cynthia back to sleep before leaving the bedroom. He closed her door behind him and pressed his forehead against it. A lone tear rolled down his cheek. It wasn't out of sadness, but joy. Though he hadn't been the one to off him, Don B. was dead and his family finally had justice. The promise he'd made standing over the grave of his little sister had been kept.

Sin made his way to his bedroom, stripped down to his boxers, and laid down for what would be yet another fitful night's sleep. As he was dozing, he heard the sounds of gunshots coming from outside. He barely stirred. It was just another night in the hood that he and his mother called home. It wouldn't be until he read the paper the next day that he would find out who the victim had been, and that the opportunity he planned to provide for Shake would never come to fruition.

CHAPTER 25

Promise felt like she had just drifted off to sleep when her eyes snapped open at the sound of a door slamming. She sat bolt upright on the lumpy couch, which had served as her bed when she graduated from the air mattress on the floor a few weeks prior. It had been a long night for her, and all she wanted to do was sleep the entire day away, but whoever had slammed the door was preventing that. She was pissed and planned to let whoever was responsible know about it.

A few seconds later, Vaughn came marching into the living room. He was a medium-height brown-skinned dude, with a handsome face. He ran his hand over his braids, anxiously, as he often did when he was irritated over something. A few steps behind him was the object of his irritation: his pain-in-the-ass baby mama.

Candice was Keisha's twin sister. She was tall and dark, with Keisha's good looks, but not her body. Having two kids in two years had put a few extra pounds on her. She was nowhere near close to fat, but thick as hell in all the right places. That would explain why Vaughn couldn't seem to stop pumping babies into her.

"Don't walk away from me, Vaughn!" Candice was on his heels.

"G'on with that, Candice. This paranoid shit with you is getting old." Vaughn paced back and forth across the living room. He wasn't trying to hear whatever she was talking about.

"Paranoid is me asking why ya balls smell clean while the rest of you is musty. I caught you coming out of the bitch's building! Just come clean!" Candice insisted.

Vaughn stopped his pacing and composed himself before responding. "Candice, I sell drugs. I go in and out of a lot of buildings. The only difference with this one is, a chick you think I'm fucking happens to live there."

"Used to fuck," Candice corrected him. "I asked around about the lil whore and heard y'all had a thing before I came along and upgraded your life."

"First of all, you didn't upgrade shit. I might not have been up like I am now when I met you, but I wasn't no slum-ass nigga trying to run up your food stamp card either," Vaughn checked her. "A'ight, so maybe, once in a while, I used to knock shorty down, but don't act like you ain't got a past either. I'm sure there's a few niggas around here that you let pipe you out before we got together."

"You calling me a ho?" Candice asked defensively.

"No, I'm saying that wasn't neither one of us no saint," Vaughn clarified. He moved in to wrap his arms around her. She put up a bit of fake resistance before letting him hug her. "Dig, wasn't none of them bitches I rocked with in the past held me down like you do. Why would I risk fucking this up over a bitch who didn't mean nothing to me, even when I was still fucking her?"

Candice's resolve wavered. There was something about the way Vaughn looked at her that always made her weak. "I told you before I had our son that I wasn't trying to be nobody's baby mama."

"And I told you that this thing between us is bigger than that." Vaughn cupped her chin with his finger and kissed her lips softly. "You gonna be my forever, girl. I keep telling you that."

"I'm waiting for you to show me," Candice countered.

"I will. With this new situation I got, things are about to change for us. No more forty-dollar eighths. I'm stepping our shit up. Just give me some time and trust."

Candice knew that he was bullshitting. This was the same line Vaughn always ran on her when he came up with a new hustle that likely wasn't going to work. The one thing she loved about Vaughn was that he wasn't afraid to go after it. He just never seemed to be able to catch it. The routine was getting old, but she loved him and wanted to have faith. "I ain't gonna wait forever," she replied instead of saying what was really in her heart. The two lovers traded kisses and intimate touches. They might've gone the extra mile had Promise not cleared her throat and reminded them that she was in the room. "And what the fuck is your ass doing over there ear hustling like this is some type of entertainment?"

"Ain't nobody ear hustling. I was sleeping until y'all came in here making so much noise." Promise sucked her teeth.

"Don't be trying to tell me how much noise to make in my fucking house. The last time I checked, you were the squatter around these parts." Candice snaked her neck. "And why the hell are you still sleeping this late in the afternoon like a damn crackhead off a bender, anyhow?"

Promise picked her phone up off the floor and double-checked the time to see if Candice was exaggerating. She wasn't. It was 3:05 p.m. "Damn." She threw her legs over the edge of the couch and sat up.

"Heard you had a busy night," Candice said with a smirk.

"I wonder where you got that from?" Promise asked sarcastically, knowing it was Keisha who had told her business.

"I love how you sitting there with an attitude when my sister was only trying to look out for you. That's all any of us have done since you two ragamuffins showed up on our doorstep."

"You mean like you looked out for Mouse when you sent her to Brooklyn with no backup?" Promise challenged.

Candice cut a glance at Vaughn who was watching the exchange. Vaughn pretty much knew all Candice's skeletons, but there remained aspects of her past and present life that she hadn't been completely transparent about. "And where is my little cousin this afternoon?" she said, changing the subject.

Promise looked to her former air mattress, which was neatly folded in the corner, and shrugged. "She was knocked out when I crashed. Maybe she had to get out early and tie up y'all's business from last night?"

"Don't get cute," Candice warned her.

"Candice, leave that girl alone and go get ready. We gotta go get the kids from my mom's, and you know how she is. We can't show up smelling like we been in the streets all night," Vaughn said, which made Promise laugh because she knew they had.

Candice flipped Promise the middle finger before heading down the hall to her bedroom.

"You need to stop provoking her," Vaughn told Promise once Candice was out of earshot. He liked Promise well enough and would've hated to see his baby mama put hands on her.

"She needs to stop fucking with me then. All her and her sister have been doing since me and Mouse moved here is come at our necks." She was getting fed up with the twins.

"You don't like it here? Do like Mouse did and find somebody else who'll let you stay with them for a little bit of pussy here and there. Outside of that, try and make this work as best you can until something better comes along," Vaugh suggested. He wasn't trying to be cruel, just putting her situation on black and white.

"Something like what?" Promise questioned. "No disrespect to my girl, Mouse, but I can't see myself trading ass for shelter. So, that's out. And the little bullshit change they was paying me at the club is barely enough for me to feed myself and still kick them twin vampires their monthly tribute, for the privilege of sleeping on this fine couch. I've been trying to stack enough bread to get my own situation, but this shit slow motion."

"What if I told you that I could help with that?" Vaughn questioned. Promise sat up a little straighter, which let him know that he had her attention. He took a quick glance down the hall to make sure Candice wasn't around before continuing. "So, you know I got a new plug, right?"

"I hope this one is better than the last dude you was copping from." Promise was speaking of Vaughn's weed connect. He had been getting ounces on the cheap from some Jamaican and was trying to get his weight up. He'd recruited Promise as one of his street dealers. She didn't know a whole lot about selling drugs, but she gave it her best effort. The problem was that the weed Vaughn was giving her to sell was weak. Vaughn ended up losing more money than he made and that's how Promise ended up working at Dirty Wine.

"Nah, totally different cat and a totally different product," Vaughn told her. He reached into the pocket of his hoodie and came out with a Ziploc bag full of pills with Superman emblems carved into them. "Everybody sells weed now. I'm moving ecstasy. It's all the rage now."

This was something that Promise knew all too well. She

knew a bunch of kids back in Newark who made E their week-
end things, and sometimes weekdays, too. She'd been around it
since forever, but had never tried it personally until she moved to
New York with Mouse. Some dudes Keisha knew had some at a
party, and Promise dropped one out of curiosity. It was the first
and last time. She found herself all over the place, trying to keep
her emotions in check. Her night had ended with her and Mouse
sitting outside on a bench in front of the building, crying over
past mistakes until the sun came up. That one time let Promise
know that it was one drug she wanted nothing to do with.

"That's out of my comfort zone." Promise held her hands
up in surrender.

"Dizzy, white girl. Nobody wants a repeat of that
emotional-ass shit you put us through over the summer," he
teased her about her bad experience. "But on the real, I'm
plugged in with some real gangsters now. Old-school cats who
are about their business. I met their boss through Candice, and
buddy is about his business. He got Westchester County and
the Bronx rocking off this shit. I can get all the weight I want
on consignment because he trusts me."

"So, some random nigga you met through Candice is just
willing to hand you the keys to the kingdom, just like that?"
Promise was suspicious.

"Let's just say I stepped up when it counted. Now I got
access to all this shit and just need somebody I trust to help
me move it. This is where you come in. You can push this shit
through the strip club. Stripper bitches, and the niggas who
trick their bread on them, love E. You're already tapped in, so
it'd be nothing for you to get these shits off during your shifts."

"Sounds like a decent enough plan, but there's one hole in
it. I quit working at Dirty Wine last night," Promise told him.

"Fuck Larry and his janky-ass spot. We get you set up

somewhere else. I'm telling you, this is easy money," Vaughn said as if it were that simple.

"That's what a nigga always says to a bitch right before he gasses her up to do something that's going to get her twenty years," Promise countered. "Thanks, but I'm good."

"I hear that," Vaughn said, in a tone that let her know he wasn't happy with her refusal. "You on your high horse now, but being that your ass is now unemployed, there's only so long you'll be able to keep standing on that soapbox before you fall and bust your head." He tucked his bag back into his hoodie pocket and went into Candice's room.

"Fuuuuccckk!" Promise threw herself back on the couch and slapped her hand across her forehead in frustration. As bad as she needed money right then, turning Vaughn down felt like intentionally cutting her own throat. She had to though. For as sound as Vaughn's plan to move ecstasy through the strip clubs was, she didn't trust him to be the one to execute it. They weren't talking about a few ounces of ditch weed. He was asking her to follow him blindly into something that came with a different kind of prison time. Vaughn was a good dude, but it would only be a matter of time before he fucked that situation up. It was just in his nature. If he and Candice planned to make the apartment ground zero for their new designer drug business, Promise knew the clock had officially started ticking for her to move the hell out. She needed to get her hands on some cash in a hurry.

No sooner than Promise laid back down, there was a knock at the door. With a huff, she got up and shuffled down the hall. She didn't bother to slip into her sweats, instead going to the door in a pair of spandex shorts and a tank top with no bra. It was probably Mouse, because everyone else who lived there was already in the apartment, and Keisha and Candice didn't allow unannounced guests. Mouse used to have a key to the place, but when she started staying with her boyfriend, Keisha made her give the key back. It didn't make any sense because Mouse was over there damn near every day anyhow. Now, whenever she came, someone had to get up and get the door for her, and most of the time, it was Promise. But when Promise opened the door, she was surprised to see who was standing on the other side.

"What the fuck?" Promise placed one of her arms over her breasts, hoping that he hadn't seen her nipples staring back at him.

"How you be, Ms. Jersey?" Sin looked her up and down. He could tell that she had just gotten up, and even on the wake-up, Promise looked good as hell.

"I be creeped the fuck out right at this moment. You following me on some stalker shit? I didn't take you for a weirdo last night, but maybe I was wrong?" Promise fired off.

"First of all, I'm gonna need you to turn all that aggressive shit down real quick. We established last night that you have a very high opinion of yourself, but me being here ain't got shit to do with you, a'ight? I got business with Keisha. I didn't even know hers was the couch you've been crashing on."

"A temporary arrangement," Promise told him.

Sin threw his hands up in surrender. "I ain't here to judge. I'm kinda glad that I ran into you today though, seeing how you slid out last night without even so much as saying good-bye. Damn, I thought we were better than that, ma?"

"We ain't nothing, Sin. And yeah, I wasn't feeling too good, so I checked out early," Promise lied.

Sin had seen her get into it with Larry, so he knew that she was full of shit, but he didn't call her on it. He figured she had a reason for lying about what really went down. "Looks like you're feeling better . . . a lot better." He let his eyes drift down her thighs, over her calves and to her pink-painted toes. He caught himself and felt like a perv, so he turned his attention back to her face. "So, you working again tonight? Maybe I'll come by and grab a drink with you."

"No, I think my time with Dirty Wine has run its course," Promise told him. "I don't think they'll be open again for a while anyhow. I heard some people got killed last night."

"Oh, word?" Sin faked surprise.

"I thought you and your boys were there when it jumped off. You didn't hear the gunshots outside?"

"Nah, we left right after you broke my heart and took off like Cinderella at the royal ball." Sin turned it into a joke. "So, being that you can't get no money at Dirty Wine anymore, I guess you got something else lined up or, at least, a solid plan to get to a bag? From what I picked up from you last night, the folks you stay with ain't the kind that are gonna let you lay around while you get your shit in order."

"I'll figure something out," Promise said, trying to conceal the worry in her voice. A plan was the one thing she didn't have.

"Or take advantage of the opportunity I'm trying to provide you with." Sin revisited their conversation from the previous night.

"You still on that?" Promise chuckled.

"You can't tell from last night how persistent I am?"

"Like a dog on a bone," Promise joked.

"I've been called worse, and that didn't make it a lie," Sin said with a shrug. "But on some real shit, Promise, I dig your style. How you handle yourself and all. I know you got some principles about you, so I wouldn't never bring no bullshit your way. I'm talking about easy money."

"Easy money gets you the most time," Promise countered.

"Touché." He gave her a mock salute. "Sweetie, I'd never sit here and bullshit you like it's a nine-to-five waiting for you at the other end of my offer. I'm a criminal. I break the law to eat every night, make no mistake about that. But I ain't no fucking purse snatcher or pill head running up in a liquor store with a broken gun."

"Then what are you?" Promise asked.

"Afraid of not having," Sin replied without hesitation. "Baby, I ain't known you twenty-four hours, so I ain't gonna pretend to have a crystal ball into your life to know what your circumstances are, but when I looked into your eyes last night, I saw the same anxious look that's in them right now. Whatever you're going through, I get the impression that time is not your friend. I've been there, so I know urgency when I see it. Help me to help you."

Promise hated the fact that he was able to read her like that. Sin hadn't told one lie in his assessment of her. Was she that transparent, or was this opportunity knocking at her door and she was too dumb to open it? "Sin, like you said, we don't even know each other like that. Why do you even give a fuck about what happens to me?"

Sin measured the question before answering. "Honestly, because, in you, I see opportunity."

"So, I'm just another come up?" Promise asked defensively.

"Everybody is a come up for someone else. I'm just one of the few who are honest enough to tell a muthafucka when I plan to use them to my benefit," Sin said honestly. "The fact that I'm feeling you might be making me a little biased in all this, but it don't change the fact that I know me and you can get some nice money together."

"Doing what?"

"Less than they were asking of you at Dirty Wine," Sin

replied. "I ain't asking you to sell your body, or hurt nobody, just follow my lead to the bag."

"I hear you talking, but you still ain't saying shit. You wanna convince me to get down with whatever you got going on? Stop trying to bullshit me and lay everything on the table." Promise stepped aside so that Sin could enter the apartment.

* * *

"Fuck is this?" Keisha asked when she came into the living room and found Promise and Sincere on the couch conspiring.

"Oh . . . hey, Keisha," Promise greeted her nervously as if she had just been caught with her hand in the cookie jar.

"Don't 'hey' me. I asked a question. What the fuck is going on out here?" Keisha looked from Sin to Promise suspiciously. She and Sin were cool, but not cool enough for him to have her in the middle of her house while she was sleeping. She knew who he was and what he was, so she would've never let him come any further than her threshold. Apparently, her dumbass squatter still didn't understand what she had been trying to indirectly tell her about him.

"Take it easy, Keisha. I came by to conclude our business, and me and ya family just got to chopping it up while I waited," Sin said with a smile.

"She ain't my family," Keisha corrected him. "And since when did you know me to do business in my house with anybody? We can have our conversation in the hallway."

"Well, good chat, Jersey. Hope to hear from you soon." Sin patted her thigh before getting up and heading down the hall.

"Leave that girl alone, Sin," Keisha said, once they were out of earshot of Promise.

"I told you, me and her were just chatting. Wasn't about nothing," Sin said innocently.

"You might be able to fool that green bitch, but I know what you are, Sin. I'm warning you. Stay away from Promise."

"Why you even care? You said it yourself that she ain't family," Sin questioned.

Before Keisha could answer his question, the apartment door opened, and Candice and Vaughn came walking out. When Sin saw Vaughn, his eyes went wide. He was wearing a button-up shirt instead of a hoodie, but Sin recognized him from the night before. He had been with the man who shot Don B.

"What up?" Vaughn asked aggressively, not feeling the way Sin was sizing him up.

"Ain't nothing," Sin replied, committing Vaughn's face to memory.

"What's up, Sin? What you doing here?" Candice interrupted. She smoothed down the wig she had just put on to make sure she looked presentable.

"I'm chilling. How you been, Candice?" Sin asked the girl, but his eyes were still locked on Vaughn.

"I been okay. I'd be better if a certain somebody would let a bitch eat with him," Candice said suggestively, as if Vaughn wasn't even standing there. She had been checking for Sin for a while now, but hadn't had the opportunity to proposition him yet. Now, here he was at her front door.

"Ain't you gonna introduce Sin to your baby daddy?" Keisha threw a block. Her thirsty-ass sister was always trying to weasel her way into someone's bag.

"Oh, I'm sorry. Sin, this is my kids' father, Vaughn. I think y'all met before at that block party a few months ago," Candice reminded him.

"Oh, right. That's where I saw you before. I knew that I knew your face but couldn't place it." Sin extended his hand. Vaughn hesitated before shaking it, and when he did, his grip didn't feel genuine.

"Let's go, Candice. My mama waiting on us to pick up the kids." Vaughn grabbed her hand and damn near dragged her to the elevator.

"See you later, Sin!" Candice called over her shoulder as she was being pulled away.

"I ain't never known your sister to be fucking no hitters," Sin said to Keisha once Candice and Vaughn were on the elevator.

"Vaughn?" Keisha chuckled. "He ain't no hitter. Vaughn is a halfway drug dealer who ain't long for the free world. That boy ain't killing nothing and letting nothing die. But fuck Vaughn. You got something for me?"

"Of course," Sin reached in his back pocket and pulled out a thick envelope, which he handed to her. Keisha took a second to thumb through the bills inside and nodded in approval. "Good looking out again on that. Without you, we wouldn't have been able to get those hammers inside the club, even though we had to end up taking the nigga down outside anyway."

"I heard. Made a real mess of things out front from the way I hear it. Messy ain't usually your style, Sin."

Sin shrugged. "Shit got out of hand. It happens. You hear any chatter on it? People talking about who might've dropped that body?"

"Who? The big dude that got laid out front? Just a loose description. You'd have to know Unique personally to know who they're talking about," Keisha told him.

"Fuck him. I'm talking about the Don. A big-named rapper

like him gets murked, the streets should be on fire right now with speculation," Sin told her. He'd had his ear to the ground all morning and hadn't heard too much, which he found odd.

"I guess it's true what they say about street niggas not reading, huh?" Keisha shook her head sadly. "Hold on a second." She went into the apartment and came back a few seconds later with her phone. She jumped on Twitter and scrolled until she found the trending topic. She clicked the hashtag and handed the phone to Sin.

Not understanding what she was getting at, Sin took the phone. He made it through the first few tweets before his knees got weak. "What the fuck?" Sin's head swam as he read through tweet after tweet. The hashtag was #TeflonDon, and it led him to a series of tweets about a failed attempt on the life of the rapper. One person who claimed to have been on the scene when it happened told a fantastic story about watching the rapper take ten bullets, roll a blunt, and then drive himself to the hospital. There were several variations of what had gone down, but the one piece of information that remained the same in every tweet and story was that Don B. was still alive.

"You didn't kill him, Sin. You made that bastard a folk hero."

* * *

When Keisha came back into the apartment, she found Promise on the couch with her feet up, thumbing through a magazine as if she didn't have a care in the world. "I hope those are the classified ads you're looking through, since you ain't got a job no more." She snatched the magazine and tossed it onto the coffee table.

Promise sat up. "Larry told you, huh?"

"He didn't have to. Everybody was talking about the show your yellow ass put on last night."

"He had it coming. I got tired of Larry's disrespect. He was always calling me out of my name. Dizzy broad this, clumsy gal that." Promise imitated Larry's country drawl.

"Where's the lie? You done broke more dishes in that man's joint than any five bitches I know. Just face the facts, Promise. That game might not be one you're cut out for," Keisha said.

"You're right about that," Promise agreed, before retrieving the magazine from the table and going back to her page flipping.

"So now what?" Keisha asked.

"What you mean?" Promise looked up at her.

"I mean what do you plan on doing about money? You know this ain't no soup kitchen."

"How can I forget? You tell me almost every day," Promise said with an attitude. She was tired, hungry, and not up for Keisha's shit.

"I wouldn't care if I told you every hour. This is my damn house. You don't like what comes out of my mouth? Find another place to rest ya head, ma."

"Relax, Keisha. You'll have your rent money. I made a nice piece of change at Dirty Wine last night, and I got a few other things lined up," Promise told her.

"Is that what Sin's ass was talking about? I swear your head is as hard as a fucking rock! I keep telling you to stay away from Sin, but you're gonna have to learn the hard way. You and my cousin Mouse are just a couple of dumbass kids from Newark, trying to play grown-up games." Keisha shook her head.

"What's the matter? You afraid of a little competition?" Promise accused. "Sin said he came by to conclude his business with you and don't think I don't know what kind of business he was talking about."

Keisha snatched Promise off the couch by her tank top and shook her like a child. "Lil bitch, you better watch your mouth. You don't know what the fuck you're talking about. Talking about things you're clueless to is liable to get your ass hurt!"

"And so will putting your hands on me!" Promise broke Keisha's hold, causing her to stumble backward. Keisha was strong, but Promise was no weakling. She was a thick girl, and the few street fights she'd had coming up in Newark taught her how to use that weight to her advantage. She hadn't meant to push Keisha that hard, but she was angry. The initial look on Keisha's face was one of hurt, but it quickly changed to anger.

Keisha's eyes narrowed to slits, and there was ice in her tone when she spoke. "Ain't no bitch or nigga never raised their hand to me in my own house."

"Keisha, I didn't—"

"Yellow whore, you got until I come out of my bedroom to be gone, or I'm surely going to prison this afternoon," Keisha promised. Without another word, she turned and went into her room.

Promise hurried around the living room, tossing her few meager belongings into a duffle bag. She had never seen Keisha that angry, and there was no doubt in her mind that she would make good on that threat. Promise had crossed a line that she knew she couldn't come back from. She stayed only long enough to make sure she hadn't forgotten anything of importance in her haste. In way of an apology, Promise peeled off $200 from the money she'd made at Dirty Wine and dropped it on the coffee table.

She sat outside on one of the benches in front of Keisha's building with her few meager belongings. She probably looked like a homeless person to the casual passerby, and technically she now was. For all Keisha's bullshit, she, at the very least, had been kind enough to let her crash while she sorted her life out. She had been the only security blanket Promise had had while in New York, and Promise had let her mouth and her ego snatch that away. She now found herself displaced for the second time in a year. She thought about calling Mouse but decided against it. She had already come to Promise's rescue more times than she could count. There was no doubt that, if she asked, Mouse would try and convince the guy she was staying with to let her crash, but that would be too much of an imposition. She was already a guest in someone else's home and trying to bring Promise in might fuck up her situation. Promise would have to solve this problem on her own.

Thinking about the tragedy that was her life made Promise's eyes water. "You better not cry, bitch," she said to herself. She couldn't eat those tears, nor could they shelter her from the elements. No, the time for weeping was over. She needed to act. She thought of the few random people she had met in New York and couldn't think of one who would let her stay with them for a couple of days, at least without wanting something in return. That was the one crucial lesson that she had learned during her time on the streets. Nothing was without cost. It was like Vaughn had predicted. She could only stand on that soapbox for so long. She now found herself with a few choices. She could rent a motel room and stay there until the money she'd made at Dirty Wine ran out or place a call that she had told herself she wouldn't. It was a hard choice, but feeling the first few drops of rain on her head made it easier. With a deep sigh, she pulled out her phone. "Hey . . . it's me. That offer still stand?"

PART III

A COUPLE OF KIDS FROM NEWARK

CHAPTER 26

SEVERAL WEEKS LATER

"Those would really bring out the color in your eyes," Mark said, leaning on one of the jewelry counters at the small Zales store inside the mall. He was a handsome man with chocolate skin and dressed in a form-fitting gray suit. Mark had only been working at that location for two months but had already proved to be one of their top salespeople. He was so good that he could sell water to a whale, but at that moment, he was trying to sell a pair of ice-blue diamond earrings to a blond.

Mark had damn near broken his neck turning around when the blond was strutting past Zales. But then again, so had every man and even a few women who laid eyes on her making her way through the mall. She stood about five nine, maybe ten, in her sleek black designer heels. She was wearing a short-cropped leather jacket and black slacks that hugged her ample hips. Fire engine red lipstick painted her thick soup coolers, and her bone-straight blond hair hung down her back, stopping just short of an ass so round it looked like it belonged on a black girl. Wearing big designer shades and dripping with swag, she reminded him of a young Amber Rose, only with hair.

Mark prayed that she would stop at his booth, and her pivot in his direction told him that God had been listening. He quickly checked himself in one of the counter mirrors as Ms. Rose approached his station. After making sure there was nothing in his teeth, he tried to cut into her. "How you doing today, beautiful? Anything I can help you find?"

"I doubt it, but if that changes, you'll be the first to know," she said without bothering to acknowledge him beyond that. This was a first for Mark. He was a slick talker and strikingly handsome, so most women were drawn to him, but not Ms. Rose. He continued to watch her as she went from counter to counter checking out the different pieces of jewelry. She stopped and lowered her shades when she came across the earrings. It was then that he saw her eyes for the first time. They were as clear and as blue as a tropical ocean. She was taken with the earrings, and Mark saw this as his window of opportunity. Her eyes really did match the set perfectly.

She paused her examination of the earrings and turned her blue peepers to him. "You have much luck running that line on chicks who come through here?"

"It ain't no line, just an observation," Mark told her. "Here, let me get them out so you can have a better look." He grabbed the key from behind the counter and unlocked the case to retrieve the earrings. He slid them across the counter to Ms. Rose. She plucked one from the velvet pillow and held it to her ear, looking in the mirror. They really did bring out the color in her eyes. "Told you."

"They're nice or whatever." Ms. Rose placed the earring back in its place.

"C'mon, you and I both know that these are better than nice. They're amazing. You see the clarity in those stones? These are of the finest quality, not that cloudy shit that most jewelers would try and charge you an arm and a leg for. These stones were carved with you in mind, and because of that, I'll give you a good deal on them."

"How much of a good deal?" Ms. Rose asked suspiciously.

Mark pulled out his calculator and punched in some numbers. "They're priced at thirty-five hundred, but for you?" He paused, mulling it over. "I can let them go for three thousand even—and your phone number."

Ms. Rose laughed. "You swear you got game."

"Can't knock me for trying, right?" Mark smiled.

"You done with this snake-oil salesman? We got places to be," a male voice spoke up from behind Ms. Rose. Mark had been so focused on Ms. Rose that he hadn't realized she wasn't alone. He was a short dude with cornrows, rocking a black shirt and black jeans. Both his hands were weighed down with shopping bags from Nordstrom, Saks, and Victoria's Secret.

"My fault, big dawg. I didn't mean no disrespect to you. I was just trying to see if your lady might've been interested in these earrings. Valentine's Day is coming up, and they'd make a nice gift," Mark said. From the dude's posture and the way he was staring at Mark, he could tell the man with the cornrows was with the shits, and Mark didn't want any problems, especially not at his job.

"That's not my man. He's my valet," Ms. Rose said dismissively, much to the disapproval of the man holding the bags.

"I don't even know what that means, but it sounds fancy as hell," Mark admitted. "You know, when I saw you walking by, I knew you weren't no regular chick. You had to be some kind of celebrity. I got an eye for the elite."

"Is that right?" Ms. Rose leaned in closer so that she and Mark were eye to eye. "Then what industry do you think I'm in?"

Mark thought on it. "With that body and those eyes? You can't be anything short of a movie star."

"You might want to get that eye of yours checked. I'm an actress, but far from a movie star," Ms. Rose told him.

"I was close! And you might not be a star yet, but you will be. I know I'd pay good money to see any flick you was in. Let me get your IG or at least your IMDb page, so I can check out some of your work."

"Stop playing with this lil nigga and let's bust a move," the valet said in an irritated tone. He might not have been Ms. Rose's man, but he was definitely giving off jealous lover vibes.

Ms. Rose shot him a dirty look and then turned her attention back to Mark. "You'll have to excuse my *boy*," she said, dragging the word out, "we were so busy today that he had to skip lunch, and it's made him a bit cranky. And getting three grand out of me for some middle-of-the-mall jewelry store is as unlikely as the prospect of you getting my phone number."

"Damn, that's cold. You act like my breath stinks or something." Mark tried to laugh off the sting of rejection.

"It ain't that at all. In fact, you smell like sunshine and rainbows, which is all the more reason that you and me can't have nothing to do with each other. I let you hitch your little wagon to this fast train that I call a life, and I'd end up feeling bad when you find out too late that you ain't built for this ride. Take this courtesy I'm about to give you and leave it." Ms. Rose then slipped into a vernacular that didn't fit her Caucasian persona. "You ain't quite slick enough to grease this pig yet, but I got a way neither of us leaves this conversation empty-handed." She paused to make sure she hadn't lost him in the spin cycle. "I got twenty-five hundred for you." She slid a Mastercard across the counter to Mark. "Two bands on the card and five cash in your pocket. Don't think about it too long because I ain't got all day."

Mark looked down at the card, which was in the name of a Mrs. Aleen Choo. "Lady, I don't know what you think, but—"

"It ain't about what I think, but what I know. And what I know is that you ain't new to this." She opened her purse to show him the bills inside. "Now stop playing and run this card before you make us both hot." She dangled the Mastercard.

Mark was hesitant. He didn't know Ms. Rose from a can of paint, but apparently, she knew him and how he got down. He couldn't believe that this beautiful movie star bitch was on the hustle! With a weak nod, he plucked the card from Ms. Rose's hand and swiped it. He held his breath, but to his surprise, the transaction went through. He placed the earrings in a box before wrapping them and presenting them to Ms. Rose. She slid him the bills and accepted the earrings. As he continued to stare at the slick blond fox, something about her nagged at him. "We know each other? Don't we?" Mark asked just above a whisper.

"You should've opened with that question. Not ended with it." Ms. Rose gave him a wink, before putting her shades back on and turning to leave.

* * *

"You playing real fast and loose lately, huh?" Sin asked once they were away from Zales and the crooked salesman. He sat the numerous bags on the ground in front of Bebe, so he could adjust for a better grip.

"Nah, I'm just being proactive. That's what you told me to do, right?" Promise adjusted the wig that she had been feeling hostage to all day long. It was heavy and hot, and the pins she had holding it in place were starting to stab at her.

"You know what the fuck I meant, and it wasn't burning through one card in one store. We spread the charges out. That was the plan!" Sincere reminded her.

"Yeah, and them bullshit small charges are why we're spending so much time moving around, instead of hitting for something of value in one shot and saving us half a day's work. It's all profit, right?" Promise countered.

"Shorty, you ain't listening. We had, at least, another day or so to play with that card, but with that two grand charge you just put on it a red flag might go off. Who are we even gonna fence those stones to and see fair value?" Sin wanted to know.

"See, it's you who ain't listening. The other night, when we were casing the after-hours spot, the kid Judah cut into some of us girls talking about how he needed help picking something out for his baby mother's birthday. Judah is getting a few dollars out here, so I'm pretty sure I can get him to spend two grand or close to it for them earrings. He's been trying to fuck me since I met him anyway, so he'll spend the bread with me just for clout."

Sin shook his head. "You've been with us for what? A month? And you think you a master at this finessing shit already, huh?"

"Three weeks, but it feels like three years," Promise capped.

"You for real a slick mouth these days. I think I liked you better when you were the clumsy white girl spilling drinks at that shithole strip club I found you in," Sin joked.

"Bullshit, because, if you did, you wouldn't have put me in position to make us so much money. Admit it, Sin. I'm your golden goose!"

All Sin could do was shake his head. Promise wasn't wrong

in her assessment. Since bringing her into the fold, Sin had made a nice piece of change. In the beginning, he had been planning to use Promise as bait to lure in potential victims for the crew to rob. Men would go crazy over those exotic features and hips. They'd follow her to hell without so much as a second thought if she shook her ass the right way. It was a thought, but just that. Promise was street-smart but didn't have enough larceny in her heart to pull that off. She fumbled one of her first jobs, and the john she'd lured to the spot had been holding nothing but counterfeit money, instead of real cash. On another outing, she'd almost gotten herself killed when the mark wised up to what she was up to and beat her up. Promise was a hustler, but being a part of their strong-arm operations was a disaster waiting to happen. Sin didn't want her blood on his hands, or to get himself locked up for having to kill somebody over Promise, so he pulled her off bait duties and brought her into his *other* business. To his surprise, she proved to be a natural at her new hustle.

Sin's primary sources of income were robbing, contract hits, and occasionally drugs, but he and his crew were getting hot on the streets. New York was only so big, and word was spreading about who they were and what they were about, which was making it harder to move with the anonymity that had given them the edge to that point. So, he had to diversify his hustles. This is how he got into scamming. He could buy profiles on the Dark Web containing people's personal information, which he would use to open up bogus lines of credit to make internet purchases. He even had machines to press up fake cards that could be used in stores. He kept a small crew that he would send into malls to burn the cards out buying things that they could move on the streets. In the beginning, the money was cool, but not coming in fast enough to force him to hang up his guns. Most of the people he used were Black and Latino, so there was always the risk of them being racially profiled in some of these high-end stores. That changed when he met Promise.

Of course, Promise being Promise, she was suspicious of the plan. Sin wasn't asking her to sell her pussy or take her clothes off for dollars, but he was still asking her to put herself in harm's way. She may not have been as likely to get killed doing this, but getting caught would carry prison time. Her fears were put to rest after she made her first purchase. Promise shook like a leaf up until the time she had made it out of the department store with the two leather jackets she had charged. What she discovered was the right makeup and those blue contacts and blond wig erased almost all traces of her African American side and gave her the appearance of a straight downtown white girl. This allowed Promise to move with impunity in and out of the most high-end stores, making fraudulent purchases without so much as a second look. It was ironic that the part of her that she resented the most was what had allowed her to finally move off Keisha's couch. Sin was putting money in her pocket, and he had even arranged for Promise to rent a room from a woman he knew. Her host had a bunch of badass kids that raised hell from sun up to sun up, but she didn't have a baby daddy selling pills out of her crib. All in all, things were starting to look up for Promise. Not just in her professional life, but her personal life as well.

"Yo, I'm starving. You've been dragging me in and out of stores all day and ain't even let a nigga stop for a food break. Let's put this shit in the car and go grab some food somewhere," Sin suggested.

Promise checked the time on her phone. "Maybe some other time, Sin. I got a move to make."

"You know this is like the third time since we've been running together that you've turned down my invitation to break bread? What? My breath stink or something?" Sin blew into his hand and smelled it.

"No, Sin. Your breath is fine. At least, today it is. When you be chain-smoking them blunts, your shit does get a little tart," Promise teased.

"I'm dead ass. Why you keep acting like you don't know I'm trying to get to know you beyond what we do in these streets?" Sin asked. He had been courting Promise since he'd met her at the club, in his own way. There were times when he got the impression that the interest was mutual, but whenever he tried to cross that line, she'd put a wall up between them.

"Sin, I told you from the beginning that I don't think it's a good idea to mix business with pleasure. I appreciate the shit out of you for everything you've done for me, and under different circumstances, I might've given your little cute ass some play. We got a good thing going and us giving into our feelings would only complicate things. I hope you understand?"

"I can respect that," Sin said, trying to act like his pride wasn't wounded.

Promise could see the frustration in his eyes, and it pained her. Sin was a good dude and had really looked out for her at a time when she desperately needed it, but there was no way that she could give him her heart. It had stopped being hers to give long before they'd met. "Would it be trash of me to leave you to get this stuff back to the stash spot on your own while I go take care of something?"

"Of course, it would, not that you would care," Sin half-joked. "The way you're rushing off, you must have a hot date?"

"Actually, no. I've got a loose end to tie up."

CHAPTER 27

Asher had one hand on the wheel and one hand on his gun when he pushed the Jeep Compass. He'd had the SUV only about a week. He got it on the cheap from a shady mechanic he knew in Elizabeth. It was a no-questions-asked purchase. Asher already hated the Jeep. It stank of cigarettes from the previous owner, needed a wheel alignment, and the check engine light came on two days after he'd purchased it. But for $1,500, he couldn't complain. The Jeep was a downgrade from his Benz, and even his Accord, for that matter, but he hadn't purchased it for style. He'd dropped the money because it would provide him anonymity. Being able to move with stealth was the only thing standing between him and the poverty line. He felt like a sucker for having to move so quietly through blocks where his presence had once been announced every time he touched the hood, but that was before Zul had stripped him of his crown and given it to a nigga who was less deserving.

For the last few weeks Asher had been trying to avoid Zul, but it had proven to be harder than he expected. Zul seemed to be able to find him no matter which rock Asher tried to hide under. He hadn't gotten at Asher directly but had been playing mind games by having his people pop up at spots Asher was known to frequent. Fangs popping up in his hood, Baby Blue eating at restaurants that Asher liked. He even thought he'd seen one of Zul's SUVs parked down the street from his mom's condo. These sightings always occurred right before Asher left one of the locations, or just before he arrived. Asher had even changed up his routine, with the same results. It was like Zul had a low-jack on him. Asher knew that this would continue until he gave Zul what he wanted . . . blood.

Handling the situation with Cal had been tough for Asher. He had known the dude since forever, so when he stepped to Zul to inform him that Cal was dead, the words tasted like ashes in his mouth. Of course, Asher hadn't really killed Cal. Instead, he'd found a way to take him off the radar. He sent him down to South Carolina to get things set up with a drug spot Asher was opening in Columbia. Of course, Cal hadn't been happy about Asher sending him out to the sticks, but Asher convinced him that it was for the greater good of their business, and Cal was the only one that he trusted to oversee the task. He also made it a point to emphasize that they were making this move behind Zul's back, and for both their health, they had to keep it quiet. Getting Cal out of town wasn't an easy task, but to convince Zul that he was really dead, Asher had to perform a feat of magic.

Zul was far from slow, so Asher knew that it would take more than a well-crafted lie to convince him that Cal was dead. He would want proof, so Asher gave it to him. The body of a young man who was about Cal's age and build had been found in Cal's car. He had been shot through the head, and the car set on fire with him still in it. Cal had left his whip with Asher to look after, while he drove the rental down south. He would be pissed when he found out what happened to his car, but it beat the alternative. This seemed to appease Zul, at least for the moment, but it still left the issue of Saud to deal with, and that was proving to be the biggest headache of them all.

Asher had played phone tag with the old-timer for a while, trying to get a line on him, with little results. Whenever they spoke, Saud was always very cryptic about his whereabouts, and whenever Asher suggested they meet up, Saud always had an excuse. Asher suspected that Saud knew something was up by then, and the last time he called him, he found that the cell phone had been disconnected. Not even Shelly seemed to know where he had disappeared to. Saud had gone so far underground that it would likely take the devil himself to root him out. Asher was about to give up the hunt when, unexpectedly, his luck turned around. This is what had him riding through Newark in the Jeep.

Saud had finally reached out. He called Asher from a number that he didn't recognize. He fed Asher a bullshit lie about having been locked up over an old warrant that he had to get straightened out. He was now ready to get back to business. He said he needed a fresh shipment, so he could get back on his feet, which meant he needed money to run. Asher could hear the desperation in Saud's voice. He told him not to worry and assured Saud he'd take care of him. Asher knew the real reason why Saud had been MIA, and this was thanks to his partner, Vaughn, who was all too willing to double-cross Saud in exchange for his position and the pipeline to the pills Asher had been supplying them with. Vaughn confirmed what Asher had already suspected. Saud had taken a swing at the devil and missed. Asher wouldn't.

Asher heard his cell phone vibrate. He peeked at the screen and read the text message: *We still good?* He smirked before replying: *Fosho*. Asher had a million things going on and really didn't have the time to entertain anything that wasn't about money or death, but he'd been trying to set this meeting up for a while. His plan of emancipation consisted of a lot of moving parts, and this was one of them. His heart beat with anticipation as he planned the rest of his day in his head. He needed to wrap this shit up in Jersey and get back across the water.

The thing that brought Asher out so early that morning was one of the few things that motivated him more than pussy, and that was money. Milk and the lieutenants had been handling the day-to-day operations of their drug business, but Asher still had a few side hustles going on. One of them was wholesaling weed. A dude he had become friendly with, the same one he had offered to introduce Cal to, had a mean weed connect. That's how Asher had originally met him, copping a little weight here and there when he was in California. Music was his main hustle, but he had access to a damn near limitless supply of primo pot. Asher had negotiated a deal where he got shipped as much weed as he could handle on consignment to move on the East Coast. Asher would then turn around and put it on the streets for double what he was paying. None of the guys he supplied complained about the overcharge because the product Asher was hitting them with was way better than anything they could ever hope to get their hands on.

Over the last few weeks or so, Asher had been making the rounds to collect monies owed to him. He had about fifty grand floating collectively and needed every dime of it ASAP. He was building a nest egg in case his plan went left and he had to take a page from Saud's book and run. Most of his clients had paid up, except for a cat they called Dirty, who was a cool cat, but he had some scandalous ways about him. They all did, if Asher was being honest. They were criminals after all. He'd been playing phone tag for the last couple of days to make arrangements to collect, but something always came up at the last minute on Dirty's end. Asher felt like the dude was trying to play him, so he decided to pop up.

Dirty wasn't hard to track down at all. This was due to him being a creature of habit. Dirty liked to eat in the same places, shop at the same stores, and fuck with the same types of females. You could set your watch by Dirty's movements—or plan his execution. Asher hoped that the latter would be the case. Dirty wasn't at the chicken spot, which is where he took his lunches most days. That meant he had a few dollars on him and told Asher where to look. Sure enough, he found Dirty at Applebee's on Springfield Avenue. Asher could see him through the window, sitting at a table and enjoying a nice meal with some sack chaser that he recognized from the neighborhood. He parked his car and went inside, totally ignoring the hostess who was offering to seat him. The girl spotted Asher first, eyes lighting. She was now in the presence of hood royalty and knew it. Dirty's reaction was one of shock.

"Oh, shit. Big Ash! What you doing down here in the slums?" Dirty, despite his name, was a very clean-cut dude. He took pride in being immaculately dressed at all times. You wouldn't even catch him with dirt on the laces of his sneakers. They called him Dirty because that's how he played in the streets. If he fucked with you, he fucked with you, but if he didn't, you could expect him to try and beat you out of whatever you were trying to buy or sell.

"Picking through the trash," Asher said coldly. "You got something for me?"

"Yo, you didn't get my text?" Dirty asked him.

"Nah, and even if I had the only thing I'd accept is you texting me to tell me you got my bread."

"Baby," Dirty addressed the hood rat, "I gotta go outside and chop it up with my guy." He made to stand, but Asher grabbed him by the shoulder and shoved him back into the seat.

"Ain't nothing to talk about unless it's you having my bread or how you wanna deal with this issue," Asher told him. He was getting impatient. He needed that money probably more than Dirty understood.

Dirty looked from Asher's angry face to the hood rat. She was watching in anticipation to see how Dirty would play it. Would he be a stand-up dude that she could brag to her friends about? Or would he go out like a sucker that she would complain to her friends about? Either way, the outcome of this confrontation would be neighborhood tea to be spilled as soon as she touched the block. Dirty thought about spinning a lie, but he didn't have enough skin in the game to go through the headache that would result from it. In a rare act, he went with honesty. "I gave it to Milk."

Asher blinked twice, as if someone had just snapped their fingers to bring him out of a trance. There was no way in hell Dirty just told him that he had given his money to Milk. "And why would you do that?" His voice was calm, but his brain was still trying to process it.

Dirty was hesitant to answer but eventually did. "Ash, you know it ain't never been no bullshit between us. We always done straight business, so I'm just gonna keep it gangsta with you. Word in the hood is that you're out and Milk's in. Ol' boy been around talking about how you on the outs with the plug. Milk found out about our arrangement and had some of the guys try and lay some pressure down over his new mandatory street tax. All independents in the hood gotta kick him up a taste to keep doing business in the area," Dirty confessed. "I'm just one man, Asher. Milk got soldiers, and I ain't getting enough money off this bud to even try to address those kinds of problems. I hope you can respect my position."

Asher nodded, while processing everything Dirty had just told him. It was just as he had feared. Zul and his divisive games had blurred the lines as to who was really running shit. It obviously didn't help that that clout thirsty muthafucka Milk was probably running all over the city pissing on Asher's name. Asher's rep was the one thing that he had left to hold onto, and he'd die before he allowed anyone to besmirch it. With this in mind, he picked up one of the water glasses from the table and smashed it against Dirty's face.

Dirty howled like a whipped slave as he clutched his face. Blood poured down his clothes and over the table, and he was fairly certain that a piece of the broken glass had made it into his eye. "My eye . . . you took my fucking eye!"

Asher grabbed the plate of shrimp scampi that Dirty had been eating and smashed it over his head for good measure. "Pussy, you're lucky I didn't take your life. Shorty . . ." He looked to the girl who was frozen in shock. "Get this piece of shit down the street to UMDNJ. If he's lucky, they'll be able to salvage what's left of his eye. And when you make it back to the hood, tell everyone you know what happened here and who did it. These streets still mine."

* * *

"Forever miiiiiinneeee . . ." Atilla sang along with the O'Jays classic blaring in his ear pods. He had a pint of Rémy Martin in his back pocket and a tall can of Coors in his hand. He cracked the beer and took a deep swig, appreciating the coolness down his dry throat. It was a little early to be drinking, but that only counted if you had been to sleep, and Atilla hadn't.

The previous night had been one of the best Atilla had had since his release from prison. This was thanks to his new position as one of the bouncers at Wiggles gentleman's club. It was a job that Asher had hooked him up with. He knew somebody who knew somebody who was willing to hire the ex-con to play the door a few nights per week. The money wasn't the greatest, but what the job lacked in hourly wages, it made up for in the free pussy that Atilla found himself buried in since he'd started working there. He'd learned that everyone loved the gatekeeper. From the dudes who would throw him a few extra dollars on the side to let them in with their drugs, to the strippers whose backs he guarded when they crept off between sets to make a few extra dollars in the backs of cars. He still hadn't managed to crack Asher's inner circle, which was his intent when he hooked back up with him, but the homie kept him in position to earn a dollar here and there. Atilla couldn't even be mad at that.

He was bending the corner to go back to the crib when he spotted Milk and a few of the homies chopping it up. Milk was leaning against a forest green Ford Explorer talking to someone Atilla thought looked familiar. What stood out about him was the fact that he was missing two of his front teeth. He knew that fucked-up mouth from somewhere but couldn't think where. As Atilla grew closer, he saw the kid with the missing teeth's eyes drift to him, just before he tapped Milk as if he was signaling him to end the conversation. Milk turned, and when he saw it was Atilla, he flashed him all thirty-two of his teeth.

"The Mad-Hun . . . what it do?" Milk gave Atilla dap.

"Maintaining," Atilla replied. He noticed the kid with the missing teeth giving him the once over and addressed him. "What's good wit you, my nigga?"

"Everything and then some," Fangs said arrogantly.

"I hear that hot shit." Atilla pulled the Rémy from his back pocket and cracked it. He took a swig, staring at Fangs from over the neck of the bottle.

"Easy, Tilla." Milk picked up on the tension. "This here is the homie. It's him and his people that keep this hood fed."

"I thought that was Asher's job?" Atilla questioned.

"Asher's been reassigned. I'm running things around here now," Milk told him. He paused to gauge Atilla's reaction. He knew that he and Asher were cool but wasn't sure how cool.

Atilla shrugged. "Players on the team gotta play for whoever the coach is, I guess?"

"Glad you feel that way," Milk continued. "Like I was telling my man over here . . ." He gestured to Fangs. "We doing like a corporate shake-up. Out with the old and in with the new. That kinda shit. I could use a man of your talents under my reign."

"For as much as I appreciate the offer, Milk, I don't wanna get in the middle of whatever you and Asher got going on," Atilla told him. Asher had never spoken on it, but Atilla was far from slow. His ear was always to the streets, so he was aware of the quiet power struggle between the two upstarts. Asher had been good to Atilla since he'd come home, but not to the point where Atilla was ready to pick a side just yet.

"Ain't but one side, and that's mine. So, nothing to get in the middle of," Milk said with a dismissive shrug. "Bottom line is, I'm in the big chair now and ain't nobody knocking me off in the foreseeable future."

The universe heard Milk's proclamation and decided to call his bluff. The Jeep Compass with Asher behind the wheel came to a screeching halt near where they were standing. Asher jumped out and stormed in their direction, jaw tight and fist balled. Atilla had never seen him like this, so he fell back and watched the scene unfold, curious as to how it would play out.

"If it ain't the prince of pennies!" Fangs greeted him. "You must've taken care of that business for the homie if you're showing your face back on the set."

"Fuck you," Asher flipped Fangs off and marched directly up to Milk. "Holla at you for a minute, bruh?"

"All depends on what kind of conversation you trying to have. You running down on me all puffed up, I need to know how you coming?" Milk capped. He was talking greasy because he had an audience and was trying to show off in front of Fangs.

"I'm coming to you as a man trying to avoid getting into some nasty shit over a misunderstanding. Dirty gave you something that was supposed go to me," Asher told him.

"To my understanding all drug proceeds made in this neighborhood go into the pot, which I have been charged to oversee. Or didn't you get that memo?" This drew an instigating snicker from Fangs.

Everyone in attendance looked to Asher to see what his response would be. Milk was baiting him. A blind man could've seen that. Normally Asher wouldn't have allowed himself to be drawn into such a petty conversation, but these weren't normal circumstances. Asher had put in too much pain for his hood to be played with by Milk or anybody else. It was time to draw a line in the sand. "Dig this. Whatever dream Zul is selling you, I can't subscribe to. My name was etched on this hood before you went to sleep, and it'll still be etched there when you wake up. Gimmie my bread and let me go my way before we have an issue."

"Shorty talking that talk, Milk. You going for that?" Fangs stoked the fire.

Milk sized Asher up. Milk had the money on him and

could've just made things right with Asher, but that would've been too much like doing the right thing, and Milk's ego wouldn't allow that. At one time, Asher had been a dude he respected in the hood. But this was back when Milk was just a solider and Asher was seated at the table with made men. He had always lived in the shadows of better men like Asher, Ab, and even Cal, to an extent. As far as he was concerned, it was his turn to sit at the Big Boy table. Zul had put him in position, but Milk still lacked the respect that Asher carried in the hood. The sucker side of his brain told him the only way to build himself up was to tear Asher down. "A'ight, so check how we make this right." Milk dug in his pocket and came up with a knot of money big enough to choke a horse. He counted off a few stacks and handed them to Asher.

Asher counted through the money and gave Milk a quizzical look. "This shit is light."

Milk shrugged. "If Dirty told you he handed over your bread, I'm sure he told you about my new street tax. Nobody is exempt, including deposed princes. It's a new day in the hood, little Ash."

"Damn, that was some gangsta shit, Milk. Somebody needs to put that line in a movie!" Fangs doubled over laughing, causing the rest of the assembled men to join in.

Asher felt his blood begin to boil as the laughter rang in his ears. He had tried to exercise diplomacy in handling everything that was going on in his life. Tried to color within the lines. But at every turn, he was being tested like he was a punk or something. A film of red came down over his vision. He looked from the cackling thugs to Milk, who was grinning smugly. All Asher could think about was how bad he wanted to wipe the grin from Milk's face, and before he could stop himself, he was in motion. When Asher's fist connected with Milk's jaw, it stunned him. The hook to the gut doubled him over. The cherry on top was the vicious punch to the back of Milk's head. Asher hit him so hard he thought he heard something in his fist snap. He was too mad to care about the pain, or the fall-out that would come from what he was doing to Milk. When he got him down, Asher started stomping him roughly in the head and face. "Trying to play me like I'm some fucking punk!" He dropped his sneaker on Milk's face with so much force that several of his bottom teeth broke loose and scattered.

Asher was so focused on his dismantling of Milk that he didn't see Fangs creeping up behind him. The knife in his hand glinted in the sun. He raised the blade intent on cutting Asher, but his arm was stayed mid-swing. Atilla bent Fang's arm behind his back and forced his face against the side of the house this was taking place in front of. Fangs tried to pull his face away but could do nothing against Atilla's grip. "Fuck is you doing?" Fangs questioned from the side of his mouth because the rest of his face was buried under Atilla's massive palm.

"Picking a side," Atilla told him.

All Fangs could do was watch while Asher beat the brakes off Milk. Asher would've probably killed him had all the blunts and Black & Milds he smoked not caught up with him and stolen his wind. Asher paused his stomping, his breathing heavy and toe hurting from the repeated kicks. "I don't give a fuck whose product is being sold out here. This will always be my hood." He spat on the ground for emphasis.

It wasn't until Atilla was certain that they had the situation handled that he let Fangs loose. Zul's number-two jerked away from him clutching his sore wrist. His hateful eyes went from Asher to the few guys that were gathered with him. "What y'all niggas just standing around for? He violated. Handle that!"

The goons looked between each other awkwardly, as if they

were uncertain as to how they should've responded to the order. One of them, a boy Asher knew as Brick, stepped forward. Asher balled his fists, ready to fight to the death if that was what it would come to, but it wouldn't. "You might be tapped into the plug," Brick addressed Fangs, "but Asher is one of us." Brick threw up their set. "It was a fair fight. Let this shit be done."

Hearing his response made Asher smile inwardly. Zul might've been the man who supplied the hood, but Asher was from the hood, and it made him hopeful that his name still meant something. If he was lucky, he might still come out of this alive. Brick and the others departed, leaving Fangs and Milk to whatever fate might've awaited them.

"Traitorous muthafuckas!" Fangs spat. "You niggas is dead, Asher. Zul gonna send everything he got at you for laying your hands on me."

"And when they come, we'll be waiting," Atilla said, before knocking Fangs out and leaving him slumped next to Milk.

* * *

"Thanks for that back there," Asher told Atilla once they were away from the scene.

"Fuck them off-brand niggas. I can't stand them crabs from up the way, anyhow. If I had a pistol on me, I'd have smoked him on the strength of them even thinking they can come through our hood talking tough," Atilla spat.

"Zul ain't gonna be happy about this. Now they're probably gonna come looking for you, too," Asher said, thinking about how he had dragged yet another one of his comrades into his bullshit.

"I hope so. All they're gonna find is a beautiful death," Atilla said proudly, anticipating the coming battle. "You know, saving your ass has become a regular thing since we hooked back up. This is the second time I had to save you from getting your shit split."

The joke stung, but only because of the truth in it. The night at Dirty Wine when they were out looking for Saud, Atilla had rescued Asher from a potentially bad situation. Seeing Promise again after fearing he had lost her forever had Asher floating on a cloud. He was so lost in his plans for her that he had been caught completely off guard when the shooting started. Asher moved more off instincts than thought when he hit the ground and rolled behind a parked car. He covered his head to protect it from falling glass as the windows were shot out. At first Asher thought that he had been the intended target and maybe Saud had lined him and got the drop. But the shooters weren't Saud or any of his boys; instead, there had been another outside that night who was the target.

Target or not, the bullets had no preference as to where they flew, and a few of them had struck close enough to Asher for him to think that he might die that night. He was caught in the crossfire of some shit that had nothing to do with him, and he was without a gun. He promised himself that, if he made it out of the situation alive, he would never go anywhere without a strap again. A shadow draped over his hiding spot, followed by a gruff voice. "Up!" the voice barked before Asher felt himself being yanked to his feet. Much to his surprise and relief, it was Atilla, and he wasn't alone. In his hand was the gun Asher had said to leave in the car. Atilla had disobeyed a direct order, and Asher wasn't even mad. Atilla placed Asher behind him like he was the president and cleared a path back to their car. Asher didn't even balk when Atilla shoved him into the passenger's seat and jumped behind the wheel of the Benz. With skills born from years of stealing cars, Atilla had them out of the Bronx and crossing through the Holland tunnel in record time.

It was after that incident that Asher came to the realization that he had misjudged Atilla and his value to Asher's cause. Cal and those in Asher's inner circle were all solid, but none of them brought to the table what Atilla did. He had proven himself to be more than just a soldier to be marched out into the field of battle. In Atilla, Asher now had what he'd been missing during his reign, a wall willing to stand between him and harm's way.

"I can't front, you've proven your worth twice over since we been running, and I promise, once I get this shit sorted with Zul, you'll be rewarded for your loyalty," Asher said.

"See, and that's part of what I can't figure about you, Ash. How did you end up under the thumb of a man who was branded an enemy of this hood? Zul couldn't come within spitting distance of Washington Street without one of these young nuts trying to peel his wig when B-Stone was still alive. It was green light on sight. Even when I was away, I would hear the stories about the little war between B-Stone and that crab nigga Zul. This is why I can't understand how every one of you ended up eating off his plate?"

Asher thought very carefully about how to respond. Atilla was a wrecking ball of violence, but he was also no fool. He was already growing suspicious of Asher's true intentions, and if Asher hoped to fully sway him to his cause, he would have to properly motivate him. "Because that's how Ab wanted it." The lie rolled effortlessly off his tongue.

Atilla couldn't hide the look of shock on his face. "Bullshit! Ab hated Zul, too."

"No, B-Stone hated Zul, and Ab did what was required of him as a loyal solider," Asher clarified. "You know, just like I do, that Ab was more about a dollar than he was the drama, and that thing between B-Stone and Zul was personal, not about money. When B-Stone died, so did the beef. The fact that Zul opened up that dope pipeline he'd been sitting on to Ab made it a little more acceptable to bury old grievances. Ab having access to Zul's plug made him a king."

"And when Ab fell, you picked up the crown." Atilla started to put the pieces together. "Asher, you're either the luckiest son of a bitch I know or one hell of a chess player."

"Does it matter if we all end up rich for our troubles?" Asher asked.

"No, I don't suppose it does." Atilla shrugged. "One thing that you ain't factored into this is, if Zul sends his people after us, we ain't gonna live long enough to spend this newfound wealth you keep promising me. Zul has got the soldiers and the reach, so this little war of yours I've chosen to fight is one we're likely going to lose."

"Unless we can end it before the first shot is fired." Asher tapped his chin in thought.

"You just said yourself that he's gonna come for the both of us behind what just happened. How you plan on calling that dog off?"

Asher smiled devilishly. "By throwing it a bone."

CHAPTER 28

This was Todd Richardson's second time bending that corner. At least, by his count. It could've easily been his third or fourth. There was really no way to be sure, considering that his brain had been on autopilot since the GPS announced that he had arrived at his destination. The more he surveyed the area, the harder it was for him to believe how low he'd taken to stooping to feed his fetish.

He pulled into the parking lot of a sketchy-looking motel that sat on the lip of the Lincoln tunnel, in the shadow of a billboard whose lights kept winking on and off. Todd slow-spun the lot, suspicious of every face and place he encountered. He could've parked in any one of the multiple open spaces that sat near the stairs leading up to the motel rooms; instead, he opted to park around the side of the building near where the office was. Hanging from the side of the building was a low-end Walmart camera. It hung on by two out of its four intended screws. Todd slipped out of the car and pulled up the collar of his overcoat to obscure his face from the camera, which probably didn't work anyway, before locking his car up and forcing himself to go through with something that he wasn't entirely sure about to begin with.

Near the stairs that led to the second level of the motel, a man leaned against a vending machine smoking something that didn't smell like tobacco or weed. He was speaking in a hushed tone to a thin white girl with stringy blond hair. Two sets of eyes landed on Todd, and he felt his stomach rumble. "Hey, handsome, you looking for some company?" the blond asked in a hoarse voice. Todd didn't reply. He kept his head down and picked up the pace heading up the stairs. "Well, fuck you then, peckerwood!" she cursed after him.

Todd ignored her. The brash whore was yet another reminder as to why he had left the Rotten Apple and now took in his sunsets out west. Todd's primary residence was in the 92008, Carlsbad, but he often found himself having to spend periods of time back east. He'd never stayed longer than he had to. It was always in and out, as the circumstances under which he left weren't the best, and every time he touched eastern soil, he was reminded of that. He was supposed to be in and out within twenty-four hours, but weather had delayed his flight, and he had an extra day to kill.

They said that idle time was a tool of the devil, and Todd didn't disagree. This is why he hated the downtime during these trips. It allowed him the space to explore some of his less quiet proclivities. One of the few things Todd loved almost as much as making money was pussy. He made good money in his profession and was well-respected among his peers. Getting pussy had never been a problem for Todd, but he had an acquired taste for a certain type of pussy . . . young Black pussy. Whenever Todd was in the public eye, you'd likely find a beautiful, statuesque blond on his arm, but behind closed doors, he craved the darker things, both literally and figuratively. Generally, he kept a few regulars in each city that he visited. Women who would entertain his fetishes in exchange for cash and their silence. His latest trip to the tristate had been short notice, so he hadn't had time to set anything up. Finding himself horny and bored, Todd did something that he probably wouldn't have if he'd thought it through. He turned to the internet to feed the sex-starved gorilla clawing at his back. This is what led him to the New Jersey motel in search of a happy ending.

Todd scanned the numbers on the motel room doors until he found the one he had been instructed to go to. He stood outside it for a few minutes and contemplated calling the whole thing off. The only thing that stopped him was that he was more nervous about crossing paths with the couple at the bottom of the stairs again than he was about facing what was waiting for him on the other side of the door. He had come too far to turn back now. Taking a deep breath, he knocked and waited.

It was only a few seconds before he heard the locks being undone on the other side, but it felt like a lifetime. When the door was pulled open, Todd was greeted by a thin black girl sporting a long black wig. She was wearing a simple terry cloth bathrobe and socks that looked like they had once been white before she'd taken a few laps around the dingy motel carpet. Her brown face was heavily made up, but you could tell that she was young. Young and tender. Just how Todd liked them. The name on her profile was Betty, but she didn't look like a Betty.

"You gonna stand there gawking at me? Or do you plan on coming in?" Betty asked.

Todd looked back the way he had come, and he could see the couple he had passed looking up at him. In was definitely better than out, so he crossed the threshold. "Sorry it took me so long. I got stuck in traffic," he lied, once he was inside the room.

"No worries, baby. It gave me some extra time to make sure I was nice and fresh for you. Come on out your coat and get comfortable." Betty motioned toward the motel bed and leaned against the dresser with the television, watching as he did as he was instructed. He tossed his coat on the armchair and sat on the bed, looking nervous. "Relax, I ain't gonna bite you," she said. "Unless you're into that kind of thing?"

"Sorry, it's just that I . . . um . . ." Todd searched for the words.

"Never paid for pussy?" Betty finished his sentence. "Don't worry about it. I ain't some common whore selling ass out of back alleys. I'm an escort. There's a difference. Now, you got that for me?"

Her so-called assessment wasn't even close to what Todd had been about to say, but he went along with it. He pulled out the five hundred in cash that he had in his wallet and counted off three, which he attempted to hand to Betty, but she refused the money. "You said three hundred, right?" He didn't understand her hesitation.

"Yeah, but you can just lay it on the dresser. That way we never made a direct exchange. You can't never be too careful," she told him.

"I'm not a cop," Todd assured her.

"It wouldn't matter to me if you were. Cops are some of my biggest tippers." She winked. "Don't worry. Betty is going to take real good care of you. Let me fix us a taste, and maybe it'll help you to relax."

Todd watched Betty as she moved to the dresser to fill two plastic hotel cups with Hennessey. Her back was to him, so this gave him a chance to check her out, at least what he could see through the robe. A few things stuck out to him about his afternoon appointment. She was thinner than she had appeared in the picture of the site he found her on. It was one that several guys he did business with used when they wanted some out-of-town thrills. Also he noticed that her nails weren't done, and she had probably applied her makeup herself or had one of her friends do it. Todd had dealt with enough whores to spy that Betty was either new to the business or a hustler trying to make a few dollars off what God gave her. She was decent enough looking, but Betty landed several rungs down from the types of women he was used to buying pussy from. He was tempted to call it off and chalk the $300 up as a loss. What was a few hundred to a man with pockets as deep as his? What happened next, though, would change his mind.

Betty sauntered back to the bed with the two cups. When she moved, her robe opened enough for him to see the lace number she was wearing beneath. Her pussy was so fat that it looked like a balled-up fist in her panties. What really turned him on were the coarse pubic hairs poking near her bikini line. She hadn't even had the decency to groom herself before meeting her trick. Todd didn't mind. The bushier the pussy the better, as far as he was concerned. Most of the Hollywood-type women he dealt with were too vain not to keep themselves well-groomed. Going down on them was like eating chicken with no skin, good but lacking something. It was the girls who weren't afraid to let their pubic hairs wolf that really turned him on. He loved to bury his face chin deep in an unkept bush, especially when they were a little tart. Not funky, but with just a little tang to it like the girl had been out running errands all day and hadn't had a chance to take a second shower before sex. Todd was weird like that.

"Here you go, baby." Betty handed him one of the glasses. It was half-full with liquor and no chaser, but it didn't stop Todd from downing it. "Slow down. I don't want you to be too drunk to perform."

"I can hold my liquor," Todd told her while trying to keep his voice from cracking. He was more of a scotch man, but the cognac did help to put him a little more at ease.

"I could give a fuck about how you handle your liquor. I'm more concerned about how you gonna handle me." Betty slipped out of her robe and gave Todd a full view of what he had previously only had a glimpse of. She was dressed in a thong and bra set that she had probably gotten from Rainbows, but it looked good on her. The straps of her thongs hugged the right angles, and the sheer bra top exposed the dark nipples of her small breasts.

Todd reached for her like a child motioning to its mother that it wanted to be picked up. Betty took her time stepping into his arm's reach and letting his hands explore her body. She straddled him, running her breasts across his chin. Todd greedily suckled at them through the fabric of the bra. Between her legs she could feel his dick harden in his slacks. She reached down and gave it a squeeze.

"Damn, baby. You're holding for a white boy," Betty told him honestly. Todd's dick felt thick and hard. She had never been with a white guy, but some of her friends who had agreed that they had small penises. She pushed back on his lap to allow enough space to open his pants. Getting his dick out proved to be a struggle, but once she got it free, she understood why. Either Todd was mixed with black or her friends had been liars, because the man had one of the biggest dicks she had ever seen.

"Yeah, just like that . . ." Todd rasped while Betty stroked him. Her hands felt like warm silk on his dick. He almost blew his load when she spat in her hand and began jerking him off. "Put it in your mouth." He tried to force Betty's head down, but she pulled away. "What's the matter?" He had shaken his jitters and was ready to get to it.

"I don't mind sucking a little dick, but you just come in off the streets. I can't let you put that thing in my mouth until you wash it." Betty climbed off his lap and sat on the bed. "Go in there and jump in the shower. In the meantime," she recovered a large dildo from under one of the pillows, "I'll be getting myself all primed and ready for you." She lay back and began rubbing the rubber cock against her panties.

Todd was already halfway out of his clothes by the time he disappeared into the bathroom. To say he was excited would've been an understatement. She waited until she heard the shower running before jumping off the bed and going back to where she had left the bottle. From behind the television, she pulled out the small bag of white powder she had stashed. She wasn't sure what it was, but it was supposed to be something that would make Todd drowsy and her job easier. At least, that's what her partner in crime had told her before she undertook the mission.

When she'd first been presented with the proposition to make some extra cash, she had scoffed at it. She had traded pussy for money before, but this was different. The stakes were higher and the risks greater than a simple exchange of pay for play. She had been reluctant at first, but all it took was some sweet words and good dick to get her to waver. The first time she had done it, her date had been asleep within ten minutes of her dosing him, and she was in his pockets and gone within fifteen. Meanwhile Todd still seemed to have all his wits about him. She reasoned that he probably had a higher tolerance to the date-rape drug and needed a little extra for it to take effect. She needed it to hurry up and kick in before she found herself actually having to let him stick that big white whale into her little pussy. He was liable to knock something loose. She glanced over her shoulder to make sure the bathroom door was still closed before opening the package. When she heard the shower abruptly stop, she panicked and dumped the entire contents of the baggie into the cup. She wanted to shake some out but didn't have time, so she hastily poured liquor over it and jumped back onto the bed.

Todd came out of the bathroom ass naked and dick swinging. His eyes were glassy, but sleep looked like the last thing on his mind. His legs looked a bit unsteady as he crossed the room, but not shaky enough for her liking. He crawled onto the bed and attempted to mount her. She stopped him. "Slow down, love. No need to rush. Finish your drink and then we can get the party started."

Todd nodded and went to retrieve his cup. He eyed her over the rim like a hungry lion as he downed it. He tossed the plastic cup aside and crawled onto the bed. His mouth and hands explored Betty's body thirstily. This second mission was definitely not playing out as smoothly as her first one had. When his mouth clamped over hers, she wanted to retch but had to hold her composure. "Take it easy," she said between the white man's sloppy kisses, but her words fell on deaf ears. Todd was amped up. The drug was supposed to make Todd a lamb, but instead it had turned him into a wolf. "Red light," she blurted out randomly.

"A little blood has never bothered me," Todd told her while prying her legs open. This shit was going downhill fast.

She wasn't sure how it had happened, but Todd had her flipped on her stomach. His hand was wrapped around her neck, with her face buried in the pillow. "Red light!" she blurted out again, this time with more urgency. Betty heard something tear behind her. She couldn't move her neck to turn and see what it was, but she found out when she saw the condom wrapper sail to the ground. It wasn't much in a way of a consolation for what was about to happen to her, but at least, he was strapping up. Fire shot through her ass and up her spine when Todd tried to shove his massive dick into her. He was too big and she was too dry. "You're hurting me," she whimpered.

"And I've paid for the privilege." Todd spat on his dick twice and lathered himself with his saliva before shoving his dick into Betty. He knew from the moment he walked in that Betty had sized him as some kind of lame trick, but it was her ass who was about to get the treat.

Betty wanted to scream, but she couldn't because her voice was wedged between the lump in her throat and the dick in her guts. The pain was white-hot in the beginning, but once she opened up it became tolerable. About six or seven pumps in she found herself overcome with shame when she creamed over Todd's dick. The white boy knew how to work his tool. "Reeeddd liiiight . . ." she moaned when her intended lick hit her spot. She didn't want to throw it back at him, but her body had disconnected from her brain and was going with the flow. The plan was to get this white boy for his money, but the way he was dicking her down made her feel like she should be paying him. Betty was mumbling in protest like she wanted him to stop, while secretly working her way to her second nut. She was at the height of her orgasm when she heard the motel room door open and felt a gust of wind roll across her ass. It was about then that all hell broke loose.

CHAPTER 29

Just as Betty was about to get off again, Todd and his dick were roughly pulled out of her. She turned just in time to see Bone, with one of his hands wrapped around Todd's neck, choking him out. To Todd's credit, he didn't go out like a sucker. He hit Bone with a nice two-piece, but they may as well have been open-hand slaps because they had little to no effect. Bone responded by punching Todd in his chest so hard that he flew across the room and knocked over the television. Todd crumbled into a heap on the floor.

"Crazy-ass white boy!" Bone cursed, shaking his hand in pain and checking to make sure he hadn't damaged his fist with the punch. "You good?" he asked Betty.

"What the fuck do you think?" Her voice no longer had the sultry, enticing pitch she had used with Todd. Betty had dropped her facade and was now Mouse again. She opened the nightstand drawer and retrieved the cell phone she had stashed in it when Todd knocked on the door. The call on the screen was still live. Bone had been on the other end secretly

monitoring the date so that he could swoop in if things started
going left and Betty gave him the signal, which was "red light."
The fact that she had to end up fucking Todd anyhow said that
Bone had been slipping. "I'd have done better screaming for
help out the damn window! Where were you?"

"I stepped out of the car to take a leak and left the phone
on the car seat. I came in as soon as I heard you call out."

"While you were attending that weak-ass bladder of yours,
this john was in here having his way with me!" Mouse scolded,
while slipping hurriedly into her jeans.

"Bitch, first of all, you need to watch how you speak to
a gangster. I ain't one of them tender dick Jersey niggas you
used to dealing with, so turn that shit down before I do," Bone
warned. "And from the way you was throwing that shit back
on him when I busted in, seems like y'all were having your way
with each other. You was really grooving off that pink pecker,
huh?"

"Never that," she replied cooly, knowing damn well Bone
had seen the passion on her face when he discovered Todd
inside her. She finished dressing and tried to brush past Bone
to get her purse when he grabbed her arm roughly.

"Tell the truth. That cracker got you off, didn't he?" Bone
asked in a threatening tone. He fronted like he wasn't into
Mouse like that, but his jealous behavior said otherwise.

"You know this pussy only gets wet for you, big daddy,"
Mouse purred.

"You better say that shit and mean it." Bone gave her arm
a little squeeze before releasing her.

Bone and Mouse's relationship was one born of random
chance and common interests. This happened shortly after
Promise had officially been brought into their crew. She had
pulled off her first successful caper with Sin, and he insisted

that she come out and celebrate. Promise wasn't really up for it, but Mouse convinced her to accept the invitation. She had yet to meet Promise's new friends but had heard quite a bit about them and how they moved. All it took was for Mouse to see what Promise had cleared from her first lick, and she knew that these were the types of New York hustlers that she needed to be affiliated with.

They'd gathered at a dive bar on the east side of Harlem for drinks and wings. By far, Sin was the most handsome of the group, but Mouse already knew not to waste her time. Promise hadn't formally laid claim to him, but Mouse could see from the way Sin looked at Promise that he only had eyes for her. Mouse set her sights on Unique, but it was Bone who claimed her. He wasn't the prettiest of the crew, but he was more Mouse's speed. He was more concerned with having a good time and a dollar than keeping up appearances like the other two. When Mouse saw Bone snatch a tip from a table that had just been vacated by a dining couple, she knew he was the one. Not because he was obviously larcenous, but because he'd likely be the easiest to manipulate in her quest to get to the bag as her girl had done with Sin.

Sin had been reluctant to involve Mouse in their business, but at Promise's insistence, he let her pick up a few crumbs from the table. It was mostly light work, like driving when they had something going on or dropping packages off, but he never let her anywhere near serious capers. Mouse made a few dollars, but they amounted to little. Sin had a million hustles going on at once, and his crew got money in a variety of ways, but from what Mouse had been able to pry from Bone, one of their primary sources of income was strong-arm robbery.

One technique they employed was the same one Mouse and Bone had just used on Todd. They would place ads on underground dating sites that were frequented by men with money, lure tricks to remote motels, and rob them. To the casual observer, this plan looked flawed because there was no way to guarantee that whoever responded to the ads would be holding enough money to be worth robbing. This is where Mouse experienced the genius of Bone's brother Sin firsthand. He had managed to procure a list containing the names of regular big spenders in and around the city and some of the sites they used, and this is where he placed his ads. The men would respond in search of a good time and end up getting fleeced. They never used the same site twice within a thirty-day span, and they bounced around to different cities when committing these crimes. They had no pattern, which made it easier for the robberies to seem more like random occurrences than an operation. Sin wouldn't allow Mouse to take part in these heists because she was still too new, and he didn't quite trust her yet, but Bone had no such hang-ups. Like Mouse, Bone wasn't content with his brother's crumbs either. It was their mutual greed that would graduate them from lovers to partners in crime.

Had Sin known what Mouse and Bone were doing behind his back, he would've surely flipped out. Sin had a nonnegotiable rule about moonlighting and running the risk of bringing unnecessary attention to the crew, which is just what Bone and Mouse were doing with their little backdoor schemes. This is why Bone constantly reinforced in Mouse the importance of keeping their side hustle a secret. She couldn't even tell Promise what she had been up to. There had been no secrets between Mouse and Promise before she hooked up with Bone, and Mouse hated lying to her friend. When she expressed this to Bone, he was quick to point out that Promise was making money from his crew's schemes and how she'd be foolish not to try and cash in as well.

When Sin pulled this trick, he rolled three deep: the girl who would serve as the bait and two shooters to watch her back in the event that something went wrong. This way, the girl was always protected by a second line of defense if the first one failed, but Bone wanted to do it two-deep. His cheap ass didn't want to recruit a third party because it would've left him with a smaller cut of the money. He was confident that he could do the job by himself and had convinced Mouse of the same. The fact that Todd had actually made it inside her showed the flaw in his plan. Mouse was fortunate that, at that time, all she'd had to give up was a little taste, but what about the next time?

"Uhhhhggg," a groan came from across the room. Bone and Mouse had been so wrapped up in each other that they had almost forgotten that Todd was still in the room. He was lying on his stomach, groaning, moving his arms and legs slowly as if he was trying to swim on the dirty carpet.

"Shut yo bitch ass up!" Bone kicked Todd in the ribs. He was still angry about finding the white man balls deep in something that he considered his property. He kick flipped Todd onto his back and what they saw made Mouse shriek.

"What did you do?" Mouse asked in a panicked tone. Todd's eyes were rolling in the back of his head and there was thick white foam bubbling from his mouth.

"Me? I didn't even hit him that hard." Bone knelt beside Todd and placed his fingers to the man's throat. His pulse was sporadic, and his skin hot to the touch. There was no way a punch to the chest could've caused this. "How much of that shit did you give him?"

Mouse was silent.

"I asked you a question! How much?"

"All of it," Mouse admitted.

"Damn it! I told you to only give him a little. No more than half the bag and that was a worst-case scenario. You done overdosed the man!"

"How? You said they were only muscle relaxers!" She had never heard of anyone overdosing off muscle relaxers.

"I told you that it was something to make him relax. You assumed I meant muscle relaxers. Jesus, Mouse!" Bone shook his head, getting up and moving to where Todd had tossed his pants. He removed his wallet and car keys. Todd was having convulsions now, and his skin had gone ghostly white. "We gotta get the fuck out of here."

"Wait . . . shouldn't we call an ambulance?" Mouse suggested.

"And tell them what? That you accidentally snuck too much drugs into his drink while you were robbing him? Bring your simple-minded ass on." Bone grabbed her by the arm and pulled her toward the door. As Mouse was being dragged outside, she spared a glance back at Todd, who had finally stopped shaking. This was her second time leaving a man for dead on the floor of a hotel room. This one hadn't hit as close as B-Stone, someone she had known her entire life. Todd had been a stranger, nothing more than just another casualty in her fight for survival. She didn't feel good about it, but at the end of the day, what effect could the death of a random stranger have on her life?

As Bone was shoving Mouse into the car, her cell phone rang. She looked at the caller ID and saw that it was her cousin Candice calling. She hadn't spoken to either of her cousins much since hooking up with Bone because he kept her busy scheming. She wasn't going to answer, but then she did anyway. The moment she heard Candice's voice, she knew something was wrong. Her cousin was hysterical. "Wait . . . slow down.

What?" Mouse continued to listen. "Okay, I'll be right there."
She ended the call, the color draining from her face.

"Everything good?" Bone asked.

"When is it ever?" Mouse punched in one of the few
numbers that she knew by heart.

CHAPTER 30

Asher gunned his Benz through the toll booth of the George Washington Bridge at a less-than-advisable speed. He was already behind schedule for his meeting and still had another stop to make before he could go there. His business in New Jersey had taken longer than he had anticipated, but he needed to make sure that all the pieces were where they needed to be before executing the next phase of his plan.

After dealing with Milk and Fangs, Asher and Atilla dipped back to Asher's where he had left his Benz parked. Asher switched cars, giving the hooptie to Atilla to hold down while he jumped in his Mercedes. Asher was trying to fly under the radar, but the flashy Benz wouldn't help with that; however, for his next move, appearances would mean everything. After making the car switch, Asher warned Atilla to stay low until he heard from him and headed into New York to meet Saud.

The old head had been blowing Asher's phone up all afternoon and into the evening. Something had him rattled, and Asher didn't have to guess what. The chatter on the streets had picked up about the shooting of Don B. at Dirty Wine. This was largely in part due to Asher feeding Shelly a tidbit of information that he was sure she would let slip. She didn't disappoint. It didn't take long for the gossip train to start moving and Saud to find himself living on borrowed time.

The riddle had been a fairly simple one for Asher to figure out. He had been there the night Saud and Don B. had exchanged words over the rapper having been rumored to be behind the death of one of his former artists, a cat called Lord Scientific. Lord Scientific had been from their hood and a former protégé of Saud's, and his death had never sat right with the OG. The only thing that had stopped Saud from getting at Don B. that night in Newark was Ab stepping in, but Saud vowed that there would be a reckoning for what Don B. had done. That reckoning had come at Dirty Wine. Asher didn't have to see him pull the trigger to know that Saud had been behind it. The pieces fit too perfectly for Saud to have coincidentally been at the same place where Don B. had been shot. Saud going underground immediately after was confirmation of Asher's suspicions.

The solving of one mystery had also created yet another. Who were the other dudes Asher had seen gunning it out with Don B.'s camp outside the club? They weren't Newark dudes, this much Asher knew, nor did they fit the profiles of any of the New York cats Asher set Saud up with. Could the Don's luck have been that bad to where two assassins had been set on his ass on the same night and Saud had just had the luck of the draw? Saud was the only person who could fill in the blanks, and sadly Asher didn't suspect that the OG had enough time left on earth to do so. Saud had gone from a calculated gamble to a liability. He was now marked in New York and Newark, and it would only be a matter of time before one side or the other caught up with him and put his lights out, which was why Asher had to get to him first.

Saud had suggested that they meet somewhere out in the open, but after what Asher had walked into at Dirty Wine, he wasn't trying to hear it. They settled on meeting at a neutral spot, Shelly's apartment. It would still put Asher in a potentially dangerous situation on foreign soil, but at least, by meeting at Shelly's he'd still be able to control the narrative, at least, to an extent. He spotted Saud's Cutlass parked on a side street near Shelly's apartment building. Asher spun the block twice to make sure there were no surprises lurking before parking on the next avenue.

Asher pulled on a dark hoodie, which he kept in the trunk of the Mercedes for just such occasions. He then walked the block to Shelly's building. She lived on a main street, so the block was teeming with activity. Dudes loitered in front of the corner store, drinking, smoking, and shooting dice. Asher could feel their eyes on him as he passed but never looked up from the folds of his hoodie. As he crossed the lobby, the elevator pinged, just before the door slid open and a man stepped out. He too was wearing a hoodie, but it hadn't completely covered his face. As they passed each other in the lobby, Asher caught a glimpse of a tattoo that he thought he had seen somewhere before. The man must've felt Asher staring because he looked up. When his dark eyes landed on Asher, a cold chill swept over him. Asher was the first to look away. Not because he was afraid, but because he didn't have time to deal with the kinds of problems that a staring contest with this kid would surely bring. The young man snorted victoriously before exiting the lobby and disappearing into the night.

Asher decided to take the stairs instead of the elevator. The last thing he needed was to step out into something unexpected.

Whatever might be waiting for him at this meeting, he needed to be able to see it coming. It was a short hike to the third floor, where Shelly's apartment was. Asher paused outside the door and listened for a few ticks. Inside he could hear music blasting as if someone was having a party. He raised his fist to knock and then paused. Something didn't sit right with the scene. It took a moment for it to register what it was. There was music, but Asher couldn't hear any voices. What kind of party were they having where there was absolutely no chatter?

He drew his gun before checking the door and finding it unlocked. Cautiously, Asher crept inside the apartment. He could smell lingering weed smoke, but it was weak, like someone had been getting high earlier. As he crept down the hall, he felt something slick under his foot. He looked down and realized that it was blood. Upon closer inspection, he noticed a trail of bloody footprints that led from the bathroom to his left to the front door. With his gun raised, he pushed the door open and that's where he found Vaughn. He was slumped on the toilet with his pants around his ankles and a magazine on his lap. There were two nasty-looking bullet holes in his chest. To die while taking a shit was literally one of the nastiest ways that a man could go. Initially Asher thought that maybe this had been the work of Saud, trying to clean house before he vanished. Since Asher had known him, the old-timer had never been one to leave debts unsettled. That theory died when he ventured deeper into the apartment.

There were three additional bodies in the house, all spread out in different poses of death like mannequins in a department store window. Asher surveyed the scene, trying to piece together what had happened. Laying on the floor across the entrance to the living room was a young man with a bullet wound to the neck. From the amount of it pooling, the shot hadn't killed the man. He'd probably bled out from the wound. There was another body hanging halfway out a partially open window. He'd sought to use it as his escape route until the three slugs he'd taken to the back thwarted his plan. Not far from where he lay was Shelly. She was curled into a ball as if that would protect her from the hail of bullets that ripped through her body. Of all the deaths Asher had caused in his life, this was one of the few he felt bad about. He had dragged her into this, so her blood was on his hands.

The crown jewel of the scene was the older man sitting on the couch, Saud. His head was lolled slightly to one side as if he were simply taking a nap, but the bullet hole in his head said that it was a sleep he would never wake from. One of his hands sat limply on his lap, near the gun tucked in his waistband that he'd never had a chance to reach for. Plastered across his face was the signature scowl that had terrorized Asher and all the rest of the young kids from the hood when Saud was still running things. This hadn't been an execution, but a massacre.

Asher approached Saud's corpse and began rifling through his pockets. He had a few loose ecstasy pills on him and a few hundred dollars in cash. He took the cash but left the pills. He'd searched all Saud's pockets and still hadn't found what he was looking for. Pulling his sleeves to cover his hands so he didn't have to touch the dead man, he pushed Saud's body to the side. There it was, wedged between the cushions of the couch. Saud's cell phone and the only thing that could connect him to Asher.

He took a minute to make sure he hadn't left any traces of his passing in the apartment before creeping back out. He replayed the crime scene over in his head on his way back to his car, and nothing about it made sense. The fact that Saud had never drawn his gun was what tugged at him the most.

Saud was a soldier, so there was no way he would allow some-one to get the drop on him without, at least, getting off a shot or two. This could only mean that Saud had known his killer. That was the only way Asher could see Saud letting anyone get that close up on him. He never saw it coming. Asher had set out with the intent of murdering Saud, but once again, the universe had done his dirty work for him. It was too soon for the Big Dawg crew to have tracked Saud down, and there was no way it could've been Zul's people because only he and Saud knew where Shelly lived. If none of them had killed Saud, who the hell had?

CHAPTER 31

Zod stood in front of a massive office window, looking out at the city skyline. From there, he could see clear across Manhattan. The sun had long ago set, and the moon floated high over the city. This wasn't his first time observing the moon from that view, but somehow it looked different that night. It was like the moon shone just a little bit brighter, just like his future.

"What are you doing in here?" a voice called from behind Zod.

"Counting my blessings," Zod said without turning around. There was no need. He continued watching the sun until the overhead office light flicked on and ruined his peaceful moment.

"You know Don don't like nobody in here when he's not around." Devil stepped into Zod's line of view. Devil, or Red Devil as he was sometimes called, was built like a muscle with a mouth and eyes carved into it. He wore his head shaved and sported a faint beard that was starting to show the first signs of gray. Zod had known Devil since he was a kid and first came into the services of Don B. He was now Big Dawg's head of security.

"I think me being in his office is the least of my uncle's concerns right now," Zod said before turning to face Devil. Zod's eyes were glassy and red, due to lack of sleep. He'd been up for nearly forty-eight hours and wanted nothing more than to crash, but there was still work to do. "I could ask the same of you being here, especially since you've been missing in action lately."

"I just came from seeing the Don, and Tone needed me to come here and grab some files."

"Any change?" Zod asked.

"Nah." Devil shook his head. "He's stable, but still not out of the woods, so they think it's best to keep him in that medically induced coma for a time longer."

"It's been nearly a month already."

Devil shrugged. "That's what the doctors are saying."

Zod was silent for a few ticks. You could see the frustration on his face. "Somebody is gonna bleed for this. You know that, right?"

"That goes without saying. Niggas can't touch the Don and get that off like that." Devil fumed.

"So how come my uncle's is the only blood staining the sidewalk so far?" Zod asked.

"Trust, we gonna find out who did this sooner than later and make it right."

"Streets talking yet?" Zod asked.

"A lil something, but mostly cap or shit that's being posted on the internet. You know, when a major figure like Don B. gets hit, everybody and they mama wanna take credit for it."

"But everybody and they mama didn't shoot my uncle. I wanna know who did," Zod said.

"Tone thinks he's got a pretty solid lead. Some dude from out of Jersey," Devil revealed. He watched Zod's face for a reaction. The young man remained unreadable.

"Give me his name, so I can pay him a visit."

"Nah, can't do it. This is a delicate situation because of mutual acquaintances. Tone wants to make sure all our ducks are in a row before we make a move and the last thing we need is you jumping the gun and causing a gang war," Devil told him.

"Fuck the gang! That's my family laid up in there. Y'all don't trust me to handle it?" Zod asked defensively.

"No, he don't trust you not to make a mess of it. You a hot head, kid. You shoot first and ask questions later. That ain't what we need right now," Devil told him. "Zod, you been around us long enough to know that we ain't shooting at each other on corners no more. The game is played differently at this end of the field."

"Yeah, but the game is still the game, ain't it?" Zod asked. "How long can you all really expect me to sit on my hands and do nothing while a man I love is in ICU fighting for his life?" Zod ran his finger along the top of Don B.'s bloodred office chair, which sat behind a large cherrywood desk.

"For as long as we tell you to," Devil replied. "This whole situation is a mess, and it's gonna be up to me and Tone to clean it up. Had I been there, none of this would've fucking happened!"

"And that's the same thing I keep saying to myself." Zod slid into the chair and made himself comfortable. He placed his cell phone on the tabletop and folded his hands behind his head. From the look on Devil's face, he could tell that he didn't appreciate the slick response. This was just the reaction Zod had been looking for. He'd nudged Devil off balance and gravity would do the rest.

"And what's that supposed to mean?" Devil was defensive.

"Only that, for as long as I've known you, D, I can't ever recall you missing a day of work. On a night when my uncle needed eyes in the back of his head most, you come down with a tummy ache and hand your responsibilities over to someone else." It wasn't an accusation, more of an observation.

"First off, it wasn't no stomachache. When I woke up that morning, I had chills and a bad case of the shits. With Covid tagging people left and right, I didn't want to put the team at risk by coming around. You know nothing short of death or a serious illness would've kept me from the Don's side."

"Forever the loyal soldier, ain't you, Devil?"

"Shorty, I don't like what you're insinuating. Any nigga talking to me like that better have a pistol on him," Devil warned.

"I do, but I don't want no trouble with you, OG." Zod raised his hands in surrender. "All I'm saying is, none of this shit sits right with me. One of the most polarizing men in the music business—who made his bones off gangsta rap—not only lets a muthafucka close enough to shoot him, but there was no immediate retaliation. The wolves are hungry, and they're looking at it like, if Don B. can be touched, then so can any of us. Only be a matter of time before we hear the sounds of wolves sniffing at our backdoor. Shit was already getting shaky over here, but after this . . ." Zod shook his head sadly. "We may as well wave the white flag because it's looking like we've rolled over and died."

Devil wanted to argue with Zod, but he couldn't. The Big Dawg brand had indeed been struggling, and people were starting to notice. Don B. and Tone did what they could to keep up appearances, but a buzzard could smell a rotting carcass from a mile away. Whether Don B. pulled through or not, the fact that Mr. Untouchable had been touched was a blow to their whole image. "So, what do you suggest we do?"

"It's simple. Somebody has to fall."

"But we don't even know for sure who shot him yet."

"Maybe, maybe not," Zod said suggestively. He let the uncomfortable silence linger for a few beats before continuing. "I'm fairly certain that whoever was really behind this will get exactly what is coming to them. That goes without saying, but if we want to save face, we can't wait. We need to make a move now."

"I do know, man." Devil was hesitant. "Tone said—"

"You let Tone keep making his statements to the media. We'll make ours on the streets. My uncle has no shortage of enemies to choose from, but plucking one of them out at random won't serve any purpose other than making us hot. This has to be someone who not only stood to benefit from the death of the Don but had a big enough ax to grind against him."

"I could think of at least ten dudes off the top of my head who might've wanted to see the Don dead," Devil said, rolling over Zod's plan in his mind.

"Of this, I'm sure. But this has to be someone heavy enough that the entire city hears it when they hit the ground. This will send a message to the vultures circling and waiting to pick over the bones of what the Don has built, that we're still the biggest dogs on the yard."

Devil measured Zod's words. He had to admit that the little nigga had balls. That was one of the only things that Devil liked about Don B.'s ambitious young nephew. "Sounds like you've given this a lot of thought. Let's say I buy into this little plot of yours. You got somebody in mind to send this message?"

No sooner than Devil asked the question, Zod's phone rang on the table. He looked at the screen and read the text from an unknown number: *Red Light.* "As a matter of fact, I do. I gotta bust a move, but keep your phone close." He got up and prepared to leave.

"Don't do nothing stupid, Zod."

"Only thing I'm gonna do is what one of you niggas should've had the balls to do a long time ago." Zod had just reached the office door when Devil stopped him.

"Is that blood on your shoe?"

Zod looked down at the splotches of red on the sole of one of his crispy white Nikes. "Nah, man. I was eating a pizza and must've dropped sauce on them. Keep your phone close," he repeated before leaving.

* * *

The first thing Zod did when he came out of the Big Dawg offices was to find a homeless person and give him the shoes right off his feet. The man was so happy to receive Zod's gift that he burst into tears. He thanked Zod for the blessing, never knowing that he was really passing off a curse. God help him if the police ever stopped him and looked too closely at his new kicks. That wasn't Zod's problem though. He could only imagine how crazy he must've looked walking back to where he had left his car with nothing but a pair of white ankle socks on his feet. There were too many other pressing things on his plate for him to care. He had somewhere to be.

Running into Devil at the office had been an unexpected blessing. Devil was definitely on his list of people to see, but he hadn't expected it to be quite so soon. This turned out to be a good thing, as he had now managed to sway the muscle behind Big Dawg to his cause. He'd counted on as much, after doing a bit of digging through Don B.'s private files at the office. He kept them on flash drives in a floor safe under his desk. Zod had discovered it one day when he had found Don in the office, passed out drunk and the safe left ajar. It took

Zod three weeks of sneaking into Don B.'s office when no one was around to figure out how to crack into the safe. The code was simple enough to figure out because Don B. was a simple enough man—0-3-1. Once Zod had access to the safe, he would frequently visit the safe and pour over the information inside. It was what he had learned there that would plant the seeds for the weeds that he had been growing.

Zod doubted that anybody, including Tone, knew the Don secretly kept files on them all. Inside the safe, Don B. documented the lives, personalities, and potential weaknesses of everyone he proclaimed to love. There was all kinds of damning information about Don B.'s entire inner circle. Zod had even found three life insurance policies on Big Dawg artists that listed Donald Bernard as the sole beneficiary. He had initially taken the collection of this information as an indication of what people were saying about Don B. slipping deeper into his paranoia as his company faded and bank accounts dried up. But Zod came to realize that what he was really looking at was a testament to his uncle's genius. He had protected himself from enemies both foreign and domestic, considering almost every eventuality except the one that had almost knocked him out of the game for good. It was sheer luck that he had survived the assassination attempt, but even alley cats only had so many lives, and his uncle had wasted eight of his nine.

Devil had been one of several people on Zod's list who he had planned to pay a call on, and who had proven to be the easiest to manipulate. This was thanks, largely in part, to one of the first lessons that Don B. had taught Zod when he brought him into the fold. No one was easier to manipulate than someone who had something to hide. They'd pretty much go along with anything you said if they felt like it would bury their secrets deeper. Zod had only been fishing when he engaged Devil back at the office, but the fact that he had so willingly bit the hook, confirmed what, until then, Zod had only suspected. The fact that such a loyal dog was suddenly willing to keep secrets from its master told Zod that they were on the same page. The winds of change were suddenly picking up speed.

Reflecting, Zod realized that he wouldn't have been able to get as close as he was to his ultimate goal had it not been for the man he had come to affectionately call his Perfect Patsy. He'd discovered him quite by accident, meeting through a dude named Vaughn that Zod copped pills off from time to time. They didn't know him as Don B.'s nephew, only a disgruntled executive at the label who Don B. hadn't been playing fair with. Saud saw this as an "Enemy of my enemy is my friend" type of situation, and Zod used this against him. Saud was so blinded by his hatred of Don B. that he didn't think twice when Zod made him an offer that was too sweet to pass up. Zod had given him one job. One simple task and it would've been a win for all parties involved. Saud had fucked it up and now Zod was forced to alter his plans. It was time to clean house.

Zod's ruthless nature was the main reason why Don B. had named his nephew the heir to the Big Dawg throne. He was willing to do what most wouldn't to ensure the survival of the label, but even the Don had no idea how far Zod was willing to go in order to get what he wanted. He was truly the flesh of Don B.'s treacherous flesh. The current leadership of Big Dawg was the reason for the once mighty label's rapid demise. They were echoes of Big Dawg's dark past, and it was now up to General Zod to march them into a brighter future. There was only one more domino left to fall; then, the usurping of his uncle would be complete. In his mind, he rationalized his actions as not a betrayal, but a cleansing.

CHAPTER 32

Promise sat at a small table in the back of the Upper Westside Café. It was probably one of the tiniest tables in the place and sat too close to the bathroom for comfort. Every time someone went in or out, she was able to pick up on the scent they had left behind. It wasn't the most ideal seat in the house, but it gave her the best vantage point of the street beyond the window. Sitting with her back to the window was a habit that she had picked up since running with Sin. Whenever they went somewhere, he refused to sit with his back to the windows or door. It didn't matter if they were in church. Sin would receive the word of the pastor over his shoulder because he would be facing the door. This paranoia was born of a lifetime of doing dirt.

She had learned quite a bit from Sin in her short time running with him, but the most important thing was probably the content of his heart. Sin was an outlaw, and his first loyalties would always be to himself. Promise held no illusions about this, but Sin also had a big heart. She saw how hard he went, not only to take care of his crew, but anyone around him who he saw needed a little help. Promise was proof of that. He had picked her up at a time when she had been flat on her ass. Of course, Sin benefited from Promise's services as well, but the gesture itself counted for something. Sin was the definition of a real nigga, one of those dudes who would go above and beyond for those he cared about. That was the kind of man that most chicks would be grateful to have, and he had offered himself to her, only to be rejected multiple times. What was wrong with her?

That was a question that she already knew the answer to. The line she had been running on him about not wanting to mix business and pleasure had been half-true. Promise fumbled every opportunity ever presented to her and was hesitant to do anything to affect the flow and Sin's rhythm. Not even from the money aspect, just from finally being able to find a dude who was down for her. Like really down to see her win! The moment she laid down with Sin, it would all be shot to hell. Not because she didn't believe they could be good for each other, but because she doubted she could ever give herself to him completely. She would always have one foot in and one foot out of their relationship, while certain doors to her past remained open.

Her cell phone buzzed on the table. She looked to the caller ID expectantly, but that quickly died away when she saw that it was only Mouse calling. She decided to ignore the call. Mouse would likely ask where she was, which would lead to her having to explain herself. It was a conversation Promise didn't feel like having right then. Staring down into the bottom of her second cup of green tea, she heard her mother's words in her head: "The definition of insanity is repeating the same mistakes and expecting different results." Was she insane? Had to be if she kept setting herself up for the bullshit.

The bathroom door swung open. A chubby young man with thick glasses and starter-kit dreadlocks came out adjusting his pants. The smell he left in his wake told Promise that he had obviously eaten something that hadn't agreed with him. That was all the motivation Promise needed to abandon her foolish experiment. Lightning had struck twice, and she was a fool to think that it would hit for a third time. She threw her sunglasses back on, collected her purse and her phone, and stood to leave. She was upset, but more at herself for showing up than the fact that she had been stood up. The universe was sending her yet another sign, and this time, she would take heed.

Her cell phone rang. It was Mouse again. She had just decided to answer when the bell above the café door jingled, announcing someone had just come in. When she looked up and their eyes met, she forgot about her phone, Mouse, and everything else. The only thing that existed in that moment was him.

* * *

Asher made his way into Manhattan from the Bronx. He was feeling pretty good about himself, all things considered. This changed when he received a call from Cal. Asher almost crashed his Benz when Cal told him that he was back in New Jersey. Apparently, something had happened with his sister, and he'd hopped on a plane back to Newark. Cal didn't go into detail about what had brought him back, but he sounded pretty upset. If Zul or any of his boys spotted Cal, Asher would be fucked with a capital F. He told Cal not to do anything rash until they had a chance to talk. They made arrangements to meet at one of their trap spots, where Asher planned to lay everything that had happened on the table to his friend. By that point, he no longer had much of a choice. He couldn't keep him in the dark any longer and risk him getting caught slipping. Asher didn't want that on his spirit.

Cal popping back up unexpectedly complicated things, and besides that, he knew he would have to still deal with the fallout from what he and Atilla had done to Milk and Fangs. Things were still quiet on the streets, but they wouldn't be for long. The shit was going to hit the fan, but before that happened, Asher needed to make sure he had all his ducks in a row. This meant getting everyone he cared about out of harm's way until he figured out how to deal with Zul.

His first priority was his mom. He needed her not just out of the house, but out of Newark. At least until he got everything sorted out. Normally, getting Linda to take days off from work would've been like pulling teeth, but luckily, she had a birthday coming up, and he was able to use that to his advantage. As an early gift, he surprised her with three tickets for an all-expenses-paid cruise of the Southern Caribbean for her and two of her closest friends. Because of the history Zul shared with Asher's mother, Asher doubted Zul would make good on his threat to hurt her. He'd likely only said it to scare Asher because Zul knew his old bird was the only person in this world that he truly loved. Zul was a nut, but he was also honorable when it came to such things. Still, Asher wasn't about to take any chances. Linda would spend the next eight days drinking herself silly and soaking up sun in tropical paradises, while Asher tried to clean up the mess he had made in Newark.

By the time Asher made it to his destination in New York, he was already thirty minutes late. Of course, he couldn't find any parking on the west side, so he took a chance and left his Benz parked near a hydrant. If he happened to get a ticket, he would just eat it. The hundred and something dollars the city of New York would hit him for would be well worth it if things worked out as he planned.

Asher paused just outside the café, giving himself the once over in the window's reflection. He had ditched the hoodie and smoothed out the wrinkles in the button-up he wore beneath as best he could. He popped a fresh piece of gum in his mouth before stepping inside the café. The patrons consisted of mostly older white folks and a few college-aged looking kids on their laptops. He scanned the faces, yet none of them looked familiar. He did, however, lay his eyes on a beautiful blond who was standing near a table in the back peering at him from behind a pair of dark glasses. She was checking him out, and under different circumstances, Asher would've entertained her, but he wasn't there for that. He was focused on his mission. He glanced at his watch again. He was forty minutes late and knew she had probably tired of waiting for him. He couldn't say that he blamed her. He was disappointed, but he understood. This wasn't the first time he had left her dangling in the breeze, but apparently it would be the last. Asher was about to turn and leave when he heard someone speak his name.

"Really, Asher?"

He turned and found the blond glaring at him, arms folded and lips twisted. Asher was confused at first as he was sure he didn't know her, but then he took a closer look and realized he did! "Promise?" He didn't recognize her in the blond wig and draped in designer. She looked like a totally different person than the girl who used to watch him from afar back in Newark, begging for his affections. No, this wasn't his Broken Promise, but a well-kept young stallion.

"And who else would be fool enough to sit around and wait for your ass for nearly an hour?" Promise asked.

"My fault, I just . . . I didn't recognize you in all this." Asher motioned toward her disguise. "You look different."

"I am different." Promise flipped her wig confidently. She'd actually forgotten that she was still wearing the getup, but seeing his reaction to the image Sin had curated made her feel good. It felt like, for the first time since they'd known each other, he was actually *seeing* her.

"Miss, are you still using that table?" one of the baristas asked Promise. She had a spray bottle and some rags with her and was prepared to wipe the table down for the next guests.

"Yeah, we're going to hold onto it for a few minutes more," Asher answered for her. After dismissing the barista, Asher walked Promise back to the table, watching her hips sway all the way. This was definitely not the Promise he knew. Something had changed in her, and he liked it. She reached for her chair, but he beat her to the punch and pulled it out for her. Promise smiled in thanks before taking the seat. Asher flopped in the wooden chair opposite her.

"You know I was sixty seconds from saying fuck you and leaving, right?" Promise asked from across the table.

"Then I'm glad I made it here in fifty-nine," Asher capped. "Blame it on my hectic schedule and not my heart."

"I see you're still the same old Asher, out here chasing things beyond your reach." Promise shook her head.

"See, that's where you got me fucked up. You act like you wasn't listening when I told you that I was up. I done caught everything I ever chased except you," Asher said seriously.

"Cut the bullshit, Asher."

"Nah, this real shit, and it's long overdue. How long we gonna keep acting like we ain't meant for each other?" Asher asked seriously, tiring of the games he had been playing back and forth with Promise since they'd known each other. With the way his life was currently set up, he knew it could end forty years from then as easily as it could end in forty seconds. He was on the clock, and this is what pushed him to place all his cards on the table at once.

"For as long as it takes you to realize I ain't built to be no side bitch," Promise countered. She too was ready to push her chips in.

Asher didn't answer right away. He studied Promise, trying to get a read on her behind the designer shades and tightly crossed legs. "Would it be too cliché if I told you that it was complicated?"

Promise sucked her teeth and rolled her eyes as if to say "cut the bullshit."

"I'm only messing with you, Promise. Damn, what happened to that sense of humor I loved so much about you?"

"You killed it, along with my spirit."

"C'mon, Promise. You still on that? How many times do I have to say that I'm sorry?" Asher asked.

"As many times as I need you to. At least, if you were serious about all that shit you've been kicking to me since we got back in contact," Promise challenged.

This was the second time she'd seen Asher since moving to New York, but they'd been speaking and texting quite a bit since the night he gave her his number. Promise didn't reach out right away, though she desperately wanted to. She had to let him stew for a bit so as not to come off as too thirsty. She'd opened up with a simple *"You know I still can't stand your ass"* text. To which he replied: *"Allow me the opportunity to change your mind."* They went on like that for a while before she finally broke down and accepted his call. He'd been blowing her up, but she wasn't ready just yet. Their first conversation was filled with more awkward silence than actual words, but she eventually opened up. Promise did most of the talking, while Asher patiently listened. She told him about her life in New York, and what she had been up to. She didn't say too much about her business with Sin, but she did share with him her adventures on Keisha's couch and the events leading up to her untimely eviction. Asher seemed especially interested in Vaughn and his pill business. When Promise questioned him about it, Asher dismissed it as just an opportunity to make a few dollars. Vaughn was a dealer, and Asher was a supplier. Promise shut that idea down. She wanted nothing to do with Vaughn's foolishness, and besides that, he already had a mystery supplier. Asher didn't press her further with questions that he already knew the answers to.

"Promise, I can tell you until I'm blue in the face that I'm a changed man, but the only way for me to make you a believer is if you let me show you," Asher said.

"And how are you supposed to do that?"

"Come away with me. I'm planning on taking a trip to the West Coast on business, but we can make it about pleasure. Like a mini-vacation."

"Asher, I got too much going on right now to pick up and run off to California with you. Besides that, if I don't want anything to do with your drug business on the East Coast what makes you think I'll have a change of heart getting caught up on the West Coast?"

"Nah, it ain't that type of party. My business in California has nothing to do with drugs. It's totally legit. Well, for the most part. Think about it. Me and you soaking up that California sun. Eating the best food and smoking the best grass. It'll be a vibe. We can even hit up Disneyland."

"Wow, I can't believe you remembered that." Promise chuckled. This was something she had told Asher when they were still running around Newark. Promise had always wanted to go to Disneyland. It was one of the places her dad was supposed to take her when he sent for her and her mother to move them to the West Coast. Yet another promise that wasn't kept. That had been the story of her life.

"Of course I remember!" Asher continued. "I know it might not have seemed like it back then, but whenever you talked, I listened and digested every word. You taught me a lot, believe it or not."

"Like what?" she wanted to know.

"For one thing, you taught me how to dream," Asher admitted. "You were the one person from our hood who saw the world as bigger than those run-down blocks we were killing each other over. In a way, I have you to thank for setting my sights west and the amazing thing I'm building out there."

"And what exactly is that?" Promise asked suspiciously.

"Allow me to show you." Asher held out his hand.

Promise sat there, just staring at it for a few beats. She wasn't exactly sure how to respond. Asher was saying all the right things. Things that she had been wanting to hear from him since the first time she laid eyes on him, but he had broken her trust once, and it had devastated her. She wasn't sure if she would be able to recover from that kind of heartbreak a second time. Her mind was telling her *"No,"* but when she looked into those beautiful brown eyes of his, her heart screamed *"Yes!"* She didn't think it was possible, but Promise found herself falling for Asher all over again. Without even realizing she was moving, Promise placed her hand in his.

"Well, if this ain't the sweetest shit." Asher heard a voice coming from behind him that made his blood run cold. Zul hovered over the table, smiling wickedly at the two lovers. He saw Asher move and pushed his jacket back to expose the butt of the gun tucked in his slacks. "You're fast, youngster, but not faster than me. Don't do it to yourself." Asher wisely placed both hands flat on the table. "Smart."

"What you doing here?" Asher asked through clenched teeth.

"I could ask the same of you. You a little far from home, ain't you?" Zul pulled out a chair and invited himself to sit down.

"Had some shit to take care of on this side of the Hudson," Asher told him.

"I can see." Zul gave Promise the once over. "And what's your name, beautiful?"

"That ain't your concern," Asher said defensively.

"Oh, you think I'm trying to poach your little girlfriend? Shame on you, Asher. You know I'm more of a gentleman than that. It's just that I can't help but to feel like I've seen her somewhere before."

"Nah, you don't know her. She's just some chick I met a little while ago," Asher lied, which got him a dirty look from Promise.

"You're from Newark, ain't you?" Zul ignored Asher and kept his attention on Promise. He was toying with her.

Promise looked to Asher, who looked like he was about to shit his pants. Something was wrong. "Is there a problem?"

"No problem, love. I'm just making small talk. That's all." Zul continued to study her. "Yeah, I know I've seen you before. Your name is Passion or something like that, isn't it?"

"Her name is none of your fucking business," Asher answered for her. "As a matter of fact, she was just leaving. Take a walk, shorty," he said, dismissing Promise with a coldness that threw her off.

"Asher, you good?" Promise asked nervously.

"You hard of hearing? Bounce, bitch!" Asher snapped.

Asher's words cut her like a knife. It was like he was a totally different person than the one who had just been promising her the world moments prior. No, the monster sitting across from her was far more familiar. "I should've known better." She snatched up her purse and stormed off. She felt tears welling in her eyes but wouldn't give him the satisfaction of letting him see her cry. She had shed enough tears over Asher to last her a lifetime.

Asher watched helplessly as Promise walked out of his life for what was likely the final time. He wanted to stop her . . . to tell her that his handling of her had been a ruse and he was doing it to keep her safe, but he couldn't. Promise represented a weakness. One that he knew Zul would use to hurt him if he felt like he could. So instead of going after one of the best things that had ever come into his life, Asher suffered in silence.

"I hope you got the pussy already because, if you didn't, you probably never will after how you handled that fine young thing. You a cold muthafucka, Asher." Zul laughed.

"Fuck you, nigga!" Asher spat.

"Yeah, you've been trying to fuck me, which is why I'm sitting across the table from you, trying to think of a reason not to paint the walls of this café with that devious-ass brain of yours. You know Fangs is calling for your head behind that shit you and your jail bird homie pulled, right?"

"Fangs can eat a dick or a bullet. Don't matter to me at this point," Asher said flatly.

"You know I love it when you talk spicy, Asher," Zul said in an amused tone. "The fact of the matter is, the only reason I haven't let Fangs and Baby Blue put you on the treadmill is because you are the dog I trained, so it falls to me to put you down after you've bitten your master's hand. Now, to your credit, I heard about those bodies the police found in the Bronx, but you still owe me a life and the deadline for that has come and gone."

"You asked me for two lives, and I gave you two," Asher countered.

"No, you gave me one and a possible. This ain't a game of spades. You're playing with your life right now," Zul warned. "In the beginning, I was skeptical about you doing the right thing for once without trying to put some sneaky shit in the game. I even found myself impressed when word came back that you had served justice to them two traitors, especially Cal. I knew that couldn't have been an easy thing for you. I respected the fact that you actually went through with it. I even started to believe that the blood of an honorable man might still pump somewhere in that black heart of yours. But something kept nagging at me, and I couldn't let it go."

"Zul—" Asher began, but Zul cut him off.

"You ever seen a miracle, Asher? I have. Just the other night in fact. I sent Baby Blue by the place where Cal's mama and them stay." Zul paused to make sure he had Asher's undivided attention. "He was supposed to ask a few harmless questions, but you know that boy overdoes his job sometimes. No worries, everybody is whole, but Cal's sister might've gotten knocked around. I reprimanded Blue for that already. Not long after is when I saw the miracle. A dead man crawled clean up from his grave to be there for his family. One of my people saw Cal in the hood, enjoying a cold brew like he didn't have a care in the world. Asher, I'm so disappointed in you."

"I couldn't do it," Asher said honestly. The truth was all he had at that point.

"I figured you wouldn't be able to. For as cold as I am, even

I couldn't go through with something as heinous as that," Zul confessed.

"Then you should understand why I lied," Asher said.

"The fact that you couldn't go through with it is something I could've lived with. Honestly, if you'd just kept it a buck, I'd have put it on Fangs or Blue and spared you the heartache. It's the lie that has you on the shot clock for what's left of your life. You've bent the truth with me too many times, Asher. So, I'll tell you what's going to happen next. Me and you are going to get up and walk out of here, and drive somewhere nice and quiet, so I can give you a quick death. Which is more than you deserve, considering."

"Or you can hear my counterproposal," Asher offered.

"Asher, you've crossed and played me at every turn since this shit started. Nobody short of Jesus can stop me from murking your grimy ass at this point."

"Then allow me to turn water into wine." Asher removed an ink pen from his pocket and scribbled something on one of the café's napkins, which he slid across the table to Zul.

Zul looked from the address scribbled on the napkin back to Asher. "What the fuck is this?"

Asher looked out the café window in time to see Promise getting into a taxi before answering. "A bone."

CHAPTER 33

"Big bro. You've come up with some nut-ass plans over the years since we've been doing this, but I think this one has got to be the most reckless," Bone said from behind the wheel of his car. Not long after dropping Mouse off in the projects, he had gotten the text from his brother. *All hands on deck*, followed by an address. He knew that meant Sin had a job for them, but he wasn't prepared for what he would hear when he arrived.

"Scared money don't make no money," Sin replied.

"But this ain't about money, is it?" Bone questioned. Sin didn't respond. He just continued staring aimlessly out the window, as he had been doing for the last hour or so.

Bone wanted to argue his point further but knew it was pointless. Sin's mind was made up, and there was nothing he or anyone else could say to sway him.

Sin ignored his brother's chattering and fired up another blunt. He had been chain-smoking them back-to-back all night. He should've been high as a kite by that point but found that he was only just mellow. Probably due to the seemingly endless supply of adrenaline that was coursing through him. He spared a sideways glance at his brother and noticed something unfamiliar . . . worry. Bone was a rock who wasn't easily rattled. In light of the circumstances, he couldn't say that he blamed him. This would be either the most gangsta shit Sin had pulled or the dumbest. Either way, it had to be done.

His phone rang. It was Promise on the line. He started to answer but decided against it. She would be a distraction, and at that moment, he needed to be laser-focused. No sooner than the phone stopped ringing, he got a text notification: *Need you when you have time.* Now she wanted to talk? He wouldn't say it, but he was still in his feelings for the way she had curved him earlier. It had taken a lot for Sin to work up the courage to tell her how he felt, and she had dismissed him. Whatever she had to say could wait.

A few minutes later, Unique emerged from the entrance of the building they had been watching. He moved cautiously across the street, scanning in both directions. Tucked under his arm was a parcel that he held onto with the security of a running back heading for the end zone in a playoff game. The car door barely made a sound when he slithered into the back seat.

"How we looking?" Sin asked over his shoulder.

"Like three niggas about to do some shit that's gonna get us life in prison or killed," Unique half-joked.

"Sounds like another day at the office to me." Bone reached back and bumped fists with Unique.

"If y'all two are finished jerking each other's dicks, I got something to do," Sin said seriously.

"Pretty much everybody is gone for the day, but one nigga is still lingering. Muthafucka looked like he was half-sleep, so I can tell he ain't no soldier, just a warm body," Unique updated him.

"He'll be a cold body in a few." Sin checked his gun to make sure a round was chambered.

"Sin, you sure about this? Maybe we should wait until this shit dies down some and try our luck again then," Unique suggested.

"We all out of luck. This ends tonight." Sin grabbed the parcel that Unique had been carrying and checked the contents. Everything was in order. "If I ain't back in half an hour, y'all peel the fuck out."

"Hell no. No man left behind. You know the rule," Bone reminded him.

"This is the exception. I mean what I said, a half-hour and no more," Sin reinforced. He made to exit the car, but Unique stopped him.

"You ever gonna tell us what this was really about? Ain't no amount of money can make you take a gamble this big," Unique said.

Sin measured the question. "Ask me again when I get back." And with that he was gone.

* * *

The hospital was relatively quiet that night. Of course, the ER was a shit show of people who had come in to receive medical attention and the overworked and understaffed nurses and doctors who tried to attend them. A young mother held a wailing baby in her arms while trying to explain to the triage nurse that she had been waiting for two hours and her child's fever still hadn't broken. On the other side of the room, a couple who looked to be on drugs were engaged in an argument. The woman had a gash on her forehead, covered by a bloodstained bandage that needed to be changed. Her male companion rocked back and forth on the hard-plastic chair with a look on his face that said he'd rather be chasing whatever was in the streets calling him than making sure his woman got the proper care. The ER was a symphony of chaos, which made it that much easier for the Shadow to pass unnoticed.

The Shadow caught the elevator door just as it was closing. Inside was a young Black orderly, with a patient on a gurney. The patient was a pale, older woman who didn't look like she was long for this world. Her weary eyes drifted to the Shadow. There was a moment she saw it for what it was . . . death.

"Not you, sugar. Not today," the Shadow assured her. She gave the Shadow a smile of relief before the orderly wheeled her out onto the second floor.

The elevator pinged before the doors slid open on the seventh floor. That was the floor where they treated their high-profile victims. Those who wanted to keep their business out of the streets. During the day, it was well-guarded against the paparazzi and potential threats, but during those hours, they operated with a skeleton crew: three doctors who worked in rotation to attend to the patients and a handful of nurses and one uniformed police officer in case something jumped off that the hospital security couldn't handle on its own.

The Shadow paused when he spotted the duty nurse behind the desk speaking with the officer who was assigned to the floor that night. He was leaned in whispering sweet nothings into her ear. When the nurse noticed the Shadow lingering, she whispered something to the cop before leading him to the supply closet where she would keep him occupied until the Shadow had done its work. She was risking her job by leaving her station, but the Shadow had compensated her handsomely for her troubles. The Shadow continued down the hall between the hospital rooms. At the end, near the last room, a young man wearing a gold chain sat on a wooden chair. He was scrolling through his phone, eyes heavy, trying not to doze off. When he spotted the Shadow, he stood.

"What you doing here?" the man wearing the gold chain asked. He extended his hand in greeting and was met with a knife plunged up through his heart. The Shadow cradled him tenderly and dragged him into the room he had been guarding.

After securing his victim in the bathroom, he turned his attention to his real target. Stripped of all his jewelry and bravado, Don B. looked like an ordinary man, instead of the demon he was. He was unconscious with tubes monitoring his vitals. The Shadow stood over the sleeping rapper for a time, watching the rhythm of his chest rise and fall in time with the beeping of the machines he was hooked to. For the briefest of moments, doubt crept into the Shadow's heart. Was he doing the right thing? Betraying the man who so many depended on to eat, including him? Probably not, but it was a necessary evil. The death of the Don was the only way to ensure the survival of the company.

Pushing down his emotions, the Shadow gently removed one of the pillows that had been propping Don B.'s head up. Shooting him would've been easier, but this way was more humane. When they found Don B. they would think he had passed away quietly in his sleep. "Goodnight, sweet prince," the Shadow whispered and prepared to smother the Don. Just as he laid the pillow across his face, he heard something just outside the hospital room that gave him pause.

* * *

Sin's heart beat so rapidly in his chest that he was sure the woman standing next to him in the elevator could hear it. He spared a glance in her direction, but she continued to stare down at her phone, more concerned with it than the man dressed in hospital scrubs and a face mask, pushing a laundry cart. The hospital gear had been what Unique had in the parcel. He'd stolen them during his casing. The laundry cart had been a bonus, something he'd found discarded outside the elevator before he got on. The elevator dinged, and the woman got off without so much as a backward glance.

By the time Sin made it to the seventh floor, he found himself sweating like a hooker in church. His disguise had gotten him past the guard in the lobby, but the seventh floor was likely to be heavier on security. This is why he found it so surprising to find the floor deserted. The nurse's station was empty, and even the guard outside the hospital room door that Unique had warned him about was absent. The only signs of him were an empty chair and an abandoned cell phone. He peeked inside the room and found Don B. unconscious in his hospital bed, but as near as he could tell there was no one else in the room. Why would someone as high profile as Don B. be left unguarded? The situation felt off, and Sin's good mind told him to abort the mission, but he was so close. This was his best and last chance to kill the man who had violated his mother and caused the death of his half sister. The Don had to die.

Sincere gave one last glance down the hall to make sure it was still all clear before sitting the cart outside the room and stepping inside. He drew his pistol from the pocket of his scrubs. He was so excited that his hands shook as he screwed on the silencer. The moment he had been anticipating since he was a kid had finally arrived. He raised the gun and pointed it at Don B.'s head. "This is for my family."

"And this is for the team," Sin heard someone say from behind him. He turned in time to see Zod step from the bathroom he had ducked into when he heard the squeaky wheels of the laundry cart.

Sin was raising his pistol when Zod's first bullet struck him. It struck him in the chest, stealing his breath. His legs felt like noodles, and he feared that they would give out on him. He ignored the pain and the armed man with the tattooed face, keeping his focus on the Don. He had to pay for what he had done, even if it cost Sin his own life. He managed to get a shot off, but his aim was shaky, and the bullet struck the pillow right next to Don B.'s head. Sin wasn't sure how or when it had happened, but he ended up on the floor, bleeding from his chest wound. He tried to raise his gun, but no longer had the strength. Sin watched helplessly, gasping for air as Zod moved to stand over him. "You don't understand . . . he has to die . . ." he rasped.

"This we can agree on, but his life isn't yours to take," Zod told him before pulling the trigger.

Sin's last thoughts before the end came for him were that he hoped that Bone would take care of their mother after he was gone.

CHAPTER 34

Gone . . . that was the word Promise would've used to describe Candice's state of mind. She sat near the window, rocking back and forth, staring off into space and whimpering. Every few minutes, she would stop her rocking long enough to scream the name of her murdered lover, as if it would bring him running from out of the bedroom like it normally did. Her sister Keisha consoled her as best she could, but there was nothing that could ease what she was feeling. She had suffered a tragic loss, the father of her children.

After being unceremoniously dismissed by Asher, Promise turned to the only person she could always count on to pick her up when she was feeling down, Mouse. She had called Mouse looking for words of encouragement, but instead found her best friend going through something of her own. Mouse rarely cried, but when she picked up Promise's call, she was bawling. Mouse was so emotional that, at first, Promise couldn't even understand what she was saying. The only thing that she was certain of was that something terrible had happened. Promise didn't even continue to try and decipher what Mouse was saying. She immediately jumped into a taxi and rushed to be with her friend during her time of need.

When Promise got out of the taxi in front of the projects, she could feel the dark cloud looming over it. Promise made hurried steps toward the building. Out front she found a cluster of locals, young men and women who she knew only in passing from her time staying with Keisha and Candice. They all wore looks of great sadness. Whatever had gone down had caused a ripple effect that was felt not just by the occupants of the twins' apartment, but by the whole hood. One girl who Promise recognized as an associate of the twins stopped Promise as she was entering the building and embraced her in a hug while offering condolences. Promise only nodded and said, "Thank you." She still had no idea what had happened and was too afraid to ask.

Promise bypassed the elevator and took the stairs up to the floor of Keisha and Candice's apartment. From the other side of the door, she could hear someone wailing, and it made her stomach lurch. She prayed that nothing had happened to one of the twins. Though they had both treated her like shit most of the time, they had still opened up their home to Promise when she had nowhere else to go. Timidly, she knocked on the door. She only had to wait a few seconds for someone to answer it. Standing on the other side of the door was Mouse. Her eyes were red and swollen, and her makeup was streaked with dried tears. Seeing her friend in that condition, Promise knew that, whoever had died, the death hit close to home for her.

"I'm so glad you're here." Mouse threw herself into Promise's arms.

"I wish I could've gotten here sooner, but I was caught up. What happened? Are the twins okay?" Promise asked nervously.

"I wish I could say they were. C'mon." Mouse stepped aside and allowed Promise to enter the apartment. "Why are you dressed like that?"

"Long story." Promise shook her head.

Mouse gave her a suspicious look. "Now you know you can't throw no shit like that out there and not give my nosey ass the details. You and I are going to talk."

Mouse allowed Promise to hold onto her secret for a time longer and led the way into the living room. This was where Promise found Keisha and Candice. Candice was in shambles, and Keisha was trying to hold her together. She stroked her sister's hair and whispered to her that everything would be okay. This was a state of vulnerability that Promise had never seen either of the twins in, especially not Keisha. Ninety-five percent of the time, she was vicious, so the other five percent that Promise was seeing was new to her. When Keisha saw Promise standing there, she glared at her, and for a minute, Promise saw that wicked side of her peek through. Promise hadn't forgotten how things had played out between her and Keisha, and neither had the twin. The fire burned in her eyes for a few seconds before smoldering out, and Keisha turned her attention back to her sister.

"What happened?" Promise asked just above a whisper.

"Vaughn got killed," Keisha said softly, as if she was afraid Candice would hear and go back into her fit of screaming. "They found him and those Jersey niggas he'd taken to running with all of them dead in an apartment in the Bronx a few hours ago. I warned Vaughn that Newark don't breed nothing but snakes." She gave Promise a dirty look.

Promise caught the dig but was too focused on Keisha's last statement. She thought back to her last conversation with Vaughn about this new connect that was supplying him with pills. She had learned from her nightly chats with Asher that he had expanded into pills and knew that he had dealings in New York, but she never cared to dig deep enough into that side of his life to find out with who. Then there was Asher's seemingly harmless interest in Vaughn. She knew that Asher was a devious dude, but could he have been that low to try and pump Promise for information just so that he could get close enough to kill Vaughn? Was that why, when the man in the suit popped up on them earlier, Asher got so nervous? All kinds of wicked shit started running through Promise's head, none of which she wanted to believe, but it was all hitting too close to home for her to dismiss as coincidence. "Newark ain't but so big. Any idea who Vaughn was dealing with from that side?" she asked, dreading the answer to the question.

"I never let any of them snakes get close enough to me to ask," Keisha replied.

"Saud," Candice spoke up. This was the first piece of information to come out of her mouth in the last two hours.

The name hit Promise like a slap across the face. She knew exactly who Saud was and what he was about. She hadn't seen him in over a year, but the mention of his name still had the same effect on her as a kid who had sworn they'd seen a monster under their bed. She felt her legs threaten to buckle at the revelation, and how it connected to her recent misadventures, but she managed to hold her balance and her game face. Against her better judgment, she turned to Mouse, who wasn't as adept at keeping her mask in place. The color had drained from her face, and her lip quivered nervously. They both knew the implications of Saud being found dead so close to the place they had fled to. If for no one else in the room, for Promise and Mouse, this was bigger than Vaughn getting killed.

"Something y'all wanna add to this?" Keisha asked the girls. She had caught whatever it was that had passed between them.

Promise looked to Mouse, who appeared about to break and spill it all. "Nah, Keisha. It's just all a little overwhelming. Me and Mouse gonna put our ears to the streets, and we'll bring whatever we hear back to y'all."

"You be sure to do that. Vaughn might not have been the most well-respected nigga in the hood, but he was fosho well-loved. A dude like that goes missing, and there are sure to be questions," Keisha said.

"And I hope that, the next time we see each other, I'll be able to help you get those answers. Condolences on your loss," Promise said to the grieving twin before going back the way she had come. On her way out, she tapped Mouse to follow.

Mouse lingered for a time. She turned to her cousin Keisha who was glaring at her like she had a grudge.

"You don't hear your massa calling? Go on and see what she wants," Keisha dismissed her cruelly.

"Fuck you, Keisha. I'm my own woman. You ain't shit for suggesting otherwise," Mouse shot back.

"Maybe, but I'm gonna keep feeling that way until you show me different. Y'all might be girls but don't forget whose blood pumps through your veins."

* * *

Promise was outside, leaning against one of the project fences smoking when Mouse came out of the building. She looked pissed. "Your cousin is a real trip."

"Did you know?" Mouse asked.

"Know what?" Promise was confused.

"That Asher was going to kill Vaughn?"

"Mouse, you're starting to sound just as crazy as your cousin. Why would Asher kill Vaughn? And if he did, how would I know?" Promise questioned.

"Because I know you've been seeing him," Mouse revealed. Promise opened her mouth to speak, but Mouse waved her silent. "Promise, we ain't never lied to each other, so let's not start now. I knew that you and Asher rekindled whatever it was you thought y'all had in Newark. I was just waiting for you to keep it real and tell me. Your ass has been floating on a cloud lately, and there's only one person I know who can have you running around like a lovestruck little girl, and it ain't Sin."

Promise was busted. Mouse knew her better than anyone, so she had been a fool to think she could hide something like that from her. "Yeah, we talked, and I met him earlier, but it ain't what you think."

"Then what is it, Promise? Asher pops up in New York, and all of a sudden, Saud gets clipped. Shit, I didn't even know he was in the city. Do you realize what would've happened if he'd caught up with us?" Mouse was livid. Promise remained silent. "Well, I guess we ain't gotta worry about that now, thanks to your little boyfriend."

"I know that I kept seeing Asher from you, and I was wrong for that. As far as Saud being here, I had no idea. That's on my mom. And we don't know for sure that Asher killed him. They used to get money together, so what would be his motive to kill him?" Promise argued.

"For one, Asher is a double-crossing snake who would step over his mama for a dollar. And for two, if Saud is dead that would mean you were safe. You said, when y'all first hooked, he told you that you didn't have to worry about that business in Jersey anymore, right? How could he be so sure unless he knew that anyone who would want to see us dead wasn't around anymore?"

Mouse raised a good point. Promise hadn't looked at it that way, but the more Mouse talked the more sense it made. When Asher kept asking about Vaughn and who his supplier was, he had likely been fishing to see how much Promise knew before he made his move. Once again, he had used her. "Damn" was all she could say once the realization had set in.

"Damn is right. Now, I had no love for Saud, and I can't say that I'm mad that he's gone, but Vaughn didn't deserve that. There is going to be a shit storm behind this," Mouse told her.

"You think Keisha and Candice are going to go to the police?" Promise asked.

"The police?" Mouse chuckled. "Hell no, but the law is going to be the least of Asher's worries if my cousins put two and two together."

"And what's that supposed to mean?"

"It means, even though Vaughn was a fuck-up and half-ass hustler, he comes from a family tree of certified psychopaths. His cousin is a heavyweight, and I don't mean a boxer. He is going to scorch the fucking earth behind Vaughn getting killed, and God help anyone he thinks was involved."

There was something about the tone of Mouse's voice that made Promise very, very nervous. "Who is this cousin?"

"I don't know his real name, but on the streets, they call him the Outlaw."

CHAPTER 35

Cal sat behind the wheel of his car, sucking the life out of a blunt. He checked the time on the dashboard and saw that it was well after midnight. Asher was late, but that wasn't unusual. The boy would be late to his own funeral, if he showed up at all. What was troubling Cal was the location where Asher suggested they meet.

The Pit, as they called it, was really an abandoned housing project off MLK Boulevard in Newark. Back in the day it had been home to dozens of underprivileged and working-class families, but now it was just another victim of Newark's gentrification project. It was one of the many housing projects that they had torn down, displacing families while trying to make the city a more appealing place to live for the influx of transplants that were now calling Newark home. The abandoned projects were now home to mostly junkies and rats. Asher had turned it into an open-air drug market where their crew could sell drugs and not have to worry too much about the police because the law didn't care what went on in that area.

"Say, man. You holding?" A drug addict approached Cal's

car. He was a shabbily dressed man wearing a tattered overcoat and a hood pulled over his head.

"Man, get your hype ass away from my ride!" Cal barked on him.

"Fuck you, too, nigga!" the dope fiend spat before going back to join two other junkies who were huddled around a fire burning in a trash can.

Cal watched the man shamble away toward the others. He was easily the biggest dope fiend Cal had ever seen and looked like he might've been a football player before the drugs got ahold of him. If shit had gotten crazy, Cal would've had to shoot his overgrown ass. This was yet another reason Cal hated being in The Pit. The junkies were more treacherous out that way. Normally, they let the young boys, who were a little on the wilder side, work The Pit. They had less to live for than a man like Cal who was getting to the money.

He checked the time again. It had inched closer to twelve thirty, and there was still no sign of Asher. Cal was now starting to get concerned. Asher had been acting strange lately. He was more paranoid than usual and barely came through the block anymore. The last time Cal could remember Asher moving like that was when Zul had first put him in a trick bag to kill B-Stone. There was definitely something going on, this Cal was sure of, and he had decided that would be the night he confronted his friend and demanded that he tell him what was going on. This is why he had chosen to roll with his big .45, instead of the baby 9mm he usually carried. He and Asher were like brothers, and he didn't think his friend would double-cross him, but he imagined that was the same thing B-Stone and Ab had thought until they both found themselves in the ground.

In his rearview, he saw headlights turn onto the block. He

recognized the blue-tinted LEDs that Asher had fitted his Benz with. The car pulled directly behind where Cal was parked. He waited for a few minutes, expecting Asher to get out, but no one emerged from the car. He just sat there. "Fuck is going on?" he thought to himself. He grew tired of waiting and decided to get out, after he secured his gun in his waistband.

At the same time Cal got out, the driver's side door to Asher's Benz opened up. He'd killed the overhead light, so Cal couldn't get a good look into the car. "Man, you had me out here waiting all night. I thought . . ." Cal's words trailed when he saw who had climbed from behind the wheel. It wasn't Asher.

* * *

Asher had it all mapped out. Get rid of Saud, reconnect with Promise, and then put the nail in his enemies' coffins. Giving Zul Cal's location was the final piece to the puzzle, but what he hadn't planned for was Zul taking him hostage and forcing him to ride along. He didn't know why he hadn't seen that coming. Zul knew Asher too well to trust him blindly.

"You awful quiet back there," Baby Blue said over his shoulder. He was behind the wheel of Asher's Benz, and Zul occupied the passenger seat. Asher was in the back sandwiched between Fangs and Whisper.

"He's probably trying to think of how he can weasel his way out of this one," Fangs said. One side of Fangs's face was covered by a large bruise, and there was a knot just below his eye that was the size of a baseball. Atilla had caused all that damage with just one punch.

"No worries, Asher. It'll all be over soon. I'm a man of my word," Zul assured him.

Asher didn't like the sound of that. Zul had promised him that, once the traitors had been eliminated, they could get back to business as usual, but Asher was no longer so sure. His heart began to thud in his chest when they turned onto the block and he saw Cal's car idling. They sat there for a few minutes, waiting. On what, Asher wasn't sure. Asher had done some low things in his short time on earth, but this ranked as the lowest.

Baby Blue pulled the Benz directly behind Cal's car, before reaching up to switch off the overhead light.

"You try anything, and I'm gonna let Fangs have his way with you," Zul warned.

"Please try something. I want you to," Fangs pleaded.

Asher watched helplessly as Cal got out of his car and approached the Benz. If only there was a way for him to signal to Cal; maybe there was still a chance to get out of this. There was no way. Asher knew that, at the slightest wrong move, Whisper and Fangs would make lunch meat of him, so he sat there quietly while his friend walked to his death.

* * *

"What the fuck?" Cal cursed when he saw Baby Blue get out of the car. He made to reach for his gun, but Whisper and Fangs jumped out with their weapons drawn. They had him.

"Go on and toss that piece over here before this shit gets messy," Baby Blue told him. Reluctantly, Cal did as he was told. "Good boy," Baby Blue spoke to Cal like he was a dog.

Zul was next to emerge from the car. He paused at the backseat and motioned for the last occupant of the car to get out. Cal's heart dropped when he saw it was Asher. "You set me up?" he asked.

"Cal . . . let me explain . . ." Asher began, but Zul cut him off.

"Of course he did. Ol' Ash here traded your life for his. I don't know why you're surprised. Your boy has a history of doing dishonorable shit. And the way I hear it, some of his grease ball ways have rubbed off on you. Did you think that I wouldn't find out what you were up to?"

"Zul, I have no clue what you're talking about," Cal said honestly.

"Lying-ass snake!" Baby Blue snuffed him, dropping Cal to one knee.

"Blue!" Zul barked his name, signaling for him to relax. Baby Blue mumbled something under his breath before backing away.

"Zul, I don't know what this lying muthafucka has told you but don't believe it," Cal said, glaring at Asher. Asher couldn't hold his gaze.

"Asher's might've led me to you, but it was your actions that put you on my radar. How long were you feeding Saud off my plate?" Zul asked.

"Saud? I ain't seen or spoke to that dude since not too long after B-Stone died," Cal told him.

"It's okay, Cal. Zul knows everything," Asher said. "He knows all about you supplying Saud for his operation in New York. Might as well confess."

"You dirty muthafucka!" Cal lunged at Asher, but Whisper clocked him in the side of the head with his gun and dropped him.

"So, we're square now, right, Zul? You said that, once I took care of Cal and Saud, we were all good," Asher reminded him.

"You took care of Saud only because the Outlaw couldn't seem to find what hole he was hiding in, so don't be so quick to pat yourself on the back. I did promise you your freedom, Asher, but I also told you that, if you dragged your feet with handling the task, your ass was out, too," Zul said. "Asher, you must take me for a fool if you think I don't know about the sneaky moves you've been making, trying to line me up. The first chance you got, you planned to double-cross me. You're a good earner, but I can't break bread with a man I can't trust."

Fangs grabbed Asher and shoved him to the ground next to Cal. "Looks like we're getting a two-for-one special," he snickered.

"Looks like this is another fine mess I've gotten us into, huh?" Asher half-joked to Cal.

"Fuck you, Asher! I should've cut your ass off when I saw what you did to Ab!" Cal spat.

"I never meant for it to go down like this, Cal," Asher said sincerely.

"I know, you planned to leave me for dead and ride off into the sunset," Cal accused.

"Cal, you're my brother. I'd never betray you," Asher said.

"And what do you call this? My only regret is that I can't put a bullet in your head before I die."

"Man, y'all cut all that fucking whispering," Baby Blue kicked Asher in the stomach, doubling him over.

"You're gonna wear that, you little imp!" Asher threatened as he tried to catch his breath.

"Not likely." Baby Blue laughed.

"Man, you boys over here looking like new money." The dope fiend who had approached Cal earlier was back. He was looking at Asher's car in adoration. "I know one of y'all can spare a few dollars to help me get a blast."

"Take a walk, junkie," Baby Blue ordered.

"I resent that remark. I ain't never been a junkie a day in my life," the dope fiend said indignantly.

"Oh, yeah, then what the fuck are you?" Baby Blue asked with an amused smirk on his face. The smirk faded when the junkie produced the shotgun he had been hiding under his coat.

"An Ape!" the junkie announced before pulling the trigger. The shotgun blast took Baby Blue off his feet and sent him flying over the hood of Asher's car.

Everyone assembled was stunned to silence when the junkie removed his hood and revealed his face. It was Atilla! Once again, he had come to Asher's rescue, and he wasn't alone. The two junkies who had been with him drew weapons also. On the back of one of their hands was the same tattoo that Atilla sported on his face, a snarling Ape.

"Well played, Asher," Zul nodded in approval.

"I learned from the best," Asher said proudly.

Their moment was broken up by the sound of Whisper's gun going off. He was shooting at any and everybody who wasn't one of his people. Asher, Cal, and Zul managed to find cover behind a car, but one of the Apes that had been with Atilla wasn't so lucky. Whisper hit him twice, once in the head and once in the face, ending him. Then the world was thrown into chaos.

* * *

"That's three you owe me now, Asher," Atilla joked, handing him the spare gun he'd had in his coat pocket.

"I'll pay you back in spades if we get out of this alive." Asher popped from behind the car and returned fire, before ducking back down.

"You used me as fucking bait?" Cal asked in disbelief.

"What? You thought I would really cross my day-one homie?" Asher asked. Cal's silence was all the answer he needed.

"You two can kiss and make up later. Let's kill these niggas and go home," Atilla said, rolling from behind the car with his shotgun. He let off another shot, this one hitting the windshield of Asher's car, sending glass flying everywhere.

Zul and Fangs took cover behind the car, but Whisper made his stand. He found himself trapped between Atilla's shotgun and the remaining Ape. Whisper fired, managing to catch Atilla in the shoulder and slow him, but the big man kept coming. He was like a force of nature. The other Ape got cocky and tried to close in so that he could be the one to make the kill shot. This was a mistake he wouldn't live to regret. Whisper waited until the Ape was almost on him before opening fire. He had to pump several rounds into the man before finally dropping him. It was just him and Atilla now. Atilla was out in the open, and Whisper saw this as his opportunity to take him down. He raised his gun and pulled the trigger, but to his horror it clicked empty.

"Gotta keep track of your ammo," Atilla told him before blowing Whisper's head off.

* * *

"What are you doing cowering back here with me? Get out there and fight!" Zul ordered Fangs, who was damn near under the car and quivering.

"But Zul—"

Zul pulled a small pistol and pointed it at Fangs's face. "You either eat one of their bullets or one of mine. Pick your poison."

Reluctantly, Fangs crawled out from under the car. His plan had been to blast his way out and make a run for it, but that plan died when he saw Asher waiting for him. His gun was pointed at Fangs's face.

"Asher, you can have Zul. Just let me slide. It ain't gotta be like this."

"That's where you're wrong, Fangs. I told you, Newark was and always will be mine." Then Asher put three bullets into Fangs.

"That nigga is trying to make a run for it!" Asher heard Cal shout. He looked up just in time to see Zul hauling ass down the block.

"Not today, Satan," Asher said and took off behind Zul.

* * *

For a man wearing hard bottom shoes, Zul was incredibly fleet of foot. He had a half-block head start on Asher, but the young man was closing in. Zul fired blindly over his shoulder, but Asher kept coming. Zul had nearly made it to the corner when pain exploded in his leg and sent him skidding face-first to the ground, jarring the gun from his hand. He had been hit. Zul tried to stand, but it was nearly impossible with half his kneecap missing. He rolled over onto his back and waited for the inevitable.

"And so the student becomes the teacher," Zul said, as Asher stood over him.

"This is what you made it, Zul. We could've kept getting money together, but your ego and need to control everyone around you fucked it up," Asher said.

"This wasn't about ego. This was about seeing if you really had what it took to be a king. The fact that you couldn't bring yourself to kill Cal tells me that you don't," Zul said, shaking his head.

"That's where you're wrong. A good king understands the importance of protecting his subjects, not trying to set them against each other."

"You kill me, then who are you gonna get your dope from? You're gonna starve on them streets without my plug," Zul warned.

"No, I don't think I will. One thing I learned from you is, never get complacent. Always want more, and I want it all.

Drugs are a thing of the past. I've got my sights set on the future."

"I'll see you in hell, Asher!"

"Maybe, but not anytime soon." Asher raised his gun, but before he could pull the trigger, he was blinded by the headlights of a car coming straight at him. He barely got out of the way before the car jumped the curb where he was standing, coming between him and Zul.

Zul had thought the driver of the car was another one of Asher's people, but found out differently when the door swung open. "If you wanna live, get your ass in!" the driver shouted.

Zul was hesitant. This could be another trick of Asher's, but at that moment, it was the only play he had. Zul had barely pulled himself completely into the car before the driver was speeding off down the street, leaving Asher and his comrades in his wake.

* * *

"Tell me that nigga Zul is up the block with his brains leaking on the sidewalk?" Atilla asked when Asher rejoined him.

"He got away. Somebody snatched him before I could get off the kill shot," Asher admitted.

"I still can't believe you used me as bait," Cal said, the shock of what had happened was now wearing off.

"It was the only way I could make sure I got Zul and his crew in one place to take them out. I planned on being here with Atilla and getting the drop when they came for you. Me getting snatched wasn't a part of the plan," Asher explained.

"Your little plan could've gotten me killed!" Cal shouted.

"But it didn't," Asher countered.

"You know, being that Zul got away, we're all as good as

dead if we stay in Newark," Atilla pointed out. Zul was a very dangerous enemy to have.

"Fuck Newark. I got bigger plans for us, fellas," Asher said with a sly smile.

EPILOGUE

ONE WEEK LATER

"Welcome back to the land of the heartless," Lobo greeted his guests when they stepped out of the terminal of Los Angeles International Airport. Lobo was a tall, handsome fellow with curly black hair and a thin mustache barely connecting his goatee. With thick lips and a wide nose that sat slightly off from the center of his face, most people assumed that he was Black at first glance, but Lobo was one hundred percent Washington Heights–bred Dominican. "How was your flight?"

"Long," Asher replied before giving Lobo dap. He unzipped his sweat jacket and fanned himself. It was much hotter in California than it had been when he boarded the flight in Newark during the wee hours of the morning.

"As much as you swing back and forth, I'd think you were used to it by now. I don't know why you don't just go ahead and make this your home, instead of blowing your money on plane fare every two to three weeks," Lobo suggested.

"In due time, my man. In due time," Asher said. "Let me introduce you to the guys." He motioned his friends forward. "Of course, you already know Cal, but this here is the homie Atilla. He's from the old neighborhood."

"Sup?" Atilla greeted Lobo, but his eyes were following a big-breasted blond in a short tennis skirt who was jumping into a Bentley coupe with a dude who looked twice her age.

"Your first time, huh?" Lobo asked, noticing the star-stuck look on Atilla's face. It was always like that when dudes from the east landed in Cali for the first time, Lobo included. He had the same look in his eyes when he had stepped off the Greyhound in LA several years prior. He didn't have to think twice about planting roots there permanently.

"Only broads I seen in the last few years that weren't in magazines were wearing prison guard uniforms, and they damn sure wasn't built like that!" Atilla thumbed at a shapely Black girl walking toward the taxi stand. He was like a kid in a candy story. "What they feeding these hos out here?"

"Dreams," Lobo said with a wink. "If you think this is something, you ain't ready for what I'm about to show y'all. But first, somebody has been waiting to see you, Asher."

Lobo led them to the curb where two SUVs and a classic car waited on them. He opened the back door of one of the SUVs. Seated in the back, smoking a blunt, was a man dripping in heavy jewels. When he saw Asher, he smiled, revealing a mouth full of gold teeth. "The conquering heroes," he greeted them with a southern twang.

"What is this?" Cal asked suspiciously. After what he had gone through with Asher over the past few weeks, he didn't trust anyone or anything, including Asher.

"This is my business partner," Asher revealed. "Fellas, I'd

like to introduce you to the man who is going to help enrich our lives. They call him the Kingmaker."

"That's what niggas call me who I make rich, which is what I hope to do for all of you. For now, you can just call me Trap."